# THE HOUSE OF THE BLACK RING

# THE HOUSE OF THE BLACK RING

## A ROMANCE OF THE SEVEN MOUNTAINS

FRED LEWIS PATTEE

*With an Introduction by Julia Spicher Kasdorf and Notes by Joshua R. Brown*

THE PENNSYLVANIA STATE UNIVERSITY PRESS
UNIVERSITY PARK, PENNSYLVANIA

Publication of this book has been aided by a grant from the Center for American Literary Studies.

Library of Congress Cataloging-in-Publication Data

Pattee, Fred Lewis, 1863–1950.
The house of the black ring : a romance of the seven mountains / Fred Lewis Pattee ; with an introduction by Julia Spicher Kasdorf and notes by Joshua Brown.
p. cm.
Includes bibliographical references and index.
Summary: "A reprint of a 1904 novel by Pennsylvania State College (now University) professor of English Fred Lewis Pattee, set in the 1890s in central Pennsylvania. Includes a preface by poet and essayist Julia Spicher Kasdorf and endnotes by Joshua R. Brown"
—Provided by publisher.
ISBN 978-0-271-05420-9 (cloth : alk. paper)
I. Kasdorf, Julia, 1962– .
II. Brown, Joshua, 1956– .
III. Title.

PS3531.A8H68 2012
813'.52—dc23
2012007192

*The House of the Black Ring* originally published by
Henry Holt & Co. in 1905
Author's preface originally appeared in 1919

Printed in the United States of America
Published by The Pennsylvania State University Press,
University Park, PA 16802-1003

It is the policy of The Pennsylvania State University Press to use acid-free paper. Publications on uncoated stock satisfy the minimum requirements of American National Standard for Information Sciences—Permanence of Paper for Printed Library Material, ANSI Z39.48–1992.

This book is printed on Nature's Natural, which contains 50% post-consumer waste.

# CONTENTS

# ACKNOWLEDGMENTS

For recognizing that *The House of the Black Ring* remains a provocative product of its time, and for returning it to contemporary readers, thanks go to Penn State Press director Patrick Alexander and to Kathryn B. Yahner, assistant acquisitions editor extraordinaire. The project would not have been possible without the support of the English department, which Pattee served for so many years, and especially the help of associate professor of English Sean X. Goudie and the Center for American Literary Studies, which he directs. James L. W. West III, Edwin Erle Sparks Professor of English and director of the Penn State Center for the History of the Book, and Professor Robert Caserio generously contributed their expertise. Thanks also go to Joshua R. Brown, who worked diligently on the notes while completing his doctoral work in German and applied linguistics and gaining his first academic appointment. And finally, we very much appreciate the support of Barbara I. Dewey, dean of the University Libraries, and Nancy Eaton, dean emerita.

# INTRODUCTION

*Julia Spicher Kasdorf*

Fred Lewis Pattee had never traveled west of New York City when he set out to interview for his first college teaching job in the spring of 1894. As the train snaked along a single track through the isolated valleys and rocky mountainsides of Central Pennsylvania, he glimpsed "a new world, arousing all that was romantic" in him, as he would recall many years later when writing his memoirs. The landscape that inspired the thirty-year-old New Englander on that first visit to the region became the "indescribably lonely and wild" setting of the novel you now hold in your hand.

Today scholars remember Pattee for his early and important contributions to the study of American literature as advocate, historian, and critic. But in light of recent enthusiasms for "the local," *The House of the Black Ring*, long out of print, deserves a fresh look. What personal and literary concerns led the transplanted Penn State professor to write it? How was it received when it first appeared more than one hundred years ago? And perhaps most important, why read the book now?

## *The House of the Black Ring*

What Pattee called "romantic" in that view outside his train window has a particular literary meaning that may be useful in understanding this book. "Novels" in Pattee's day were commonly understood to be imaginative stories set in the real world, but "romances" were more fantastic works of fiction set in remote or exotic places with characters engaged in heroic dramas, passionate loves, or supernatural encounters—or, as in the case of this book, all of the above!

Whereas *The House of the Black Ring* follows many of the plot conventions of a mid-nineteenth-century romance, its setting and characterization belong to a later genre: local color. Those works were not usually driven by dramatic plots; instead they sought to depict realistically the place and everyday life, humor, and language of remote areas where people still lived close to the land. Nostalgia for simpler times sometimes inflected local color writing. The books were largely judged in terms of authenticity and for their ability to represent distinct identities and places accurately. The best examples of the genre celebrated the nation's multicultural and geographical diversity; the worst exploited their rustic subjects and exposed them to ridicule. In one of his literary histories, Pattee identified the decades between 1880 and 1920 with regional writing. *The House of the Black Ring,* published in 1905, is one such work.

Among local color authors, Pattee especially admired Sarah Orne Jewett, who is remembered for her vivid sketches of life along the border between New Hampshire and Maine. Pattee mentions Jewett in his memoir, relating her concern for the "invasion" of summer boarders from the cities to his own childhood memories of encounters with urban vacationers in the White Mountains. He quotes her on her motivation for writing her first novel, *Deephaven:* "I determined to teach the world that country people are not the awkward, ignorant set those people seemed to think. I wanted the world to know their grand simple lives; and so far as I had a mission, when I first began to write, I think that was it."

One of the "country people" himself, Fred Lewis Pattee was a writer and scholar whose career was shaped by his rural roots and modest means. He was born on March 22, 1863, the son of Lewis Franklin Pattee and Mary Philbrick Ingalls, on a small farm on Pattee Hill, adjacent to his grandfather's property, in Alexandria, New Hampshire. He attended public schools in Bristol and South Alexandria. At sixteen, he went to work as a laborer on a nearby lawyer's estate and there discovered the squire's library. Like many American authors before him—Benjamin Franklin, Mark Twain, Walt Whitman—Pattee's literary interests led him to work as an apprentice in a print shop. He dreamed of gaining more education and becoming a journalist, a vocation more broadly concerned with literary pursuits in those days than now. Toward that end, he enrolled in preparatory courses in classical languages and literature and worked as a printer and waiter at resorts on the coast to raise funds for his college education.

In 1888 Pattee graduated from Dartmouth College with some debt. One year later, he married Anna Lura Plumer, a neighbor and childhood friend who had studied art in Boston and then worked as a schoolteacher. Financial constraints prevented Pattee from pursuing graduate studies. (In 1902, on sabbatical leave in Germany, he attempted to earn a doctorate, but apparently never found the credential compelling enough to divert his attention from pioneering projects in American literary study already under way.) He worked as a reporter and teacher during the couple's first years of marriage. During the summer of 1890 he served as a census enumerator in Alexandria.

Those months spent talking with local folk, visiting the working and increasingly abandoned farmsteads near his home, richly informed his first work of fiction, *Mary Garvin.* He set the novel on his home farm and populated it with characters based on his own family members and acquaintances, engaged in activities common to nineteenth-century farm life. He recalled, "I wrote it, dialect and all, out of myself." Working as a professor in Pennsylvania, he felt he could see and value the essential elements of home most clearly from a distance. "All my best poetry is youthful dreams and homesickness—a vain striving to win back the gleam. Alone of all my fiction *Mary Garvin,* my first novel, has *me* in it."

The character most certainly modeled on Pattee is protagonist Luke Farnum, a native son who leaves the farm to study law in Concord, New Hampshire. After graduation, but before taking up his profession (which the farmers find morally suspect), Luke returns to rake hay and work in his father's blacksmith shop. Throughout the course of that summer, his affections are torn between his robust, "sunny" local fiancée and a frail, darkly sophisticated young woman from the city who has come to the country for a rest cure. The visitor calls herself a "realist" interested in studying local dialect and folkways; she dubs Luke her "romantic" guide to the region. In the end, Luke chooses homegrown Mary Garvin, who in the meantime manages to lose her regional dialect through a couple of months' study in Boston.

On a personal level, the love triangle expresses a central tension in Pattee's life, divided between the simple materiality of his farm background and the ideas and high culture of his vocation. Years later, in a memoir that offers few personal reflections or revelations, Pattee described himself as one who "had become, all unknowingly and all unwillingly, estranged from my tribe, uncomprehended by my kin" because he had left the ways of his home place. At the same time, for all his scholarly industry and striving, Pattee never felt he fully belonged in the academy. His childhood home contained four books: Webster's dictionary, *Lives of Eminent Christians,* a biblical geography, and a Bible, all used for religious instruction, the chief purpose for literacy in many rural families at that time.

Pattee wondered, "Was there not a gulf impassible between the world of my first two decades and the world in which Oliver Wendell Holmes had been reared with books and culture heaped upon his very cradle?" Not only their different geographical locations, but also different financial and educational circumstances made Pattee feel "grafted" onto the cultural universe that Holmes, an author, physician, and Harvard dean, inhabited with ease. Perhaps only in the United States is this kind of social mobility possible, but even here, Pattee keenly felt that migration comes with a cost. Cultural gain implies a loss of home: "Can one climb out of the rut that has been worn ages deep by one's ancestors? It is easier in America, but to break from one's tribe even here brings inevitable penalties. Leave behind you the old totem poles, begin to doubt in your heart the worth of the old rituals, and there is no return possible. One makes of himself an Ishmael, at home nowhere."

Pattee dedicated *Mary Garvin* to his parents, "with memories of a happy boyhood." Published in 1902, the novel sold some thirty-five hundred copies. Royalties from the project that had returned Pattee to his New Hampshire home in his imagination enabled him to buy the family farm and, in fact, return to it—albeit as a professor who made his living elsewhere. In 1902 he purchased his inheritance, a seventy-acre property of fields and woodland edging Newfound Lake. His parents then retired and moved to Bristol. Thereafter, with his wife and daughter, Pattee joined the urbane outlanders who flocked to the New Hampshire countryside in the summer. Each year he spent three idyllic months at the farm picking berries, raking hay, and reading and writing. In early fall, crates of potatoes and apples traveled back with the family to their residence on campus and later to their home at 210 East Nittany Avenue.

The success of *Mary Garvin* set Pattee onto a number of other fiction projects; he seemed constantly to be writing, rewriting, submitting, and suffering rejection for stories and novels, even as he maintained his work as professor and literary historian. For the next major effort, *The House of the Black Ring,* he drew on Centre County's landscape and people to create a local color romance "made of note-book jottings and research" instead of personal memory. He recalled that he "grubbed steadily for materials," eavesdropping and "jotting down dialect" quite different from his own and that of his colleagues on campus, who were largely recruited from New England and the East. In those days, at the turn of the twentieth century, "at every gathering of faculty people there was always presented a new string of funny 'Dutch' localisms." In his memoir he recalled once seeing this note on a door: "The bell don't make. Bump."

The term *Pennsylvania Dutch* refers to the language spoken by descendants of Swiss, Alsatian, and Palatine Germans who emigrated before the American Revolution. These people spoke inflected English as well as a wholly distinct New World language derived from several German dialects, which Pattee could not comprehend even though he had taught German at the academy and studied in Germany. Prior to World War II in eastern and central Pennsylvania, the language was commonly spoken by "fancy" as well as "plain," or sectarian, folk. Although Pennsylvania Dutch people had lived in the United States for more than 150 years, it was not until after the Civil War that historians and writers from these communities began to document their own history, culture, and contributions to the nation. For print sources, Pattee no doubt turned to publications of the Pennsylvania German Society, founded in 1891 to preserve the language and history of the group, and to books such as Oscar Kuhns's *The German and Swiss Settlements of Pennsylvania: A Study of the So-Called Pennsylvania Dutch.*

He also gathered information from his students, half of whom, he estimated in the fall of 1894, were of Pennsylvania Dutch heritage. In those days, Pennsylvania State College enrolled about three hundred students, approximately doubling the population of the surrounding village, which was composed of little more than a few houses along unpaved streets without sidewalks or sewers. Several pigs roamed freely in the mud on Lemont Pike (now College Avenue) when Pattee first visited for his interview, and he was so taken by the sight that he described it in his memoir. Fellow faculty members who found the place to be a "cultural borderland," according to Pattee, referred to it as "Pigsylvania."

Hired to teach the writing and speaking of English with an "incidental" bit of rhetoric, Pattee constituted the *entire* English department faculty in 1894. He found that most of his students, a majority of whom studied some branch of engineering, arrived from public schools "ludicrously unprepared," with "no training in language, even their own tongue"—by which Pattee meant English. Following the conventional pedagogy of the day, Pattee assigned his students to write compositions, stressing the use of standard diction, syntax, spelling, and punctuation. He complained that he spent countless hours marking about a hundred student papers a week. For one full year, however, he made use of their content. To gather material for his literary project, that year he assigned his students to write their themes on such topics as "strange nooks in the Pennsylvania mountains," "queer dishes served by Pennsylvania housewives," "some Dutch superstitions," "queer people I have known," "Dutch weather signs," "a funny happening in my home neighborhood," and "Dutch localisms."

During the spring of 1904, Pattee worked hard to complete a revision of his Pennsylvania Dutch novel, *The House of the Black Ring,* which he then submitted to Dodd Mead. That summer, he wrote very little on the farm. In August, he received word that the novel had been rejected, so he immediately sent it on to Henry Holt. In October the New York publisher offered to publish *The House of the Black Ring,* but only with significant revisions, including a rewriting of the final chapter. Throughout November, Pattee worked. He wrote in his daybook, "There seems to be no end to the amount of revision this story will stand. I am thoroughly sick of the whole thing." He sent off a final draft in December, and it finally went into production—after having been rejected in various versions fourteen times.

When it first appeared, *The House of the Black Ring* was reviewed in newspapers across the country. Although some reviewers had reservations about the romantic style or about Pattee's use of the time-worn plot of a forbidden love between heirs of two feuding houses, most praised the detailed descriptions of life among these odd people, hidden away in the mountain nooks of Central Pennsylvania. Many reviewers focused on the dramatic feud between the lovers' families. A *New York Times* writer called Pattee's sparkling heroine Rose Hartswick a "Pennsylvania Juliet."

*The House of the Black Ring* is especially interesting when viewed as a product of its time and as a book of ideas, the work of a man who was more successful as a historian of literature than as a writer of fiction. Set in the 1880s or 1890s, the novel demonstrates the tensions that arose as the unified nation struggled to achieve its highest ideals. A common convention of local color novels is the educated outsider—like Fred Pattee—who engages with local rustics, characterized as "peasants" early in this book. In Hell Bottom, Al Farthing (far thing?), a newcomer from the Philadelphia suburb of Paoli, Pennsylvania, clashes with the irascible local landlord Ira (ire?) Hartswick, who has been "bleeding" the tenant farmers dry. Farthing brings free trade to the valley and compares the economic conditions of his neighbors with those of Southern slaves, announcing, "I fought in the war against slavery, and I'll fight again 'fore I'll see slaves around me."

The book also expresses the fresh century's hope for emancipation in domestic relations. Romantic heroine Rose Hartswick is the "new woman": articulate, educated, strong in both spirit and body, and smart enough to defy her father's will. Her handsome suitor at first wonders how he will prove his worthiness now that the Civil War is a distant memory, but he embodies the "strenuous life" that Theodore Roosevelt advocated. Through brain, brawn, and mastery of his own passions, he wins his desire. When the couple is caught in a reckless sleigh race, he is self-confident enough to admit that Rose is more skillful with the horse, and so "Jim passed the reins over like a woman, and she took them like a man." Nonetheless, freethinking Rose, who "would have her way in love," as advertisements for the book announced, wonders, "Why should I want to marry *anybody?*" (To consolidate familial wealth, her father insists.)

When a series of mysterious robberies and a murder befall the valley, the local folk attribute these deeds to witchcraft, but unflappable Farthing and Amos Harding, a no-nonsense New Englander, insist there must be a rational explanation for the events. In the end, feudalism is undone by free trade and justice, superstition is displaced by reason, the veils of fear and blinding tradition are lifted through rational discourse, and the people are delivered from their primitive past.

But not so simply, at least not for the book's most thoughtful readers.

Local color writing has been dismissed as the domestic labor of quaint preservationists; indeed, it often was also the work of women. A group of contemporary literary theorists now reads these novels as expressions of cultural anxieties at a time of great change in the United States: demographic shifts, industrialization, westward emigration, immigration, and consolidation of the nation. *The House of the Black Ring* is as much a romance driven by the liberating forces of progress as it is a "spook story," to use an old phrase from this region. Anxiety is often expressed as obsession, as haunting, and this book is haunted in several ways.

Most immediately, the old German settler's cabin on the edge of a gap at the foot of the Seven Mountains is said to be haunted by the devil. The locals cite plenty of evidence to support that story: the black ring around the cabin where snow won't stick in winter, the eerie red glow at night through the windows, the terrifying cries that come from inside. Settler Matthew Heller had built the cabin in the days of King George III, but after the Revolution, John Hartswick, holding a new deed to the land, usurped the pioneer's claim to the valley. Old Heller calls the devil on Hartswick and his heirs until the valley is restored to its rightful owners, but who is the rightful owner? The primary haunting is an anxiety as old as the arrival of Europeans in the New World.

During the eighteenth century, Delaware and Shawnee Indians traveled on paths through the ridges and planted corn in the valleys of this region. Their memory persists only dimly in the late nineteenth century, echoing in local place-names and romantic tones in this novel. When wildfire traps the most vital characters, Rose and Jim, in the mountains, they camp overnight in the forest and eat fish from the stream. Far from the limits of familial convention, Jim says, "Oh, we're Indians now." A stronger suggestion of the prior human habitation appears in the last paragraph of the book, as the old Heller deed, tacked to the cabin wall, becomes illuminated by "the ray of the Indian summer, increasing as the sun sank lower in the west."

Other strangers and histories haunt the valley as well. In his discussion of powwowing and hexing—dark arts of purely European origin—Pattee erroneously states that the practices derived from Native American, African American, and Palatine German sources, thereby conflating all early non-Anglo (and darker-skinned) inhabitants of Pennsylvania. Elsewhere he compares local farmers to Southern slaves or sharecroppers. Amos Harding, the one New Englander in Hell Bottom, regards the frightened, superstitious Dutchmen with disgust. At one point, he accuses the "grown white men" of talking like "nigger wenches," as if African slave women, not children, represented the antithesis of white manliness. Lona, the frightened, dark granddaughter of a gypsy and local powwow doctor, is apparently the sole survivor of the Heller clan. Mute, she expresses the loss and violence that has befallen her clan, but also carries secret wounds of psychological and possibly sexual abuse. She haunts the mountainside, linked to the land "as if she had sprung from the earth."

Set against these shadowy, troublesome figures, the New Englander says, "I'm mighty glad I'm a Yankee and ain't superstitious." Immediately Dutchman Lem Fisher, "to whom the world presented as many devils as ever it did to old Cotton Mather," reminds Harding that only in Salem were witches ever hanged. At least we "hung" them, Harding replies. The past is not passed, but presses onto the present. The narrator attributes regional rivalries between Pennsylvania and New

England to colonial times, when northern Pennsylvania was part of Connecticut: "The old antipathies and resentments . . . are still to be found in the Teutonic portions of the State, where they cling even yet like persimmons." The only character who manages to rise above the frightened rabble in the valley moves away and, for one of the mystery's linchpins, changes his family name from German to its English equivalent.

Pattee's biographer, James J. Martine, has identified the most significant textual haunting in *The House of the Black Ring* as Hawthorne's *The House of the Seven Gables*, observing that Squire Hartswick is a dead ringer for Judge Jaffrey Pyncheon. Pattee drops several clues that point to Salem in the text, but a relationship between the two stories runs deeper than that. Hawthorne's romance takes place around an ancestral house, and the plot turns on an old dispute about land ownership, matters of inheritance, witchcraft, and a curse. In his introduction, Hawthorne states the moral of his story: "The wrongdoing of one generation lives into the successive ones and . . . becomes a pure and uncontrollable mischief," which also describes the trouble in Hell Bottom. In both places the mischief finally resolves through a love match and surprising disclosures that break ancient spells and liberate the living. Literary history haunts the professor-author. However, Martine finds that Pattee never achieves the mythic power of the nineteenth-century master. In Martine's words, *The House of the Black Ring* is "all motion and no motivation."

In his preface to the 1916 reprint, Pattee admits as much: "The characters are types rather than studies of particular individuals." His romance is driven by dramatic episodes and anecdotes, inspired by the haunted landscape and by odd details from his students' unwitting collaborations, instead of by the psychological depth or complexity of more realistic writing. In this way, Pattee follows in the tradition of Hawthorne, who wrote in the preface to *The House of the Seven Gables* that the romance "sins unpardonably, so far as it may swerve aside from the truth of the human heart." Yet Hawthorne insisted upon "a right to present that truth under circumstances, to a great extent, of the writer's own choosing or creating." *The House of the Black Ring* rushes ahead with rigorous activity—windblown forest fires, robbers, murder, attempted lynching, and breakneck sleigh and horse races. All this "motion" may be counted among its pleasures, too. A reader can't help but agree with cool-headed Yankee Amos Harding when he surmises that "life indeed was becoming strenuous in the little valley."

For today's readers, the book's pleasures also include vivid images of a long-ago landscape and linguistic artifacts carefully collected by a fascinated outsider. Those familiar with the area now commonly called Happy Valley will enjoy seeing how Pattee transforms the local terrain into a mysterious and highly charged setting for his romance. They will flip to the map that appeared in the original edition as they almost recognize various spots. The fire at Wild Meadows and the primeval forest beyond must be at Bear Meadows and the old-growth forest at Alan Seeger, along Standing Stone Creek. Hartswick Hall might take its name from the Hartswick Farm that once stood on Hartswick Avenue in present-day College Heights. It's also easy to imagine the Squire and his family in one of the old limestone homesteads, such as the one still standing at Oak Hall. The haunted cabin could have sat on any of the runs or creeks in the gaps on the Tussey ridge between Pine Grove Mills and Potters Mills. The train station at Lemont or the post office at Pine Grove Mills surely figures into the plot.

People who live in the region will also find in these pages a number of names that belong to long-established families in the area: Corl, Bowersox, Dreibelbis, Fisher, Hubler, Kemmerer, Krumrine, Kuhn, Miller, Siebert, and Tressler. Anyone who grew up among the "thrifty Dutch" of Central Pennsylvania will see for the first time in print familiar colloquial phrases or terms that we have encountered only in spoken discourse: "onion snow," for instance, or "redd up," or the word *all* to indicate that something is "gone" or "finished."

The past is also another place. This book preserves detailed descriptions of a rural community engaged in the chores and celebrations of everyday life long ago, such as butchering, the annual moving, or "flitting," day, and young people's sleigh rides. The farmers plant their crops by the signs of the moon and almanac, and they ascribe power to the supernatural folk practices of hexing, that is, casting a curse, and powwowing, or magico-spiritual healing. (For a brief discussion of hex and powwow practice that is more accurate and respectful than Pattee's, I direct you to Joshua Brown's endnotes.) These are not the sophisticated Pennsylvania Dutch of southeastern Pennsylvania, who responded to urbanization and cultural homogenization after the Civil War by printing newspapers and writing verse in their own language and publishing revisionist histories that traced the origins of the nation to Pennsylvania instead of New England. These are rubes in the northern reaches of Appalachia, where "nobody can 'fire a stone' at random in any of the 'Dutch' valleys and not hit his second cousin," and where "Baer's almanac and the tradition of the fathers rule Central Pennsylvania with despotic sway."

Pattee's portrayal of the dim-witted, hardworking, superstitious farmers in Hell Bottom reflects tired stereotypes of the time, according to Earl F. Robacker, who reserved one sentence for Pattee in his 1942 study of Pennsylvania German literature. Robacker describes the evolution of this sturdy type who helped to build the nation by cultivating the land in remote rural locations. Consequently the Dutchman "developed those characteristics which the world outside has often found so distasteful: the substitution of temporal prosperity for spiritual welfare; the reversion to a belief in magic and witchcraft which had long antedated the pious teaching of his immediate ancestors; and the lack of interest in intellectual pursuits which led to the opprobrious appellation of 'Dumb Dutchman.'"

In 1904, while Pattee was working to complete *The House of the Black Ring,* Harrisburg author Helen R. Martin published her first local color novel, *Tillie, a Mennonite Maid,* which went into twenty printings and was made into a silent film. The immediate success of *Tillie* might well have encouraged Pattee's publisher to take a risk with *The House of the Black Ring.* Martin, who had been publishing stories about the Pennsylvania Dutch in *McClure's* since 1902, made a long career of producing formula fiction that promoted "dumb Dutch" stereotypes: the frugal, authoritarian father; the work-worn, submissive mother; the dull children; the crude, unappealing suitor; and the one smart, beautiful heroine who escapes her repressive background through education or marriage to an intelligent outsider, often from New England. A committed socialist and feminist, Martin outlined her political agenda in interviews and made no apology for creating grotesque caricatures and endlessly repeating the same plot. Robacker lamented, "No single writer has done so much to exploit the Pennsylvania Germans; and time alone can alter the picture she has created."

A newspaper clipping of Martin's obituary survives among Pattee's papers. Her readers would probably have appreciated *The House of the Black Ring.* The "dumb Dutch" epithet—suggesting both stupidity and silence or failures of articulation—may have come to Pattee's mind as he surveyed his ill-prepared, reluctant pupils who were more concerned with designing concrete structures than with literary study. In his memoir, however, he wrote that the longer he lived in Pennsylvania, the more he came to admire the Pennsylvania Dutch for their honesty, thrift, genuine religion, and hard work. "They are more American than I," he wrote, "for they were permanent settlers before the first pioneer of my own line had left England." He at once admired their stubbornly traditional ways and was taken aback by their ignorance and superstition. This conflicted response runs parallel to the attitude he must have felt toward his own rural background.

Like Martin, Pattee chose to write in the local color genre—which describes and even romanticizes the folksy—only to refute those folkways by the end of his book. (More than a century later, given new studies of powwow healing, it is harder to dismiss the practice as mere superstition, as Pattee does.) Martin's politics are obviously at odds with traditional life, and the Pennsylvania Dutch make easy foils for her reforms. Pattee, a progressive Christian, valued democracy, rational thought, individual choice, civilization and education, and individual deliverance from "bondage" of all types. Those ideals would have also undermined traditional folk life in Hell Bottom.

The tension between genre and content in both Martin and Pattee may be partly the consequence of timing. Whereas the American South and West and New England had become established subjects for local color writers by the 1850s, the people and places of Pennsylvania Dutch country did not attract the attention of regional writers until after the turn of the twentieth century, when a very different spirit gripped the nation. As Pattee recalled in his memoir, "The century began as a new century should, in major key." He recalls Theodore Roosevelt and "action now, 'the strenuous life, 'superman' after [the] Nietzsche pattern, 'men with the bark on' as Frederick Remington expressed it, men who had listened to the 'Call of the Wild' like Jack London." And the new century saw "new women" who were just as vigorous and capable as the men.

*The House of the Black Ring* was published in 1905. That year also saw publication of Martin's second romance, *Sabina, a Story of the Amish,* which recounts paranormal activity in a Lancaster County Amish family hosting a landscape painter from New England. Also in 1905 Elsie Singmaster's first published short story appeared in *Scribner's Magazine.* In the decades that followed, Singmaster's more restrained and complex short stories and novels about her background came to represent the finest examples of historical and realistic local color writing about the Pennsylvania Dutch from this period.

Meantime, Pattee ensured that *The House of the Black Ring* remained in print. In 1911, when Henry Holt stopped publishing it, he obtained the copyright and printing plates. He promoted later runs through the 1920s, mostly in Central Pennsylvania. According to a note in his memoir, the plates for this and most of his other books were melted down during World War II. In the middle of the twentieth century, it seemed that there was no hope for subsequent editions of much of his work. Current technology and new ways of reading, however, have returned *The House of the Black Ring* to us. (For a detailed description of the book's publication history, please see the note that follows this introduction.)

## Fred Lewis Pattee, Professor of American Literature

Teaching—a financial necessity while he was a college student at Dartmouth—became Fred Lewis Pattee's vocation. Shortly after he married Anna Plumer, he took a position as principal, and she as preceptress, at Coe's Northwood Academy in Northwood Centre, New Hampshire. In 1891, Pattee published a booklet titled *Literature in the Public Schools*, which outlined strategies to help teachers incorporate English and American classics into the secondary school curriculum. Two years later he also published a collection of verse, *The Wine of May*. Both volumes accompanied his application for the job at Penn State.

When he arrived at State College, he felt that he was "entering the trenches of a revolution." The Pennsylvania legislature had accepted a grant to establish the university but "was as yet unsettled as to whether the State had thereby obligated itself to support the institution, to maintain in all the coming years the child it had fathered." The Morrill bill of 1862 established land grant schools for the children of the working and merchant classes, aiming for "the unity and democracy of education" that was to be both "liberal and practical." But how this curricular balance would be achieved remained to be seen.

Although he came from a farm background himself—or perhaps because of that—Pattee bemoaned the decline of the study of Latin and Greek classics. As a student at Dartmouth, he mocked the introduction of practical subjects like agriculture. At Penn State, he found himself at a school that had been called the Agricultural College of Pennsylvania when it was formed in 1862. Postwar industrialization drove growth in the mechanical arts, and when Pattee arrived in 1894, fully 123 of the 178 full-time undergraduates studied some aspect of engineering. All other disciplines fell into a category college president

George Atherton flatly referred to as "the general side," although he hoped eventually to offer courses in literature, history, and philosophy.

At Northwood Academy, Pattee had begun to develop a curriculum in the history of American literature. That subject suited his Penn State students, who were preoccupied with practical concerns and largely untrained in literary study. During his second year, he offered the college's first course in American literature, one of only fourteen college professors in the country to teach the subject at that time, according to Martine. The same year, 1895, saw the birth of his only child, Sarah Lewis Pattee.

Drawing on class lecture notes, in 1896 Pattee published *A History of American Literature: With a View to the Fundamental Principles Underlying Its Development*, a textbook that situated the study of this country's literature in relation to the people, place, and times that produced it. Pattee's enthusiastic *History* sold a quarter of a million copies. That year he also published a manifesto titled "Is There an American Literature?" in the *Dial*, a Chicago journal of politics and literary criticism. One language can produce two distinct literatures, he argued, counter to the common sense of the day. After three hundred years, it was time to part ways with England and honor writing produced by the unique conditions in the New World—not just in a different landscape also but under the influence of such dramatic and formative experiences as the Revolution, westward settlement, and the moral dilemmas of slavery and the Civil War. This literature must embody "the soil, the spirit, the individuality of the people."

Pattee was not alone in making the case for American literary study in the late nineteenth century, but he wrote with the devotion of an aspiring practitioner of the new writing and with the zeal of an admirer of Emerson, Poe, Cooper, Hawthorne, Whittier, Lowell, Whitman, and Twain. His passionate piece drew public rebuke, published in New York's *Nation*, Philadelphia's *Saturday Evening Post*, and London's *Author*. Pattee also received a number of critical, sarcastic personal letters. Although his tone and views were tempered through the years, Pattee always insisted on the necessity of studying American literature as a field distinct from English literature, and on the importance of considering literature in relation to culture and geography. (It would take at least another century for literary historians to recognize that American literature might also be written in languages other than English.)

From 1897 until 1901, Pattee wrote or edited four more volumes on American and English literature and prepared entries on the history of American and Canadian literature for the *Encyclopedia Britannica.* A major new scholarly project—gathering and editing the collected works of Philip Freneau, the poet of the American Revolution—took him to archives on the Eastern Seaboard, and he was tempted to accept an editing job in Philadelphia. In 1901 he wrote a song that became the Penn State alma mater, but he felt "restless" at the dawn of the new century. Finally, he decided to devote himself to what he called "the most cherished field of my ambition, fiction."

While he continued to work on the three-volume Freneau editorial project, Pattee devoted much energy in the first eight or nine years of the new century to writing fiction. Among his early projects, however, only *Mary Garvin* and *The House of the Black Ring* were published. In his memoir, he confessed that as a critic he had condemned the enthusiasm for historical novels at the turn of the twentieth century, but as an author he rushed to publish one before the fad passed. He repeatedly revised and submitted another novel, *Old Second Street: A Romance of the Revolution.* In a 1908 datebook, he wrote, "I have been refused more times than any other author in America, and I have rewritten my work and studied and planned with infinite patience. . . . I doubt if I ever try another novel if "Old Second Street" does not win. After a man has had 5 novels killed under him it is time for him to try another vehicle."

Pattee's most reliable vehicle would always be literary history. In the fall of 1909 he embarked with his family on a sabbatical journey to Europe to observe research and teaching practices at great universities. While abroad, his wife became gravely ill and was diagnosed with tuberculosis. She did not regain her strength until the family returned to New Hampshire in the spring of 1910. During this time, Pattee pursued his interest in pedagogy and worked mostly on religious materials. In 1909 he published *Elements of Christian Pedagogy,* a book that applied current ideas in child psychology and education to religious instruction. In 1908 he agreed to edit a journal called the *Adult Bible Class and Teacher Training Monthly* for a year. Long before coming to Penn State, Pattee had been licensed as a Methodist minister; from 1905 until 1925, he served as Sunday School superintendent at St. Paul's Methodist Church in State College. From 1912 to 1927, he also acted as campus chaplain, his chief duty being the delivery of brief devotional remarks at compulsory services held for the students each morning before classes.

Some of those devotions he crafted into a small book, *The Compelled Men,* published by the YMCA in 1913. The booklet sheds light on Pattee's personal piety, which was profound but expressed largely in private practice and institutional service, as described by his biographer. The booklet is consistent with the progressive Christian ethic of cultivating the whole man—strong mind, strong body, strong spirit—that inspired the YMCA, popular at the turn of the twentieth century on American campuses. The Y is associated with "muscular Christianity," a British literary, social, and religious movement that aimed to revitalize both the domesticated Victorian male and the weakened empire. If a man could master himself through exercise, he could gain control of the playing field—or the globe. Theodore Roosevelt, with his "strenuous life," represented a secular form of this ethic. In *The Compelled Men,* Pattee argued that the Christian man exercises free will and that his consistent choice of "the higher things," both culturally and morally, ultimately becomes his fate. He is thus compelled to choose the right and good; compelled by inheritance of family and nation; compelled by a sense of responsibility, self-respect, and ultimately love of God and others, which in turn compels him to perform acts of service. Everything turns on self-mastery. Pattee wrote, "We begin always by being our own masters and we can always be masters if we will."

During these years, Pattee worked on a novel of literary realism about a chaste relationship between a minister and a prostitute. The story functioned mostly as an allegorical critique of hypocrisy and organized religion. Published in 1912 by Small, Maynard and Company, *The Breaking Point* did not sell well or receive significant attention. Later, Pattee wrote, "But the daily correcting of student themes for years turns a poet into a critic, into a scientist armed with established laws and ascertained facts. Gradually the poet dies." From his college days until his death, Pattee continued to read and write poetry for himself most Sunday afternoons, and for sixty-two years he published literary criticism and histories. At the age of forty-eight, however, he concluded his career as a writer of fiction.

In 1915, he published his best-known work, *A History of American Literature Since 1870.* The book set forth criteria for the development of American letters and surveyed an impressive range of literary and popular titles. In its preface, Pattee argued that the Civil War served as the greatest catalyst for the development of American literature. Out of that struggle, authors turned to their own land for material and inspiration. And that land produced bountifully.

During the 1910s and 1920s, Pattee's reputation grew along with the number of his publications. On campus he was regarded as a beloved professor who rarely lectured from notes and who engaged students in informal conversations about literature in his office classroom. Although he was often called to teach and speak elsewhere—at Dartmouth, Bread Loaf Summer School at Middlebury College, Columbia University, and the University of Illinois—he continued to serve as head of the English department. Between 1918 and 1920, a territorial conflict between the dean, Pattee, and another professor of English nearly drove him to accept an offer at Urbana. In the end, he decided he was too old to move a household, and the title "Professor of American Literature" was bestowed on him along with a sizable raise—not so much as an honor as to settle the dispute.

Anna, Pattee's wife and companion of almost forty years, died in September 1927. Their daughter had married and moved away, and Pattee was suffering from pernicious anemia, a disease that had taken the life of his colleague and close friend Joseph M. Willard. Fourteen months after his wife's death, he married Grace Garee, a church worker and widow of means who lived in Florida. At the age of sixty-five, he resigned from his position at Penn State and moved south, where he annually taught one course in American literature at Rollins College and continued to write and publish until his death in 1950. He was buried at Homeland Cemetery near Bristol, New Hampshire.

With Pattee's retirement from Penn State in 1927, the English department was divided into two programs: Literature and Composition. The split reflected significant departmental growth and expressed a practical division in the discipline of letters. Moreover, it marked the end of an epoch shaped by a man who once had literally embodied the entire departmental faculty and who, throughout his career, managed to bind together the divergent interests of English studies, because his work as a historian, critic, and teacher drew on his practice as a writer of poetry and fiction. In 1929 Pattee departed from an institution and a town that bore little resemblance to the village where he had begun his career as a professor thirty-four years before. With characteristic irony he described his parting glance in an essay about university life in the prosperous 1920s: "The college Babel with its hundred-thousand-dollar 'frat houses,' its million-dollar stadium and its young barbarians all at play, with its budget-making Prex and magisterial deans, its blacksmith shops and soil analysis and concrete structures; with here and there a book, and here and there a lusty 'professor' who once in high school possibly studied Latin grammar."

Of course, Pattee was the "lusty 'professor'" without a Ph.D. who had studied Latin grammar in high school. When he arrived, the paucity of literary titles in the Penn State library confounded him, so he took on book-reviewing assignments to help build the collection. When he retired, he bequeathed to Penn State his personal library, which included more than one thousand books and literary manuscripts, the core of today's strong holdings in American literature, housed in the library that now bears his name. Nevertheless, he chose an agricultural metaphor to describe his relationship with the place: "I never took root in Pennsylvania," he wrote, "though I lived there more than thirty years." Nor were his roots deeply grounded in the New Hampshire farm. The title of his posthumously published memoir points to an uncomfortably divided professor-farmer identity, shaped and defined by the two places he inhabited and served for so many years: *Penn State Yankee.*

# NOTE ON THE PUBLICATION HISTORY

Fred Lewis Pattee's *The House of the Black Ring* was first published in March 1905 by Henry Holt and Company—printed on faux laid paper with a frontispiece (a map) on glossy stock, and with a pictorial cloth binding of green linen stamped in black, white, and brown. Holt kept the book in print over the next six years, binding up sheets as they were needed in variants of this same cloth.

In 1911, when the trade run of the novel was finished, Pattee acquired the copyright and printing plates from Holt. This was a typical arrangement for the time. Theodore Dreiser, for example, purchased copyright, back stock, unbound sheets, and plates of his famous novel *Sister Carrie,* originally published in 1900, from the originating publisher, Doubleday, Page and Company, in 1907. Thereafter, Dreiser leased the plates to other publishing houses, maintaining control of the text and monitoring print runs for the rest of his career. Pattee adopted a similar strategy. He had *The House of the Black Ring* reprinted from the Holt plates three times: in an "Author's Edition" in 1916, a "Penn State Edition" in 1924, and an "Illustrated Edition" in 1927. Presswork, binding, and distribution were handled by Mount Pleasant Press in Harrisburg. In this fashion Pattee kept the novel in print into the 1930s.

Pattee made a few changes along the way. The Author's Edition of 1916 has a new title page and a "Preface to the Second Edition" in the front matter, together with five pages of excerpts from reviews in the rear of the volume. The binding is red linen, lettered in gold. Newspaper clippings pasted into the endpapers of Pattee's personal copy, preserved among his papers at Penn State, indicate that a copy of the book could be purchased for seventy-five cents, a typical price for a clothbound reprint in the early twentieth century when there were no paperbacks as we know them today.

The Penn State Edition of 1924 includes for the first time a dedication to the students, alumni, and faculty of Penn State—and to the citizens of State College. The 1916 preface is carried over, as are the quotations from reviews. Pattee has introduced the subtitle "A Romance" on the title page. The binding is a dark blue cloth stamped in gold.

For the final outing of *The House of the Black Ring,* Pattee had Mount Pleasant Press manufacture an Illustrated Edition, with six photographic images, printed on glossy stock, tipped in at intervals throughout the volume. For this reprint Pattee altered the subtitle to "A Romance of the Seven Mountains." The photographs are of landmarks or geographical features fictionalized by Pattee in the narrative. The dedication, preface, and reviews are carried over from the first two reprints; the binding is black cloth, stamped in red and white with the image of a rustic cabin.

The present edition, freshly typeset, brings together elements from the various incarnations of the novel. The map from the Holt edition is restored; the preface from the Author's Edition is retained; the dedication from the Penn State Edition is included; and the subtitle from the Illustrated Edition, "A Romance of the Seven Mountains," appears on the title page. A few typographical errors in the text have been mended. Otherwise, the narrative is presented here as Pattee originally published it in 1905.

James L. W. West III
Department of English
The Pennsylvania State University

# THE HOUSE OF THE BLACK RING

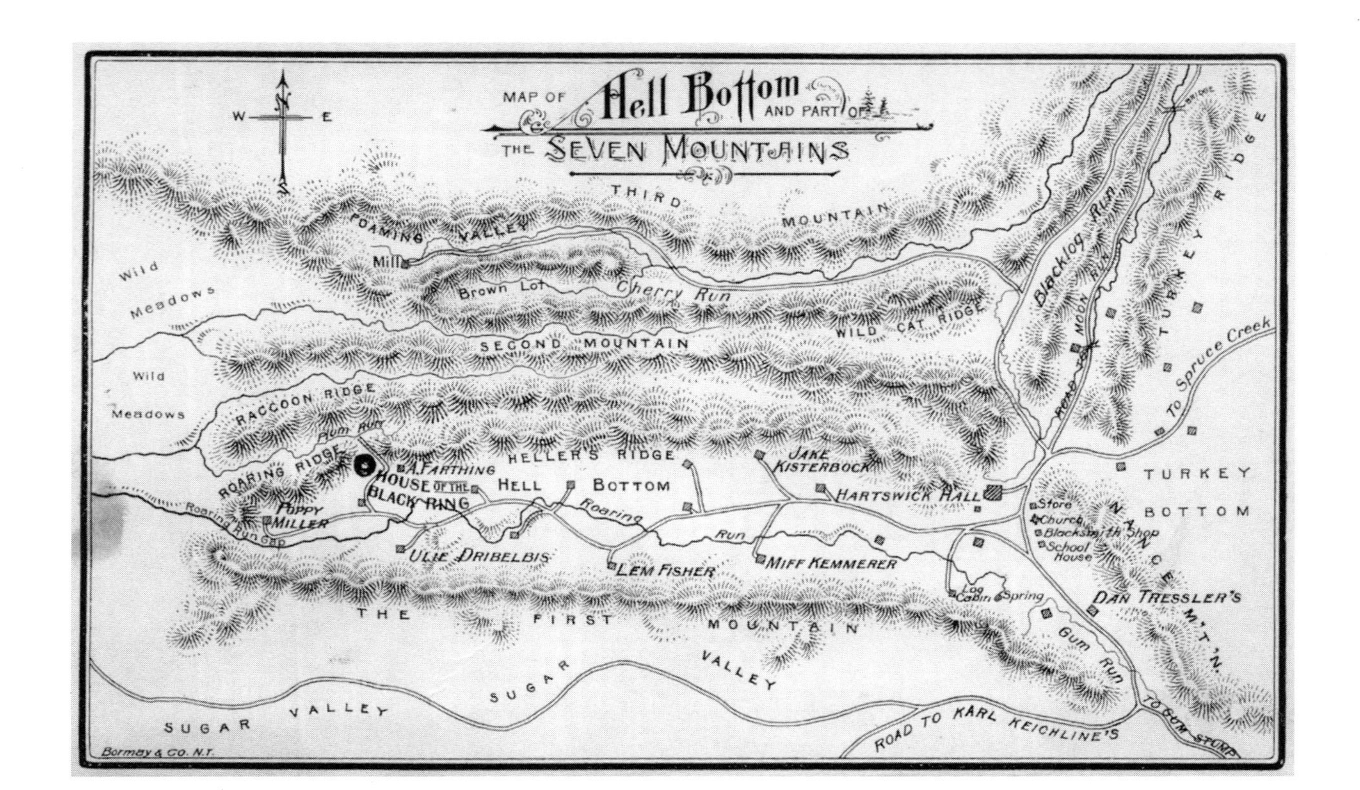
MAP OF Hell Bottom AND PART OF
THE SEVEN MOUNTAINS
W
E
N
S
THIRD MOUNTAIN
FOAMING VALLEY
Mill
Wild Meadows
Brown Lot
Cherry Run
WILD CAT RIDGE
SECOND MOUNTAIN
Wild Meadows
RACCOON RIDGE
Rum Run
ROARING RIDGE
HELLER'S RIDGE
A. FARTHING
HOUSE OF THE BLACK RING
HELL BOTTOM
JAKE KISTERBOCK
HARTSWICK HALL
POPPY MILLER
Roaring Run Gap
Roaring Run
ULIE DRIBELBIS
LEM FISHER
MIFF KEMMERER
Log Cabin
Spring
THE FIRST MOUNTAIN
SUGAR VALLEY
SUGAR VALLEY
Blacklog Run
MOON RUN
ROAD
BRIDGE
TURKEY RIDGE
To Spruce Creek
TURKEY BOTTOM
Store
Church
Blacksmith Shop
School House
NANCE M'T'N.
DAN TRESSLER'S
Gum Run
ROAD TO KARL KEICHLINE'S
TO GUM STUMP
Bormay & Co. N.Y.

To the students, alumni, and Faculty of Penn State
—and to the citizens of State College

—FRED LEWIS PATTEE, 1924

# PREFACE TO THE 1916 EDITION

The House of the Black Ring was first issued from the press of Henry Holt & Co., New York, in 1905. During the following year it appeared serially in several papers, notably The Syracuse Herald and The Washington Star.

It has been out of print now for some time, and a steady demand for it, especially by Pennsylvanians, has brought about this second edition. That the book has been accepted as a true picture of life in the central parts of the state seems to be proved by the steady demand for it long after it has ceased to be advertised, and by many letters, of which the following is typical: "I was so much pleased with your House of the Black Ring, which appeared as a serial in our Washington Star paper, that my daughter bought me the book for a Christmas gift. Fifty years ago, as the son of a Lutheran Preacher, a Pennsylvania German, I rode all over Nittany, Penn, Sugar, and Brush Valleys, and my familiarity with the locality and my acquaintance with the characteristics of my people made your story a positive delight to me. Have you written anything else about the Pennsylvania Dutch?" etc.

In sending forth the edition, the author, mindful of many letters and personal inquiries that he has received, would explain that the background was not drawn from any one specific region. There is no Hell Bottom among the Seven Mountains, and no Roaring Run,—at least no regions that go by those names. The book, however, is as minutely true to the spirit of the region and to the general type of landscape found there as the author knows how to make it. The romancer has been granted the right to idealize his backgrounds, and to assemble in one setting physical peculiarities that Nature, less cramped for space than he, has created far asunder. The characters also are types rather than studies of particular individuals.

F. L. P

*State College, Pa.*

*February 26, 1916*

# CHAPTER I

# THE AFFAIR AT TRESSLER'S FARM

WHEN THE GREAT architect had finished building the earth, he dumped the chips and débris into the centre of Pennsylvania, and men called the heap the Seven Mountains.

They are not mountains at all, but long ridges like giant furrows plowed deep into the very sandstone and left ragged and chaotic. Straight on they go for leagues, making a right line of the horizon, the second and third ridges following as if drawn with a pantograph. Here and there is a wild slash across the furrow, a rip into the very foundations of the range, and through the rock-snarl at the bottom worms a scared little stream. It is a gap—so they call it—and if one can wriggle through the jagged litter and the rhododendron, spiked like a wire tangle, it will lead him into the next valley, which is often a narrow gut full of torn sandstone and matted scrub, where only the rattlesnake may freely go. Often there is a bend in the furrows, a mad swirl as if the primal dough had been stirred with a giant mixer. Then the furrows run straight again.

Thus the Seven Mountains, a ragged hole in the heart of the East, where the wild turkey still wakes the morning, where the bear and the deer still flourish, and where the eagle and the buzzard wing undisturbed. The ridge-sides, rising sheer, and as steep as rock débris will lie, are like the tailings of mighty stone-quarries. A few dead scrags of trees break the sky-line; here and there in the rock chaos are scrub-oak thickets blasted by fire, and in the angle of the V always a little brook filtering through the rhododendron tangle. Then come ridges and mighty breaks and jagged cliffs and right-angle turns, and sometimes there are the ruthless tracks of lumbermen,—valleys choked up with hemlock tops snarled into the rhododendron, ramshackle saw-mills long since deserted, winding "dinkey" roads rusted out long ago and half buried in the fire-growth, and the effect of it all is indescribably lonely and wild.

But the valleys are not all of them V-shaped and littered. There are places where the ridges leap far asunder leaving a ribbon of bottom land, the seat of prosperous farms. Sometimes there are small, shut-in valleys, like pockets in the range, the homes of secluded communities,—a cozy bunch of farms strung on a winding road and bounded sharply by two gaps and the stone-line at the foot of the ridges. And of these might be counted the alluvial banks of Heller's Run, better known on the local maps as Hell Bottom.

So much for geography.

It was December the fifth, Dan Tressler's butchering day, as any one in the valley could have told as early as the preceding June. The sign was right, and the moon was "in the up." Squire Hartswick, lord of the Bottom, had butchered on Thanksgiving Day, as he and his fathers always had done; Jake Kisterbock had duly followed, and now by every valley right it was Dan Tressler's day. Things are not done by chance among the thrifty "Dutch." Baer's almanac and the tradition of the fathers rule Central Pennsylvania with despotic sway.

There was no lack of help. A "meetin'" on Sunday at the Bottom church brings out a goodly number, if the weather be fine; a funeral gathers the old people; a "schnittin'" in the fall, the young; but a "butcherin'" calls for everybody not "bed-fast," be the weather what it may. Not that all the inhabitants, hit or miss, are called.

"Invitations
For your 'lations"

goes the valley proverb, but the rule bars no one; for another valley saying is to the effect that nobody can "fire a stone" at random in any of the "Dutch" valleys and not hit his second cousin.

It promised ideal butchering weather.

As early as four in the morning lanterns were dancing like fireflies. All was bustle and din. Water was heating in copper kettles,—the valley's supply of kettles; scalding-tubs were rolling upon temporary blockings; scraping-tables were arising; knives were grinding, the sound coming up a dull creaking from behind the corn-cribs; and boys, eager and excited, were scurrying hither and back in the half light, shouted at and commanded until they were like "hens with their heads off." In the kitchen the housewife, calm but pale, was presiding like a general at the outset of a campaign, for the valley eaters, like a flock of buzzards, were to descend at noon, and she well knew that her dinner, good or bad, would be a topic for a year to come.

It was one of those clear, crisp mornings when there is a steel ring in the air and one's breath floats out like whiffs of smoke. An inch of frowsy snow had whisked over everything the day before, and it had grown colder during the night. In the east over the black silhouette of Nance Mountain, hung long iron bars of cloud, untouched as yet by the approaching dawn. From the valley there came up a faint murmur, which, on the vibrant air, soon became distinguishable as the grumble of wheels over a frozen road. Dan Tressler caught it and straightened up over his grindstone.

"Bet yeh that's old Miff still. Yas? Hear them wheels clunk?" He ran his thumb critically over the knife edge, then slopped the stone with water from a gourd. "Old Miff 'd set up all night 'fore he'd let anybody get to a butcherin' 'fore he did wunst. Turn 'er right up smart, Jakey."

He was a picturesque figure as he crouched over the flying stone in the uncertain light, his grizzled beard almost sweeping the knife in his hands and his eyes blinking small and sharp behind iron-bowed spectacles. He wore a "warmus," which fitted tightly at the waist, and a woolen cap pulled down over his ears. He was an eager little man, who on great occasions like this went about on the dog-trot. A wagon drove heavily into the yard, and with a nervous jerk he wheeled about to meet it, the long knife flourishing in his hand.

"Wal, now, who'd 'a' thought it wunst? It's you sure enough, ain't it now, Miff? And you here, Maria? Wal, by Chimminy! How gehts? Jump right out now; the woman's in there crazy 's a bed-bug still. Better go right in and help 'er out. Here, puht yer hoss right in the barn, Miff. There you be." He was bustling jerkily about the wagon.

"That's a fine day, Dan."

"Yes, Sir-r-r-r! By Chimminy, here comes Lem!" Another farm wagon drove into the yard, and then another and another. The crowd was appearing. The little man fairly danced in his progress "from rig to rig, like a weasel in a trap," as Lem Fisher phrased it.

The bustle was increasing. Roadside and yard were filling rapidly with farm wagons of all varieties, and with horses. No time was lost: each man had brought some implement that it was his especial duty to furnish at a butchering,—pulley-blocks, hooks, kettles, knives,—and each knew his part and went at it instantly without orders. The women and the girls went straight into the house, where they took their places with an order and despatch gained by the experience of many butcherings.

"Ah, here's old Poppy a'ready. Here, let me help you out, Poppy. Chust you wait a minute wunst." But the old man did not hear. Horse, wagon, and man seemed incredibly old. Without a word he hoisted himself over the wheel with unchecked wheezes and groans, then straightened up slowly and looked about him. Then he hardened into a stiff pose, with his gaze fixed intently on the south.

"What is it, Poppy?" asked Dan anxiously. "That's going to be a fine day? Yas?"

"Pet day, young man; t'at's a pet day. Chust you remember what I's a-tellin' yeh still. Chust you look t'ere wunst." He stretched a wavering hand out toward the south. "Beware of goat's hair in t'e sky a'ready. Ummmmmm!" He said it in the same awful tone that the soothsayer must have used when he said "Beware the Ides of March."

Despite the dire prediction, the morning was breaking clear and sharp. The iron bars over old Nance were softening into copper and bronze; the black smudge in the south was growing into the semblance of a wooded ridge, cut sharply against the pale sky.

A belated vehicle drove into the yard, and a shout greeted it.

"It's Ulie, boys! Here's Ulie a'ready."

"Sleepy! Oh, my! Jest you see them eyes wunst."

"Get home in time for breakfast, Ulie?"

A plump, middle-aged man climbed from his wagon, and proceeded with preternatural gravity to tie his horse to the fence. Apparently he had heard no word of the raillery. It was as if the undertaker had arrived at the funeral, and was arranging the hearse. As he turned, however, a sheepish grin began to spread over his face, and at the sight of it the crowd began to laugh.

"Think you're dretful smart still, now don't yeh?" he snapped, pulling off his big coat with vigor, and taking his customary place. Then the chaffing fell sharp and thick, like rice at a wedding.

"Who was it, Ulie, last night? Come tell us. Dew."

"Say, better get your courage up quick, Ulie. The rule for sparkin' is that the gal's jest as afraid of you as you be of her."

"Oh, pshaw, Ulie! Finish it right up slap and be done with it. It's awful bad on yeh, this settin' up so late nights when you're gettin' along in years. Boys can stan' it, but it's death on you old critters."

When a country gathering gets started on this track there is no logical end. No quarter is given, nor is it usually asked. Shouts of merry laughter went up at every hit. The victim seemed irritable and angry; he snapped and growled and bustled over his work with unnecessary vigor, but a close observer might have detected that in reality he was enjoying the raillery.

"Pretty smart, ain't yeh? Heh?" he spluttered. "'Spose you mind your own business awhile? I've known folks to get rich jest by minding their own business." He was greeted with snickers. "Wal, then," he exploded, as if hopelessly at bay, "let me tell yeh one thing wunst. I *was* out last night, and I seen something that would scare the very devil himself." The snickers broke into guffaws.

"Lord! is she that ugly, Ulie?"

"You jest wait a minute, fellers. I was out last night till midnight,—on business, you know,—and—" Again they interrupted him. Ulie Dribelbis, as all knew, had as his first business the securing of wife number three.

"Strike a bargain in yeh business, did yeh?"

"I—was—out—on—business," he repeated with studied deliberation, "and at just twelve o'clock, midnight, I was in sight of the old Heller house, and," lowering his voice, "I seen something."

"What was it, Ulie?" A strange hush had fallen over the crowd. They had all to a man stopped working, and were looking at him in a curious way.

"Tell us, Ulie. What was it?"

"Oh, nothing much." He was working away as if unconscious of the interest he had suddenly aroused.

"Say, this is a good hog, Dan. Spring wuts, wan't he?"

"Ulie, what was it? Tell us what you seen."

"Oh, boys, don't ask me about it. Please don't. It makes me creep all over. Oh, my lord! I wouldn't go through that again for a thousand dollars. No, suh,—a thousand dollars." He glanced up with a shade of terror in his face, and he shivered perceptibly. "How many hogs you got, Dan?" He changed the subject with a visible effort. "Reckon we can do 'em all to-day?"

"Come, out with it, Ulie. What was it, Ulie?" They had gathered about him, and were looking into his face with round eyes.

"Kind of a reddish, sickish light in the winder wunst, that kept sort of wa-a-a-verin' and beckonin'."

"Is that all? That was the moon shinin' on the glass still. You was scairt, Ulie."

"Cloudy night last night, and you-uns knows it. Dark 's the devil's pocket a'ready. Wan't even any stars, and you-uns knows it. And that light shined wa-a-a-ay out on the snow, makin' it look jest like blood. Oh, my lord! And don't you ask me what I heard. I can't stan' it. My god, men!—say, le's talk about something else. Say, Dan, when did yeh begin to feed these hogs? Did ye—"

"What was it, Ulie? What did yeh hear?" There was an awed tone in the voice.

"Well, suh, I heard most an awful noise a'ready. An awful noise!" He lowered his voice to a shuddering whisper.

"How did it sound, Ulie?" Lem Fisher's face had turned to a tallow white.

"A great, long laugh, like a crazy man's laugh,—a laugh that never come from no living man's mouth; no, suh. It made my hair go right up straight like a cat's back. Then I heard the awfulest swearin',—a kind of a hollow, gaspin' swearin' and cursin', as if somebody was being strangled to death. Somethin' seemed to take right hold of my throat and grip it up hard, so I couldn't breathe. I never heard no voice like that, never in my life." There was no doubting the honest horror in the man's face.

"Oh, pshaw!" came a disgusted voice. "Somebody was up in that old shanty,—tramps probably. If you're looking for ghosts, you'll find ghosts, I'll tell yeh that. Folks shoot bear that are loaded for bear."

"You look ahere, Amos Hardin,' wunst. What do you 'spose I seen this morning? Heh?" The company gathered nearer. "When I come over this morning I went up clost, and, suh," his voice breaking, "there wan't no track in the snow anywhere round it,—nothing but that black, dead man's ring a'ready. All round the house that awful black ring, but there hadn't been no track."

"Han't been no track in there all winter, yetst," spoke up a voice. They all fell to work again in silence. There was a look of horror on all faces.

"Wonder if Al Farthing has saw anything?" Lem Fisher was the first to speak. "Wonder what he thinks of this devilishness?"

"Bet you won't never know. Al's the most closest-mouthed man I ever seen still. If he'd saw old Heller with his own eyes a'ready, he wouldn't say a word about it. No, suh."

"Say, did yeh ever think there might be something strange about it?" Lem Fisher half closed his eyes and looked knowingly at the group.

"Now, don't you go to hintin' about Al. Don't you do it. He's square 's a die. Yessuh." Dan Tressler bustled instantly, as if the remark was a personal thrust. "Al's a square man, and the best friend we-uns have got in this walley still. Yessuh. He sayes as how he'll pay five cents a bushel more for our corn than the Squire will, and he's going to have a big load of flour come for fifty cents a berrel less than what we-uns are a-paying. Yessuh. He sayes it is a mean shame the way Ira Hartswick's been bleedin' us. He's been out and saw things, Al has, and he knows what prices is a'ready. Yessuh. I inwited him over to the butcherin' to-day and he's coming until eight."

"You inwited him?" They all straightened up and looked at the man.

"Yessuh, I did," doggedly. "It's a mean shame to leave him out every time jest because he ain't relation and the Squire's kreiseled at him. I inwited him, and his boys too."

"But you know Squire Hartswick—"

"I don't care a chincapin. Nosuh." There was a note of bravado in the voice. It was the tone of the small boy at noonday bragging about ghosts. "If Squire Hartswick don't like Al Farthing, I can't help it. Al's done the fair thing by me, and I'm going to do it by him wunst."

"Al may be all right, but it ain't safte in this walley to butt up against the old Squire. I'll tell yeh that. You'd better go slow, Dan."

"There's going to be a tarnation big explosion in this here walley if Al Farthing keeps on. Puht that down in your awmnick a'ready. There can't be two kings in this Bottom still. You mind waht I tell yeh."

Dan started to retort, thought better of it, and relapsed into silence.

Allen Farthing had moved into the valley the preceding April, coming from no one knew just where. He had bought the old Heller farm from a real-estate agency in whose hands it had been placed by Squire Hartswick, and had started in with energy to bring up the place from its forlorn condition. He had found the fences flat, the buildings in a ruinous state, and the land fast running to cockle-weed and bushes. In one season, however, he had got the old place into a fairly respectable way.

But the advent of the new family had troubled the valley. Allen Farthing was a singularly silent man, and his boys were like him. There was an element of mystery in the affair that was maddening to the little community, accustomed as it was to know all the minutest details of neighbours' lives. The Farthings, in spite of many subterfuges, and of sly traps set to learn of their past, disclosed nothing, and the whispers rapidly grew into open gossip. Who were these people? Why had they moved to this secluded little nook? Why had they bought, of all places in the world, the notorious Heller farm that for years had kept a tenant only for a few months at most? Why had they not complained of the ghostly revels in the deserted cabin not a quarter of a mile away? There was something mysterious and even uncanny about these people.

One thing, however, was clear: the Farthings were certainly kind neighbours. They were the first to volunteer aid in times of sickness; they were hospitable and generous; and they seemed anxious to make friends of all in the valley. Had not the three, when Dan Tressler had had typhoid, gone down and worked all day on his grain? And there were other good turns of which the valley could tell.

But the silence of the man and the strength of his personality fanned more and more the curiosity of the little community. He was probably not under fifty-eight, yet so vigorous and well-preserved that one might hesitate to set him at forty-five. He was a man of masterful temperament, one could see that at a glance. His sharp, black eyes looked one straight through. One felt instinctively that here was a man not to be trifled with, a man whom one might be glad, very glad, to have for a friend, but whom one might well hesitate to have for a foe. He was a man of great activity. He had adapted himself quickly to his new environment; he soon knew everybody in the region; and he seemed to understand as if by instinct all the problems and conditions of the little valley. The farmers were not getting enough for their wheat. Squire Hartswick, who owned many of the farms, and who had a monopoly of the valley trade, dictated the price, and there was no appeal. They were paying him too much for their groceries too, and Farthing had rebelled. He had decided to market his own produce and send for his own groceries, and he had invited his neighbours to join him.

"But don't you suppose Al knows about the old house?"

Ulie wiped his knife and looked over his glasses.

"Told him myself a'ready."

"Oh, you did?"

"But Al can hear and see for himself if he ain't deef and dumb and blind. No use to tell him," snapped Ulie.

"Then why don't he do something about it wunst?"

"But what in time *can* he do about it?" Lem Fisher was facing the crowd half defiantly.

"Burn down the old coop, hide and hinges." The suggestion came from a tall slab of a man who was very busy with the pulley-blocks. A scornful laugh burst from Lem Fisher.

"Now, that's good. That *is* certainly good. Just you hear Amos, boys. Burn out the devil! Fight the devil with fire! Oh, my! That's something new, ain't it a'ready yet?"

"Dry wood 'll burn, devil or no devil. You touch a match to that old shebang and see what happens. If it don't burn, then you c'n go and harvest my head 'long with the rest of your fall pun'kins."

"Now, don't you be too sure, Amos Hardin,' wunst. And don't you go to makin' big talk about what the devil can't do still. 'Tain't safte. Nosuh." He had a threatening tone, as if his own personal prowess had been made light of.

"Oh, pshaw!" Amos turned in disgust and walked away.

"Do you think that cabin could be touched by fire? Do yeh?" raising his voice to follow him. "Where's he gone? You see he's afraid to talk. Amos, he ain't nothin' but jest a Yankee still, but he knows I'm right. I tell you I knows what I'm sayin'—can't nobody go over the dead line around that house but jest the devil and them he lets go. Nosuh!" The oracle straightened up and looked about him like one who has won his debate.

"But what I want to know is why ain't Al scairt? Why don't he say something wunst? Why don't he tell what he sees nights? I tell you-all still there's something strange about this,—something strange." Ulie wagged his head mysteriously.

"Yas, yas, somesing strange," echoed old Poppy Miller, who had sat till now in sphinx-like silence. The unexpected words caused a thrill to go over the company. They all stopped short and looked at him.

"What is it, Poppy?" There was a breathless silence.

"Somesing strange," mumbled the old man with a vacant, far-away look in his eyes. "Somesing stranger 'n you sink a'ready. Somesing strange."

"H-s-s-s-s! Here comes Al." Dan Tressler warned the group in a penetrating whisper. Then he called out in unfeigned welcome:

"How d' do, Al? Mighty glad to see yeh, mighty glad." He shook hands with the stranger and a few of the others did also.

The day was breaking clear and sharp. The sun, peering through the bars over the mountain, was transmuting the bronze into incandescent gold. It lighted up the far horizon in marvellous shades of red and russet, and it fell on the long ridges that bounded the valley, showing in sharp relief the snags and scrub-oaks on the sky-line.

The Farthing boys plunged at once into the work with muscular vigor. They were broad-shouldered, brawny fellows, both of them over twenty, with good nature in their faces, and a self-reliance and mastery of affairs, come as they might, clearly inherited from their father.

"Smart boys you've got there, Al. Good workers, ain't they?"

"Oh, yes. Yes, Sir-r-r!" There was a hearty ring in his voice. "They're willing to work and I'm willing they should." He rolled up his sleeves and took his place in the line. He was a goodly man to look at, square-shouldered and straight, and he went into the work as if he loved it.

The business moved on merrily.

At ten o'clock Squire Hartswick with a whirl and a flourish drove into the yard, and the climax of the day was at hand. The men looked up nervously, then fell to work again with redoubled vigor. The old man made it a point to oversee carefully all butchering operations on his farms, and he criticised shabby work without mercy. The hogs were to be sold to him. He seemed to be a thick-set old man as he sat in the buggy, square and forceful. His face was smooth and florid, and under white, shaggy eyebrows glittered beady eyes that were never still a moment. In the corner of his mouth, as if it were a part of him, was gripped tightly the stub of an unlighted cigar. He was holding his horse with difficulty. Horses were his one weakness. Counting in his work teams, he had twenty-seven, and he had long held the county records in nearly every class. In races he always drove his own horse, and it was a sight to stir the blood to see him then. If anything had ever kindled within his hard old soul the passion of love, it certainly was his horses. It may be doubted if even his only child Rose, the one hope of his old age, aroused within him the tide of sentiment which was called forth by his magnificent stud of pure bloods.

The great bay stallion which he was holding by main force was pawing, and dancing, and snorting.

"Can you get out, Rose? Whoa there, Bill! Whoa! Behave there! Say, one of you fellows, come and help Rose out, won't yeh? Don't stand there with your mouths wide open. Whoa, I tell yeh!" Half a dozen sprang forward eagerly.

"I don't want any help." She arose impulsively and vaulted from the buggy like a boy, alighting with grace and spring as if she always got out that way. Then with a ripple of laughter at the discomfited swains, and a girlish flirt, she disappeared into the house.

"Too slow!" burst out the old Squire with a great, gurgling laugh. "You fellers 'll have to wake up if you want to help her out. Ho, ho, ho! Say, Dan, have somebody take this hoss and stand by him. He's full of ginger this morning. How're yeh getting along?"

"Good. Here, Sam, you and Jakey take the Squire's hoss. Come out and see 'em, Squire; they're neat ones, I tell yeh." The old man alighted briskly and went with Dan.

"Wal, wal, wal, boys, you have done well. That's a good job. How're they dressing up, Dan? Good?"

"Prime, Squire. Never had a better lot of hogs up by the heels, never. Jest you look 'em over, Squire, wunst."

The old man examined them with critical eye, and found nothing to criticise. Dan expanded volubly on the merits and the history of each in turn, and swallowed greedily the patronising words which the great man deigned to let fall. The Squire was indeed a man of commanding presence, a man to inspire awe and even fear in the peasant mind. There was that in his every tone and attitude which suggested mastery,—the stamp of the man who is often called upon to decide, and who is accustomed to be looked up to and obeyed without murmur. He turned from the hogs and threw a quick glance over the men in the yard.

Instantly his brow darkened.

"Say, Dan,"—he turned sharply,—"is that Al Farthing? How'd he get here?"

"I inwited him." There was a dogged tone in the answer.

"Humph! You did, did yeh? Getting pop'ler, ain't he?" No answer from Dan.

The group was preparing for dinner, which is served ever at a butchering at eleven. Four of the boys had gone into the house to help the women extemporise the seats and tables from planks and boards. The others had been watching furtively the progress of the great man.

Many of them feared him beyond expression, and they had cause. Some were in debt to him beyond all hope; others were his tenants without power to release themselves even if they would; still others were dependent upon him for work. Few there were who could oppose him with impunity.

He walked straight up to Allen Farthing, the jealousy and hate which had been gathering for weeks written on every feature. As he grew older his power of self-control, never large, grew feebler. So accustomed had he been all his life to undisputed supremacy that the slightest opposition angered him unreasonably. He found his man sitting by the corner of the overshot and clearing the ashes from his corncob. The others looked on with rising excitement. They knew the man; the fire and tow which had been so long preparing had at last come together.

"Changed yeh business, so I hear. They tell me you've set up in produce and groceries." The sneer in the man's voice and the curl of his lip made the speech positively maddening.

"You've been misinformed, Squire." He calmly knocked his pipe against the barn to free it from ashes, and proceeded with deliberation to find his plug of tobacco. His coolness acted like a red rag on the choleric old man.

"Hain't ordered a car-load o'flour? Oh, no! Hain't bought two car-loads o'corn and one o'wheat? Oh, no! Think I don't see what's going on, heigh?"

"You don't in this case, it seems. It's three of corn and two of wheat, perhaps three." He pressed the tobacco into the pipe bowl with his thumb, and began to search his pockets for a match.

"Who's selling yeh this grain, I want to know? Who in this valley's selling it to yeh?"

"Who's selling it?" He echoed the question in mild surprise, looking up curiously through the first white puffs of smoke.

"Yessuh, who's selling it? There's some here that can't afford to sell you their wheat. They'll find mighty quick that they can't afford it." He turned and cast a glowering look over the men. "And flour!" he continued with rising passion, his face fairly purple. The man's coolness was like a whip-cut. You think you can cut under me in flour and make money? Flour! Going to add dry-goods, and millinery, and five-cent counter stuff?" The sneer in his voice was changing to a hard, menacing tone.

"Why, it's possible, Squire; it's possible," admitted the man meditatively. "Folks here seem to be paying big prices and getting small returns for their produce. I may get a car-load of farming tools next month. I find the price-lists very interesting."

"To hell with your interest! Think you're going to run me out of business, do yeh?"

"I don't intend to injure a living soul, Squire Hartswick. I haven't the slightest intention of interfering with anybody's honest business, not in the slightest."

"Honest! You call me dishonest to my head, do yeh? You stand there and insult me, do yeh? Heigh? You be mighty careful, young man." He swung his hand angrily within a foot of Farthing's nose.

"I haven't called any man dishonest, as you know very well, Squire, but if you want to wear the coat I can't help it. You are doubtless aware of your own failings." He was as serene as if the conversation had been about the weather.

"Look here, Al Farthing." Realising suddenly that he had gone too far, he made a great effort to control himself. "It has taken me forty years to work up a business in this valley, and nobody ain't going to take it away from me without the biggest fight they ever had in their lives. You remember that. These people here owe everything they've got in the world to me-e-e. If I wanted to, I could turn half of 'em out of house and home. I'm putting the bread and butter into their mouths and I'm the best friend they've got in this world. They know that. Now what do you know about people here? What do you know about their needs? Not one thing. You come here a stranger and think you're going to run the whole show here and make things all over. You can't do it. All I want of you is to mind your own business and I won't trouble yours."

"Competition's the life of trade, Squire. You han't got no patent right to the exclusive business of this valley, have you? If I can sell flour for fifty cents a barrel less 'n you can and pay five cents a bushel more for grain and then make money, I don't see how I'm injuring these people here. I don't want to go into business; I came here to farm, but I'm going to see fair play among my neighbours. I rather think I shall keep right on,—that is, if you still continue present prices, and the people want to take advantage of my bargains. I'm not in this to make money."

"All right, suh!" The words came out with a metallic snap. "We'll see what happens. We'll see. But let me tell you one thing: you'd better go slow,—you'd—better—go—slow, or you'll get into trouble. You remember that. If you don't want the biggest heap of trouble you ever had in your life, you'll mind your own business and let other people mind theirs. Remember that. I've given you fair warning."

"Ummmmmm!" He took several deliberative puffs at his pipe, then calmly knocked out the ashes. "So I hear. But I shall go right on as I have done, and I sort of reckon there won't be any trouble. It's been a long time, Squire, since I wore anybody's collar and chain on my neck, and I reckon I'm too old now to learn. I fought in the war against slavery, and I'll fight again 'fore I'll see slaves around me. I don't owe you one cent, Mr. Hartswick. I own my farm clear, and you can't intimidate or boss me. If you pay fair prices for things, I'll quit the business and be glad to. Whatever I do I'll be fair and square and aboveboard, and I shan't injure nobody that's honest. I reckon that's all the speech I need to make just now. By Jimminy," turning his back on the Squire and changing his tone completely, "I'm glad to hear that dinner bell. I could eat a burnt boot." The big farm bell on the kitchen roof was clanging merrily.

"All right, suh!" The Squire's jaw sprung like a rat-trap. "We understand each other. Now, you remember what I told yeh. Don't you forget it, suh. You've tackled a hard man to beat—a hard man, suh." He wheeled and strode stormily away toward his horse and buggy.

"Goin' to stay to dinner, ain't you, Squire?" called out Dan anxiously.

"No. I don't want no dinner." He sprang into his buggy and a moment later was driving furiously down the road.

The company filed into the long kitchen in silence. They seemed awed and frightened. Only Farthing and his boys were self-possessed, and they speedily became the life and soul of the dinner-hour, joking and chaffing and telling stories till the others joined in perforce.

The mood of the company, however, did not delay the meal. The brown turkeys disappeared in a twinkling; the stewed chicken ebbed low in the milk pan; and the potatoes and vegetables were shovelled into hungry mouths as fast as iron knives could be made to work with safety. Great slices of bread were spread thick with apple-butter, and stowed away like coal into a stoke-hole. There were five "spreads" on the table, headed by the "Pennsylvania salve," without which no meal is complete; there was a gallon of cold slaw and a peck of krout. Then came the cider, great glasses of pure juice made late in October and fit for a king. In twenty minutes it was all over, and the women were alone with the wreck.

There was but one theme for conversation on the homeward ride that evening. Al Farthing had defied the Squire. Men and women discussed it in awed voices. Not one of all those at the butchering thought much of any other topic, save, perhaps, young Jim Farthing, who had seen a pair of black eyes.

## CHAPTER II

## WHERE THE DEVIL TREADS, WHO LOOKS FOR SNOW?

THE VALLEY OF Hell Bottom lies like a giant stocking at full stretch among the ridges. There are three ragged holes: at the heel, Bald Eagle Gap, walled in on one side by Nance Mountain, and cut deep by a little stream; at the toe, Gum Run Gap, leading into a populous valley beyond the clutch of the ridges; and at the top, which is puckered almost to a point, Roaring Run Gap, the vent of a small river fed from a spring from near the instep of the stocking.

The scenery of this last gap is wild and chaotic. Huge limestone hulks, weathered into weird patterns, protrude from the soil, or lie scattered about as if the place had been a workshop of the Titans, who had flung aside these colossal gargoyles spoiled in the making. In places the gnarled blocks are piled helter-skelter, forming grottoes and ragged hollows about which grows a scurf of junipers and laurel scrags,—a place to be avoided at all times, and especially after dark. A few rods further on, the stream, breaking in a panic from the alluvial, slinks whimpering down a wild gorge, and lies sluggish and exhausted beyond.

This chaotic five acres was old Poppy Miller's farm. One lot was under the plough, a ragged little patch hugging the ridge as for protection, and guarded at every avenue by the weathered rocks, which leered hideously, like totem-heads. Many there were who walked softly when they went to Miller's, and they averred there was reason. It was an uncanny hole surely, and unfitted in every way for agriculture, but old Poppy was reputed to have other and sufficient revenues, of which more later.

There was another rip in the hosiery, well up the ankle, a gaping tear through the ridge, known as Heller's Gap. It had been through this opening that Matthew Heller, purely by accident, had burst into the valley one December afternoon in the days when the land was King George's, and he had been greatly pleased with what he found. In the very jaws of the gap he had built him a cabin, and in the spring he had brought thither his young wife to make of it a home. He had hewed out a little farm along the run and had built him a barn, and all had gone well until the day when he had heard the sound of axes in the pines down by Gum Run.

There are traditions still vivid as to how the first band of settlers, who had come in from Sugar Valley, had been startled on the second day of their clearing by the apparition of a man grizzled and gaunt, who had proclaimed that he was sole owner and proprietor and king of the valley, and who had ordered them roughly to be gone.

Then John Hartswick, leader of the clearing band, had challenged the man to show his title deeds, which the old settler had done promptly, and the intruders, after looking wistfully at the goodly land, had left the region that very night.

Then ten years had gone by, during which time occurred the struggle along the eastern seaboard known as the Revolutionary War.

As to what happened next, tradition is vague. It would seem that on a certain April day, John Hartswick had come again into the valley, descending upon the old settler in the evening as he sat at the door of his cabin, and producing a certain paper which rendered the original document worthless. As to just what means he had taken, tradition says nothing at all, for the valley population, who alone preserve the story, know little of law. That there was a serious defect, however, in the older title is clear, and that it was of real moment and well-nigh self-evident to one whose attention was called to it, is proved by the fact that Matthew Heller then and there had been forced to admit the worthlessness of the paper, though the admission left him not the ground on which stood his cabin.

Then had followed a half-hour that even after a century is vivid in the little valley.

The old settler had sat at first in silence. Then he had expostulated. Morally and really the land was his. A mere technicality could not deprive him of land on which he had resided for twenty years. It was his even by squatter's rights. The letter of the law could never destroy the spirit. He had the right on his side; he would fight the matter in the courts; and no jury in the world would decide against him.

The younger man, however, had remained firm. The land was his; he alone had a clear title. Justice by the law was an expensive business, and he would see that this case was no exception. He had not been idle during the war; he had money and to spare; and he would fight for his legal right as long as he had a farthing. Then suddenly he had assumed a benevolent look. He would not be hard on him. He would give him a clear title to his cottage lot and to the few acres which he had cleared about it. Really he was injuring him not at all, for he was giving him all that he had ever used.

The patronising tone in the younger man's voice had pierced the free-air-loving old woodsman as with a knife. His helplessness, his total unpreparedness to fight a legal duel involving great expense, the perfect justice of his claim, and the barefaced wrong forced so brutally upon him, sent the hot blood leaping to his head. He had burst into a paroxysm of helpless rage, and had cursed the man with his whole soul. He would accept not one single inch of the land which was his own, but nevertheless he would stay where he was. It was useless for him to fight, for he had no money, but none the less he would hold his claim.

Then, in a paroxysm of rage, he had called on the devil to guard him and to bring evil upon every Hartswick, or Hartswick emissary, henceforth and forever, who should dare to come near him. He warned the man to beware of an infernal patrol which henceforth should surround his premises, and which would blast and destroy any of his name or blood who might ever enter the accursed circle. As for himself, he would never, so long as he lived, defile his foot by treading on the land that the law decreed to a Hartswick. If the court sustained the infamous robbery and gave him clear title, then, if ever once he, Matthew Heller, set foot on one inch of the disputed land, might the devil pounce upon him and bear him bodily away. Then, according to tradition, the old man had called upon all the powers of evil to make the valley a curse to Hartswick forever. Might he never have male descendant who was not a devil and who would not live in hell even before he died; and might the curse never be removed until he, the real owner, or his descendants, should get their rightful due and be kings of the valley lands.

Then, so runs the story, had come a ghastly stench of brimstone and fire, and Hartswick, seized by a panic, had fled for his life, leaving his coat-tails in the hands of a fiend who had snatched at him as he bolted for the door. A rifle shot, a mad laugh, and a volley of curses had followed him out into the forest.

Thus ran the valley tradition.

That very winter the crew of men which Hartswick had put in to cut the pines had noted a strange thing. All winter long there was no track in the snow to the Heller hut, though a smoke arose daily from the chimney. And they noted with horror that in a circle some twenty feet wide about the house there was no trace of snow, though it lay piled deep over the rest of the valley.

That was the beginning of strange things.

Not once in the twenty years that he lived was Matthew Heller seen in the valley, on land outside his little circle. What he did, where he obtained supplies, how he lived, no mortal outside his home ever knew. None visited him or his wife or his strange, wild son. It was as if they did not live in the valley at all, save that they furnished abundant food for conjecture and for superstitious awe. Many averred that they had seen the old man during hunting trips in distant valleys even in winter, and some were positive that they had run across the whole family on the ridges in berry time, but no one ever saw any of them on the valley lands, and, strange as it may seem, though smoke arose daily from the chimney of the old hut, no track, year after year, was ever seen through the snow to the dwelling. Furthermore, in all the century during which the valley folk had known the place, not one flake of snow had ever lain within the strange circle about the cabin.

At length the old man had been seen no more, though none knew when he died, or if, indeed, he did die. Then the old wife came no more to the blueberry ridges in midsummer, and the son, a dark, silent man, lived alone in the hut. After a few years he had brought from no one knew where a dark-haired wife, who said little and who encouraged no advances by the valley folk. Then, after years, the grandson of Matthew Heller, a man of ambition and energy, had rebuilt the old cabin, and later, in the early forties, had bought of Thomas Hartswick, heir of the original John Hartswick, fifty acres of land at the entrance of the gap, and had built on the little stream near by a set of modern farm buildings,—those now occupied by Allen Farthing. At first he had prospered. His elder son, Andrew, who had inherited the shy, hermit traits of the family, had retired in early manhood to the ancestral cabin, where he had lived much as his grandfather had done, but the younger son, a forceful fellow like his father, had remained at home until an unfortunate affair had forced him to flee from the valley.

It would seem from local tradition that this younger Heller had possessed a singularly winning and masterful personality, and that he had won with ease the leadership of the valley boys. As a result, however, he had stirred up a venomous hatred in the breast of young Ira Hartswick, son of the great estate, and hereditary heir to the valley lordship. It was impossible that there should be two leaders in Hell Bottom, and the result was a war, waged on one side with unutterable meanness and on the other with a stout defence in the open. The climax had come suddenly. In a burst of passion over a taunt about his ancestry, young Heller had given the Hartswick scion a thrashing so severe that the old Squire had had him arrested at once for assault with attempt to kill.

The plight of the young fellow was then indeed a serious one. There was no lack of witnesses who would swear to anything the old Squire desired, and it was hard to get a jury in the whole county who would bring in a verdict against his expressed wish. The outcome was not doubtful. Thereupon, with the impetuousness of youth, the young man had promptly fled the valley, a fact which naturally prejudiced his cause. It was known after a time that he had enlisted in one of the Pennsylvania regiments, for the Civil War was in progress, and after Gettysburg his name had appeared on the list of the Union dead. Thus he had disappeared from the annals of the valley.

Old Hartswick, however, had not been balked of revenge. The son having escaped him, he began to persecute the father. In five years the farm was in his hands, and the parents, crushed down by calamity after calamity, had both died in the old cabin where they had begun their married life. The elder son lived on alone, but late in life he married the daughter of old Poppy Miller. Both had died of sudden fevers some years later, leaving twin children, a boy and a girl, to be brought up by the grandparents. The boy, Leon, a headstrong fellow, had disappeared one summer day, drowned in a foolish attempt to run in a boat the whirlpool of Roaring Run, though his body was never found; and now the girl, Leonora, the last of the Hellers, was living, a strange, seldom-seen creature, with her grandparents in the Gap.

So much for tradition and family history.

As for the Hartswicks, they had been men of property,—hard, grasping drivers of business, who had answered in the full the wild prayer of old Matthew Heller. And of them all the hardest had been the present Squire, Ira Hartswick, owner of the village grocery and half of the valley besides.

The centre and the focal point of Hell Bottom was this store at the heel of the stocking, under the shadow of old Nance Mountain, in the jaws of Bald Eagle Gap. Near it were the little church of the community, the blacksmith shop, and the schoolhouse, all on the mountain side of the road, and on the other side, to balance it all, was the farmstead of Squire Hartswick, a village in itself.

First, there was the mansion,—Hartswick Hall,—built when the century was scarcely of age, of blue limestone and native mortar, a venerable old structure half hidden among the locusts and horse-chestnuts. Behind and around it sprawled a motley collection of buildings. The original log cabin, a tumble-down affair, used now for a hog-pen, stood not far from the spring, and near it was the structure indicating the second stage of the family,—a larger building partly framed, which was occupied now by Amos Harding, the farmer of the estate. Around these, in picturesque lawlessness, were smokehouses and sheds and sheep-pens and corn-cribs, the huge Dutch oven, after half a century still in active use, and the great barn, the chief pride and glory of the estate.

Altogether the effect was homelike and satisfying. It was like a Southern plantation, a little community in itself, almost self-supporting and independent. There was an antique atmosphere about the old trees, about the rambling paths and drives, and the old mansion itself, weathered and bleached and overgrown with Virginia creeper and honeysuckle. It had sheltered five generations of one family, a thing not common in America.

The grocery store was also a striking bit of architecture. It had grown little by little during many years. The owner, instead of tearing down and building larger as his business and his worldly goods had increased, had added bit by bit to the original structure. The whole mercantile history of the valley was written over the face of the building, every stage of growth from the original log shop to the large frame addition of only five years before.

Here it was that Squire Hartswick was most often to be found. Despite his abundant property he was a close reckoner of dimes and nickels, and he could keep but a single clerk, a nervous, bloodless lad, who worked early and late for the bare privilege of learning the business. Thus the Squire was obliged himself to be often behind the counters, especially of evenings, when the farmers dropped in and the mail was to be "disturbed." It saved the wages of another clerk, and paid well in the long run.

Thus, on a blustering night, some six weeks after the affair at Tressler's, the old man was in his place, a stout apron covering his entire front, an old Derby hat, much battered, askew upon his head, and the usual unlighted cigar-stump in the corner of his mouth. The store was well lined with the loafers usual of a winter night. In a ragged line they circled the stove, facing the Squire, who was perched, as was his custom, on a projecting shelf, opposite them, his feet on the counter.

"Now, what do you folks know about this ere Farthing?" he was asking with solemn earnestness, leaning far forward and holding his forefinger poised before the group. There was an expression on his face that seemed almost affectionate. It was like a father in earnest expostulation with his sons. "Have you ever thought how a'mighty little you know about him? Have yeh? Who is he, and where 'd he come from? Now, somebody speak right up quick."

"Jim Kemmerer sayes he come from nigh Philadelphy still," volunteered Dan Tressler.

"Humph! What does he know about it? Wal, le's 'sposen he did. What's he out here for, hiding in this hole in the mountains? What's he here for? Did ye ever stop to think that Philadelphy folks don't very often buy farms in these here mountains, unless there's some mighty good reason? Heigh? Now, what's Farthing down here for?" He paused impressively for an answer.

"He's mighty tight-mouthed," observed Lem Fisher, falling in with the Squire's line of thought. "He don't say a word about himself, and you can't make him."

"That's it. You've hit it right on the head. Now, let me ask you one question." The old man leaned toward the group impressively and spoke almost in a whisper. "Why is it that folks don't talk about themselves? When a man that you don't know won't say nothing about himself, what's probably the reason? Did you ever know a straight man in all your life who wan't always giving you something from his own experience? Did you, now? It's human nature to talk about yourself, and just you recollect now that this Farthing's been here going onto ten months and he hain't let drop one single word. You fellers think of that a minute or two."

"Al's all right," burst in Dan Tressler, with a spasmodic spurt of courage. It took courage to oppose the Squire's dictum. "There ain't a kinder man ever come into this walley still. Nosuh! Jest you see what he done for me when I was bed-fast last summer. You think of that. He didn't leave me lay, way some folks done, but he and his boys come right down wunst and went to work. Yessuh. Jest cause it tain't natural for him to keep his mouth going like a krout-knife every minute ain't ag'in him, now I'm tellin' you that. If some of you fellers," sweeping his glance over the group about the stove, but not including the Squire, "if some of you-uns quit your yammering wunst and didn't work yeh jaws so much, it would be better for you and everybody else in this walley still." He resumed his pipe and smoked furiously.

"Now, that's all right, Dan,"—there was an indulgent tone in his voice,—"but this Farthing's carrying it too fer. Wouldn't it be jest natural now for a man that's moved into an out-of-the-way hole in the mountains for *some* reason,"—there was a certain squinnying of his eye and accent of his voice that made the word significant,—"and who don't want to say much about his past for *some* reason, wouldn't it be jest like him to overdo the Good Samaritan business at first? Wouldn't he want to get on the good side of people and pull the wool over their eyes? Mind yeh, now, I ain't talking about this Farthing. I'm just 'sposing a case."

"I tell you Al's kindness ain't put on," maintained Dan doggedly, nettled at the Squire's insinuations. "If I ain't a nixy clean through and through, then I never seen a kinder-hearted man in my life. Nosuh. He jest seen his jewty and he done it, and I ain't the only one nuther. He don't go cacklin' all over town every time his old Buff Cochin lays an aig."

"Say, boys, ever think of one thing?" continued the Squire placidly. "You've been seein' some strange sights up to the old cabin lately, hain't yeh? There's always been queer stories about that place, but you didn't hear of much going on there till Farthing moved onto that farm, did yeh? Now stop to think of this latest cuttin' up; hain't every bit of it been since he moved into town?"

"Wal, you can't lay that onto Al." Dan squared about argumentatively. "There hain't been no track into that cabin all this winter yetst, and you-all knows it still." He addressed his arguments to the crowd, as if it were they who were combating him. "He told me himself when I asked him, that he had other business nights than laying awake watchin' for ghosts still, and that he hadn't saw a thing in the old cabin a'ready. He said he slept nights and went at his sleepin' early."

"Wal,—now—I—don't—know." The Squire again winked knowingly. "Ever notice what a sharp little black eye he's got and how it looks right through yeh? You don't see eyes as sharp as that very often." The old man understood perfectly those to whom he was talking.

"Yar! Now you're gettin' at it," burst in Lem Fisher. "It's an eye that can weave a brauch 'round yeh. First thing some of you-uns 'll know you'll be gettin' haexed; your kids 'll be liver-growed, and have the rundown and oppnehmer. You be careful, you-uns; that's my word to you a'ready." He had lowered his voice almost to a whisper. Ulie took up the theme instantly.

"That's jest what I've been a-tellin' of yeh. The devil knows what's what. There's a reason for the doin's up in that old shanty, don't you forget that. The devil don't have to walk when he wants to get over snow and,"—lowering his voice mysteriously and half closing one eye,—"a haexer and a pow-wower don't nuther. You-all think of that wunst."

"Recollect how strange old Poppy Miller acted down to Dan's butcherin'? Heigh?"

"How'd you dast to stan' ag'in him so, Squire, and say what you did right in front of him? Won't he haex yeh? Won't he send Rose into the oppnehmer? Ain't yeh 'fraid something 'll happen to her?"

"Naw! Not a bit. I carry words ag'in *him*. He can't touch me or mine. I've saw to that."

"But he's a deep one." Lem Fisher was on his own ground now. "He's jest the worst one we-uns ever know'd here."

"I don't believe it!" exploded Dan. "Al ain't no more of a haexer than you be, Lem; not one bit. And I don't believe that none of you have really ever saw anything up to that cabin wunst. Nosuh. You're jest like my old mare when she goes acrost the railroad track. You're so blamed scairt and you expect to see such an awful thing that you don't know what you do see, and you shy and kick and snort for all the world as if there was something there."

"Humph!" retorted Ulie scornfully. "'Spose I don't know still what I see with my own eyes? Humph!"

"Oh, I ain't questioning but what you think you see it. My boy come in one day and sayed that he seen a snake as long as the hay-ladder still, and I hain't the slightest doubt but what he thought it really was. Where's Amos? He'd knock the whole thing higher 'n a kite."

"Look here, Dan," the Squire spoke up sudden and sharp, "I'll give you ten dollars and pay it in money if you'll go up to that cabin right off *now* and touch it with your hand. Now, that's business." The Squire knew his man.

"Yessuh; now, that's business, and I'll dare yeh to do it," added Ulie importantly. "You talk big still, but you don't dast to do it. Nosuh. We've got you now, Dan. It's go up or shet up."

"Where's Amos? I'll go if he'll go with me wunst." The man was clearly in distress. He had half arisen, and was wavering perceptibly.

"Amos don't count in this bargain. Amos ain't here. Now you go up there or you quit your everlasting yammering about this here Farthing. I'm sick of it."

"All right, suh." He spoke with a quiver of excitement in his voice. "I'll go." Loyalty to his friend was struggling with innate superstition, and loyalty was for the moment the stronger. He arose like the leader of a forlorn hope and took a tottering step.

"Now," said the Squire briskly, "I want Ulie and Lem to follow behind and see that he does it." The crafty old man knew with whom he was dealing. Fear is as contagious as disease. The two men hesitated a moment, then arose doggedly and buttoned up their coats. It was always best to obey the Squire even when he asked hard things.

"Come back and tell us how you make out," shouted the old man as they were plunging out into the night.

"All right. We won't be gone long, I'll tell you that," called back Ulie, and then they were lost in the darkness.

There was a swirl of rattling snow in the air. The wind came in puffs and eddies, whirling the sharp grist into the faces of the men. A dismal roar, sullen and steady, rolled from the distant ridges, and from the near gaps came a succession of snarls and shrieks. The snow modified the darkness into a ghostly light in which nothing was distinct.

The three men struggled on in silence. At length they reached the place where the road turned off toward Heller's Gap, and they struck into it without a word. The buildings of Allen Farthing were in complete darkness; the family had gone to bed. Then they turned into the little lane that once had been the main road to the Heller cabin. By day a clear view of the hut could be had from this point, but the ghostly light revealed nothing as they peered through the bushes.

Suddenly a thin, wavering shriek rang through the air, far off like the cry of the Banshee. It stopped the three dead in their tracks. Lem Fisher turned and took several hasty steps.

"Oh, come on, boys," spoke up Dan stoutly. "It's only the wind in the gap. I've heard it blow that way before. Come on." They paused a fearful moment, then crept tremblingly after him. The outlines of the cabin were now dim ahead, and a few steps further left it clearly defined. At the sight of it Lem and Ulie stopped as if arrested by an invisible hand.

"Now go ahead, Dan, if you're goin', but I adwise you not to. I wouldn't go another step for all the money the Squire's got. This is all the farther we're goin', I'll tell yeh that." The three huddled together like children at night after a ghost story. Then Dan gripped his fists hard and crept ahead as if stalking some fearful wild beast. Ten steps and he stopped short with a sudden drawing in of the breath.

"Ah!" Before him stood the cabin with a black ring around it like the rope-mark about the neck of a hanged man. His knees smote together, but he started on. Again he stopped in utter terror. Was that a spark that had floated up from the old roof? And, oh, horror! The windows seemed to have a light in them,—a ghastly red that seemed to him to flicker balefully like phosphorus marks on a wall.

Pshaw! It was his imagination. He forced himself to take another step forward. He would make a run for it and have it done with. But his heart gave a mighty leap into his throat and stuck there, beating furiously until he could scarcely breathe. The light flickered suddenly brighter, a dark shadow seemed to glide before the window, there was something black and sinewy writhing at the corner of the cabin as if for a spring. Then suddenly there rang out a gibbering laugh the like of which he had never even dreamed of, then a string of curses that bubbled and cracked like boiling brimstone.

The man was no longer free to act. His brain no longer guided him. When next he could think his legs were flying beneath him as never before in his life, and he was hurtling down the valley faster than the winds, which, shrieking in fiendish glee, were chasing him from the Gap. But fast as he ran he was far in the rear of two other figures which never once stopped until they arrived, breathless and spent, before Squire Hartswick's store.

# CHAPTER III

# ROSE HARTSWICK

SINCE ROSE HARTSWICK had come back from her three years at the seminary, the life of the whole valley somehow had been changed. In the old days she had been simply one of the valley girls, a freckled, sunny-faced tomboy, the leader in every prank and frolic, but she had returned a full-blown woman, so changed that her neighbours hardly dared to speak to her. The little brown chrysalis had turned suddenly into a magnificent butterfly.

Then all in a moment their surprise and apprehension vanished, and they awoke to a new delight. The change was all in the outward. The Squire's daughter was still one of them; she was the same joyous, unspoiled country girl as when she had gone away, and she was glad to get back, glad all through and through; for the hills were home, and she had been homesick, she averred, every moment of her stay. Her joyousness had overflowed until the whole valley had shared it, and the young fellows had lost their heads like dandelions on a lawn.

But Rose was not a girl for lovers. There was about her no slightest trace of sentimentality. She had been fortunate in inheriting the best traits of both her father and her mother. From the old Squire had come her active, practical bent, her self-reliance, and her instant readiness of resource, and from her mother, her tender heart and her sunny, laughing soul. She was a girl with enthusiasms, spontaneous and magnetic; a girl who helped her mother because she liked to do it; a girl who was busy all day and who had no time for lovers. The anxious swains who sighed and stammered filled her with glee. They seemed to her inexpressibly funny, and they aroused in her instantly a desire to make them sweat, to torment and startle and embarrass them until they were at their wits' end. They were ludicrously in awe of her; never for a moment were they sure of her next move. When they began to grow serious she would laugh until they would blush like girls and grow confused and even angry. Then, before they could collect themselves or expostulate, she would be off on another tack, and they could only wonder if all girls were like that.

One saw her oftenest in the afternoon, rattling helter-skelter by on a long-geared mustang which had been her chief crony since she was a girl of twelve. She was no timid rider. It was a sight to thrill one to see her plunge down a mountain road, or to have her sweep in mad career full upon one around a sudden bend. A cheery hail, a sunny ripple of laughter that made one feel for an hour afterwards that the world was good, a clatter of hoofs, and she was gone. Few there were, young or old, who would not turn at the sight, and follow the trim figure, rising and falling in perfect harmony with her mount, until it faded in the distance.

"Mercy on us!" they would chuckle, "that girl will break her neck galloping in that crazy way." But they would smile softly, and the day somehow would seem brighter. It became a saying in the valley that if one wished to see Rose, the surest way was to sit beside the road for a few days anywhere within twenty miles of Hartswick Hall.

This love of horses and of the out-of-doors had come clearly from her father, and he delighted in it. There was not one of all his trotters, not even the vicious bay stallion, but what he allowed her to drive alone whenever she wished. Though she had never driven in a public race, it was the old man's boast that there was no jockey in the region that he would sooner trust in a critical moment. She knew horses almost by instinct. She loved to break wild colts and vicious balkers and halter-pullers. It was a joy to see her in battle with a stubborn beast. One who knows only the type of female who drops the reins and screams when the horse begins to back, knows little of what is possible. She was slight of figure, but she was marvellously strong in her shoulders and arms. And besides this she feared nothing in the shape of a horse. Never once in her life had she failed of her purpose, or met with an accident or a set-back.

It was about this time that young Jim Farthing began to take a new interest in horses. Five years before, his father had given him a colt, a wonderfully dainty little creature that he had bid off at a bankrupt sale. There was good blood in the colt, so the owner said. The mother had been good for two-eighteen, and the sire even better. With proper handling she ought to develop into a wonder, and Jim had tried hard to give the proper handling. She had from the first been the passion of the young fellow's life. He had trained her early in the sulky, and when she was three he had won in handsome style a two:twenty-five heat. Then had come the removal to the mountains and small chance for training trotters. There was a world of work to do: for the old farm was a chaos; the little mare had had to find her exercise on the cultivator and the horse rake, with occasional trips to Spruce Creek, the nearest railroad station. Thus it happened that during the year not one in the valley, not even Squire Hartswick, who boasted that he could size up any horse at a glance, had seemed to see her.

Suddenly, late in January, after he had seen Rose in full gallop one afternoon on the Gum Run road, young Jim made the discovery that his mare had possibilities as a saddle horse. She needed exercise, and it would be easier in the mud that lay fetlock-deep on all the mountain roads, to give it without the buggy. There was the mail to get, and there were errands to do all up and down the valley.

It was some time before he ran across Rose again. It was on a Monday afternoon. He had gone to Spruce Creek to enquire for his father's freight, and as he had cantered up to the station his heart had jumped into his mouth. There was no mistaking the supple figure on the platform with the agent. She was holding her crop jauntily before her, a hand on either end. Every detail of dress and posture and expression burned into his brain like a flash-light snap,—the glorious wealth of her hair under the riding cap, the square set of her shoulders, the dainty grace of her coat, and even the expression of her eyes as she looked up at his approach. He tipped his cap automatically, and sprang from the saddle even before the horse had come to a full stop.

"Hello! Glad to see you," he called, with hearty ring. "How's this for mud?" He looked ruefully down over his spattered clothes.

"That's nothing. You ought to ride the Sugar Valley road."

"Muddy down there, is it?"

"Muddy! Why all I could see of Pomp one time was just his ears." Her spontaneous laugh thrilled young Jim. Before he could answer, she had turned with sudden change of tone to the agent.

"We'll have the teams down here by nine. That car 'll have to be moved twenty feet,—all of it. There's no chance to swing in, don't you see? You'll be sure to have it done?"

"Sure. Anything you say. Glad to do it." There was sultry good nature in the agent's face and tone. He followed her even to the edge of the platform, suave and gushing.

"All right, then,"—with business snap,—"at nine sharp it is." She turned quickly to her horse, which was standing unhitched a few steps away.

"Come, Pomp," she called.

"Here, Miss Hartswick, let me help you." Jim sprang forward eagerly.

She turned for an instant as if to answer him, then vaulted seemingly without effort into the saddle. "Oh, pardon me," she said quickly, "I mounted before I thought." A roar of laughter pealed out from the platform.

"Too slow! Have to wake up, young feller, if you're goin' to do business round here."

"Has our freight come?" He wheeled square about and changed the subject with a snap.

"No, but it 'll be here on the evening train."

"We'll get it to-morrow." He was on his horse and cantering after Rose. In a moment he was swinging along beside her.

"Say, you've got a nice pony there, haven't you?" She turned in her saddle to examine the horse. "Can he go?"

"Well, I guess."

"All right,—good-bye."

On the instant the mustang shot ahead alike a polo pony. They were fairly out of sight behind a bend before Jim awoke to what had happened. Then he too was off on the jump.

How gloriously the girl rode! The great mustang was at full stretch, smashing through mud and water-hole, and throwing a deluge of soft mush three rods in every direction. She was leaning far forward, almost to the horse's neck, to break the force of the wind. The rider behind her never once took his eyes from her. The soft brown of her hair, an intense fleck against the winter white, was like the focal centre of all things. He urged the little mare to her utmost, and in two minutes he was right at the mustang's heels.

Then as suddenly as she had started, the girl dropped again into a canter.

"My, but he's a goer!" she burst out enthusiastically. "Say, I want to ride him. May I?"

"Why—yes——"

"All right. Whoa, Pomp!" The horse stopped instantly, and she sprang to the ground. Jim also alighted.

"Now, you hold both of 'em by the reins," he said with business decision, "and I'll change the saddles. I'm afraid yours won't fit very well, though."

"Oh, no. I can ride a man's saddle just as well as I can my own."

"Shall I help you mount?" He came very near her, so near indeed that it awed him a little. He had never been so near her before.

"Can't you get me a block or a stone or something for me to clamber up on?" She looked about her as if in distress, and involuntarily his eyes followed hers, seeking for a block. He turned to find her in the saddle. It seemed like magic. But her merriment was bitten short off. The gingery little mare knew nothing of women, and she started instantly on a mad, kicking, slewing, bucking, breakneck rush down the road. Jim's heart went into his mouth. No girl in a flurry like that could stay in that man's saddle without stirrups.

But she did. It was as if she were strapped on. She anticipated every movement and checked and reined and braced and swung, until after a moment the scared horse lighted out full speed on a straight-away trot, as if she were in a sulky and on the home-stretch. It was an experience to shake the life out of one, but the girl kept her seat. it was as if she had always ridden that way. In three minutes she had the horse in a rocking canter. Then Jim loped up on the mustang. He was perched precariously on the side-saddle, and his face was full of apprehension. She looked over at him and laughed.

"This is fine!" she cried, turning to him a face fairly radiant with enjoyment.

"Why, I'd no idea she'd do that," he began to apologise. "You see she never——"

"But isn't she a little wonder, though? My, can't she go! I had no idea you had such a horse." Her hair was shaken in curly little wisps about her face, and her cheeks were glowing. She seemed to be perched carelessly on the saddle, so that the slightest movement might shake her off.

"By George, I thought she'd kill you sure. Aren't you hurt? Aren't you shaken all to pieces? Wait, let me help you down."

"Pshaw! that's nothing. I'm going to ride some more. It's fun." She laughed up at him again in a way that made his finger-tips prickle.

"Say," he burst out, "I don't believe there's another girl in the State who could have done it. I don't believe there's half a dozen in the whole world." There was no mistaking the tone in the young fellow's voice.

"The idea! I can't ride much. But, say, this is no saddle horse. She's a trotter."

"I know it."

"Really? Then what are you riding her for? You're spoiling her."

Young Jim could have told the exact truth, but he didn't. He preferred to keep silent.

"You're too heavy in the first place. You must weigh,"—looking him over with judging eye—"all of one hundred and eighty."

"One hundred and eighty-four exactly."

"That's it, and the mare here goes barely nine hundred. And she's a fine-boned, sensitive little thing. It's risky for you to be jumping her around on these miserable roads, and besides that you are teaching her so she'll break every time just at the critical minute. Has she ever trotted to a sulky?"

"She's got a record of two:twenty-five."

"No-o-o! Why, Mr. Farthing, I never dreamed you had such a horse up there. When did you get her?"

"I've had her ever since she was a colt."

"If I had known it I should have had her out before this time, I'll tell you that." She looked up at him archly, and then laughed in mere girlish fulness of life. "Say, I want to try her in the harness some time? May I?"

"Why, yes. Certainly."

"Right off? This week?"

"It's muddy for trotting, ain't it? The roads are all like this, or worse."

"There's the Gum Stump pike," she suggested. "That's fairly hard now."

"All right. Will you go with me some afternoon this week and try her? Say Thursday. Will you?" he asked eagerly, reining his horse a little closer.

"Yes, I can go Thursday. Say, I believe if this mare's handled right she's better than two:twenty-five. Just see what a chest she's got and what a neck and shoulders, and see that clean, dainty little head. Why, her record's written all over her."

"We've been pretty busy up to our place, and I really haven't had time to exercise her."

"Why don't you let the witches do it?" she flashed up at him mischievously. "Up in the old house there? They're out, you know?"

"Are they? Perhaps I can," he laughed. "Guess you'd be safer, though; when shall I call?"

"Two, if you can. I've got to be back by five. Here we are." She drew up the horse suddenly and turned him partly around. "We'll have to swap horses here; I've got an errand a mile down this road. Here now, hootchie, don't you shy when I jump off. Here! here! See that? Haven't I got her tamed? Why, in a week she'd be just like a kitten, wouldn't she? What's her name?" She had alighted and stood fondling the horse's nose.

"Dolly,—Dolly Gray."

"Fine! Well, 'good-bye, Dolly Gray.'" She sang the words, then laughed up into his face with mere joy of life. An instant later she was on her own horse and off down the branch road. A dozen bounds and she turned lightly in her saddle.

"Good-bye,—till Thursday," she called. Then she swung around the bend out of sight.

It was a full minute before he had collected himself enough fully to realise what he was about. No wonder the boys lost their heads. Young Jim had lost his for the first time in his life. For him now there was but one thing in all the world, and that was Thursday,—but much was to happen before Thursday.

## CHAPTER IV

## THE WOOING AT HARTSWICK HALL

A YOUNG MAN in the early forties, a fleck of grey at the temples, a silver dollar at the crown, a trace of advancing corpulency in his rounding figure, but withal settled in character and income and looking confidently out upon life, is in a position to make strong arguments to a maiden of twenty. But maidens of twenty are not won by argument, and the tragedy of it all is that careful parents are influenced little by anything else.

Which is a novel in a nutshell.

Ever since early August it had been a foregone conclusion in all the region that Rose Hartswick was to marry Karl Keichline, the postmaster of Sugar Valley. The old Squire was growing old; the burdens of his great estate were beginning to weigh upon him; he needed a son-in-law who had force and judgment and tact to help him in his work, and to succeed him when he was gone. That he had chosen Keichline for this place was no secret at all; he even talked of it openly; and it was the impression in both valleys that the affair was as good as settled. As to what Rose might think very little was said. She might protest at first,—such girls usually did,—but in the end she would yield to her father's will. In a hundred years there was no tradition in the valley of a successful rebellion against the head of the house of Hartswick.

His will was law.

The campaign had opened briskly and without delay. On the very first Sunday after Rose had arrived home from school, Keichline had driven six miles to worship at the Bottom church. And no one had wondered. It would have been impossible, all conceded, to make a more perfect match. The man had force and maturity and judgment; he was a born leader, sharp at bargains, and given to holding what he had gained; he had, moreover, an impressive dignity and a tremendous self-respect.

It seemed to the old Squire as if Providence had raised up the man to take the place of the son who had been denied him. Therefore he had hastened to invite him home at the close of the service, and after the ample dinner, had smoked with him in the great front room, and had talked over the crops and the prospects in Sugar Valley and the Bottom, and the state of the grocery trade, and the outlook, and had grown every moment more satisfied with himself and with all the world. Then, after the dishes had been "dried," and the dining-room "redded up," he had called in Rose, who had sat by the west window, the sun in her hair, and she had fondled the cat, and pretended to read the story in the weekly paper while they talked, and all had seemed idyllic and as it should have been.

The personality of Karl Keichline was strong and dominating. He was self-made and therefore self-centred. He had fallen in love with Rose at first sight, as he had expected to do, and he had begun his wooing with confidence. That any woman in her right mind, be she even the daughter of the great Squire Hartswick himself, could fail to be flattered by his attentions, had never entered his mind. He owned three farms clear of debt, beside his grocery business and his home estate. But even without these material good things, his personal charms were surely enough. He was plump and cherub-faced, a man to give the impression of great solidity and importance, well-groomed, still young, he fancied, and still fascinating to the sex. Moreover, he had heard whispers of the old man's wish, and he knew the great power of his expressed desire. Truly, he held the long suit and all the master trumps, and he wooed, therefore, as he who has already won.

But, alas!

Rose Hartswick was not a girl to be impressed by mere proprieties. She cared not a snap what people expected of her, or for what was considered the proper thing. What she wanted to do she did, and the people might talk. If she took it into her head to ride her horse astride a man's saddle, she did it, and if she disliked a thing she said so flat and honest, cut where it might. She was her own sweet, unconventional self and nobody else, and the valley loved her for it.

From the first Keichline had struck her as irresistibly funny, so funny indeed that she giggled at the sight of him. His dignified, self-important air was almost too much for her, even at the Sunday dinner. She felt an unholy impulse to prod him with a hat-pin under the table to see him jump and look shocked, or to creep slyly up behind him as he sat Sphinx-like and impressive and shout in his ear "boo-o-o-o!" or to pull the chair suddenly from under him as he was taking his seat at his place solid and aldermanic, and have him come down with a crash, shaking the blancmange and the chicken jelly. She was only a girl, despite her twenty winters,—a sweet, joyous, unspoiled country girl, who had never had a sick day, and who was brimming over with the zest and the urge of joyous young life.

On Keichline's third visit to the valley the Squire had arisen after the first cigar and had gone out without a word, leaving the two in possession of the sitting-room.

It was time for the second act.

There had been an awkward silence for a moment, then the man had bristled up in a most engaging way, had wet his lips, and wheeled his chair about so as to face her. Somehow he was not so much at his ease as he had expected to be.

"That's fine weather now, isn't it?" he began unctuously, in a tone so different from that which he had been using to the Squire that it seemed almost to come from some one else.

"Yes," she said primly, fighting hard with the beginnings of what she knew was irrepressible.

"Very fine weather, very fine!" There was conviction in his voice. Then suddenly, as if he were giving a confidential tip about the markets, he added intensely, "I think we shall have fine weather tomorrow."

"Yes," she said again solemnly, hardly daring to breathe. Then she caught sight of his little plump hands clasped tightly across his stomach, the thumbs twirling very slowly, and it was no use. The giggle came out with a burst; to save her life she couldn't have helped it. He looked up with a jerk, utter surprise written all over his face. Then realising that he must do something, he forced himself to a sickly grin.

"Ah,—why, you seem to be in good humour. Ah,—that's good. I always like to see—" She caught sight again of the little fat thumbs, twirling rapidly now, fought hard with her handkerchief, then burst out again. He stopped short in dismay, and looked at her as if she were suddenly sick. Then he glanced down over his clothes, felt of his necktie, and ran his hand over his hair.

"Yes." She checked herself with an effort. "You always like to see—?" She paused interrogatively.

"Ah, yes, as I was saying, I always like to see—Ah, yes, I take the greatest delight to see—ah—"

He was "rattled"; his face flushed scarlet; he breathed audibly; and there were beads of sweat on his forehead. He cast another swift glance down over his clothes; then he tried again to speak; but there was nothing to say.

"Oh, I'm afraid my cat's got a bird," she cried, casting a quick glance out into the garden. "Here, Dick, stop!"

She dashed out tumultuously, and on the instant he was at the mirror looking himself over from every point of view. Then he peered into all the corners of the room and even under the sofa, for he had read stories of concealed small boys. He found nothing wrong. There had been nothing to laugh at.

There could be but one explanation. He knew the sex chiefly from what he had read, and he had read somewhere that girls always giggle when they are embarrassed. The thought relieved him; she would soon get over that. He strolled out into the yard, and forgot his woes in contemplation of the fatness and glory of the old Squire's heritage.

When next he saw Rose she was serving the supper,—a prim, tall figure that moved with decision, and that set things around with a snap and deftness worth watching.

"Rose is a good housekeeper," the old Squire was saying jovially. "She just about runs this house. Things have snapped around since she got home. Why, she got every bit of this supper alone; wouldn't have her mother come down at all; and she did it in thirty minutes. How's that?"

"Fine, fine!" he gurgled, looking with experienced eye over the bounteous table and rubbing his hands together in anticipation. Rose came in just in time to see the movement, and a lightning impulse possessed her to pour water over the plump hands as he rubbed them, but she took her place with preternatural gravity. There was little conversation; the supper required the undivided attention of the guest.

"Of course you'll stay to the service this evening?" the Squire spoke up at length. "There's a good moon, and it 'll be a glorious ride down the Run."

"Why, yes, perhaps I will,—perhaps I will." It was as if he had just thought of it. There was a tone of concession in his voice, as if he were conferring a favour by staying.

"I don't go much in the evening," the old man continued. "I don't feel quite sure of my footing now after dark, and I like to have the woman stay at home with me, but Rose never misses a service. She's organist, you know. She'll take you right along; you and she can start off together any time now. It takes up at seven. Here, Rose, 'most ready, are you?" He had taken a step to the door, and was calling up the stairs.

"Yes, all ready," came the cheery voice from above.

"You going, Pap?"

"No, but Mr. Keichline is. He's all ready."

"Yes—yes." He came forward suavely as she appeared at the door. "I shall be glad to escort you; very glad indeed." He was bowing unctuously, his hat in his hand. "I'm at your service. Shall I have the pleasure?"

"Oh, land, no!" she burst out with a laugh. "No time for ceremonies. Got to get there and practise that old anthem. It's late now. There goes the second bell. I must hurry. Good-bye." She waved her glove at her father, and tripped girlishly down the walk. Keichline stood looking at her blankly.

"You'll have to get used to Rose." The old man turned full of apology. "There isn't a better-hearted girl in this world, but she's young and impulsive yet. She doesn't mean any harm. You know girls,—they've got just about so much silliness in 'em, and it's bound to come out. You'll get along with her all right when you understand her. She's a good girl,—good 's gold. She's never once disobeyed me, and she never will."

"Yes, yes, I understand." And he had gone on to the church, mollified and encouraged.

As he sat and watched her at the organ, her figure full of supple and slender grace, her movements rapid and decisive, and her whole attitude whispering of hearty and joyous life, he forgot his vexation and was glad that he had come. He studied her during the sermon: her brown wavy hair; her eyes that seemed darker than they were; her cheeks and throat, girlish in their outlines; and he resolved to stay every Sabbath evening to the service. He would go home with her through the twilight, and perhaps he would whisper to her something on the way. Perhaps.

He lingered at the door while the audience straggled out after the service. It was embarrassing, for all the young fellows of the neighbourhood were lined up for several rods down the walk, either waiting for their "girls" or else curious to observe what was going on. He would not do it again; he would go forward and speak to the pastor, and then take Rose as she came down with the choir.

The row of youngsters grew thinner about him; there were only half a dozen; and now he was alone. What was keeping Rose so long? Doubtless the choir was arranging for a rehearsal. He would walk in and see; it was not proper for her to go home alone in the darkness.

The church was empty, save for the janitor, who was extinguishing the lights.

"Rose Hartswick—" he blurted out. "Has she gone?"

"Land, yes; long ago. She went out of the side door there."

He turned, dazed and angry. As he reached the step, a voice from the shrubbery opposite bellowed lustily:

"Too slow!" and a great, roaring laugh followed from a dozen throats.

He did not see Rose again that night. He rode down the valley vexed and peevish, and it was two days before he recovered his old confidence.

Thus it was in the weeks that followed. He came every fair Sunday and remained for the evening meeting, and the girl tormented him until often, as he rode back the long, dark journey down the Run, he vowed that he would never go again. He was at her mercy.

He was never quite sure as to what was to happen next. If she complied with his request, it made him suspicious. One perfect January afternoon, for instance, he had invited her to a walk.

"Fine!" she had cried joyously. "It's just the thing; it's just the day for a walk."

"Ah, it is; it is," he had gurgled, hardly daring to believe that she had really consented. They would saunter out in the clear, warm air, and would sit at length in a sunny little nook, and he would settle the whole matter once for all. His heart beat high at the thought.

"I've wanted to go for a long time," she went on radiantly. "We'll go over to the old Heller cabin. There's all sorts of stories flying around, and I've wanted to see it all winter. It's just the day. Come on."

"Not afoot? You don't mean to *walk* clear over there?"

"Sure. I feel just like walking. Come on."

"But the roads are all mud,—it's awful walking," he had persisted.

"All the more fun. I ain't afraid of mud, are you? Get on your gum shoes. We'll be there in no time." There was no escape.

"Don't run," he puffed at length. "Let's just saunter along. There's no rush."

"We'll have to hurry to get there and back before meeting-time. Come on," and she had flitted on before him, while he puffed and waddled and tried to keep up.

The day was perfect. The sun, low in the south, poured in a mellow flood that was like the Indian summer. There was no snow, but along the whole road there was that which was tenfold worse,—a river of that yellow, Centre County mud that sticks closer than a brother. There is no shaking it off; indeed, it is difficult to separate it from the shoes even with a stick.

Rose, picking her way lightly and daintily, now by the roadside, now on the crushed stones, avoided it almost completely, but Karl, ploughing along heavily, kept ever in the middle of the road. His feet increased to the size of peck baskets. In vain he kicked and scraped. His rubbers came off, and he ruined his shoes.

"Don't hurry," he pleaded, hot and panting. "There's no hurry."

"Call this hurrying?" she called back over her shoulder. "Why, we're only crawling. We must walk faster than this." And he stumbled on after her in desperation.

His collar became a wet rag. The sweat soaked through the band of his best hat, making a broad, yellow stripe. His feet weighed a hundred pounds apiece and were increasing every moment. It was like walking with a ball and chain. The mud smeared his trousers nearly to his knees, but he puffed on.

"Come, come," she called gaily. "We're losing time. It's getting late. We won't make it. Come."

"Wait!" he gasped. "Stop,—wait! Let's rest." He sank upon a stone, too exhausted even to try to reduce the round mud balls which were his feet.

"Rest!" she cried scornfully; "why, who's tired? We've only just started. Why, I've walked twenty miles lots of times. Come on; I'm going." She started on briskly. He hesitated a moment, then panted after her half on the dog-trot.

When at last they had cut through the scrub-oaks and stood in sight of the old house, he was in a dry pallor. His mouth and throat were like pieces of paper.

"See! See! The old house!" she cried.

He gasped out something like a "Thank God," and collapsed upon the nearest stone.

"It's a wild, lonesome place, isn't it?" she went on, almost excitedly. "See how the gap hangs over it. And look,—the black ring! What do you suppose makes it? Can you see it?"

"Yes," he puffed.

"It seems almost like a perfect circle, doesn't it?"

"Yes."

"It's something that's growing; some kind of a moss or grass, don't you think? I'm going down and see. Come."

"No, no. This is all the farther I'm going," he said with decision.

"Then I'm going down there alone."

"No, no, no!" he gasped. "Remember what they say. You know it's death for any Hartswick to go inside that ring."

"Oh, gammon! As if I believed that!"

"It's safer to stay away."

"I want to look into the window."

"This is all the farther I'm going," he announced decisively. "Besides, you wouldn't see anything if you tried. Don't you see how there's a shutter over the window?"

"But the ring?"

"Oh, the Hellers put some kind of a chemical there, and a devil's crop of some sort or other comes up on it."

"But why don't the snow lie there in winter?"

"I don't know. Probably they sowed some kind of a plant that melts snow just the same as salt does. Say, I'll bet it is salt."

"But that would kill everything and make the ground bare and dead, and see, it's a sort of black, matted moss."

"Well, there's some chemical about it, I'll bet a dollar." For a time they looked in silence at the old structure.

It was a log-house, some twelve feet square and two stories in height. The eaves projected far out, giving it an unusual appearance. The crevices had been caulked with some black material, which in places had begun to crumble out. A great chimney of irregular blocks of limestone arose at one end. There was no path leading to the house and no clearing save the black ring, which surrounded it and upon which there grew no trees or shrubs.

"Hark, what's that?" They both straightened instantly. The sun was near the top of the western ridge; all was deathly still save the growl of water in the near-by Run.

"Didn't you hear something?" Then the faint voice of the church bell came to them over the valley.

"My! That's the first bell. We've got just an hour. Come, we must walk now; we can't crawl the way we did coming up. Come on."

She sprang lightly down the rocks and out upon the pike, and he followed as best he could. Through the puddles and into the mud, thick and sticky as sodden glue, he ploughed, puffing and blowing and wallowing, while she tripped daintily ahead.

They arrived at the church just as the last bell was tolling. Darkness had fallen, for which Keichline was profoundly grateful. It allowed him to drag himself through the church-going throng unrecognised, and to get safely to Hartswick Hall.

He was faint and feverish; his legs almost refused to obey him; and his breath came in gasps that rattled and gurgled in his throat. An hour later, when he appeared in a complete suit of the Squire's that was three sizes too small for him, and sat down to the long-delayed supper, he found it impossible to eat.

"Oh, Pap," Rose burst in from meeting, "we had a glorious walk. Didn't we, Mr. Keichline? We went over to the old cabin, and it was fine. We'll go again, won't we?" She took her place at the table as fresh and unruffled as if she had spent the whole afternoon in her room. One glance at Karl in his tight-fitting costume, an imperceptible flutter for a moment at the corners of her mouth, and she finished her supper with great solemnity.

Keichline said very little. He was aching in every joint, and his dignity had suffered. When at ten o'clock he drove out of the yard he was beginning to be really angry. The game was not worth the candle. Without a doubt he could win her in the end; he felt sure of that, since the old Squire was on his side; but was it worth the while? With every mile down the Run his slow-kindling, fat-man's rage grew hotter. He would never return; not even the Squire's great property was sufficient to repay him. He would go there no more.

But before that very week was over he made a discovery,—a most unforeseen and unaccountable discovery: he had really and honestly fallen in love with Rose, wildly and unreasoningly in love with her. He awoke all in a moment to the fact that life without her was inconceivable, and that he must win her, be the price what it might.

## CHAPTER V

## THE HORSE-RACING ON MOON RUN

IT HAD BEEN an open winter. For six weeks the roads had been half-spoke deep, not with mud, but with that thick, yellow smear that clings like birdlime. There had been flurries of snow when the wind had roared and when the black ring about the Heller cabin had stood out sharp and vivid in the drifts, but there had been no sleighing. The snow had gone as quickly as it had come, flooding Gum Run Gap until it roared like a mill-race over a quarter-mile of road, and barring Karl Keichline from his Sunday service for weeks at a time. The valley creek had spread far out on the bottoms, and the voice of Roaring Run, always a dominating note, had become a hoarse bellow that echoed even into the remotest nooks of the valley.

On the evening of the day on which Rose had discovered Jim Farthing's little horse, the winter came on in earnest. It began in a smother of wet snow,—a foot of it—like raw putty. A cloudy day when roads had packed hard and smooth, a fierce drop in the night of forty degrees, and on Wednesday morning the sleighing was perfect.

It is not sure who first thought of the trip; it may be doubted if any one did. It was one of those spontaneous affairs where all awake at the same moment and find that they are thinking the same thought. Why not a sled-ride over Moon Run and a chicken and waffle supper at the old Snyder House at the Cross Roads? On Tuesday evening not one had dreamed of it; on Wednesday evening every young person in the valley was ready.

When Jim Farthing got the news his first thought was of Rose. He would take her with his colt; he would drive right down and invite her now. Within ten minutes he was in front of the Hartswick mansion.

Front door or back? It called for nice judgment. Front doors are of little use in the Seven Mountains; they are for the minister and the doctor and funerals. But this was Hartswick Hall, and he hesitated. Only a moment, however. Who was he that he should go to the front door of a week-day and in the forenoon? He heard a brisk, light step, seemingly started by his knock, then Rose herself stood framed in the door.

"Ah, good-morning." She looked down at her costume and laughed. Her sleeves were rolled to the elbow; and her dress was concealed by a gingham jumper. There was a touch of flour on her cheek, and more than a dusting of it in a little lock that had straggled rebelliously from its moorings.

"Come right in. Want to shake?" She held up her floury hands, laughing the while.

"Think I'm afraid of flour?" he asked jovially, seizing her hand with hearty grip.

"Take this chair, Mr. Farthing." She pushed him a kitchen rocker.

"No; no chair. I'm not making a call. Keep right on with your work."

"Oh, I'm going to." She looked up at him with bright eyes and laughed in a way that thrilled him mightily. "I'm making bread; and you can't stop, you know, after once you've begun." She turned to her heap of dough and began to knead with vigour. Young Jim could have watched her all day.

"I dropped in to ask if you were going on the ride to-night." It took courage, but it was not his way to loiter and wait for hints.

"Sure! Wouldn't miss it for anything." She paused a moment and looked up at him with girlish enthusiasm. "Karl 'phoned up that he was going with his new horse."

"Oh!"

"You know,—the one he bought over Altoona way three weeks ago. They say he's a beauty,—fastest thing there is 'round here. He's a perfect bay, so Pap says; seven years old, fifteen hands high, and weighs thirteen hundred. How's that?"

"And you're going with Karl?"

"Yes. Wouldn't miss it for a farm. You're going, aren't you, with the little colt?"

"Yes,—perhaps." Somehow the day had suddenly gone dark. It came to him with a bitter rush that he was out of his place. The prosperous Keichline had every advantage. She had herself expressed the difference: the one drove a magnificent great bay; the other a little colt. That indeed was the proportion. He turned to go.

"Don't hasten, Mr. Farthing," she urged sweetly, turning from her bread and looking into his eyes as frankly as a child. "You've only just got here."

"I must go. I can't stay. I must get to work." She went with him to the door, and laughed aloud when he shook her doughy hand.

"See you on the ride," she called merrily, and he was down the path, and in the road, and driving pell-mell home before he realised just what he was about.

The cloud that was to shadow young Jim's life had arisen now, and it was racing, black and threatening, to the zenith.

The sled-ride began auspiciously. It was a beautiful night, thick at first with stars that glittered in the still cold. Then the moon came up, rolling, large and round, over the snags of Turkey Ridge, casting long shadows down the valleys, and then flooding all with that marvellous glory that comes only with the snowy night and the radiant moon.

But the focal point of all the landscape was the "bob-sled," a long-bodied affair half-full of straw, and packed tight with young folk, who sang and laughed and abandoned themselves to the witchery of the hour as only youngsters can. In front and behind were the single couples,—boys who had a "rig" of their own and a girl, and staid pairs at the critical junction between courtship and matrimony.

Up at the head of the line was Karl Keichline, with Rose beside him in his smart new sleigh. His horse was indeed a magnificent one,—a mettlesome, hard-bitted, long-geared fellow that kept his driver constantly on the alert. It was evident that the sleek postmaster remained with the group only through courtesy. A single word, a loosening of the reins, and—zip! he would be out of the landscape in a twinkling. It was understood that on the home trip Rose was to drive, and they were to have a free road.

At the rear of the procession, utterly unnoticed and unthought-of, were the Farthing brothers and the little colt. Tom was driving, and Jim sat curled down, black and silent and preoccupied. He had not even wanted to drive the horse.

Through winding valleys, between the zigzagging parallels of rail fences, into dark gaps where the songs echoed strangely from the ragged walls, out into tangles of scrub-oak and yellow pine, and through lanes of rhododendron weirdly clinging to its green foliage even among the January snows,—mile after mile wound the gay cavalcade.

> "Bright, sunny days will soon pass away,"

came the sweet chord from the sled,—girlish sopranos and altos blending perfectly with tenors and basses, for these people of the Seven Mountains can sing, like all others of German blood.

Ah, the bright, sunny days had already passed away for young Jim,—at least, so it seemed to his brooding soul. What use to think of winning her from this contented, prosperous money-bags, who basked in the favour of the old Squire and who could offer her all of the comfort and luxury that her heart might desire? As for him what had he save health, and youth, and a pair of willing hands? He had not the ghost of a chance.

> "I'm off to the wars; to the wars I must go,"

came the clear strains from the sled. "Off to the wars"—a wild impulse arose within him to do something, to dare a deed that would thrill her and win her. But there were no wars to go to, no field of hazard where a stout heart might all in a moment snatch fame and fortune,—more the pity. The old days were best; there was a chance then for all. But he must do something to win her; something indeed he must do, and at once. But what?

And thus he sat humped up and dreamy, and saw nothing of the moonlight, and the wild scenery of the gaps, and the mountains ragged and picturesque all about. And he scarcely realised when at last they arrived at the little mountain inn and the ride was over. As he helped to unspan the horses, he was still "off to the wars," daring deeds that should make her turn in disgust from the clod beside her, and fly to him,—ah, to him!

The inn had little stable room, and they were content to fasten the horses under a long shed protected on all sides save one. The time would be short; it would scarcely pay to go out among the farmers for better accommodations.

Then they sought the house, great boys that they were, pushing and slapping one another, joking and chaffing, full to the brim of animal spirits and laughter and whole-souled enjoyment of the night. The girls were already inside, taking off hood and wrap, disclosing pink cheeks and sparkling eyes, as full of life and spirits as the boys themselves.

Then came the chicken and waffle supper, with its wonderful accompaniment of "spreads" and other good things,—a repast to dream about. It was no cold, correct dinner party with myriad courses and noiseless waiters and velvet voices; where the diner in dress-suit nibbles daintily at this and that and exchanges epigrams and soft nothings with the exquisite creature at his right. Every one was completely at home and wholly at his ease. He had come to enjoy himself to the utmost, and that was the business of the hour. The stewed chicken, tender and brown, swimming in a gravy fit for gods, came again and again into the circle of destruction, and still there was call for more. Great, brown piles of waffles, blistering hot, were brought in steady stream to the tables to disappear like water into sink-holes. They were pitched two at a time on empty plates, drenched with syrup or chicken gravy as from a hose, cut deftly into quarters and eighths by swift shearing of knife and fork, and stowed away—one,—two,—three. And all the time there was laughter of boys and giggling of girls, and jokes and banter, and clashing of knives and forks and dishes. Cold formality and the "Mr." and "Miss" of polite society were miles away over the ridges. It was "Bill" and "Dan" and "Hat" and "Liz." Will dared May to eat another waffle, and she smeared one with apple-butter on the instant and "put it where it belonged" amid roars of laughter. Then it was her turn to challenge him. And thus the supper galloped to its close.

Up near the end of the table sat Karl Keichline and Rose. He was an imposing-looking man as Jim saw him from far down the board,—square and solid, with a clean-shaven, cherub face, which had not line or shadow. "A man of pork," Jim growled in his throat; yet he could not but recognise the strength of his rival. A man who through his own efforts has secured a competency at forty, and who, moreover, has gained a ruling place in his native county, is not one to be ignored from any standpoint. By every valley standard the match was a perfect one, and Jim recognised it. But, after all, what could a girl like Rose see in a mere tub of a man like that?

How bewitching she was as she sat there with the scarlet geranium in her hair! He had never seen her eyes so deep and dark before, and he had never seen her in such joyous mood. Her every movement, the flash of her little hands, the ripple of her laugh, bewitched him more and more until he was scarcely conscious that anything existed in all the world save her,—and *him*, ah-h-h-hg! He ground his teeth. See, she was smiling up into his face, actually beaming up into that great full moon. He clenched his fingers into his palms as if he were strangling something.

Then they cleared the room of its tables and chairs, and danced with might and main even as they had eaten. The old fiddler, scraping away for dear life, keeping time with head and foot and bow, called out the changes of the dance like the boss of a river crew loading a boat.

"All salute your pardners! First couple forward and back! First couple balance and swing! All-l-l-l-l-l—shashay," and so on and on, while the lusty dancers obeyed orders with a vigour that threatened the tavern floor.

Those elaborate mortals whose ideal of the dance is to float languidly through some dreamy waltz, scarce touching their partner's sleeve, would gain new conceptions of the Terpsichorean art could they but see a whole-souled, primitive dance like this,—the vigour and unction of those bouncing girls, the pigeon-wings and capers of those strapping boys, and the muscular energy of the balance and swing. In an hour the faces of the maidens were glowing with the exercise.

It was midnight and time to start over the mountains. The boys paid the bill and bustled out for the horses, leaving the girls plenty of time to adjust their wraps before the cracked mirror in the hall. Ten minutes passed and no sign from without.

"Say, I believe something has happened." It was Rose who spoke. "I'm going out to see."

"Oh, don't. They'll be right along." It is woman's place always to wait and wonder.

"No, sir. I'm not going to stay cooped up here another minute." She bounded through the door and out into the darkness.

"Say, what's the matter?" she called, approaching the circle of lanterns.

"Karl's lost his hoss. Somebody's stole him."

"Stole him?"

"Yes; or else he's got away."

"Was the halter broken?"

"No."

"Any sign of the halter dragging?"

"No."

"Where's Karl?"

"Gone down to Corl's farm to hire another rig wunst."

"Here, show me where the horse stood." She took a lantern from one of them and began to examine the ground.

"See, there's his track," she cried. "He backed out this way and took that swing there."

"Oh, we saw that first thing," they chorused.

"Yes?" She followed the trail carefully far down the road until it entered the beaten track and was lost. "Ah, but you didn't see this." She held up a shred of rope. "He's dragging his halter and stepping on it. He's got loose, that's all, and he's started out for home. Say, I've got half a mind to get a saddle-horse and light out after him. Bet I could catch up with him."

"But where'd you get your saddle-hoss?"

"Now don't you worry about that. Say, there's no use for you boys to wait. Better start right out with the girls. I'll overtake you."

There really was no need for waiting, so one by one the sleighs drove up and took from the group on the door-stone. Then the bob-sled arrived and Rose stood alone.

"Better pile in here with us," came a voice from the sled. "Tight squeeze, but we can make it."

"Don't you worry about me," she laughed. "I never got left yet. Good-bye! See you later." They burst into the song,

> "Good-night, ladies, we're going to leave you now,"

and drove hilariously away.

"Say, Mr. Snyder,"—she turned abruptly to the landlord,—"do you know of any good saddle-horse around here?"

"No, ma'am. No saddle-hosses round here still."

"But do you know of any horse that 'll go, saddle-horse or no saddle-horse?"

"W'y' le's see. Cal Lorah's got one,—an ole tearer, down here a half mile or so. He's awful ugly, though. He ain't no woman's-hoss."

"Then he's just the horse I want. I'm going to have him." She started out decisively.

At that instant a sleigh leaped into the yard and drew up before the door with a flourish. Even before it stopped a stalwart fellow had leaped out, and now he stood deferentially before the girl.

It was young Jim.

"You'll go with me, Miss Hartswick," he said calmly. "There don't seem to be any other way. Come on." He held back the lap-robes and turned as if to help her in.

"Oh, no! I'm going alone. I'm going to get a horse down to Lorah's."

"But you'll ride with me," he said firmly, "at least down to Lorah's? You'll ride that far?" There was a masterful, confident ring in the voice that somehow appealed to her. She hesitated a moment.

"Come on," he urged.

"Why—yes—I'll ride with you down to Lorah's." She sprang into the sleigh, and the colt darted out of the yard like a swallow. A shout arose from the sled as they went by.

The horse had been standing in the cold and was frisky. She flung the snow-balls merrily, and skimmed down the flat like a skater down a stream. It seemed only a minute before they met a sleigh with a solitary driver coming rapidly.

Rose gave a little cry at the sight of it.

"Why, that's Karl's rig," she shouted. "See? That's his bay. Somebody caught him and is driving him back." Jim ground his teeth together and said nothing.

"That's Lorah's house there, see?" she called. "Here we are. I'll get out now and wait for Karl. I'm going to drive that horse of his home. He'll find him in a minute or two, now, and come right along."

Jim said nothing. He leaned over and rattled the whip. The little mare shot out like an arrow.

"Why—why, aren't you going to stop?" There was a sudden thrill of surprise in her voice.

"No."

"Not going to stop? Why—why, what do you mean?"

"What I say. I'm going to take you home."

"But Karl's coming. He'll have his horse inside of five minutes."

"Let him come."

"And you're not going to stop?" She could hardly believe her ears.

"No! I've started out to take you home and I'm going to." His jaws set like a trap.

She stole a look up into the rigid face and settled back without another word. After all a woman likes a masterful man, one equal to emergencies, one who will fight for her to the last ditch. It is doubtful if there are many women even to-day who would really object to being eloped with, if it were done strenuously enough, and if the affair could end when they said the word.

At that instant, however, Jim became aware of an obstacle all but insuperable. He had caught up with the other sleighs, and by all that was unlucky, it was at the point where the road first enters the mountains. Scrub-oaks and yellow pine dwarfs, thick as the bristles on a brush, came down to the very wheel-ruts. It was foolishness to think of driving by, and the sleighs were crawling at snail pace to allow the sled to overtake them. He held the impatient colt to a mincing trot, fretting all the time and fuming like a trapped bear.

Soon from the distance behind came the echo of bells. Rose caught it instantly and turned to look back.

"My, but that horse of Karl's is coming, though!" she cried. Then she laughed in his ear, a most bewitching little ripple. It was evident that she was enjoying his dilemma.

He did not answer. The furious driving behind was becoming more evident. The driver in a minute would be right upon the hind sleigh, and Jim would be forced to stop and explain. He looked right and left at the bush tangle, the wild desperation of the cornered animal in his eyes.

"He'll be here in just half a minute," she laughed again in his ear. He turned to catch the twinkle of mischief in her eyes, and it smote him like a spur.

Then came a loud hail from the rear:

"Hold on there, Farthing. I've got my horse now. Hold on there."

"Not by a long chalk!" The words fairly hissed.

"Say, you're not going to try to drive by?" She straightened up in real alarm.

"That's *just* what I'm going to do. Heigh, there!" he yelled to the sleighs in front. "Turn out there, quicker 'n lightning. Turn out there! Turn out, I say! I'm going by on the right. Sharp there, or I'll smash into yeh! Hold tight, Miss Hartswick. Here she goes!"

The road had grown slightly wider, but it was inviting certain disaster to try to run by in such a place. Automatically the sleighs ahead jammed into the opposite wall of scrub, and the colt, struck with the whip, darted forward like a wild thing. Instantly the sleigh was crashing and grinding into the horny tangle. It reared on one runner and rocked and plunged at a maddening angle amid a chorus of exclamations from the sleighs. The snaggy branches raked and gouged. They bit into the driver pitiless as barbed wires, but he sat stiff as a linch-pin to trim the sleigh and shelter the girl. His hat was smashed off by a sprawling branch, but what's a hat? A jagged limb, cruel as a fish-rake, clutched into his face and hair; another snatched at the colt, and caught a sinister finger into the harness, but the straps held. In a minute it was all over, and they were spinning along with a clear road.

"There," he cried exultantly; "think he'll follow, Miss Hartswick?"

"Mercy, no!" she burst out. "Say, that's the most reckless driving I ever saw. I don't believe you could get through there again in a thousand times."

"Perhaps not," he retorted grimly, "but I started out to take you home, and it'll take more 'n bushes to stop me." There was bitterness in his heart. The girl beside him was his only by capture. Her heart was in the sleigh behind. That was evident.

She did not reply. This was a new type of man, truly. She glanced up again furtively to catch a glimpse of his square jaw and warlike figure. The glance startled her.

"Why—why," she exclaimed, "your face is all blood."

"Only a scratch," he answered lightly. "Bush struck me back there."

"But let me see." She spoke imperatively, and he bent over toward her.

"Why, there's a regular gash, and it's bleeding terribly. Here, let me wipe off the blood."

"No, no; not with that," he objected quickly, but she paid no heed.

His heart began to beat almost audibly. He would have his face carved like a German student's if she would but bend over him like this and stroke away the blood with her handkerchief.

His exultation was short-lived. By a curious chance no sooner was he clear of the bush than the road became suddenly wide enough for two teams abreast. The man behind delayed not an instant, but dashed by the line of sleighs, and now it was a straight-away race, with Jim handicapped by a hundred pounds. Soon the breath of the great bay was spouting down the back of his neck, and a lusty voice was shouting almost in his ear:

"Heigh, there! ain't you going to hold up? Stop, I say!"

"Not by a long chalk!" Jim wheeled and flung back the challenge in hot wrath.

"Heigh? What's that?"

"I've started out to take her home, and by gum I'm going to!"

"What do yeh mean?" snorted the man, the true inwardness of things beginning at last to filter through his consciousness.

"I mean exactly what I say." There was no mistaking the man's tone. "If you want her, come and get her."

"By mighty; so that's the game, is it? You just wait a minute!" came roaring back the answer, a sweep of wrath smiting him in the face like a whip. But it is not an easy matter on a narrow road to rescue a purloined maiden from a sleigh ahead, especially when the etiquette of the race forbids shooting. For a mile it was a stern chase, and it threatened to be a long one.

"What are you going to do when he catches you? Fight?" There was a suspicion of fun in her voice.

"He hain't caught me yet," he snapped, rattling the whip again in the socket.

"But he will on Moon Run flats. He'll run right round you."

"You wait and see."

"But you're handicapped, and you can't expect to beat that great bay. He's got the best horse, and—"

"Yes, and he's got the best everything," he answered bitterly. "That's just what's the matter. I don't have the ghost of a chance in—anything. But by king!"—the words fairly ground through his teeth,—"he hain't got the best horse, I'll tell him that."

At that moment they came out of the rough, bush-bound road upon Moon Run flats, where for a mile or more the road was level and double. Karl Keichline saw his chance. He would drive by, then turn and head off the fugitives. With whip and voice he urged his horse into a great burst of speed, and in a moment he was right alongside.

"Thought you was going to run away from me, did yeh? Heigh? Think you can beat me with *that* little runt of a hoss, do yeh? Heigh?" he sneered almost in Jim's ear. The two men were so near together that they could have touched each other.

Then it was that Jim Farthing's colt showed the stuff that was in her. As if catching for the first time the spirit of the race, she let out a burst of speed that astonished even her owner. Neck and neck they raced, the little mare and the long gelding. Karl, excited now to fever pitch and boiling-mad, jerked at the reins and urged and stormed, and the lank beast with mighty strides swung along like a giraffe. Jim spared whip and voice, but he held the colt firmly in hand, and watched eagerly for something to happen.

He had not long to wait. Suddenly Rose gave a cry.

"The bridge; remember the bridge. We're almost there." The excitement of the race made her forget all else. The bridge, a wooden affair wide enough for only one sleigh, stood near the lower end of the valley. It would be the goal. Keichline heard the cry of the girl, and realised the danger the same instant as Jim. He broke into whoops like a Comanchee.

"Ha-a-a-y, Bill!" he yelled. "Ha-a-a-a-a-a-y, there! Get ap! Get ap! Get ap! Hay-a-a-a-a-a-y!"

The gelding sprang to his utmost. Steadily he began to nose ahead of the mare. Jim did his level best, but he could not equal that steady, onward rush that was putting him foot by foot into the rear. The great horse was swinging along with ten-foot strides pitiless as a machine. He was a neck ahead,—half a length, and gaining with every bound.

Then something happened.

"Here!" came the command so sudden and eager that it startled Jim. "Give me them reins! Quick, there! Quick!" There was something in the tone and manner of the girl that compelled instant surrender. Jim passed the reins over like a woman, and she took them like a man. She was in her element. The thrill and excitement of the contest had entered her soul; for the moment there was nothing in the whole world but this single race; and the little mare must win.

Instantly there was a change in the driving. That nameless thrill that flashes between horse and jockey went quivering down the reins into the struggling little racer. The girl had suddenly sprung into life. Jim watched her like one fascinated. She had thrown back her wrap and hood, and now she leaned far over, her bare hands clutching the reins, her hair fluttering about her face, and her slim body tense with energy. The sleigh jumped, and rolled, and pitched like a thing of life, but she rode as if she were a part of it, as if the reins were steel rods holding her in place.

Then arose above the roar of hoof and sleigh the wild cry of the jockey,—that shrill, penetrating falsetto heard on every race-track at critical instants, a cry that goes to the heart of a struggling racer like liquid fire.

"Hi! hi! hi-e-e-e-e-e-e-e! Hi! hi! hi! hi-e-e-e-e-e! Hi! hi! hi! Hi-e-e!" The little horse flattened herself almost to the ground and put out the very last ounce that was in her. She gained back her loss in twenty strides, and then nosed inch by inch ahead of the great gelding, who was rolling and swinging like a runaway.

Head straight out, heels smashing snowballs into the dash-board, flew the little mare. Great chunks of ice and snow zipped spitefully about the girl, but she was utterly oblivious of all save the flying horse.

Now it was a neck ahead, now half a length,—Jim almost yelled in his excitement, but the girl gave no sign of emotion. She was as cool as steel; her whole soul was centred on the little mare; and the horse knew it. The bridge was just ahead, coming like an express train, and she held the centre of the road as true as a die.

Karl Keichline, yelling now and even cursing, was on his feet in furious eagerness. He leaned far over the dash-board and screamed at his horse. He yanked out the whip and began to ply it furiously. Sharp and thick fell the cruel blows. Then, with a mad fling of the head, the gelding gave up, broke into a rocking gallop, and fell a length behind the sleigh.

He had lost.

There was nothing for Keichline to do but to pull down his horse by main strength, and prevent him from crashing into the bridge rail. But furious with anger he continued to ply the whip.

"Hurrah!" yelled Jim, more excited than he had ever been before in his life. "Hurrah, we've beat him!"

"Hurrah!" echoed the girl, still alert, but with an excitement as great as his own.

"It's you; it's all you," he cried generously. "I never could have beat him alone. There ain't another girl in the world could have done it." There was no time for reply, for at that instant came a sickening crash from behind.

"What's that?" She wheeled instantly.

"Guess he's hit the bridge," he replied grimly.

"Here! whoa! whoa! there!" She pulled the little mare down by main strength and turned him about. "We must go back instantly. Perhaps he's hurt."

"A man that's fool enough to lick a horse when he's beat fair and square ought to be hurt," he burst out with harshness.

"Oh, I hope he isn't harmed," she said weakly. "Here, you take the reins. I'm afraid he's killed. Oh, it's all my fault."

"It isn't your fault any more than the man in the moon's," he burst out warmly. "The blame's all on his own head. He was a fool, and he's paying for it." She did not answer; she was peering ahead with frightened eyes.

The revulsion came quickly. The instant they emerged from the bushes at the bend of the bridge they saw the man raging up and down the little structure, mad as the devil in holy water.

"Heigh, Farthing," he roared, "I'll have you arrested for this inside o' two hours, and you'll pay for it to the very limit of the law. By God, you can't wammel over me like this!"

"Hurt yeh horse any?" asked Jim with provoking calmness.

"None of yeh blamed business," he bellowed, stamping up and down the bridge, the living image of wrath. Then they saw the horse head down and panting. He had evidently escaped serious injury, but the new sleigh was a mess of kindling-wood.

"Can we help yeh any?" asked Jim with velvet voice.

"To hell with yeh help, you mis-s-serable skunk! You hain't seen the end of this yet. You can't come a game on me like this and not pay for it. You untied that horse up there in the shed; you know you did; and I've got a good mind to pitch yeh into the river." He made two or three quick steps toward the sleigh, but he thought better of it.

"I'll talk with you when you're cool, Mr. Keichline." Jim's voice had a provoking drawl. "But I can give you some advice now. I think if I was you I'd wait here a spell or two fer that bob-sled. It 'll give yeh time to cool off, and then you can lead that horse of yours behind,—if they don't drive too fast."

"Here, Jim Farthing!" The man was actually foaming in his wrath. "You'll crow a different tune 'fore long, I'll tell you that! You—jest—wait! I'll get even with yeh for this if it takes fifty years."

"Good-night, Mr. Keichline." Jim had turned his horse and was driving away. "Be careful you don't catch cold." A sudden turn in the road smothered all echoes of the man's wrath.

For a long time neither of them spoke. A strange embarrassment had fallen over them. He tried several times to break the awkward silence, but she seemed like one in a brown study. Down the narrow valleys they sped, through the gaps and gullies, in and out of the rhododendron and scrub, while the moon sent down its radiance and the long ridges thrust out their ragged shadows. At last they passed through Bald Eagle Gap and were in the Squire's front yard. Jim sprang out to help her alight, but the girl was on her feet as soon as he.

"I'm sorry if I've been rude to you," he said awkwardly, as she took a step away.

"Mr. Farthing,"—there was a cold ring in her voice, and her eyes looked him straight through,—"did you untie that horse?"

"No, I didn't," he said, with an honest ring, looking full into her eyes. She held her gaze upon him a cold instant, but he did not flinch or cringe.

"I believe you are telling the truth," she said slowly. "I am glad of it." Then suddenly she turned and tripped toward the house.

"Good-night," she flung back over her shoulder.

"Good-night," he echoed. Then, as he drove slowly home, he wondered if she expected him to keep the appointment for to-morrow. For on Thursday they were to try the little colt on the Gum Stump pike.

## CHAPTER VI

## THE WINDY SIDE OF THE LAW

DURING THE RIDE from Moon Run, Rose had done some rapid thinking. How was Karl to get back to Sugar Valley? The bob-sled would go no further than Dan Tressler's, and there he would be, stranded in the middle of the night, afoot, ten miles from home. It would never do to have him stay at Tressler's; the Squire would never forgive that. He must stay at the Hall if anywhere in the valley, yet how could she manage it? It would be a hazardous thing to arouse her father at dead of night, and then bring him in contact with the wrathful man. That would never do at all.

There was but one way.

At the end of the main walk she wheeled sharply, and, darting across the lawn and the end of the barnyard, came to the house of Amos Harding.

Amos was a Yankee, a native of Connecticut, who, years before, had drifted into the valley as a school-teacher, had married one of the valley girls, and after a time had worked into the position of head farmer of the Hartswick estate. He was a long-limbed, sandy-haired, active little man of fifty, shrewd and worldly wise, and very valuable to the old Squire in many ways. To Rose he was almost a father. He had been her right-hand man, counsellor, and confidant ever since she could remember, and she in turn had been to him like one of his own children.

She did not go to the door, but slipped around the corner and tapped lightly on a window. There was a quick movement inside, then a fumbling at the sash, then a tousled head thrust out into the night air.

"Heigh, there! Who is it?"

"It's me, Uncle Amos."

"Sho! Is that you, Rosie? Why, what in tarnation's happened?"

"Accident. Karl smashed his sleigh, and—"

"Sho! You don't mean it! Hurt yeh any?"

"No."

"Course it didn't. Jest like a cat, I swann! I'll bate fifteen cents, if I dropped yeh into the well head down you'd land on your feet. But how in time did you smash 'er?"

"Karl ran into the Moon Run bridge. You see—"

"Heigh? Ran into the bridge? In broad moonlight? On that wide road, dead straight? Say, sis, he must o' been awful taken up with somethin' or other. He, he, he!"

"He was racing, Uncle Amos. I'll tell you about it to-morrow. I rode down with Jim Farthing, and Karl's coming leading his horse behind the bob-sled. I want you to hitch up Tussey Boy into the green sleigh and drive up till you meet him. Then let him go home with our rig, and you take his horse here. See? You'll rub him down dry when you get him to the stable, won't you, and look him all over for cuts, and blanket him warm? He's had a pretty hard time of it."

"But who in time-nation was he racing with?"

"Jim Farthing's little mare."

"Sho! You don't mean it! And Jim run yeh into the bridge?"

"No, sir; he didn't. But you must hurry, Uncle Amos. Quick. I'll be down to the barn getting ready."

"But say, how did yeh—"

The question stopped short, for she had disappeared around the corner of the house. He dressed with all haste, but when he arrived at the barn she had the horse nearly harnessed.

"Look here, you don't mean to say that that little runt o' Jim's beat out that old slasher of Karl's, do yeh?" He began to talk the moment he got within sight of her. "Say, tell us about it, dew."

"I was driving the mare myself, so she naturally couldn't do anything but win. See?" She laughed up into his face mischievously. His perplexity was really grotesque.

"The mare? Was you driving against Karl? Say, tell a feller. 'Tain't fair; I'm jest dying to know."

"I can't stop, really, Uncle Amos. You must go. Quick. They're coming right along. I'll tell you in the morning. Now hurry." She waved her hand and darted toward the house, and after a wistful look toward the shadows where she had disappeared, he buttoned up his coat and drove out into the still radiance of the night.

It was ten o'clock the next morning when Rose saw her father. She was making apple pies, busily rolling out the top "lids" and fitting them on, when he stormed in at the kitchen door. The old man's wrath gathered easily, and it made no distinctions.

"I've heard all about it," he burst out before he was fairly in the room. "Every man's that struck the store this morning 's been full of it? It's town's talk. And now Karl's 'phoned up, raving mad. I never knew him so mad. It's damnable, damnable!" His face was fairly livid.

"Why, Ira, what do you mean?—what's happened?" Mrs. Hartswick dropped her dish and spoon and fluttered over to him in a tremor.

"Oh, it's nothing. Come, Pap, it isn't so bad 's you think,—not half." Rose looked up at him with a twinkle in her eyes. "There wouldn't have been a bit of trouble if Karl hadn't lost his head. Really, that man gets rattled as easy as an old woman." She laughed up into his face, but the old man, when he was angry, was wholly animal in his rage.

"Stop!" he roared. "Don't you talk to me like that! Don't—you—do—it!"

"Oh, don't, Ira, don't,—please." The mother came pleadingly between the two as if to avert a tragedy.

"You don't know anything about it! Stand out of the way!" he bellowed.

"But, Ira, Rose didn't mean anything; she meant it all right, Ira." There was a tired, pleading tone in the woman's voice that was almost like a whine. She was a gentle, laughing little body, but her husband had dominated her until she was cowed and shrinking. Of all things she detested controversy. She bent helplessly before the Squire's frequent storms of wrath; they depressed and worried her; and now she was a mere creature of whining protest, never standing against him for a moment, but advising ever the line of least resistance. Forty years with the choleric old man had changed her into a mere helpless voice of protest.

"I tell you it's scandalous!" he stormed, paying no heed to his wife's entreaties. "It's the town's talk! Here you go with a man who's invited you to ride, and then you sneak off home with a perfect stranger, and race him against the man who took yeh!"

"And beat him," Rose laughed up saucily. "Beat his great crack racer with a little nine hundred mare, and handicapped at that. Oh, I take after my dad,—I never could ride after a slow horse." She wrinkled up her nose at him playfully, but he was implacable.

"Stop, Rose! Stop right where you are," he ordered.

"Don't anger your father, Rosie. He knows best," Mrs. Hartswick joined in with soothing tone.

"It's an outrage to Karl and me and—all of us," he roared, drawing nearer to Rose and swinging his arm up and down like a pump-handle.

"But it was a clean race, Pap," she went on serenely. "It was fair and square, and the best horse won. Say, I'd give ten dollars in a minute, Pap, if you could have seen it. It was a thriller. That little mare certainly beats anything that ever stepped in this valley. Say, I want you to buy her for me. Will you, Pap?" Somehow the old man's wrath began to wilt a little; it was impossible to withstand her sunny enthusiasm.

"But that's not the question at all, Rose. It was a disgraceful thing. You'd no business riding with that Farthing. You'd promised Karl—"

"Oh, pshaw, Pap! What had I promised him? He asked me if I would *go* with him, and I did, didn't I?" She laughed up at him again, then turned lightly to her pie-making.

"'Twas a contemptible trick; you know it. It was damnable! He planned it deliberately; he untied that hoss on purpose; and it's a prison offence."

"He didn't untie the horse, father." There was confidence in her voice. "The horse wasn't tied right, and it got loose." The reply seemed to come to the man like a blow across the eyes.

"So you stand up for him, do yeh?" He wheeled upon her instantly. "Think he's about right, do yeh? And Karl's all wrong? So that's the way things are running!—so that's it, is it? Heigh? Well—we'll—see! We'll find what the law is on that point; we'll put him where he belongs mighty quick, and his whole damned family with him!"

"Oh, Ira, don't," protested Mrs. Hartswick in a half-frightened voice.

"But how are you going to prove anything, father?" Rose turned to him with a trace of gathering anger. There was no fun in her eyes now.

"Prove it? Prove it? Look here, Rose, you're going too far! And so you're going to stand up for that low-lived scamp, are yeh?"

"Mr. Farthing's no such man, father."

By a curious perversity she said nothing about her having been constrained by young Jim, though the mere mention of it might have altered the complexion of things considerably. No one knew of the affair save the two concerned.

"Heigh? So that's your game! So you're going to throw Karl over for that miserable puppy, are yeh? Then you let—"

"Stop, father,—stop!" There was authority in her voice. Her eyes had a flash in them that was seldom there, but he paid no heed.

"Oh, Rose! Don't, Rosie, please!" The voice was near to tears.

"I never have dictated to you, Rose, who you should keep company with or who you shouldn't, but I'll say one thing now flat and square: you—shan't—go—with—that—Jim Farthing. No, sir! There shan't no Farthing ever step into this house while I live in it. I put my foot down on that flat and heavy, and you know what that means. You—know—what—that—means!" He paused in sheer breathlessness.

"Stop, father; you're going too far." She stood straight and tall and looked him full in the eyes. "You're not yourself, or you wouldn't talk like that to *me*. I have spoken to this Mr. Farthing at just three different times. I hardly know him. And you say that to me? That affair last night was a prank,—a mere prank. You've got no right to speak to me like that. It's ungentlemanly." Her eyes were flashing with outraged dignity.

"Oh, I wouldn't, Rosie. Please don't. There, there!" Her mother put her hand soothingly on her arm, and half whispered the words.

"But, Rose, think how it looks. Think what a caper that was. Look at it as other people do. It was fearfully indiscreet. Just think—"

"Oh, bother what people think! What do I care what people think?"

"But you must, Rose. It gives you a name to be seen cutting shines with a man like that Farthing."

"And what of that? Does that change *me* any?"

"But, Rose, what do you know about those people? There's something wrong about them. You know that. I could tell you something about them if I wanted to. It's risky to encourage a man like that, fearfully risky, Rose. And it isn't treating Karl right."

"Oh, Rose didn't think, Ira. She didn't mean anything, Ira."

"Why isn't it treating Karl right?" She stood straight and rigid, facing her father. He had never seen her eyes so black before. They looked straight through him.

"You know as well as I do, Rose."

"I asked why."

"W'y, Rose, he's your—your regular company."

"Am I obliged to have 'regular company'? Did I ever invite him or encourage him? Did he ever ask my permission?"

"There, there, Rosie; please, don't, Rosie."

"But, Rose, you've known right along how he's felt toward you. Surely———"

"*How* have I known? He's never said anything to me, or even hinted at anything."

"But, Rose, you've known it. You've surely known why he has come way up here every Sunday." His glance somehow fell beneath her clear eyes.

"But how have I had anything to do about it? What if he has come; does that make me in any way beholden to him? I haven't wanted him to come. I haven't encouraged him."

"But, Rose———"

"Why have I got to have 'regular company'? Why can't I be let alone? Can't I speak to a man without his thinking I'm his regular company? Oh, I'm sick of this whole thing. I want to be let alone. I'll mind my own business if other people will mind theirs."

"But, Rose," there was a pleading note in his voice now, "I want you to be civil to Karl. I want you to like him. It's my wish, Rose. I've set my heart on your having him, Rose. You know that. It's the dearest wish of my heart."

"Rose means all right, Ira. It'll come out all right. She's just a little girl, Ira."

"But I don't want to have anybody," she burst out petulantly. "Why have I got to have anybody? I want to be let alone. I want to be just myself and do what I want to without any man trailing round after me and tormenting me. I hate him. There! I do. I hate the whole lot of 'em." She snapped around and went to rolling her dough fiercely.

"Don't say that, Rose." The anger was all out of the man's voice now. "Karl's a good fellow, Rose,—a glorious good fellow. He'll make you happy; I know it. We're getting old, your mother and I. I can't handle this business the way I could once. It's getting too much for me. I'm a broken old man, Rose; I'm not what I was once." There was almost a choke in his voice.

"Oh, Ira, Rose means all right. She'll do right———"

"Oh, don't, Pap. Don't say that. Let *me* help you. I can do it. I can run this business just as well as any man." She took a quick step and laid her hand on his arm.

"No, Rose. This ain't any woman's work. This business needs a man, and a good one. I don't know a soul that could swing it but Karl. You know how I feel about it. The old place has been handed down to us for more 'n a hundred years. Nobody ever really owned it but just us, and I can't bear having it go out of the family. If little Arthur had lived it would have been all right, but he didn't, and you are all I've got, Rose, and I want you to marry Karl. Won't you, Rose? He likes you; I know that. He workships you like a dog; you can see that. He'll be good to you. Say, Rose, you'll not oppose us, will you? Your mother and I have set our hearts on it. It would kill me if you should disappoint us. You won't, will you, Rose?" There was a quiver in his voice and he wiped his eyes hastily.

"Oh, Rose is a good girl, Ira. You won't disappoint us; will you, Rose?"

"Oh, pshaw, Pap! I believe you're getting soft-headed. Here, take one of these dumplings and get out. You're in my road. I believe you've spoiled my pies now. Come, clear out." The change was instant.

"But I want you to promise, Rose," he said, hesitating a moment and looking at her, the dumpling in his hand.

"Oh, clear out. They want you over to the store. Come, start, or I'll spatter you!" She held the dipper threateningly. The old look was in her eyes again. He went out laughing, munching at the dumpling.

His good nature, however, was short-lived. When he reached the store the group about the stove looked up expectantly.

"Say, Squire," a sharp voice piped up, "they say you're going to put the law to that young Farthing. Yas?"

"That's just what I'm going to do," he responded grimly.

"What charge you calc'latin' to make?"

"Untying Karl's hoss."

"And what law does that break, Squire?"

"It's trespassing, and it's attempted damage of property, and half a dozen things."

"You can prove it, I 'spose?"

"Prove it? Well, I should say! You just watch me. I can prove it twenty-seven different ways. Say, look here, do you know this Farthing crowd's going to change the whole tone of this valley? There's trouble ahead. You take my word for it, they're a hard lot and they'll bear watching. There ain't a doubt in my mind but what that critter was actually trying to steal the hoss. Yessuh."

"Say, look here, Squire." Dan Tressler was moving uneasily on his egg-crate. "Have you got a single proof that Jim Farthing really untied that hoss wunst? Now, have yeh, Squire?"

"Proof? What'd I say? I've got proof to burn. I can bring half a dozen fellers who'll swear on the Bible they saw him go out."

"But does that prove that he untied the hoss?"

"Well, it comes mighty near it."

"But will that prove it?" persisted the man doggedly.

"Look here, Dan. What do you mean? Of course we can prove it. He had a motive; we can prove that, can't we? He had a chance; we can prove that. He went out; we can prove that. He profited by it and without the loss of a minute; we can prove that. What more do you want?"

"And you are going to have him arrested and tried on that evidence?"

"I am going to send for the sheriff just as soon as I can telephone him."

"Then let me tell you this, Squire." There was suppressed excitement in the man's voice. "If it comes to a trial, then you'll have me for a witness. I drove that bob-sled myself last night. It was my rig. I was in the tavern room all the time and I'll swear on the Bible that Jim Farthing come in when the rest did, and didn't go out till they did. He never left the room. I know it. And I'll swear that when Karl Keichline got onto my sled at Moon Run bridge and told us as how Jim had unhitched his hoss wunst, three or four, and I can tell their names still, spoke right up and said as how they knew he didn't leave the room. Joe Hubler said that he set right beside Jim all the evening, and Joe won't lie. You'd better go slow, Squire."

"And you'll swear to that?" The old man's face was twitching with wrath. There was a threat in the tone, and Dan felt it.

"Yes, sir; I will, for it's God's truth, Squire." He was fairly trembling with excitement.

"Oh, yes, them Farthings are pretty fine birds, aren't they now?" he burst out with a withering sneer. "How long has it been since they hired you to defend their doings? Heigh? You've been hand in glove with 'em all the fall. I've saw it, and now you'll swear to that, will yeh? Heigh?"

"I won't swear to nothing but jest God's truth," maintained the man stubbornly. "Al Farthing was good to me, and I'm not going back on him when he's in the right still."

"In the right? Well, suh, we'll see. It 'll take more than your little swearing to clear up this scrape, I'll promise you that." He stormed out into the back store, slamming the door behind him.

But he did not telephone the sheriff.

In the meantime young Jim had had but a single thought. He had polished the little mare till she fairly shone. He had crimped her mane, and tied her foretop with a jaunty ribbon, and had even polished her hoofs. As she stood in her newly oiled harness, with the lambskin breastplate and the glittering nickel work, she was indeed a beauty. She showed not a trace of her hard usage of the night before: she was alive in every nerve, and full to the brim of mettle and fire.

Punctual to the minute, young Jim swung up before the Squire's front gate. He could not repress a little thrill of trepidation. How would Rose feel about it after she had thought it over? Would she want to try the horse now? And what about the old Squire?

He was not kept long in suspense.

He had hitched his horse and was just starting to the sleigh for the blanket when he heard a sound behind him. He turned to find the old man coming from the store at a shuffling run.

"Here, here, young man; what do you want?" There was no mistaking the tone or the look on the man's face.

"I am calling for Miss Hartswick. She—"

"Well, sir, you won't see her. You untie that hoss and get out of here just as quick as God A'mighty 'll let yeh."

"Why, she asked me to call," he stammered confusedly. "She wants to try the horse."

"That don't make no difference," he roared, taking a step toward him. "You get out of here, and don't you ever let me see you on these premises again just as long as you live. Clear out, I say! Start!" Without a word Jim turned to the hitching-post, and the old man, fairly quivering in his wrath, made a movement to go.

Then he caught a glimpse of the little mare, turned automatically, drew a step nearer, patted her on the shoulder, and opened her mouth with a deft movement.

"How old is she,—five?"

"Five in June."

"Sound?"

"Absolutely perfect."

"Know anything about her pedigree?" He was examining her like a judge at a county fair.

"Sired by Philly Boy out of Lucy M." The old man cocked his head instantly.

"Sure of it? Can you prove it?"

"Yes, sir."

"Say, let me feel of her a little,—will yeh?"

"Sure, if you'll let me go with you."

"Get in." He gathered up the reins with skilled hand, and they swung by the store at a rattling clip. A curious crowd was watching them.

"By George!" the old man ejaculated after a moment. "How long have yeh had her?"

"Ever since she was a colt." The Squire shook the reins over her back, and she swung down the long stretch with the ease and precision of a machine.

"Give yeh two hundred for her."

"I've refused five."

"Give yeh five-fifty."

"No."

"Six?"

"No."

"How much? What's your price?"

"She can't be bought. I don't want to sell her."

"Of course she can be bought. There ain't a thing in this valley that can't be bought. How much?"

"Five hundred and fifty thousand."

"Here, don't you get smart, young feller. How—much 'll—you—take?" He turned the mare skilfully and started on the return.

"I mean what I say, Squire Hartswick. There isn't money enough in this valley to buy her. She's not for sale."

"Mighty important, ain't yeh?" His anger flashed up like a fuse. "Mighty important folks up there, ain't yeh? Money no object. Got it by the barrel, I 'spose? Well, I've taken a fancy to this mare and I'm going to have her. You mind that."

"You won't buy her, Squire Hartswick. If you get her, it 'll be by foul means."

"All-l-l-l right, sir, we'll see. I've said it,—I'm going to own this mare; you take note o' what I say. Here, take her. I'll get out here." He drew up before the store. "Now, let me tell you one thing, young man. You may see the day when you'll be good—and—glad to sell this mare for anything you can get. You may be glad to do it. You haven't heard the last of that caper last night, young feller; not by a long chalk. And you remember another thing: You keep away from my premises. Understand? You're liable to hear from me now at any minute. Good-day, sir."

Young Jim made no answer. He drove fiercely homeward, more angry than he had ever been before in his whole life.

# CHAPTER VII

# THE FLITTING DINNER

ALL FOOLS' DAY in the Seven Mountains is the time for "flitt'ns," be the sign and the moon's phase what they may. Everywhere on this April morning you will meet long lines of vehicles loaded with household goods,—everywhere a kaleidoscope of movement: old families leaving, new ones arriving; cattle and sheep and hogs driven along the highways; "riggin's" of every pattern piled with a grotesque confusion; women and children perched high among the boxes and bureaus and dressers; old bed-posts sticking out at every angle; and reapers and mowing machines dragged along behind "hay-ladders" through the April slush. One day later you will seek in vain through all the region for any trace of a "flitt'n."

Like all other institutions in the mountains,—butcherings, schnittings, infares, apple-butterings, weddings,—"flitt'ns" are governed by certain inflexible traditions. As a rule, only near relatives are invited to a "flitt'n." Should this exclusive circle, however, not possess the requisite number of "riggin's," then others are very welcome, for it is unlucky if there be not teams enough to take everything at one grand trip. Finally, like all things else in the Dutch belt, even funerals, the affair must be crowned with an ample dinner furnished by the flitter and presided over by the good flitting wife.

So much of flittings.

Dan Tressler was moving into Sugar Valley. Six weeks before nothing had been farther from his intention, but much may happen in six weeks. It had come to him like a flash in clear weather.

"Step in here, Dan," the Squire had said to him one day in February. "Come in to my office, will you?" And he had gone in, greatly wondering.

"Your lease expires April first, don't it?"

"Yes."

"I'm sorry, but I can't renew it."

"What,—what's that?" It was as if the air had suddenly been pumped from the room.

"No; I can't renew it. You see—"

"Why, Squire, I've lived on your farm nine years. Haven't I suited yeh? I've put a lot of money out. I've taken pride in it. I've—"

"Sorry, Dan, but I can't help it. You've run it well; I haven't any fault to find, but that nephew of mine three years ago wanted the lease. I'd already made it out to you, but he made me promise I'd give him the next chance. It seems I signed a paper. I'd forgot all about it till he reminded me of it yesterday. He said he was going to hold me right to it; there's no use of my kicking. I'm mighty sorry, Dan."

"But the improvements I've made, Squire—"

"It's hard luck; I see that. But you know I didn't ask you to make 'em."

"But the farm's worth double what it was when I took it. I've sunk more 'n a thousand dollars on it in work and money; you'll—"

"As I say, that's your own matter. I didn't require it. You did it on your own responsibility. It's your lookout."

"But if I was satisfying yeh, why did you promise him the place? Why didn't you tell me?"

"The rascal's a sharper; that's the long and short of it. There's no use trying to hide it; he got the best of me, and you know mighty few can say they ever done that. I didn't realise what he wanted till it was too late, and I'd entirely forgot about it till he came in yesterday. He's got me tight and fast. There's no way out of it, Dan. I'm powerless as a child." And Dan, after a moment of protest, had given in, despite the flimsy excuse, for it is useless, however great the provocation, to ram one's head against a stone wall. Now he was moving into Sugar Valley, and twelve farm wagons stood in his yard.

The morning had swarmed with surprises. The first had come when Amos Harding had driven up with the Squire's best team; then had come Rose with her buggy full of baskets and bundles to help with the dinner,—clearly the old man was doing all he could for Dan; but the crowning sensation was Jim Farthing, who had driven in late with his father's great team of Percherons. The workers held their breaths: anything might happen now.

Young Jim was in joyous mood; he had caught a glimpse of Rose in the kitchen, and the effect had been magical. There had been small chance to speak to her since that eventful night on Moon Run. He had seen her many times; he had even been very near her, for he had suddenly become most regular in his church attendance, but with Karl Keichline at the door and the old Squire at the front, there had been no hope for him. Now, however, they were far away: the thought exhilarated him. He plunged into the work with all his soul. Perchance she was looking. And if she were, she saw a goodly sight: the great, square-shouldered fellow tugging away at the big boxes and bureaus, and holding his end against two men on the other.

Once he ventured into the kitchen for a drink of water, and found the room fairly quivering with energy; it seemed full of women.

"Come, no men folks allowed here. We're working in here." Rose was in command. There was snap in her voice, and there was fun and mischief. It set the room into a merry burst, which somehow confused him mightily.

"But I want some water."

"Oh, you do. All right, here you are." She scooped a cup into the water bucket and like a flash showered him with it. Then she laughed again. "There, you've got it; now skip. Run where you belong, or we'll take *hot* water to you." He hesitated, but there was nothing else to do.

"Here," she called, as he was turning toward the door. "Here's a dipper. Catch!" She threw it with a deft swing, and he caught it in one hand. "'Spose you try the cistern. There's where we get our water. Good-bye."

"Good-bye," he echoed in puzzled tone; then he retreated awkwardly amid much laughter from around the sizzling stove.

At eleven precisely the bell on the kitchen roof began to jangle wildly. Dinner was on time, and the men, dropping everything on the instant, swarmed into the house, a motley crowd with coats off and shirt sleeves rolled high. Just inside they encountered Mrs. Tressler, who, nervous and excited, was running hither and thither as if demented.

"Here, Uncle Jake," she was calling jerkily, "you take this here chair wunst; Abe and Lem, you set right down here. And, oh, here, Amos, here's a place for you still. Thar! And the rest of yeh, Lord! set anywhere you get a chanct wunst. Thar!" She made a side plunge for the stove where three nervous women were scooping up various things out of pot and kettle, rebounded like a rubber ball to the sink, where Rose and another were peeling potatoes, then spun about and delivered a sweeping order:

"Hurry up, quick, now," she gasped. "Quick,—they're down!" Then she swirled in a sidling flutter around the table like a June bug about a lamp.

The great rattling and scraping of chairs and feet as the men took their places was succeeded by a sepulchral hush.

"Uncle Jacob, will you invoke the divine blessing?" Dan's voice sounded solemn and funereal. The old man arose, and in quavering tones went through with the formula. Then the meal was on.

"Fall right to, boys, and do your darndest. I can't wait on yeh; I've gut my hands full right here. Let 'er go."

"All right, Dan," joined in Amos. "Here goes; sail in, boys. Don't let all this good stuff phaze ye. You hain't no idee what you can do jest by takin' one mouthful at a time."

Amos was in his element. Good cooking was his chief theme at a dinner like this, and he was at his best.

"Say, now," he began in a high, drawling voice. "You Dutch have your failin's, but you're all right when it comes to vittles. Why, take it on spreads, you beat the whole world and Centre County. I never set down to a Dutch dinner yet where there wan't at least five spreads. And they're all good too, and so's your scrapple, and liver-wurst, and ponhoss, and schnitts-and-knepff,—say, Mary Ann, this is the best schnitts-and-knepff I ever put into my old head. Pass her up again, Dan."

"I reckon we can cook schnitts-and-knepff still," tittered the mistress with pardonable pride.

"There, now, there's another thing I like about you Dutch," he went on garrulously. "When you set down to a meal of vittles in a Dutch kitchen the wimmen folks all pitch right in and tell you how plaguey good everything is. It fairly makes your mouth water whether you're hungry or not, and you eat like sin before you fairly know it. Take a Yankee woman now, she'll say nine times out of ten, even if her dinner is right up perfect: 'There now, I'm shamed to death over this here dinner. I've hed terrible bad luck, and there ain't a thing fit to eat.'" He imitated in high falsetto voice a complaining woman. "After she's done runnin' her stuff down you hain't got no more appletite than a mouse."

"Oh, chimminy! that's easy." Ulie was chuckling mightily. "Reason why Yankee women runs down their vittles still is 'cause they don't know how to cook anything that's decent. Hein? Yar-r-r! e-e-e-e-e! Oh, my! say, Amos, give us somesing hard a'ready." A great laugh rolled about the tables. The man straightened instantly.

"Wha-a-a-y, there!" he called; "'nother county gone dimmercratic! Say, is that you, Ulie? Well, let me ask *you* one: ever try a mess o'genuwine Yankee bake beans? Now I don't mean your scairt, white-livered, hard-shell beans that's been sizzled twenty minutes in a tin pan, but real, gen-u-wine Yankee beans, such as my mother used to bake in a bean-pot up to Connecticut. 'Course you never did; there never was a bean baked right this side of the Susquehanny. Then take brown-bread and Injun puddin'—Lord, now what does a Dutchman know about Injun puddin'?—all kinder brown and curdly, with a skin like satin velvet plush, and a rich juice that 'll make ye shout 'Hally-lew-yer!' like a man on the mourners' benches, spite of all you can do. Then, take a biled dish,—my stars, it makes my mouth water so I can't talk; honest, it does! Look here, if you'd ever et a mouthful of arry one of um there'd be a yarler streak this minute up in the northeast, which would be you makin' a line fer the State o' Connecticut."

"There, now, hear that wunst, will ye!" Ulie straightened up in well-feigned anger. "He's runnin' down the cookin' our wimmen does and, chimminy gracious, I won't stan' for that still! Nosuh! I won't stan' for havin' the wimmin run down, nosuh; that allus makes me mad. Yes-suh!" He stole a side glance over at the widow Krumrine. "That's jest like a Yankee, now ain't it wunst? It's jest like 'em. If I was in the desert of Saharey still I'd know a Yankee wunst. I'd know him by his brag. Yar-r-r-r! e-e-e-e-e! Oh, my! Heigh, Miff?"

Unconsciously Ulie was voicing a large area of his native State. The old antipathies and resentments described by Washington Irving as existing among the early Knickerbockers, and springing up again farther south among the Germans during the era when northern Pennsylvania was a part of Connecticut, are still to be found in the Teutonic portions of the State, where they cling even yet like persimmons.

"Look here, Ulie, what are you standing up for the wimmen so for all to once?" Amos tipped a sly wink at the other end of the table.

"Oh, Ulie's gone soft on the whole female sect," volunteered a youth.

"Say, why don't you brace up, Ulie, and get one of 'em 'fore it's too late?" broke in another. "It's comin' on spring's work, and you need a woman dretfully."

"Don't you-uns worry about me," he snapped. "I know what I'm about still. Yessuh!"

"Now, Ulie, look here," Amos leaned far over and addressed him in a fatherly tone, "I'm your friend if you've got one in the world; you know that. Now you be sensible. If you wait to get a handsum young woman, then your weddin' won't come off more 'n a Dutchman's hat at a funeral. You let me tell you something." He lowered his voice confidentially. "You jest edge up to the widder Kuhn. She'll take ye with a jump quick's a bat does a June bug, and she'll make ye a good wife. You c'n get a lot of work out of them children of hern. You go 'n see her, Ulie. She'll take right to ye like a yeller dog, and I don't believe you'd hev to do the askin'. She's kind o' hard up and discouraged; her first man, old Ezra, was awful shifless, and she havin' hard times. You take my advice, Ulie, and shine up to the widder Kuhn."

"Humph!" grunted Ulie.

Jim Farthing heard very little of the running chatter. He sat facing the stove and the summer kitchen, where the women were at work, and where Rose was flitting about from point to point, the life and centre of all the workers. Rose was a housekeeper of skill and experience, and wherever she was present at a dinner like this she was soon at the head of things. She was cool and resourceful, and she forgot nothing. At critical moments when generalship was needed: when a dish came out wrong at the moment when it must be served, or when it showed signs of giving out in the very midst of the meal, or when the next course was not ready and the men were waiting,—at such tragic moments the women ignored the hostess and crowded about Rose. It was worth while to see her then, with her cool-headed orders, her deft, swift precision of movement, and her complete mastery of the situation.

Young Jim was not the only man at the table who was furtively watching her. She was everywhere. She circled about them with the water-pitcher and filled the glasses. Then she gathered up the empty dishes and poured another helping of coffee. Every one had a merry word as she came near.

"Say, Rose, won't ye smile into my coffee wunst and save me gettin' the sugar?"

"Yes, if you'll smile into this glass of water and save me drawing more vinegar."

"Ulie been round to see ye yet, Rose?"

"Oh, I'm too old for Ulie."

"Yar-r-r-r! hear that, Ulie?"

"Yes, I hev drew the line. I can't take nobody over twenty-eight still. Yar-r-r-r-r! e-e-e-e-e! oh, my!" Ulie's laugh was shrill and penetrating, and it dominated everything while it lasted.

"Oh, shame on ye, Ulie! Rose is sixteen a'ready."

"Is she? By George, she don't look it."

"How old be ye, Rose? Bet ye don't dast ter tell wunst."

"Old's I look,—a woman's as old as she looks," and she disappeared into the kitchen in a swirl of laughter.

Thus the chaff and banter and homely country wit followed her in merry stream wherever she went. The other women seemed to be merely scullions and menials; she was the presiding goddess, the life and soul of the whole dinner.

Thus indeed it seemed to Jim Farthing. So absorbed did he become in watching her that he scarce realised what he ate or whether he ate at all. The conversation rattled about him like the monotone of summer crickets. Once he heard a voice at his elbow addressing him and he turned with a start.

"Say, don't you think Dan's doin' wrong to have his flitt'n on a Saturday wunst? It's a dretful bad sign. 'A Saturday flit makes a short sit.'"

He made no answer, for he had seen Rose disappear with the water bucket in the direction of the cistern. His indignation was instant. That Rose, with all that room full of men, should have to tug water in a bucket struck him as monstrous. He arose instantly and followed her.

There was a moment's hush about the tables, then a titter. The spectacle of a man helping a woman with her work, no matter how heavy the work may be, is always regarded as ludicrous in German regions. Clearly the man was in love. But Jim heard nothing.

"Say, you hadn't ought to do that," he called to her the moment he was out of the door.

"Why?

"That's a man's work. That bucket's too heavy."

"Pshaw! I could carry two of 'em easy." She made a little run and began pumping vigorously.

"Here, let me do that."

"All right. It's 'most full, anyway." She stood aside with a swing.

"Those great lubbers in there never think of helping a woman. They—here, here, wait." She had seized the bucket before it was fairly full and was skipping toward the house.

"Say, Miss Hartswick, wait,—I want to tell you something. Wait, please." He followed her eagerly. At the door she stopped with a flirt and looked back.

"Will you go to walk with me to-morrow at three?" he blurted out.

"To-morrow's Sunday."

"Yes; I know it—in the orchard—I'll be by the old arbour seat. Say, will you?"

She looked down at him archly for a moment, then she laughed as if he were a very small boy who had proposed to her. An instant and she swirled about and through the door. A burst of laughter greeted her appearance with the bucket.

"Too slow!" he heard a voice, and there was another roar.

He wheeled abruptly; he would go for his team; he had finished his dinner; what use to face their jeers?—the dinner was over anyway. The others appeared after a moment; in twenty minutes the long caravan of farm wagons was off towards Gum Run.

Young Jim lived the next twenty-four hours between alternate hope and fear. Would she come or not? Of course she wouldn't. Why should she? But who could tell what Rose Hartswick might do? He was in the orchard an hour ahead of time.

The place was more than a mere orchard. It was a park, with paths and evergreens and a long wind-break to protect the house from the winter storms. The old Squire for years had made a hobby of it, beautifying it little by little until now it was really notable with its fantastically arranged fruit trees, its row of spruces, and its rustic benches scattered here and there along the walks.

At the point nearest the house there was a little arbour surrounded by thick evergreens,—an ideal spot, retired, yet commanding perfectly a view of the farm buildings and yard. Young Jim sank upon the low seat, and scanned sharply every avenue of approach. If she came at all, doubtless she would come straight up the path; that was the way she did things.

Then his eye detected something that troubled him. The buggy in the yard was lighter and gayer than the Squire's. That was Karl Keichline's buggy. The sleek postmaster was in the house there now, wooing Rose,—doubtless asking her to be his wife, and she would accept. She was practical and sensible; of course she would take him. He had everything to offer her, everything a woman could ask. Why should she think of Jim Farthing, who had neither money nor prospects, who was almost unknown to her in every way? It was ridiculous. Moreover, the old Squire hated him and had ordered him off his premises.

There boiled within him a sudden hatred that was primeval in its intensity, a hatred that fumed into his soul and bit and blinded him, a hatred of this prosperous clod who was buying with gold and lands the body and soul of the woman whom God, he knew, had made for him.

It was past three now, and the minutes dragged on and on, until it was near four; but still he sat there motionless as a panther on a snag, his chin in his hands, looking at the old stone mansion and Karl Keichline's buggy. It was fate, mere blind fate, that settled things in this world. There was no justice and no God. What right had this man of pork and money to step in and buy her as if she were a mere chattel? By the eternal! fate or no fate he should not. Indeed he should not. He would stop it yet; he would gain her, if it cost him his very soul. But yet what could he do?

Thus he sat and fumed and raged and despaired and hoped and planned, and did not hear the steps on the path until they were close upon him. He turned convulsively, like one who has been caught doing a crime, and faced Squire Hartswick. The old man had been taking his favourite Sunday walk.

For a moment they looked into each other's eyes like two carnivorous beasts that have come suddenly upon each other. The Squire spoke first in a voice that was a snarl.

"What are you doing here?" The whole situation flashed upon him. The man could be there for only one thing,—to meet Rose. Could it be an appointment? The thought clutched at his throat and choked him.

"Why, I've just been walking through your orchard, Squire Hartswick. No harm, I hope."

"Say, young man,"—he came very near to Jim, a black look of wrath on his face. "Remember what I told you the other day? Did you hear what I said to you then? What are you round here for now? You tell me the truth. You came here to see my daughter. Isn't that true? Now don't you lie to me."

"Yes, sir; I did, but—"

"There's no *but* about it. You came to see her. Had she promised to meet you?"

"No, sir; she hadn't."

"Did she know you was coming?"

"I told her I was coming here."

"And what did she say?"

"She didn't say anything."

"And you are here sneaking round like a miserable cur and hiding around bushes. There's no knowing what you're planning to do. It's mighty lucky I happened onto you. I'm a good mind to arrest you here and now."

"What for?"

"Trespassing, and laying in wait to commit crime."

"Squire Hartswick," he broke out confusedly, dominated in spite of himself by the imperious force of the man, "you're taking a good deal for granted. You surely—"

"Stop it; stop right off short. I know this whole miserable business from beginning to end. Now let me tell you God's truth: if I ever see you on my property again or hear of your being on it, I'll put the law to you just as far as it 'll go."

"But, Squire Hartswick, what harm have I done? What—"

"It don't make no difference what harm you've done; I mean what I say. Don't you ever speak to my daughter again. Don't you even think of her again, or look at her, or by God I'll put you where you belong; I'll jail yeh for life."

"But this is a free country, Squire. There are some things you can't help my doing." He faced the man with magnificent courage and let free what was in his heart. "I shall speak to your daughter whenever I meet her, and I shall look at her, and think of her all I please. There's no law against that."

"Then, by God! you'll take the consequences." The old man fairly exploded in rage. His face was purple; the blue veins in his forehead swelled up like welts. "I'll jail yeh before a week. You get off 'n my land just as quick as God A'mighty 'll let yeh. Start! You'll hear from me mighty soon, young man,—mighty soon!"

Young Jim, half-smothering with rage, felt an impulse to fell the old man to the earth, but he controlled it. He controlled also the hot rush of words that boiled within him like volcanic mud and threatened to burst all bounds. This was Rose's father; moreover, he had the power to cause his arrest and have him punished for even the slightest indiscretion. With magnificent self-control, therefore, he said:

"Very well, Squire Hartswick, I'll leave your land at once," and he did not stop nor look back until he had reached the boundary fence.

Life became a dreary thing for young Jim Farthing after that. It was the age-old tale of the two and the one, and the one alone and helpless and outside,—which is hell.

# CHAPTER VIII

## THE FIRING OF HELLER'S CABIN

ON THE NIGHT of the ninth of April there swirled over the Seven Mountains a wild whisk of snow that plastered the landscape as with whitewash. Five inches deep it lay and hung and stuck. Every flake clung where it fell, and in the morning the world was a study in white,—a fluff of cloud above, like a fleece over the hills held up by the ridges, and a smudge of snow beneath, that concealed every colour and outline. It was like a world in a dream. Every twig was a main branch, every thread a cable, every fence-rail a saw-log. Saplings and branches bowed to the earth beneath festoons more gorgeous than those of Christmas. For a day and a night the Seven Mountains were a realm beyond the dreams of fairyland. Then the sun came out.

Tom Farthing saw the beauty of the morning and thought of bears, for Tom was a hunter, and the morning was one of a thousand. If the clouds did not break, letting out the sun, he felt sure of a bear, provided one had moved during the night. Therefore Tom was up in the Gap before five, making for the Wild Meadows. At six he was on the summit of Raccoon Ridge, looking toward the north, where the meadows lay smooth and white among the welter of the hills like an oil spot at sea.

Eager as he was, he paused and swept his eyes about the horizon. For a moment the poet in the man dominated the hunter. It was like a frost picture on a mighty window. At his feet, in the direction from which he had come, lay the V-like trough of Plum Run, then Heller's Ridge with its sudden gap, then the dead level of Hell Bottom with every trace of man smoothed out, then the fog. On every side a wild, chaotic world without colour or sharp angle, fantastically beruffled with the snow.

He paused but a moment, then he plunged over the ridge-crest down toward the meadows, stumbling into pitfalls, tripping over stones and brush, and drenching himself through and through with the snow from the low shrubbery. At seven he entered the rhododendron slough known as the Wild Meadows.

The details of Tom's day do not concern this tale. He killed no bears, though he tramped far; but late in the afternoon he found himself ravenously hungry, wet to the skin, tired as a young fellow of twenty ever gets, down on Roaring Run just where it is joined by the Plum Run stream. From this point there are two ways of reaching Heller's Gap: one up through the rough bottom between Raccoon and Roaring Ridges,—a rocky hole with a brush snarl like a barbed-wire tangle, and the other through the jaws of Roaring Run and out to the Hell Bottom pike.

With the smear of greasy snow over brush and rocks, Plum Run was out of the question, and the longer route through the gap was well-nigh so. Even in summer, when the green slime is dry on the rocks and when the waters that go snarling down the gut are low and harmless, it is a hard climb to follow the blind trail along the face of the precipice. For the space of several rods one must cling and balance and choose his footing with care, and a misstep when the run in spring is a wild torrent is not pleasant to think of.

But Tom did not hesitate. He buckled his rifle tightly to his back, pulled his cap low over his ears, and five minutes later stood, hot and panting, among the rocks of Poppy Miller's farm. He kicked the snow from a projection and sat down.

Suddenly, behind the rock masses along the brook, he heard a splash, then another. With the spirit of the day's hunt strong upon him, he sprang to his feet and, with gun at full cock, crept noiselessly through the snow. Almost double he inched along, then raised himself silently over the crest of the rock. An instant, and he drew back as if he had come full upon a rattler.

Right beneath him—he could almost touch her—stood a figure on the bank, a woman, a young maiden, tall and lithe, without hat or wrap, her hair ivory black,—an intense fleck of colour against the snow, her plump figure clad in a plain working dress, her hands holding two buckets dripping from the brook,—an instant only, but to Tom like a camera snap. He dodged automatically—he had not been stalking game like this—and took several noiseless steps, so as not to startle the girl. It was useless, however; escape was impossible. She was coming straight toward him, and in a moment more would be around the rock and face to face with him. He wheeled about, and began to whistle, as if he were strolling up the glen and had not seen her. A moment and they came full upon each other around the rock. She did not start or cry out, but stopped instantly and looked at him with wild eyes, as a deer will when one comes upon him on a forest path.

"Why—hello-o-o-o!" he said, bluff surprise in his voice. "I didn't know any one was down here!"

Her eyes, intensely black, had long lashes; her cheeks seemed a pale olive against the jet of her hair. She did not speak; she made a movement as if to get by him.

"Oh, I see; you are taking 'em up to Poppy Miller's?"

"Yes."

"Let me carry 'em. I'll carry 'em for you."

She put them down on the instant and started ahead. Involuntarily he stood and looked at her. She was tall and straight and full-figured, and she sprang up the rocks as agile as a fawn.

"Wait, don't run away," he called, picking up the buckets and trying to follow, but in a moment she was out of sight.

The girl was undoubtedly Lona Heller. He had never seen her before, but he had heard of her as a strange, shy creature, whom no one knew much about. There was a beaten path all the way to the cabin; it was evident that they got all their water from the creek, and that the girl carried it. Neither old Poppy nor Grannie Miller was fit for such a task.

He crossed a rail fence that lurched drunkenly across the glen, and came out into a littered yard. A yellowish horse harnessed to an old wagon dozed before the house, but there was no movement anywhere. The wildness of the place with its chaos of rocks, its ragged trees, and its strange architecture did not impress him. He was looking for the girl. What should he do with the buckets? As he stood deliberating, the old man himself, hoary white and much bowed, appeared at the door.

"Leave 'em set right there," he quavered. "Are yeh going down the road wunst? Chump right in." Tom jumped in, and the old man laboriously followed. There was a movement out by the barn.

"Huh! T'at peeg's out a'ready. Wuts, wuts, wuts, wuts! Here, peegy! Hey, Loney! Lo-ney-y-y-y! Huh! She can't hear nothing still. Let 'im go it. G'up, t'ere!"

He slapped the reins viciously on the old creature's back, and, after awaking, it began to shamble down the moderate slope. Tom watched the house narrowly. No sign of life. They reached the end of the yard; by a sudden impulse he turned again.

Ah! the upper window was open and he caught the glimpse of a face. At that moment the sun, just over the ragged tear of the gap, broke through the cloud-bank, and a slanting ray fell full upon the girl of the brook, lighting up her face with a strange momentary transfiguration. An instant, and she had disappeared.

"Clear t'morrow," observed the old man oracularly. The shambling horse turned the corner, and the house was lost.

It was not far to the Heller's Gap road, and little was said, that little being from the old man and about the waywardness and perversity of "peegs." Tom heard little and cared little. He went home and, after the manner of young fellows of twenty, dreamed about black eyes and a certain picture framed in a window. And Poppy Miller resumed his reflections on "peegs," just as if he were not a pow-wower and didn't know that something had happened.

The circle about the Squire's stove greeted the old man warmly. He came to the store but seldom of evenings, and when he did come it was an event. It is always comforting to have an undisputed authority on things supernatural close at hand for ready reference.

"That's a fine day, Poppy, a'ready."

"Mmh-huh!"—a sharp accent on the first syllable, which meant "no." Otherwise accented it would have been "yes." "T'is ain't no saplin'-bender; it's the onion snow a'ready, and

'Onion snow 'twixt nine and twenty,
Drooth and trouble and a plenty.'

"Mh-h-h-h-h!"

"Gut your garden planted, Poppy?"

"Mmh-huh! Signs ain't right still."

"Right for onions, ain't it? Yas?"

"Mmh-huh!—yas,—plant 'em in the down so t'ey'll strike down wunst."

"Oh, pshaw, this moon business makes me tired!" burst out Amos Harding. He was sitting on a chair by the stove, both of his legs folded up before him, his heels on the front of the chair-seat. In this position he resembled nothing so much as a long-geared letter Z which has been sat upon.

"Heh? heh?" The old man bristled up and turned shakily.

"I plant by the sun, not the moon."

"'Spose I'm blind, do ye? 'Spose I hain't been seein' t'ese sixty year, heh? You plant by t'e moon, young man, and you plant by t'e signs if you want to reap. Mh-h-h-h-h-h-h!"

"What are the signs for planting, Poppy? Tell Amos."

"Plant your taters and turnups in the sign of t'e scales if you want 'em to weigh. Plant cowcumbers in t'e sign o' t'e twins, but don't yeh dast to plant taters t'en or t'ey'll all be runty and scrotchy, and don't for t'e Lord's sake, plant 'em in t'e fishes wunst, or t'ey'll be so watery you can't eat 'em still. I done it wunst and I knows. Everysing t'at strikes down you must plant in t'e unnergehende, but beans and peas and such truck must be put in when t'e moon's in t'e up. I wouldn't plant beans in t'e down of t'e moon more 'n I would clean out a stove-pipe in t'e down,—not a bit more. Plant cabbage in t'e Lion still, so t'e juice of the krout 'll in t'e crock. And you-uns all remember t'is: t'at all kinds of wegetables and garden truck is best if t'ey's planted by a man. Mh-h-h-h-h-h!"

"Pshaw!" snorted Amos. The old man did not hear. He drew his chair nearer to the stove, unwound several lengths of the red scarf from his neck, fumbled for his pipe, which at length he succeeded in lighting, then sat in wise contemplation of the group.

"Dan tells us the post-office at Gum Stump was broke open last night and everything took. Heern tell of it?" Dan Tressler had come up on business. He was staying with Amos.

"No-o-o! Dew tell!" cackled the old man.

"Say, this is gettin' sorter kinder close, as the darkey said when the mule kicked him," observed Amos. "This makes five breaks to my certain knowledge: Snyder's over to White Deer Valley; the post-office in Blair's Gap; McCormick's on Bottle River; and two weeks ago the store at Green Briar Creek. Better keep your eye peeled these nights, Squire. You'll be next. There's a regular gang at this."

"Say, Ulie," observed the Squire, ignoring Amos, "ever stop to think there hain't been a robbery in this section for thirty years 'fore the Farthings come in here? Mind yeh, I ain't making no charges, but have you thought of it?"

"Oh, pshaw, Squire!" ejaculated Dan, who was much bolder now he had nothing to lose. "You've got Farthing on the brain. There ain't no honester man in Pennsylwaney still than Al Farthing. Nosuh! You're mad at him jest because he's got a little of your trade still, and you've made up your mind to ruin him wunst."

"If he's all right I want to ask you a few questions: Where does he get all that money? I offered 'em six hundred dollars for that little mare and they said they wouldn't take two hundred and fifty thousand. Money ain't no object up there. They've gut it to burn. Then where does he and one of his boys go dodging off to every few days? Where does all that store stuff come from that he's trying to sell you fellers? Mighty little freight comes for him down to Spruce Creek. Then why do these store robberies begin jest the minute he gets here, and why does the trouble up at the old cabin take up at jest the same time? Heigh?"

"Now, that's pretty thin evidence, I call it, Squire," retorted Dan. "'Fore I tried to take a man's reputation away I'd get something better than that."

"Oh, no; you don't believe nothing about that old house! Oh, no!" Lem Fisher had straightened up on his nail-keg. "You don't believe there's something strange about that old house? Never seen a thing there, did yeh? Oh, no!"

"Say, Dan," tittered another, "I heard they measured your jumps next morning, and some of 'em was twenty-three feet a'ready."

"Puht yeh hand right onto the house, didn't yeh wunst?" A burst of good-natured laughter echoed about the stove.

"Wal, I did see somesing," admitted Dan hesitatingly; "but as I have told yeh a dozent times, I hain't saying as to how it's a ghost still. I run 'fore I knowed it. One don't have to be a ghost to swear yetst." The tone was that of the man defending his last ditch.

"Humph! You can't get out of it that way," broke in Lem in high key. "You know there hain't been no track in there all winter. You know it, and,"—shuddering,—" you know about that awful black ring."

"Fiddlesticks! Cats and a fiddle!" burst in Amos. "Of all the old grannies! I'm going up there some day and tear that old shanty down, hide and hinges. Darn'd if I ain't. I'm good and sick of all this tarnal nonsense I've been hearin' here night and day. Ha'nted house!—Oh, lord!"

"You go slow, Amos Hard'n; you go mighty slow. We-uns knows what we's a-talking about. Yessuh! Against the time you've been up there some dark night and been into that house then you can talk. But you keep still against that time, for we-uns have saw this with our eyes wunst, and heard it with our ears. Yessuh!"

"Huh!" snorted Amos.

"Now the whole matter is jest here," continued Lem impressively. "We might as well speak it right out as to be all thinking about it. Al Farthin's a haexer." He lowered his voice and looked about the room furtively, as if some fearful creature might be lurking in a dark corner. "He's a haexer and a pow-wower; I know it. You can tell that jest by lookin' at his eyes,—kinder sharp and beady, like a weasel's, and they never keep still a minute, but they're all the time shiftin' quick's lightning this way and that way. I tell you-uns that ain't an honest eye still. And you needn't tell me he don't know what's going on in that ole shanty. If he ain't noticed it and hain't tried to find out what's up, then he's a fool, and whatever else Al Farthin' is he ain't no fool. Of course he knows it, and of course he's at the bottom of it. And he's a pow-wower and a haexer,—you mind what I sayes, and you watch out sharp how you run ag'in him." He wagged his head in solemn warning. It was evident that the man was in fearful earnest and that he believed all that he had said. It was plain too that the little circle also believed it. To Amos, however, the matter was a red rag.

"Pow-wower!" he exploded, straightening up and glowering about him. "If somebody'd pow-wow a few brains into your old Dutch skulls it would be the greatest thing that ever happened in this valley. I can pow-wow jest as well as Al Farthin' can. If he's a pow-wower you git him down here some day, and I'll pow-wow the pow-wow out of him in three minutes."

"I wouldn't make a speech like that, suh, for no amount of money. Nosuh!" Ulie lowered his voice solemnly. "I've saw pow-wowing and haexing, I have 'fore now, and you've saw it, Poppy."

The old man mumbled a decided "Mmh-huh," and nodded impressively.

"I tell you," went on Ulie, "pow-wowing ain't to be spoke of in that way. It's a mighty serious thing, pow-wowing is. I could tell enough cases to fill a book as big as ten awmnicks, and Poppy here could tell yeh twict as many more a'ready. I tell you it's an awful thing to go against a haexer wunst, an awful thing." He rolled out the words in sepulchral tones.

"Yessuh, he's right," chimed in Lem Fisher, who was the valley archives on things occult. "What was it that give the oppnehmer to Katie Barndollar? What was it that drawed the lightning on Andy Bowersock's barn? What was it that killed Luke Snyder,"—he spoke in a shuddering whisper—"down in Turkey Bottom and left the great black ring 'round his neck? What was it? You-uns all knows what it was. And I tell you, Amos Hard'n, you watch out still. Don't you run up against Al Farthin'. Don't you dast to." A shuddering silence had fallen over the group. They were looking furtively over their shoulders and into the dark corners.

"Yessuh. It's jest as I'm telling yeh," repeated Lem impressively, attributing Amos's silence to acknowledgment of defeat. "If there's devilishness going on in these walleys still, Al Farthing knows it. What do you think, Poppy?"

"T'ere's somesing strange about it," muttered the old man absently. "Somesing strange."

"He's a haexer; now, ain't he?" he asked eagerly.

"Um-m-m-m-m-m," the old man mumbled, a far-away look in his eyes. "Somesing stranger 'n you sink."

"You see, it's jest as I say," went on Lem, with added confidence. "There's haexing and pow-wowing at the bottom of this. The devil is making his headquarters in that old shanty since Al Farthin' come here, and he's going to rave and rare up and down these walleys till we-uns is all at our wits' end. Yessuh! Ain't that so, Squire?"

"Begins to look that way." Things were going in precisely the direction he wished."

"Say, you, now, darned if it don't seem as if I was in some nigger shack down South." The disgust in Amos's face and voice were really ludicrous. "I vum I can't, if I die, believe I'm listening to white folks talkin'. Now, there hain't nothing more the matter with that old shanty up there than there is with the Squire's old smoke-house, that's ha'nted with the ghosts of four hundred hogs that's been hung in it. It makes me mad clean through and through to hear grown white men, that ought to be civilised, talkin' like a pack of nigger wenches. Pow-wowin'! Oh, my lord!" He got up and took an angry turn around the store.

"Say, Amos, you talk big; how'd you like to go up there some midnight wunst and walk acrost that dead line? Doin's one thing and talkin's another. Now, I reckon you'll be satisfied in takin' it out in talkin'." Ulie's voice fairly shook with sarcasm.

"The Squire hain't took back his offer yetst, not's I've hearn tell of," spoke up Lem sneeringly. "It's ten dollars still, ain't it, Squire, to the man who puhts his hand on the old cabin wunst after dark?"

"Ye-es," said the Squire hesitatingly. He knew Amos, and he knew Ulie and Lem and Dan. It would not do, however, to back down on his offer.

"I'll dare yeh and double dare yeh to go up to that house to-night," jeered Ulie. "Now, you've been talking big for a long time a'ready. You go up now or you shet up. That's fair."

"Oh, he won't go," sneered Lem in a tone that sent the hot blood to Amos's face. "Perhaps he'll take Dan along to give him courage." The Squire was keeping strangely silent. Things were not going just right. He knew Amos.

"I thought he'd weaken," scoffed Ulie. "He hain't gut as much sand as Dan has."

"Now, look here, folks, there hain't any reasonable call for me to go up to that old house to-night in this mush of snow, but you and nobody else ain't going to dare me. I ain't afraid, and you all know it. I'm good and sick of this whole thing, and the sooner it's settled the better. Here, Ab, get me a larntern. I'd jest exactly as lives go up there as to go to the Squire's barn. I want you to go with me, Dan, for a witness."

"All right; I'll go." He arose instantly and buttoned up his coat.

"Better strip good for racin', Dan," jeered Ulie.

"All right, suh!" Amos was getting angry. "I'm goin' up there, and what's more I'm goin' inside, and I'm goin' to fire the tarnal old shanty. I'm sick and tired of it." Amos had not a particle of superstition in his make-up. Moreover, he was a man of courage, one who seldom backed down when once he had taken a position. Clearly something was going to happen.

"Don't you do it, Amos." Old Poppy Miller had shakily arisen to his feet and was holding out a palsied hand. "Don't you dast to do it, Amos." His voice was a tremulous falsetto.

"I'm going to kill two birds with one stone: I'm going to earn ten dollars; and I'm going to get red of the biggest nuisance in this valley, that's jest what I'm goin' to do. Got that larntern most ready, Ab?"

"No, no," quavered the old man with singular intensity. "Fer God's sake don't you do it, Amos. You don't know what you're a-doin' of." His excitement was increasing visibly.

"Huh!" Amos was coolly helping himself from the store matches.

"If it's the last word I ever have to say," begged the old man, his voice cracking in his excitement, "don't yer dast ter do it. I knows what I's a-sayin'. It's death, Amos; death, death, death!" He had taken a step forward, and with his palsied hands was waving a shaky circle toward the bustling man.

"Come on, Dan. Ready? I em." They strode out together. "Watch for a fire in jest sixty minutes," he called back confidently.

But there was to be no fire that night.

"All right, t'en; all right, t'en," mumbled the old man incoherently. He was still making weird circles in the air with his shaky hands. Ulie and Lem Fisher stood behind him as far as they could get in the narrow store and watched his movements with ghastly faces.

They knew what it meant.

Those about the stove could hear the dollar clock beating on the shelf over the cloth counter. It fairly bellowed through the room. The old man was staring with vacant eyes out into the darkness and mumbling disjointedly. Then he began to wind the long scarf about his neck.

"Too bad; too bad; too bad," he was saying. "I warned him. He brought it on his own self." Then suddenly he started for the door. No one spoke or disturbed the silence, nor was there a sound in the store until the "clunk-clunk" of the old wagon had died away in the distance.

Amos and Dan walked rapidly down the pike. It was a perfect spring night. The clouds had entirely disappeared, leaving the sky brilliant with stars that scintillated coldly. Low in the west, over the ragged scar in the range, the thin curve of a new moon lay pointing upward with sharp horns. Far off in the stillness they could hear the warning growl of Roaring Run, but it only made the silence more complete. They said nothing as they strode down the pike, and they turned into the Heller's Gap road without a word. The awful warnings of Poppy Miller were echoing in Dan's ears; he was walking like a man in a dream.

A dim light burned in the Farthing kitchen, but they heard no sound, save the rattling movements of some creature in the barn. Then they struck into the old lane to the cabin.

The world still wore the fantastic garments of the morning, though much of the snow had dropped from the trees during the day. It was a weird, silent scene, and both of the men were impressed by it. The great shadow of the Gap was over them; the walls on either side loomed up like ghostly columns as they saw them in the uncertain light.

"Darn creepy place," observed Dan at length.

"Huh!" sniffed Amos, striding on stoutly in the lead.

Then they came in sight of the cabin, and stopped a moment to reconnoitre. The old house loomed up black and sepulchral amid the scrubs. A livid ring, unnaturally distinct, surrounded it. Dan called his companion's attention to it, but Amos only grunted.

"Come ahead, Dan," he said gruffly.

They strode rapidly to the edge of the snow line, then both stopped instantly as if they had run into an invisible wire. There was a light in the cabin, but one so diffused and indistinct that it was impossible to see anything within. Dan Tressler turned in a panic, and was on the point of fleeing, but Amos gripped him by the arm.

"Brace up, Dan," he hissed in his ear. "We're going to see this out if it takes a leg. You stay right here; I'm going to find out how many's in there." He started out cautiously in a circle around the cabin, veiling his lantern with his coat and examining the snow with extreme care. At length he came around to where he had started.

"Say, Dan," he said with a trace of excitement in his voice, "there hain't a living soul moved in or out of there since the snow."

"Good lord!" gasped Dan. "Say, le's make a rush and touch the old shanty and run." His nerves were rapidly getting beyond his control.

"Not by a long chalk! They probably went in there before the snow came the other night. You wait a minute. I'm going to look in."

He crept nearer. Then there came from within a shrill laugh, fearfully startling in its weird distinctness. Involuntarily Dan gave a nervous cry, and on the instant they saw a face at the window, a face strangely white and thin, with a framing of hair that even in that uncertain light showed up inky black. Instantly there echoed from within a shriek so ghastly that it shook the nerves even of Amos Harding. It was in a shrill falsetto, seemingly feminine. He dropped his lantern, so suddenly did it ring out and so frightful. But his panic was only for an instant.

"Some of them Farthin's are in there, trying to scare us," he shouted. "Here, I'm coming in! You can't scare me! You've got the wrong man, I'll tell yeh that! Here, open up!" A sudden fury seemed to have seized him. "Open up! Open there!" he yelled. Then he ran against the door full tilt, but it did not yield.

A livid stream of curses in what seemed to be an old man's cracked voice followed. Amos took a back step, and hesitated. Then a recollection of the group in the store came upon him, and he faced the cabin again.

"Come on, Dan. It's only the Farthin's trying to scare us. Stand by me, Dan," he shouted. "Get a stone. I'm goin' to stave in the old door." Dan took one step and stopped short; but for Amos he would have turned and fled for his life.

For another scream came from the interior, a scream that must have come from a woman's throat, and yet no living woman's; then a flash of light, intense and blinding, filtering through the crannies like red fire. For the space of a minute it bathed the scene in a lurid hell-red. Even Amos felt his hair creeping, but his blood was up and he would not have turned back now even if the devil himself had confronted him.

The bright light showed him a jagged piece of limestone at his feet within the dead-line. He seized it and began to batter the door. It held out strongly; he threw all of his strength into the work. Then the cabin became utterly dark; it was deathly still now; but he battered on. The bar began to give way; a couple of blows more and the door swung wide open.

But Amos did not enter.

He held up his lantern and peered within with quivering interest. Nothing was in sight; nothing moved; but there was a thick smudge of smoke and a ghastly stench of sulphur. He stood still and listened. No sound save far behind him the gurgle of Roaring Run, like the rattle in the throat of a dying man.

"Come on, Dan," he ordered excitedly. It was too late to back out now. "I'm going right in there hellbent, darned if I ain't. Come on. Don't go back on me, old man." Dan was no longer master of himself. He moved as in a stupor; the strong will of the other man dominated him. He hesitated, then took a faltering step toward the door. Amos was out of sight.

"Hey, Amos! Where be yeh?" he quavered. He caught a choking breath of the sulphur reek and his knees well-nigh gave way beneath him.

"Here! This way, quick!" he heard Amos calling. Blindly and automatically he rushed in. He found Amos, the stone still in his hand, looking about him warily. The cabin, as they saw it by the light of the lantern, was furnished apparently as the last occupant had left it years ago. There were two rooms, and in the larger were a bedraggled sofa, several kitchen chairs, a cupboard, and a few smaller pieces of furniture. In the kitchen was a stove which gave evidences of having been lately used. There were cooking utensils scattered about. Both rooms were utterly deserted.

"Here, they're upstairs," Amos yelled. "Here, you, come down." After a moment he sprang up the rickety stairway, but the rooms were empty.

"Then they're in the cellar!" The door was standing ajar.

"Come on," he shouted. "They're not goin' to fool me. I ain't goin' to back out now, darned if I am. Here!" he shouted down the stairway. "Come up and show yourselves, or we'll go down. There's a whole gang of us up here, so you don't stand no show. Who are yeh?"

No answer.

"All right; here goes!" Amos had his blood up.

"Don't go, Amos; for God's sake, don't. It's an aw-w-w-w-ful hole down there."

"Come along!" he shouted as if in anger, and Dan automatically followed the lantern: better down in the cellar with the light than above without it.

There was no one in the cellar.

They stood in speechless amazement, a shudder of superstitious horror beginning to creep over even Amos.

"They're hid," he cried, though the idea was not very plausible. They began a systematic search. They even prodded the limestone walls for a hidden exit.

There was no one in the cellar.

They went at length up the stairs again, and searched with minute care through the two rooms and the chambers above. There was no secret hiding-place,—the cabin was deserted. There could be no doubt of it. Amos stood a moment in blank amazement; then a sudden thought struck him.

"Here, I have it. They skinned out the back way while we was upstairs,—that's jest what they done. Hold on a minute; let me look for tracks." With Dan at his heels, he circled the cabin again.

No one had left the house. The creatures, whoever they might be, were still in the cabin.

"Wal—I'll—be dum—buzzled!"

"Come, le's go," pleaded Dan in a convulsive whisper. "Le's get out o' here. Oh, lord! jest look at that!" He pointed with shaking hand at the livid ring around the cabin, which seemed to glow and waver with a sort of phosphorescent light.

"For God's sake, le's run, Amos, while we can!" He was on the verge of nervous collapse, looking around him fearfully as if something were close behind him and peering over his shoulder.

"Not till I've fired this hell-hole!" There was a ring in the man's voice that held Dan involuntarily. "Hold the larntern here till I get some kindling wood." Amos broke up a chair and ripped open the tick of the old lounge. Then he arranged the straw with the wood above it.

"Wish I had a can of coal-oil. But I guess this 'll go." He struck a match, but the straw was damp. He tried another and it failed.

"Hold on; I've gut a paper here in my pocket." He drew out a newspaper which he had received in the evening's mail, opened it, crumpled the sheets together, and arranged it under the straw.

"Say, I'm going to slop a little of the oil out o' this larntern." He unscrewed the little filler, and carefully saturated the paper and the straw without extinguishing the light. Then he scratched another match.

"What 're you doing here?" growled a voice at the door.

Both jumped as if the last trump had sounded in their ears. Dan Tressler let out a yell that vied even with those of a few moments earlier. They turned and saw Allen Farthing.

"What's going on here?" he demanded. "What are you doing?"

"I'm goin' to fire this old hell-coop; that's jest what I'm goin' to do." Amos had dropped his match, but he felt deliberately in his pocket for another.

"Oh, that's you, is it, Amos and Dan? *You* the ones that's been making all this yelling?"

"No," spoke up Dan. "This house is ha'nted. It was the ghosts yellin'."

"Oh, pshaw! You don't take any stock in such nonsense as that, do you, Amos?"

"Stock or no stock, I'm goin' to fire this old hell-kitchen. That's jest what I'm goin' to do." He was sheltering the match-flame with his hands.

"Here! Hold on! This is my property. Don't you fire that straw, Amos."

"Reckon I shell."

"All right; go ahead; but it's a serious matter to burn a man's buildings against his consent. Do as you please, gentlemen. But you'll pay the penalty if you do." He disappeared in a twinkling in the darkness. Amos dropped the match and gave a whistle of astonishment.

"Wal—by—gum!" He seized the lantern and went out quickly. Al Farthing had disappeared as if into the air. For a moment they looked bewilderedly about them, then they started down the road without a word. Once only before they reached the store did Amos open his lips:

"Wal—I'll—be—dum—buzzled!"

# CHAPTER IX

# THE FIRE ON CHERRY CREEK

THE "SAPLIN'-BENDER" was followed by a week of perfect weather. It was unseasonably warm. The yellow mud, half-spoke-deep on the back roads, began to harden into brick-like welts and ragged pits and ruts; the wheat fields had emerged from the snow a livid green, most intense as viewed against the dun corn lands, and the usual spring fires, the bane of the Seven Mountains, were beginning to creep here and there on the ridges and to throw over the landscape a gauze of smoke that blurred all outlines.

It was Sunday afternoon, and a silence like that of the Indian summer lay on the valley. The sun, a rim of old brass, hung lustreless over the smudge that was Roaring Run, and a cozy twilight was creeping on, even with the sun full in sight.

Whether it was the spring day, or whether it was the memory of the Sabbath before when he had tried his best to propose and had been managed out of it, something, it was evident, had stirred Karl Keichline mightily. As he had ridden up the Run that morning there had been desperation in his heart. He would settle it before he ever went back again. He had tried the gradual approach long enough; he would be abrupt now and stormy. He would make a sudden dash, and demand *yes* or *no* without alternative.

The day, however, had passed without progress. She had not evaded him; on the contrary, she had been with him even more than usual; but somehow there had been no chance. It had not seemed her fault. There had been sudden accidents and interruptions and intrusions until it had seemed as if Fate itself were against him. And all day the fever in his heart had burned higher. He had never seen her so joyous and irresistible, and sweetly feminine; she had awed him, and thrilled him, and captivated him until he was intoxicated and helpless.

But every man has his chance.

Suddenly he saw Rose make a dash across the garden toward the cherry trees. Her cat had caught a robin.

"Here, Dick! Here, here, here!" she was calling excitedly. He leaped from the porch and together they succeeded in cornering the cat in a nook beyond the trees. It made an attempt to get through the chicken-wire fence, then dropped the bird, and dashed by them. The robin lay still a moment, but as they approached, it fluttered into a shrub.

"Oh, do you think it's hurt?" she asked eagerly.

"Not a bit. It's only scared," he responded with conviction.

"But just see how the poor little thing shakes. Just see how he's rumpled up." There was a pathetic quiver in her voice.

"He's only frightened, that's all. He's all right. But, Rose,"—he changed his tone abruptly,—"I want you to marry me. Will you, Rose?" She gave him a swift, startled look, then sidled hastily toward the shrub.

"Oh, see, his wing must be broken. Just see how it hangs down. Oh, see!"

"No, it isn't. See him fly? But will you marry me, Rose? Say, will you?" He came close to her. There was a tragic, do-or-die look in his face.

"Oh, my dishes 'll get stone-cold. I must go right back." She started off decisively, but he kept close to her almost desperately.

"But your answer,—will you marry me?"

"Why, what a question!"

"*Yes* or *no*, will you marry me?" he repeated doggedly.

"No."

"You don't mean it, Rose. You can't. Say, will you, Rose? You will, won't you?" He came nearer. Somehow she had no desire to laugh now: the affair was becoming dangerous.

"But why? Why should I want to marry *anybody?*" She looked him full in the eyes.

In the Dutch belt of Pennsylvania maidens are taught that their hearts are shaped very much like a purse, and that love awakes in its true ecstasy only at the sight of the substantial things readily convertible at the county bank. The rural swain, therefore, seldom advances the flimsy logic, "I love you, and therefore you should wed me," but he advances boldly with the more convincing argument, "I have fifty acres and a thousand cash; is that not enough to make you my wife?" Thus it was that Karl Keichline at the critical moment began to argue.

"I can make you happy, Rose. I have—"

"I'm happy now. I don't ask to be any happier."

"Yes; but think what we can have, Rose. I'm not poor. I'll build you a house that'll beat anything in this whole region, and you shall plan it and furnish it. And you shall have the best horses that money can buy, and a stable for them that's right up to date. I can afford it, Rose. Say, will you?"

"I've got everything I want now. I don't ask for another thing better."

"But what about a few years from now? Your father and mother are getting old, Rose."

"And what of that?" She was looking at him sharply.

"I know,—but, Rose, you'll need somebody to look after you—"

"Do I look as if I needed somebody to look after me?" She stood very straight and tall before him.

"But you surely are not going to live all alone by yourself your whole life, Rose?"

"Oh, possibly not. I may marry somebody years and years from now." She said it as if she were yielding a great point.

"It shan't change your life in the least, Rose. You may be as free as you are now,—just as free, and even freer. But I want you, Rose; I love you. I can't live without you. And I want you *now.*" He was looking into her face with an eagerness that was almost pathetic.

"I'm sorry," she said, a little wave of pity somehow beginning to creep over her tender heart. "But you know really I can't marry anybody,—not for years and years."

"Perhaps I've been sudden, Rose. I won't press it just now. I'll ask you again next Sunday. You'll give me your final answer then, won't you?"

"I've answered you now."

"No, no. You don't mean that, really. You'll think it over and give me the final *yes* or *no* next Sunday. You will, won't you, Rose?"

"No."

"Rose!"

"A week is not a great while," she said evasively. An image of her father had come before her,—eager and pleading. She knew well that it was his dearest wish to have the marriage at once. He wanted Karl to help him even with the present spring's work. The thing was inevitable after all, and what was the use? As well him as any one; yet somehow she shrank. "You may ask me in a year,—five years," she added quickly.

"No, no. I want you *now.* I'll make it two weeks. I insist on two weeks."

"You may ask me again on the first day of June, if you insist upon it, but not one day earlier."

"But, Rose—"

"Not a day earlier."

"But that's six long weeks, Rose."

"If you object again, I shall make it the first of August."

"Very well. Then I agree; but, Rose—"

"And you are to promise not to say one word about it till then."

"But, Rose, I can surely—"

"Not one word. Promise me."

"Yes—yes; I promise. And you'll promise to give me the final answer on June first?"

"Yes; and it will be *no;* I can tell you that now."

"Oh, no, no, no, Rose. Don't say that. And, Rose, if it's *yes,*—and it will be, I know it will,—we can have the marriage on June fifteenth, can't we? I shall insist on that."

"But I shall say *no;* mercy! I must go; my dish-water 'll be cold as ice." She darted away suddenly through the shrubbery, and before he realised it she was out of sight. He stood a moment looking after her in a bewildered way, then went again to the porch, where he found the old Squire smoking his evening pipe.

The sun had faded out in smoke; a grey dark was creeping among the trees. Near at hand in the spruce top a flock of blackbirds were cackling and scolding with raucous voices, and farther away in the maples by the barn, the robins were chanting their vesper hymns. Here and there in the mountains to the south were the dull gleams of fire creeping in fantastic, snake-like figures along the ridges. The smoke had been deepening all day, and it was bringing on the night a full hour ahead of time.

The interview with Rose had cheered Karl. When a woman hesitates and temporises, there is but one ending possible, and he realised it. Of course she would accept him in the end. It was the way of maidens to be coy and to say *no* at first; one must expect that. Therefore, as he and the Squire sat in the twilight with their pipes, he was in jubilant spirits. He felt almost like confiding in the old man, but that would be premature. He led the conversation at length up to the subject of house-building. Which was best, a solid blue-limestone house or a solid brick, and what in his opinion would be the relative cost?

"Building it for yourself or to rent?" asked the old man, sending out a feeler.

"Why, for myself?"

"When would you want to begin?" The Squire had a way of getting at the heart of things at once.

"W'y, I don't know. You see our house is small and is getting old. I'd like to begin right off and have it boarded in by the time snow flies."

"Want my honest opinion?"

"W'y, of course."

"Don't do it."

"Don't do it?" He turned suddenly and looked at him.

"No. Don't think of it. 'Fools build houses and wise men live in 'em.' Now, Karl, don't you think of building a house till you hear from me. I've got pretty definite ideas about house-building, and I want to go over the matter carefully." He turned the subject with abruptness, and although Karl was mystified, he rode home through the Gap well content, satisfied that life, after all, is good and that merit in this world ever finds its true reward.

When the Squire came in from seeing Karl off, he found Rose alone in the kitchen scolding her cat.

"You're a bad, bad boy," she was saying, holding him up by the front paws and putting her face close to his. "You're a naughty cat to catch poor little birds. Aren't you ashamed of yourself?"

The old man seemed to be in a great good humour.

"So you've settled it, have you, Dot? Ho, ho, ho!" He chucked her under the chin, and cocked his head at her jovially. "Oh, you can't fool your old Pap."

"Settled what?" She put down the cat and turned to him curiously.

"Oh, Karl's told me all about his fine new house. Going to have it boarded in before snow flies, heigh? I know what that means. Now, Rose, you don't want to build any house. Don't do it."

"Why, father, what—"

"We can't have you living way down there in the valley, Rose," he went on feelingly. He had blown out his lantern and had come very close to her. "Mother and I want you here. You won't go and leave us, will you, Rose? I want you to bring Karl right up here to live. I'll give him a share in things, and it shall all be yours when we are gone, every bit of it." There was feeling in his voice.

"Why, father, I haven't said anything to Karl. I haven't promised him a single thing."

"Oh, but you will. Of course you will, Rose."

"He asked me and I said 'No' square and flat, and I meant it."

"Oh, no, no, no, Rosie. Don't say that."

"I did."

"But, Rose—Say, is there some one else, Rose?"

"No; there isn't."

"You're quite certain?"

"I don't want to marry anybody. I don't see why I've got to be tormented every minute by somebody wanting to marry me."

"But, Rose, you must be married sometime."

"Why must I?"

"Wal, one thing is because your mother and I aren't going to be here long. You'll be left alone then with this great house and this great property."

"But it 'll be years and years, Pap," she said impulsively. "You'll live years yet, and I'll get married sometime of course,—if I must. There's no hurry, Pap."

"There are some things you don't know, Rosie. I'm going quick when I do go. I'm liable to drop off any time. You know about my dizzy spells; I've got all the symptoms your grandfather had, and he died a younger man than I. We all go that way. I'm failing up, Rose. I can feel it. I'm a broken old man." His voice choked.

"Oh, don't, Pap. Please don't." She threw her arms about him impulsively.

"I've got only one great wish now," he went on feelingly, "and that is to leave the property all right and whole. I can trust Karl. Say, Rose, won't you, to please me?"

She did not answer.

"You won't have me long, Rose, or mother, either. It seems as if you'd like to please us when we ask only one little thing, and it would kill me, Rose, if you should disappoint us. Promise me you'll take Karl the very next time he asks you. Won't you promise?"

"Oh, Pap, there's no hurry."

"Indeed there is, Rose. I want it *now.* I can't sleep nights until it's settled. Something's liable to happen any minute. Won't you, Rose?" She glanced up into her father's face and there were tears there. It thrilled her and touched her to the heart. She had never seen tears in his eyes before.

"Come, Rosie, won't you promise?"

"Yes. I promise," she said waveringly.

"Thank God. That makes me happy. I can trust you, Rose. You've never deceived me yet. It's coming out gloriously,—gloriously. Karl's a good fellow, Rose, and he'll make you happy."

And Rose went to her room and sat long at the window in the fragrant night, looking over at the fires which, like long, shapeless monsters, were crawling up the mountains. It was Fate after all. One must obey the great laws of life, and the greatest of all is that which makes us what we are, and fixes forever our metes and bounds before ever we have found ourselves, or know aught of life's meaning.

On Monday morning the smoke was thicker than ever. The Squire had business at Sinking Springs that would engage him until late in the night, and Amos was going with him. At breakfast, held always in the Hartswick home in the morning twilight, he had said to Rose:

"I don't like the way that smoke's coming. It looks to me jest as if the fire might be working over toward the Brown lot on the third mountain. I wish Amos didn't have to go with me. I'd send him over."

"But I can do just exactly as much good as Amos can. I'll hitch up Pomp after dinner and run over. If it's getting dangerous, I can raise a fire-gang just as quick 's a man could."

"All right; but don't go too near, Rose. It's awful dry, and fire 'll run like the very mischief."

"Now, don't worry about me, Pap. Nothing's ever caught me yet." She laughed up at him in her old girlish way.

"Sure enough, Rosie, and there won't; I'll bet on you against all of 'em. Ho, ho, ho!" He chucked her under the chin, laughing mightily. "But look out for the fire, Dot. Don't go to running any risks. Them narrow valleys are awfully dangerous. Well, good-bye, Dot. Look out for yourself."

At one o'clock, therefore, Rose was driving with Pomp along the second pike. All the morning it had been suffocatingly warm. The sun had poured down on the cover of smoke as on a tin roof, and the dense blanket had seemed to retain all that it received. Before noon there had not been a breath of air; now, however, a little breeze was springing up, though at first it seemed only to increase the heat.

To Rose the experience was not new. Every spring since she could remember, fires had swept here and there among the valleys and ridges and there had always been a week or two of smoke. Often a fire, driven by fierce winds down some funnel of a valley filled with a rhododendron snarl, and the dry wreckage of the lumbermen, sweeps with terrific heat over miles and miles, licking up every trace of organic matter and leaving behind it only blackened rocks and sterile stone-powder, from which nothing save the bird-cherry and the blackberry can ever spring.

By two o'clock Rose was beyond the second range, in the chaotic valley known as Black Log Run. Here at length she left the road, which had become little better than a trail, and struck into a wood-road that some years before had been worn smooth by the lumbermen. This branch valley was Cherry Creek. Three miles further on in a side spur from this valley lay the Brown lot, a magnificent bunch of pines which the Squire had kept thus far from the axe. The fire, as Rose judged from the drift of the smoke, was some distance to the right in the second valley parallel to the one she was in. If the wind, which was rapidly increasing, did not shift, there seemed to be little danger to her father's lot. It was hard, however, in the thick smoke to judge accurately.

It was a wild, lonesome region that she was traversing, one seldom visited save by the trout fisherman in the spring. The ridge-sides on either hand were steep and chaotic, mere jagged heaps of sandstone litter, and the valley bottom, scarce a hundred rods wide in places, was snarled full of the skeleton tops of old trees and of down logs,—a dreary mass of ruin which a great jungle of rhododendron was doing its best to conceal. The valley stream, still full from the melting snow, nosed its way bewilderedly down through the tangle and in places overflowed the crooked little trail. Rose, however, kept on.

Two miles further up the valley a man loomed suddenly out of the tangle. He was right by the horse's head before she saw him. It startled her: there is no telling what wild characters one may find in these remote valleys. A second glance, however, showed her young Jim Farthing.

"Why, is this you?" he blurted out in a startled voice.

"Yes. I'm up to see if the Brown lot is in danger," she replied in business tone. "Do you know how the fire is running?"

"Why, yes; and it's bad." He had come forward and was leaning over the front wheel. "I was up on the ridge only a minute ago, and it looked to me as if the fire was striking right for this valley. The wind's getting higher every minute. I think there'll be a thunder-gust."

"If it gets in here, will it go on to the Brown lot?"

"Can't help it," he answered positively.

"Then I must drive right back and scare up a gang." She straightened up briskly.

"And I think you can't get out of here any too quick. It's really dangerous here. If the fire is driven over the ridge down there by Black Log, it will sweep this valley like a hurricane right up through here. You could climb over the ridge, but the horse couldn't. I'll turn you right round. You mustn't lose a single minute." He took the horse by the bit and turned him almost roughly.

"There, run him out just as fast as you possibly can. Don't lose a second." She looked at him half incredulously. She was not easily scared; his nervous solicitude appealed to her almost humorously.

"But really, Miss Hartswick, there's danger. If I'm any judge at all, the fire's liable to get into the valley here any minute. The wind's getting higher all the time." She fell into driving attitude instantly and shook out the reins.

"Won't you ride?" she asked, as if by a sudden thought. Without a word he slid his axe into the buggy and sprang in beside her. Then they began to bump down the wild trail as fast as it was safe to trot. The tense anxiety of the man, written in every feature, became at length contagious. She threw her whole soul into her driving, as if the fire were an assured fact and she were racing with it. Young Jim watched her with hungry eyes, noting her every movement as she reined the horse past stones and logs, and through sloughs and gullies. In his admiration he forgot for a moment all else. How alert and agile she was, how instant her decisions, how perfect her control of the horse. A sudden cry from the girl aroused him.

"Look! See there!"

The smoke had deepened until they could scarce see beyond the horse's head, and now clots of soot the size of leaves were falling all about them. One that lighted on the lap-robe had the glint of fire in it.

"Hold up quick!" he ordered sharply, and she pulled the horse onto his haunches. "Hark!"

A spluttering roar, mingled with fierce cracklings and shrieks, was right ahead of them. Something hurtling in mad panic up the trail almost crashed into the horse. It veered into the scrubs not six feet from the buggy, a deer with antlers. A rabbit in mad delirium scurried under the very wheels. The horse began prancing and snorting, rearing and pawing the air, then backing and lurching and crashing into the rhododendron. The girl did not lose her head.

"Here, quick," she ordered sharply. "Jump and get him by the bit. Quick; I'll hold him. We must get him round." Young Jim leaped from the buggy and tried to turn him, but the creature was frantic with fear. It seemed every instant as if the buggy must upset.

The wild gleam of the fire, dull through the smoke, was in full sight now, and the roar was like that of the sea. The wind was sweeping it up the narrow gut, lashing on the flames like a bison stampede. They fell upon the dry tops, licked them up as if they were oil and tar, leaped agilely into the live hemlocks. roared up their trunks, and stood waving in air, mad flags, twenty feet above the topmost twigs.

The terror of the horse was almost beyond control. He tried madly to plunge forward and throw himself into the fire; it was all both of them could do to keep him from breaking away. They could hold him but an instant more.

"Jump!" he ordered fiercely. "We must leave him and run for our lives. Jump!"

"No, sir! Here, take the lap-robe and wind it round his head." She threw it to him with deft swing. "Quick!" He obeyed automatically. In an instant she was beside him, and she too had the horse by the bit.

"Here! let me take him!" she ordered sharply. "Now lift the buggy round. Sharp, there!" It was turned in an instant.

"Get in," she commanded, and he obeyed her with a jump. "Take up the reins there! Quick!" She led the horse a few steps, then bounded back and sprang into the buggy like a cat.

"Give 'em to me!"

Again they bumped and rolled and slewed along the mad trail. She was driving now for her life, and it was a sight to stir the blood. Young Jim almost forgot the ghastly death that was leaping after them as he watched this woman in action. She had grown cool and watchful, and every movement of muscle and tone of voice counted. It is no small thing to drive a panic-stricken horse with fire all about him. He was in a mad scurry, shying and rearing and plunging and ready at every instant to smash them into a wild heap, but she held him true. She talked steadily,—soothing, threatening, coaxing, urging, now in high key, now in low, and the horse seemed to understand her. They were back now to where she had met Jim, and now they were crashing beyond. As to what might be at the end neither had a thought. Their one impulse was to fly on and on, like the deer and the rabbit.

All at once the horse stopped short, almost pitching them over the dashboard. A great tree-top, bristling with dead snags, lay right across the trail.

"I'll fix that," he shouted, leaping from the buggy and laying hold of it mightily. But the thing was braced and anchored. For a single moment he writhed with it, then he leaped back and caught up his axe from the buggy. A dozen swift strokes, a pitching of the severed branches right and left, and he turned excitedly.

"You can get over the log," he yelled. "I'll run ahead to see if there are any more." An instant and she saw him fall with frenzy upon another top. The relief was only for a moment. Thicker and thicker grew the tree-tops across the road until all at once they culminated in a grand tangle that a day's work would not penetrate.

They had come to the end of the trail; there was no possibility of advancing another foot.

He ran hither and thither excitedly, but there was no exit. Then he turned in desperation.

"There's only one chance," he cried. "Leave the horse and try to get over the ridge."

"No, sir; we don't leave Pomp," she shouted half angrily. "Can't we build a counter fire?"

"There's too much wood. We'd roast between two fires."

"If we take Pomp out of the buggy can't we pull him up the rocks?"

"It's too steep. Can't be done. I've been there." Indeed it was impossible. It would be like taking a horse up the great pyramid.

"But we'll try it all the same." There was a snap to her words that made opposition useless. "Come, help me take him out."

She was by the side of the horse now, freeing him deftly from the buggy. The roar of the flames made talking almost impossible; the smoke was like a blanket; their eyes, smarting and quivering in the reeking atmosphere, could scarcely distinguish the nearest objects. Once a spark set fire to her dress, but he extinguished it with the lap-robe. Then he threw the robe over her shoulders, and she tied the ends under her chin.

"Come on. Follow me," he shouted. He fell upon the underbrush for dear life. The one cry of his heart, frantic and wild, was to save her,—at any cost. "She mustn't burn! My God! she mustn't burn!" poured from his heart like a mad prayer.

The girl, her hand linked into the bridle of the horse, staggered on in the path he was crashing down. A few steps and he stopped abruptly.

They were walking directly into the fire. They had struck for the more exposed side of the valley, and the wind had driven the flames ahead of them. The other side was their last hope.

"Quick! Turn back!" he yelled. "It's our only chance." They wheeled about like frantic creatures into the opposite brush. He was slashing at the tangle like a giant. Right and left flew the axe, smiting and crashing and lopping,—the very embodiment of destruction. Once he glanced back and saw the slim figure of the girl wrestling with the horse and the thickets. He caught a glimpse of her face, smoke-stained and eager, her glossy hair torn and streaming about it, and his whole soul sent up the mad cry, "She shan't burn! My God! she shan't burn!" But the flames were racing before a wild hurricane.

There seemed not one chance in a thousand for the fugitives.

# CHAPTER X

## THE MILL DOWN FOAMING VALLEY

AFTER A MOMENT they found themselves by the brook in a place where a deep pool was overhung by a limestone ledge. Rose, struggling with the frantic horse, saw nothing. She was crashing through the brush just a step behind Jim, with only one impulse. He too had but one impulse: he would reach the rocks and save her, if he had to tear her hand from the bridle and bear her through the flames in his arms. She shouldn't perish; she mustn't perish. He would fight for her till he died.

As his eye fell upon the pool in the brook he stopped short. If they could stand in the water to their necks there might be a chance. He had heard of such escapes. Then something about the ledge caught his eye.

"This way," he yelled suddenly. "We can make it yet. I know where we are." He turned sharply to the left, his axe still flying like a steel maul.

"We can make it,—Pomp and all," he shouted over his shoulder exultantly. "Come on!"

And she came on, though the horse reared and plunged, lifting her from her feet again and again, and swinging her about in the cruel tangle, tearing her clothes and hands and hair. But she clung fast and kept ever close behind Jim, who was slashing and stamping and smashing like a Viking in battle. Ten rods more and they came to the brook again, but at right angles to its former course.

"Foaming Valley Stream," he shouted lustily. "We're out of it; we're in Foaming Valley, and it's high time."

He was right; it was high time. Swept on by the gale, the flames were leaping like wolves from bush to bush, and scurrying in the dead leaves not two rods behind. A minute more and the roaring cauldron would have been all about them, but they had reached now the mouth of the little valley at an angle from the flame-swept funnel.

"Here we are in a regular turnpike!" he shouted. "It can't catch us now. It 'll run slow up this valley."

They were on the little dinkey road which years before had taken the lumber down to the Cherry Run trail. It was plain sailing now. But the panic still on them, they scurried ahead like rabbits.

The valley grew narrower. A mat of cherry sprouts, all in full blossom, and of raspberry and blackberry tangle, bound in the road on either side. The ties had begun to decay; the iron rails were thick with rust; and there were places where floods had gullied widely into the road-bed. The smoke became less and less dense until it was possible to see several rods in advance. The wind was blowing toward the fire and sweeping it in the opposite direction. The valley grew narrower; at length the ridge-sides, steep and ragged, a mere mass of torn stone, drew into a sharp V with the dinkey road raised on trestle work at one side. They passed through with difficulty.

"We're all right now," he announced cheerily. "The fire might back up as far as the Narrows here, but it can't jump through."

"Yes, but we're in a trap." She was looking about her critically.

"I don't think there *is* any outlet to this valley," he said slowly. "We could get over the ridge there, but Pomp couldn't. I know where we are now. We were up this way fishing last summer, and I caught a twelve-inch trout under the rock at the entrance down there. That's why I knew where we were the minute I saw it."

"That was a close call, Mr. Farthing,—an awfully close call." She was looking down at him with solemn eyes. "I don't think we had over a minute's margin."

"It did look close there one time, didn't it?—at least for Pomp?"

"Yes, and for us, too." She drew a long breath. "Well, never mind; we got out." She was not a girl to dwell on morbid things. It was not her way to shudder and live over and over the past danger.

"But we are not out of the woods, though, yet," she went on, looking up at the steep ridges on both sides. "I've heard of this valley; it's father's; but I don't know much about it. If we could only get Pomp over that ridge, I know a path all right. 'Spose we could get him over?"

"No; I don't. The only way I see is to leave him here a day or two and climb out ourselves."

"Hark! What's that?—the fire?" She turned her head and listened intently. She was still sitting on the horse, which, recovered from its fright, was cropping the bushes contentedly.

"That's thunder. Hear it? I've been looking for a thunder-gust all day and I'm afraid it 'll be a hard one, it's been so hot."

"Father's got an old mill up here a mile or so," she spoke with sudden decision. "Come, le's try for it. Come on."

"All right."

Again they started up the dinkey road, he striding stoutly ahead. There was something strong and masterful and self-reliant about this young man that appealed to her. Unconsciously she watched him,—his broad shoulders, his firm-set neck, his easy, muscular swing; it is always good to see a man.

They reached the mill just as the first large drops began to patter on the leaves. It was a ramshackle old structure, a mere roof to shelter the engine and the sawing apparatus. A great tangle of cherry trees and brush hemlocks had sprung up about it, and, mingling with the rhododendron by the stream, concealed it until one was right upon it. It was warped and windowless, half-broken down at one end, and full of a gloom and silence that were uncanny. On the side nearest the stream there was a small board addition, which had been used by the crew for both kitchen and sleeping chamber. Off against this arose a blackened pile of sawdust twenty feet and more high.

"Here we are," he called cheerily. "We can make it."

Indeed they were just in time. The first big drops were splashing on the dry leaves. She sprang from the horse, and they made a helter-skelter dash for it.

"Ah, we made it!" She flung open the rickety door. In a moment the drops had increased to a torrent which roared and pounded on the shingled roof.

"Let it rain!" he cried in high spirits. "This is tight 's a cup."

"Isn't this our lucky day, though?" she echoed. "This comes in just the nick of time. This is father's mill, but I was never here before. Isn't it a funny old place?" She began to explore with all the curiosity of a youngster. The room was in good condition. There was a rude table, a rusty stove with a stove-pipe chimney, and on one side several bunks made of pine slabs. She poked into an old cupboard, and pulled out pans and old dishes and odd contrivances, which she speculated over eagerly.

"Pokerish place," he commented after a time. "I don't believe anybody's been here for years."

"Yes, they have; trout-fishers camp here every spring. Didn't you camp here?"

"No. We didn't get up this far."

"Let's go through into the other part."

"All right," and he followed her as she disappeared through the door at the side.

For the next two hours it poured and drizzled, but there was not much lightning. They explored for a time in the old mill, then they sat and watched the rain and the retreating flashes on the horizon.

"The question now is how to get home," she spoke up at length. "Do you think the rain has cooled off the Run?"

"Oh, no, indeed. It would take half a day to cool that fire. The only way I see is to strike over the ridge."

"But it's twelve miles."

"Every bit of it, and it's through the Wild Meadows. Ever been through?"

"Dozens of times."

"Then you know. It's a regular snarl. That's where I was just before I met you. I was looking out for our timber lot in there. It's soaking wet there now. Every bush has got a gallon in it."

"What time is it?" she asked suddenly.

"Five o'clock."

"Then it's out of the question. It would be dark before we got half through."

"There's only one way left then."

"Risk Cherry Run?"

"No; that's impossible. It's stay in the mill all night and strike out in the morning. I think the Run will be cool enough then."

"I'm afraid that's the only way," she said with a trace of wistfulness in her voice. It was not her way to quarrel with the inevitable.

"All right. That means a fire." He started up and seized his axe. "I'm going to build a rouser by the brook here and keep it going all night to keep off spooks, and I'm going to have one in the old stove here to get supper by."

"Supper?" she echoed incredulously.

"Sure. Ain't you hungry?" She looked at him a moment, then burst into a laugh.

"I wonder if my face is as black as yours is?" she asked.

"I believe there *is* just the slightest trace of smut." He looked down at her a critical instant, then turned away abruptly, almost rudely.

"I'm going to try for a trout," he announced. "I've got a fly in my hat here, but what sticks me is a line. Ah, I have it," with sudden inspiration. "Old Pomp,—just the thing." He sprang off into the bushes and after a moment returned with half a dozen long horse-hairs which he proceeded to plait into a line.

"Good; now for a pole." He lopped down a slender cherry sprout, trimmed it with his knife, and was ready.

"Back in a minute," he called, and disappeared into the rhododendron. What a cheery, resourceful, fellow he was! One couldn't help liking him.

She went to the stream, and glancing coyly in the direction he had gone, began to wash her hands and face and to arrange her hair in the mirror of the pool. In half an hour she heard his hail up the dinkey road.

"Got six neat ones. Look at 'em." He held them up on a stick, six mountain trout that glistened like jewels. Her bright face and newly arranged hair gave him a quick thrill. His tongue quivered with a remark, but he only said:

"That's our supper."

"How are we going to cook them?" she asked in puzzled tone. "We haven't any dishes."

"Oh, that's easy. We're camping out, you know. I'll cook 'em. Ever see it done this way?" He dressed the trout, and, embedding three of them in a yellow clay, buried the mass in the hot ashes. The remaining three he impaled on long spits and roasted them over the coals. Then with the axe he hewed out plates from the pine slabs. Supper was ready. The clay was poked out of the ashes, and broken open, and the trout, leaving their skins in the shells, rolled out a clear yellow, and done to a turn.

"How do you like 'em?" he asked.

"They'd be good if we had salt," she said, tasting critically.

"Oh, we're Indians now, and Indians, you know, don't eat salt. You want to imagine with all your might that we are Indians, and you'll forget all about the salt. That's the way to enjoy things in the woods." He began on his share of the fish with evident relish, and she stopped nibbling and ate as hungrily as he.

"I'll get a string in the morning that 'll be enough," he declared boyishly. "Now for the chores." He sprang out into the thicket and began to lop down the hemlock scrubs and strip them of their soft sprigs. "Have to dry 'em a little, but they'll be all right. I'm going to fix up one of them bunks for you, and I'm going to stay out here and tend the fire."

"And I'll put things to rights a little in here." She arose and began to move about the room briskly. He paused a moment involuntarily to look at her.

How bewitchingly cozy and domestic it was, the rude old room with its housewifely figure flying about and setting things in order! How marvellous to have her there, busy helping at his housekeeping!

The early twilight was coming on. As it grew darker the whole sky toward Cherry Run turned to a dull brick red. The smoke hung on the ridges like a fog, and the air was full of flakes of charred leaves. The rain had not quenched the fire; it was burning as fiercely as ever. The dark came on early. It was evident that black clouds had rolled up again. The wind howled about the old structure, and roared on the ridges. Despite the afternoon's shower it was a dry, sultry wind, the breath of a week of scorching weather. The fire by the brook was almost unbearably warm, but it was needed for cheer and companionship. It was an excellent chaperon too, and young Jim kept it going steadily. He sat on an old pine block near it, and she perched precariously on the slab-heap near the door.

The conversation centred about the fire and their escape, then wandered to other fires and other escapes.

"Did you ever hear," she asked solemnly, "of the time when the fire came down in the night through Heller's Gap and threatened the valley?"

"No."

"And you don't know what stopped it?"

"No. I've never heard of it."

"It got as far as the black ring around the old cabin and didn't cross it."

"And the valley people of course thought it supernatural."

"Some did."

"But it was all perfectly natural; don't you see it was? That short, green stuff that grows around the cabin don't burn easily."

"What makes it grow there?" She was looking over at him half reprovingly.

"Oh, it's some sort of wild grass. I 'spose it was sowed there sometime?"

"But why don't the snow lie on it?"

"I haven't seen but what it does. It's possible that the sun comes in onto it in a curious way and melts it quicker. It's on the south slope, you know, and under the rocks."

"But snow never lies there, even on the north side, no matter how deep it may be elsewhere."

"Oh, that's superstition, pure and simple. The stories about that old house are really laughable."

"But Amos isn't superstitious. He's seen it; and you know about what he heard the other night,—he and Dan?"

"Pshaw! You don't seriously believe there's anything supernatural about that old house; now, do you? He looked over at her laughingly. "I didn't suppose that anybody nowadays really believed in ghosts until I came into the valley here. I never dreamed of such a thing."

"Amos don't believe in 'em."

"No; but it makes all the difference in the world who you're with. He and all the rest of you have been thinking about this thing so long that you're nervous, and you actually imagine you see and hear things."

"But Amos isn't nervous."

"Well, I know this,—that every region has got a haunted house, and people you wouldn't think of believing in such things can be found by the dozen to say they have seen the ghost. Now, do you know Tom and I watched there three nights running after that last scare and never saw or heard a thing out of the way? It's all superstition, you take my word for it."

"Perhaps so," she said doubtfully. Then for some reason a silence fell between them. After a time he glanced shyly in her direction. She was leaning far forward toward the fire, her elbows in her lap, her chin in her hands, gazing demurely into the flames.

The picture thrilled him: the dim background of hemlock and rhododendron in which the shadows played fitfully, the tottering old mill faintly outlined, and the girl with the firelight in her hair. He gazed at her rapt and breathless. It was the moment of moments for confession: the man and maiden miles and miles from all other human life, the steep encircling ridges,—a little world, and only they two. A wild impulse seized him, but he crushed it instantly. He would make no avowal now. She was with him wholly by accident; it had been against her will. He had the advantage, but he would not use it. Not one look or one word of love to embarrass her now, if he could master himself, and he could. He would seek her some other time when she was free to do her whole will, and he would pour out his heart as a man should.

"Homesick?" he asked, with a suspicion of fun in his voice.

"Not a bit!" she said scornfully. "But think how they are worrying down home. They won't sleep a wink, will they?"

"Can't blame them if they don't, but it's nothing we're to blame for."

"I think I'll go in now," she said solemnly.

"Good-night," he said, and she disappeared.

He threw on more wood and took his place again on the log. For an hour he gazed fixedly into the flames. Another hour, and he had not changed his position except to pile on fuel.

Then he heard a low growl over the ridge and sat up with a start. Another shower was coming up. The lightning, at first mere spurts of light across the west, gleamed red and sinister through the smoke. The wind plunged over the ridges in wild panic, bellowing and shrieking. It fell upon the rickety old mill and wrenched it with violence till it groaned and rattled and roared. The thunder grew louder with every peal; the lightning flickered and streamed balefully. Young Jim seemed oblivious of it. He heaped the wood ever and anon upon his fire, and continued his steady contemplation of the flames. Then some subtle magnetism drew up his glance and there she was in the doorway, looking him full in the eyes.

"I'm not just sure that the mill's safe in all this wind." She came up to the fire, so near to him that he could have touched her. There seemed to be a wistful note in her voice.

"Oh, it's stood worse blows than this. In the winter, when the leaves are off, the winds sweep down these valleys fearfully."

"It'll put out our fire, won't it?"

"Shouldn't wonder; but we can have one inside. Let it go. Believe I'll get in some slabs while I have a chance." He fell to the work with energy. "Aren't you afraid of thunder?" he called out cheerily. "I hope not, for this is going to be an old rattler, ten times worse than the other."

"No-o; I'm not afraid." There was the slightest note of doubt in the tone. No wonder; the surroundings were indeed strange and fearsome—the shuddering old mill; the intense darkness; the fire, lighting everything weirdly; and the nearing crash and bellow of the storm.

"This will cool off the Run, won't it?" she asked almost eagerly.

"Sure. We'll get out in the morning all right." He was flying back and forth between the slab pile and the mill.

"I hope we can," she echoed with a suspicion of wistfulness. "But can't I help?"

"Oh, no; I've got enough. Better come in now. Hear the rain come down the valley there! Glorious, ain't it? I just love a night-gust like this!"

The storm was indeed breaking upon them in full force. The thunder, with crash after crash, broke over their very heads; then it bellowed and roared and tumbled from ridge to ridge. The continuous volley with its rip and roar was deafening. The lightning, almost blood-red from the smoke, shook its fingers in their very faces. The rain came, not in drops but in sheets. It roared on the mill roof as if hurled from a steamer house. It hurtled down the wind in watery wrath, dashing wild floods as from buckets. There seemed nothing in the whole landscape save water and blinding gleams and crashing noise. The fire by the brook struggled fitfully for a time and then hissed out. The stream began to rise by leaps and bounds until it was almost by the door.

The mill roof had been well made; it leaked only here and there, and they kept dry. Jim had a roaring fire in the stove, which made the little room really cozy and homelike. He chopped at the slabs and fed them into the flames, while she sat on a bench and watched him. His confidence and cheery good fellowship were contagious. What a glorious, self-reliant fellow he was! The thunder and lightning were nothing to be nervous about; he laughed at them. And, somehow, despite the wildness and the crash without, she did not feel frightened or even ill at ease.

At length the storm began to subside. The thunder rolled off into the east; the lightning came in sheets rather than in blinding bolts; the rain began to slacken. In an hour it was all over.

"Did you sleep any?" he asked suddenly.

"I had just got to sleep when it began to thunder."

"Well, it's all over now. You must get some more sleep; it's a long time before morning. Say, I'm going inside the mill there. If you want anything, pound on the boards. Good-night."

Before she could answer he was gone. She lay down again in the bunk, drew up the lap-robe, and the next thing she was conscious of was the sound of voices outside. It was broad daylight.

"So, you're at the bottom of this, heigh? Where is Rose?" It was her father's voice, angry and threatening.

"She's in the mill." Rose sprang out instantly.

"I'm all right, Pap," she cried.

"This is a pretty trick!" She could see at a glance that he was angry through and through. "Here Amos and Ab and I've been hunting these mountains all night long, and your mother's almost wild, and you up here with that scamp."

"Why, father, he—"

"I don't want to hear a word about it,—not a word. If he's up here, then it's on account of you. I know that. He's sneaked up here after you, and got you in ahead of that fire on purpose to show off. I hain't a doubt he set it himself. I'm going to look into this pret-t-t-ty close, young man. Now, you start. Clear out of here this minute. I can take my daughter home alone." His anger almost choked him. Young Jim shouldered his axe without a word and turned to start.

"Wait, Mr. Farthing. Here, father—"

"Not another word. I—"

"Father, I'm going to speak." There was a flash in her eyes and a ring in her voice that silenced the man. "Mr. Farthing was here in the mountains to look after his wood lot. He met me wholly by accident in the valley down here. If he hadn't, I think I should have burned: for I wouldn't have left Pomp till it was too late. He knew the way into this valley, and we came just in time. And there was no way out last night. You know that. You've got no right to speak as you did."

"We'll go home." he said gruffly. "Come along with me."

"Not till I thank Mr. Farthing." She went impulsively to where the young man was standing and took his hand. "I want to thank you for what you have done, Mr. Farthing. I owe you everything."

"Oh, it's nothing," he said with affected carelessness, but there was a look on his face that even the Squire noticed.

"Come along, Rose," he said with an angry snap.

"Good-bye, Mr. Farthing." She turned and waved her hand at him girlishly.

"Good-bye," he echoed, then he plunged over the ridge toward the Wild Meadows.

The two strode on in silence till they reached the entrance of the valley. Suddenly a cry of horror burst from her lips. She halted instantly and rubbed her eyes. The valley, which yesterday lay a great mass of vegetation through which one could see for only a few rods in any direction, lay swept as clean almost as a room. A few scattered snags, still smoking feebly, a blackened log here and there, but aside from these nothing but fire-cracked rocks and bare earth. They could see the whole length of the valley to the Black Log road, and it was a mere blackened trough in which the flooded stream was visible its entire length.

"It made clean work, didn't it?" she said at length.

"Yes," he mumbled.

"Ah, there's the buggy." She stopped again near a heap of twisted red iron.

"Yes, imagine how we felt when we found that. We looked every inch of this valley over for what was left of you and Pomp. There's Amos and Ab. Hello-o-o-o! Found her! Now get in."

They drove in silence down the valley and out through the gaps. Rose knew her father, and she realised that the less she said in his present mood the better it would be. Only once did the old man speak and that was when they were almost home.

"Remember, Rose, what you promised me." He turned and looked her full in the eyes. "You can't break that, not if you are my daughter."

She did not answer. She was looking with far eyes out over the range which lay veiled and dim on the horizon.

# CHAPTER XI

## LONA HELLER

EVEN IN THE remotest mountain cabin one may find comeliness—roundness of figure, and lustre of eyes, and even perfection of colour and mould of feature. But beauty is quite another thing. It is an atmosphere rather than a contour and a colour; it is a subtle blending of all things together; and it is more. There is heredity in it,—the cumulative charm of a long line of fair mothers and fairer daughters. The essence of it eludes analysis; it is the bouquet of rare wine, indescribable and indefinable. When one finds it in the wilderness it whispers of old tragedy. It is the full-blown Jacqueminot among the jungle thorns. There has been a rude transplanting; there is a romance to tell, though perchance it has been forgotten.

No one could deny that Lona Heller possessed beauty,—a wild, barbaric type of beauty perhaps, yet one that attracted attention instantly and held it by a force that was little short of uncanny. A single glance marked her as an exotic, a child of the South, of the Latin lands—with cheeks of pale olive, with eyes such as only the daughters of the Mediterranean ever possess, and with hair abundant and soft and glistening in its perfect blackness. With the sun full upon it, it was still an absolute black. The supple figure, lithe and cat-quick, the arms rounded for the dance, for the fling of the tambourine or the castanets, the feet and limbs light as the daughter of Herodias, the neck and head for toss and coquettish pose,—every line and feature was of this earth, a joy to see, but of the moment alone. A curious type for old Poppy Miller's cabin in the Run, a type clearly not evolved amid the Seven Mountains.

No wonder that the valley folk, who had caught only glimpses of this girl, whispered among themselves, and no wonder that Tom Farthing, alive and twenty-one, went home from the Run in a flutter. He spent a day in searching for a pretext for seeing her again, and he found one.

It would require tact, he mused, to conquer her shyness. Doubtless he would find difficulty in seeing her at all: for she was wild as a forest creature and as timid. But the evening changed the face of things. She had not avoided him at all; she had been self-possessed and at her ease; and there had been in her every attitude and intonation the stateliness of one who is condescending graciously. He was the menial and she the daughter of the house. It mystified him and haunted him. As he walked home through the twilight he could think of nothing else. How could a woman like that live at Poppy Miller's, in that squalid cabin?

That was the beginning of visits. He went almost every night. He carried her water from the creek; he sawed her wood; he walked with her in the twilight. Then all in a moment she changed like an April day. As by an impulse she dropped her aloofness and reserve and made a comrade of him. It took his breath away. It sent him home powerless to banish her from his thoughts. He was as wax in her hands; he changed with her every mood, and her moods were infinite. Now he was joyous and confident,—he could win her yet, for she loved him, it must be; then swiftly he would despair, for she was infinitely far away and he was but an episode; then for a tense moment he would feel like one who awakes in a grip that holds him rigid, fight as he may,—but it was only for the moment.

Once he found her dressed in a strange, clinging costume of yellow, brilliant and glittering, her arms bare to the shoulders, and her feet in curious sandals. Her hair was knotted in wild, gipsy fashion. A dash of color at the crown, a sparkle of beads at the throat,—he could only stare at her.

"Don't you like the dress?" she called.

"But what is it?"

"Just a dress. See!" She sprang up and spun around till the short skirt stood out like a bell. "You never saw me dance. Look!" She caught up a tambourine-like thing with fluttering streamers, flung up her arms in joyous abandon, and glided and flashed and spun. Her eyes were full upon him. They seemed unnaturally large and brilliant, and always looking straight into his. A moment and she sank upon the rock.

"Wonderful! wonderful!" he burst out, strangely exhilarated. He could not take his eyes from her.

"But what kind of a dance is it?" he asked eagerly. "What is it?"

"It's just a dance."

"But where could you have learned it?"

"I never learned it."

"Ah, but you must."

"It's in the blood. It's like breathing."

"The blood?—what do you mean? What blood?" He leaned forward intensely.

"See; here's another." Again he watched the flash and weave of her bare arms, the twinkle of her feet, the cling and swing of her garments. The rhythmic *thump, thump* and chatter seemed beating in his throat. The streamers, floating and circling about her head and throat and breast, or leaping in exultation above her, dazed him. He began to feel strange and unreal, infinitely far off, and ever those eyes were full upon him. They seemed to be growing larger and more black. When she stopped he drew a long breath, but he did not move or speak.

"We call that 'The Fling,'" she volunteered.

"We? But who—?"

"'The witches' fling.' Did you like it?"

"It was beautiful, beautiful!" he half whispered, still looking full at her. There seemed to him no past nor future, no here nor there, only now and her,—and it was enough just to look.

"Ah, see!" With her arms flung above her head, and the ribbons flashing and twisting, she was dancing swiftly backward down the path. He tried to follow her, but he seemed to have no power to move. Her eyes were still full upon him.

"Lona," he called.

"Good-bye." She waved the streamers gaily, then disappeared into the house. Would she come back? He watched the door eagerly until the twilight had deepened into the darkness, but he saw her no more.

The next day was Saturday. He went down earlier than usual; the sun was still in sight over the ridge, though dimmed by the smoke to a mere plate of brass. The old cabin lay dead and deserted. The blinds were drawn close; there was not even a smoke. He hesitated a moment, then rapped at the back-door, and after a long wait he rapped again. No one there. He turned and scanned the path to the creek. Perhaps she was getting the water. No movement. Ah! as he turned again, there she was, not two steps away. She had opened the door without noise. He jumped almost guiltily.

"Why—why—you here?" he almost gasped.

"Come in," she said gravely.

"Why, no. Perhaps we can—"

"Come in." He followed her without a word.

The kitchen was quite dark when she closed the door. A few coals glowered in the stone fireplace, but they furnished no light. Without a word she threw on a handful of something that rustled softly; then he heard no sound. The silence was awkward.

"That's been a fine day," he observed at random.

"Yes."

"Had the spring fever?"

"No."

"I have. Had to drive myself to work. Jim's had it, and it makes him blue. It makes father work. I never saw him work so."

There was no reply. Then the flame leaped up among the twigs; it climbed rapidly; and lighted up the whole apartment.

He saw only the girl. She was sitting on a stool at the side of the hearth, and the fire brought out every detail. Then a great cat appeared from the shadows and began to rub against her. She fondled it absently, and began talking to it the artless nonsense that girls talk to cats. He was awakened by a rattling in the shed-room adjoining. Some one was coming.

"Say," he spoke up quickly. "Have you brought up the water yet?"

"No."

"All right then, come on."

"No, no; sit here. We won't get any water tonight."

"Of course, we will." He arose impetuously and started for the door.

"No—don't." There was a note of command in her voice, but he did not notice it.

"Come on. It won't be dark outside for an hour yet. Come on." He swung out through the door, and after a wavering moment she followed him. From the porch they went through the back yard with its litter of old wood and farming tools and decaying odds and ends. Suddenly, before they had come to the path by the rail fence, she stopped.

"Let's sit awhile," she proposed, sinking upon a limestone fragment. He turned with a puzzled look, then arranged one of the buckets for a seat. A fringe of ragged cedars gave them almost the seclusion of a room. For a time neither spoke. A strange new mood was upon her, and it awed him.

The sun disappeared, snuffed out even before it reached the horizon. The dull bellow of the Run, swelled high with its spring flood, came up steadily from below. The twilight, vague and unreal amid the half-seen smoke, was deepening fast. A chorus of frog voices spattered shrilly from along the stream; robins and blackbirds were in full swing with their evening songs.

"What's the matter, Lona?" he asked after a while. "You're not like yourself."

"Ah?"

"No; you're not."

"How am I different?"

"I don't know. It seems almost as if something was troubling you."

"What could?"

"I don't know; but don't you get lonesome here? Say, why don't you get out more? Why don't you?"

"Oh, bah! The valley people! They're cattle!"

"But, Lona, you forget; I'm one of them, and so are you."

"I'm not!" She turned and faced him defiantly.

"What do you mean?"

"And you're not; you're different."

"Different?"

"You're like me,—and we hate 'em. We just hate 'em!"

"Lona!" There was a look in the girl's eyes that frightened him.

"And you'll know sometime!"

"Lona!" He arose and took a dizzy step toward her.

"Oh, Lona, I—"

"No, no, no—don't!—Come!" She arose swiftly and turned toward the path. "It's getting darker; we must go for the water." He followed her breathlessly. By the creek side she paused for an instant, while he dipped the buckets; then she turned and ran up the path again.

"Come, quick," she ordered in a penetrating whisper. It was as if some fearful thing were lurking somewhere in the glen.

"Wait!—please, do," he gasped after they had scurried half-way up the hill. "Can't we stop a minute?" She turned instantly and faced him.

"No!—at the flat stone—come!"

Again they hastened up the path. At the stone he sank down breathless. The girl wheeled instantly, and, standing straight and rigid, peered back into the Run. She was very near him. How perfect she was as she stood there in the twilight,—a woman to dream about, "Fair as a jonquil, tall as a bride for the high gods mete."

"Lona," he whispered, "what is it?"

"Nothing."

"But you're strange. There's something the matter. What is it down there, Lona?" He felt like shuddering, he knew not why. It was as if something were hovering over them.

"It's nothing; it's the evening. Let's keep perfectly still. Don't you hear it?"

"Hear what?"

"The evening. It's a concert. Hark!"

It was not hard to imagine. The evening hymn of the May day was swelling all about them, but above all, and dominating it all, was the gribber of the Run just below them. There was something strange about it, something that crept over him more and more like a premonition of danger: the gloom of the place, the dark forms of the cedars, the imprisoning tangle of the rhododendron, and the smutches of black above,—the ridges converging into the Gap. He began to look about him almost stealthily. Then he caught a glimpse of her, and something all in a flash thrilled him as with fear.

She was looking with wide eyes, every muscle and nerve in her body tense, down through the laurel tangle to where the waters of Roaring Run break through the Gap. Automatically he turned in the direction of her gaze, but he saw nothing.

"Lona, what is it?"

"It's nothing,—come!—quick!" She dodged with lightning movement as if some unseen thing had struck at her, then darted away. One instant and she was gone.

Scarce realising what he did, he sprang after her. He looked eagerly right and left, behind every cedar and tangle. She had vanished utterly.

"Lona!" he called in a fearful whisper. "Lona!" Then he raised his voice and shouted, "Lona!"

"Hush! Sh-h-h-h-h!" She was right at his elbow, as if she had risen from the earth. "Come—quick!"

"But, Lona, what is it? For God's sake what's this all about? Lona!"

"Quick!" she whispered tragically. "Quick!" She seized his hand as if he were in danger, and tried to pull him along.

"But, Lona," he pleaded, the touch of her hand thrilling him mightily, "what is it?—I love you—"

"No, no, no! You *must* go.—You must never come back. Come—quick!" There was an intensity about the girl's words that frightened him.

"Lona,—what is it?"

"Go,—I command." She hissed the words in his very ear. "If you speak, it's death. One word and it's death. Come." Her hot breath was in his face. She was pulling him along as if in a panic. Then, as by magic, she was gone. He stopped for a moment in his tracks.

Everything was unnaturally silent. Even the frogs for some mysterious reason had ceased their chorus. He found himself listening breathlessly for he knew not what. A ghastly fear was creeping over him. Something black and awful was lurking right near him. The air was hot and stifling; it was difficult to breathe; his head seemed bursting. Cautiously he began to pick his way; then he began to walk rapidly; then to run; nor did he stop until he had reached his father's door.

The next morning all was normal again. The night seemed like some confused dream, far off and vague. He laughed at his panic, and all day long the passion in his heart grew more imperious. He would go down again; he would go that very evening. But he found no life about the old house that night, nor the next. For a week he tried to see her, but the whole place seemed deserted. There was no response to his rappings at the cabin; it was as if the family had moved away. He went down into the Run and sat on the flat rock until long after twilight, but there was no sound or movement. Then for a time he went no more into the uncanny hole, but tried to smother out his thoughts by the hard work of the spring planting.

# CHAPTER XII

## THE PLAY AND THE CHORUS

DURING THE DAYS following the fire, Rose seemed sober and preoccupied,—a new mood for her. She did not laugh and sing as of old, and she did not go out of afternoons to drive. Therefore she is sick, reasoned her father, and he knew the cause. It was the inevitable reaction. A girl cannot be snatched from the brink of death without a shock. An experience like hers has often completely unnerved a woman and made her a physical wreck for life. He insisted on calling Dr. Kuack, but she scorned the idea.

On Sunday, when Karl Keichline drove into the yard, she declared that she would not see him. Somehow the very sight of the man repelled her. She wanted to go to her room and stay there.

"But, Rose, you need to be cheered up, and no one can do it like Karl," the old Squire had burst out. "Of course you'll see Karl."

"No, I won't," she snapped. "I don't want to see anybody."

"But you'll see Karl, Rose."

"And why?"

"Oh, come, come, Rose. Of course you'll see him. He'll put you in good spirits in no time. He's jolly 's a lark this morning. Mother and I are going to meeting and leave you two to keep house. Of course I wouldn't have you go to church feeling as you do."

"No, no, father. Don't. I want to go——"

"Of course you don't. I know all about it, you rogue! I know girls. Take good care of him, Dot. Ho, ho, ho!" He went out in great good humour, and Mrs. Hartswick joined him at the door. Then Karl came in, simpering and solicitous, and she ushered him into the front room.

Somehow she felt no desire to laugh at him now, though he had never appeared more ludicrous. Bolt upright he sat in a straight-backed chair that creaked dolefully under his every movement, and twirled his fat thumbs, and told her of his week: his sales of this and that; his hopes of this and that; his plans, and his profits, and his ideas. The abundance of his prosperity seemed to keep him in a continual state of mild astonishment. She did not laugh nor remark; she sat by the window, her eyes on the distant range, which still had a ghost of smoke upon it, and rocked to and fro with nervous jerks, while he droned on with his tales of prosperous endings and moving accidents by store and farm.

To-day she loathed the man. It seemed to her as if she had never really seen him before. Something all of a sudden had opened her eyes. He was a mere clod of a creature, intent on money and acres. And he was to be her husband! Her father's will was like iron, when once it was set, and he had willed it. There was no escape; only five weeks more,—five weeks more! She stopped rocking and looked with far eyes out over the ridges. He had never known her so still.

"You are not well, Rose," he said at length, with calf-like tenderness. "You are not yourself."

"No; I'm not myself," she snapped suddenly, turning full upon him. "I think I'd better go to my room." In a twinkling she disappeared, leaving him to wonder and speculate, and spend the forenoon alone.

After the dinner, which was patriarchal in its quality and its profusion, the Squire took the young man to a ramble over the estate. He instructed him as to the different plots and their time of rotation, and he mapped out the spring campaign of plantings and sowings. The fences were in perfect condition; the corners and bounds were carefully marked; the wheat was free from winter-kill and "fly." Then he exhibited the barns and out-buildings and stock as if Karl were a prospective buyer. And the young man viewed it all with huge approval and made hard-headed suggestions that pleased the Squire. Here was a son-in-law after his own heart.

They sat long over the evening tea, so long that Karl missed the evening service. He was in high spirits. He laughed and joked and beamed upon Rose, and the old man reflected his joy; he fairly purred in his content. Things were moving smoothly. It was perfectly natural that

Rose should be sober. She had gone through an experience that was enough to fill a lifetime with shudders,—but it would end all right. She needed diversion, and merry company, and she was getting it.

That night, as she started for her room, he spoke to her with unusual tenderness.

"The day has done you good, Dot." He put his hand on her shoulder and looked at her admiringly. "I haven't seen so much colour in your cheeks for a long time. Oh, we know all about it, you rogue. You can't fool us. Ho, ho, ho!" He chucked her under the chin playfully.

"But, father——"

"Oh, come, come now; don't say a word about it," he cut her off jovially. "I know just how it is. Girls have to go through just about so much nonsense. It's born in 'em. Ho, ho, ho! But you go to sleep, and get rested, Dot. Sleep just as long 's you want to; that's what's going to put you right onto your feet again. Don't you worry one bit. Wal, good-night." She wavered a moment as if about to speak, then turned and ran quickly up the stairs.

Her room was on the garden side. She blew out her light as she entered. She would sit by the window in the cool night air. She wanted to think. A young moon was casting in a weird twilight, and the thrill and odour of the growing spring were breathing up from the garden like a greeting.

She had hardly closed the door when something dropped with a little crash near the window and rolled with metallic tinklings into the centre of the room. Her first thought was that she had pushed something from the bureau, and half automatically she groped to pick it up. A moment and her hand struck it,—a pine-cone. How came a pine-cone in her room? It must have come in at the open window. There was a paper on it,—a note. *He* was out there; it was a message from him. Her heart went off in a flutter, and her hand trembled so that she could hardly disentangle the dainty little missive. What did it say? To light the lamp and examine it was out of the question: he would know at once what she was doing. A moment and she went into the opposite room, closed the door and struck a match. A candle was on the little table.

> "Dear Miss Hartswick:
>
> "I am in the garden under your window. May I see you for a moment and speak to you? I must see you sometime. The other day in the mountains you were with me only by accident, and I would not take advantage of the accident to tell you what I must

tell you. May I see you, if it is only for a moment? I am sitting on the bench by the crocuses and waiting for you.

"I am, honestly yours,

"James Farthing."

She blew out the candle instantly, as if in spite of the inner room he could see her; then she stole back. As she entered again, the sweet thrill of the April night stole up and greeted her like the breath of a lover. Then she sat for a moment on the side of the bed and tried to think.

The note was still in her hand. After a time she went into the opposite room again, and, re-lighting the candle, read it twice over. There were fairness and passion and boyish honesty in every line. How gentlemanly he had been and how considerate! "You were with me only by accident, and I would not take advantage of the accident——." She tiptoed to the head of the stairs and listened. No sound. Her father and mother were already in bed and doubtless asleep.

Another wavering moment and she went to her room, found a soft, white shawl to throw over her shoulders, and then stole down the back way into the night,—the throbbing April night, where young Jim, trembling with eagerness, stood amid the crocuses.

Now the age-old drama of two men and a maiden, if played in the madness of the city, may escape all notice until the culmination brings its short-lived wonder, but in a little pocket of the hills it is vastly different. The play goes on before a hundred spectators all eager to note the slightest flutter of heart or eyelid, and every idle gathering in store or shop or horse-shed, like the chorus of the old drama, discusses and comments and speculates.

Many of the whispered tales of Karl and Jim and Rose came surprisingly near the truth, and many came surprisingly far from it, but near or remote, the whispering never ceased. At every gathering one was sure to hear the conclusions of the old, who viewed the play objectively; or the comments of the middle-aged, who looked upon it not coldly, but curiously; and the exclamations of the young, who philosophised not at all, but speculated with eagerness.

Thus the chorus droned on in the interludes.

The Bottom church, a great square block of a building, stands alone, full ten rods from the store on one side and the schoolhouse on the other. Along the road on either side extend for many rods thick poles spiked to the tops of posts, to be used for hitching places. On a fair

Sunday these rails are crowded from end to end with horses and "rigs" of every description, some of them there after a journey of six and even eight miles. It is always a thrilling experience to the stranger in the valley to come suddenly, amid the perfect silence of a Sabbath, around the curve of the road upon these two long rows of motionless horses, with no other hint of human life in the vicinity.

Country worshippers come early to church on fair mornings, and they delight to gather in knots, the men about the horses, and the women in the vestibule, to talk until the arrival of the preacher. On the thirtieth of April, the Sunday after Jim had thrown the pine-cone, the group was especially large. Its nucleus and oracle was Amos Harding, who was seated sidewise on a wagon-seat, his feet roosting precariously on one of the wheels.

"Say, that drove of old hogs there by the meetin' house looks hansum, now don't it?" he was running on garrulously. "Runnin' wild right in the street,—by Moses, I wonder what they'd say up to Connecticut? Ever think of it, the name of this State is *Pen*-sylvania and there ain't a tarnal pig-pen in the State! Say, do you know a feller once told me the rule for findin' latitude in the United States? You multiply the number of hogs running loose on a mile of road by the average number of rods of rail fence to the square mile of land and you'll have the distance in miles from the Connecticut River, countin' north and south. He, he, he! Better rule than that, though: You multiply the average number of pints of paint to a house in any region by the number of square inches in the average front yard and if you're careful of your fractions, you'll get the exact distance in rods to the nearest point on the Gulf of Mexico. Fails in Centre County, though; all rules do. W'y, we're miles north of the paint-line and miles north of the average hog-line, but in spite of all that, if you apply arry one of them rules it lands us right off of the tip end o' Florida."

"Jest you look o' there wunst," spoke up a voice in a low whisper. All turned instantly. Rose Hartswick was walking up the path with her father and Karl Keichline.

"Looks kinder pale, I take it; don't seem to be as chipper as she was once." There was a note of sarcasm in Lem Fisher's voice. "You folks can't see a hoss-fly unless he's lit right onto the tip-end of your nose. I tell you Rose ain't long for this world still. She's got the oppnehmer if ever I seen any one have it yetst. Wasn't that the way Katie Barndollar looked at first? And what did I tell the Squire last winter? What did I ask him wunst? Now jest see what's er happenin'."

"And what's happenin'?" asked Amos curtly.

"Yes, I'd ask that if I was you." He looked scornfully up at the man. "You hain't saw, I 'spose, how Al Farthing's spell-bound her to Jim? And Karl's the best match for a girl there is in this county still. She'd never want to get shet of a man like Karl if she wan't spell-bound and haexed. Nosuh."

"And who sez she wants to get red of Karl?" asked Amos sternly.

"Oh, pshaw! if I was as blind as you be I'd get some glass eyes wunst. Hain't she made him wait till the first o' June a'ready before she sayes the word? Why's that now? It's jest because she don't dast to run plumb against her father still, and because she's spell-bound to Jim. Are you fool enough to suppose when it comes time she'll give Karl the *yes?* Not by a long shot. She'll outen his light and Jim 'll be high line. You jest wait and see." He squinnied up his left eye and nodded knowingly at the crowd.

"But won't Karl fight?" inquired Uncle Jake in an old man's shrill quaver. "Karl ain't no baby still."

"Oh, no; there won't be no fight. Oh, no!" The oracle was nothing if not cock-sure. "There'll be jest a little pow-wowing that nobody 'll know nothing about, and pop! over 'll go poor Karl with a stroke, or something else, his eyes bulging out like he'd saw the devil wunst. Or perhaps he'll have the oppnehmer or the run-down or something jest as Rose has got it. Oh, I tell you, Karl's goin' to be out of it come June still. You-uns see if he hain't."

"Plain 's the nose on your face a'ready," chimed in Ulie.

"Plainer 'n two and two," continued Lem with growing conviction. "Jest you see here wunst. Al Farthing falls out with the Squire 'cause he wants to be king. That's number one. The Squire falls out with Al Farthing 'cause he wants to stay king. That's number two. Both of 'em's mad at each other as their skins can hold. That's number three. Al Farthing's a pow-wower, and what does a pow-wower do when he gets mad? Heigh? W'y, he jest goes and gets his Bible and key and silk threads and all that kind of stuff and he ups and pow-wows wunst. That's number four. Rose is the only child the Squire's gut a'ready, and he sets more store by her than anything else in the world still. Now that's five,"—counting on his fingers. "Now, you-uns look here. When he pow-wows who will he pow-wow? Won't it be Rose? Hein? Ain't that clear 's mud? Now you jest think of it a minute. He spellbinds Rose and makes her fall crazy in love with Jim. Can't you hear the old pow-wower laugh over that? Don't you see it's for the old man to kick Rose out of his house and home or else leave all of his property to the

Farthings? Hein? Oh, I tell you, a long old head ciphered that out, and I'm willing to bet my leg still that it was planned up in the old Heller cabin. Slick? Oh, my, ain't it slick?"

"You folks make me sick, by gor-ri-fus!" snapped Amos, who had been keeping remarkably still for him. "I can't, if I die, help thinking I'm in a nigger shack down South. Pow-wow! Cat's foot! Say, what do you know about Rose and her doings, anyway? Pshaw! I don't want to hear another word about it. I'll tell you one thing, though: Rose ain't in no danger of breaking her heart over any man; not this week. She's mighty capable of taking care of her own business, and that's jest the point where you folks is weak."

"Say," spoke up Lem again, utterly ignoring Amos, "have any of you-uns noticed how Tom Farthing's been shining up to Loney lately? Noticed that, have yeh? How do you cipher it out?" He waited an impressive moment. "Wal, suh, want to know my idea? I can see it jest as clear 's mud. I could tell a mighty good deal if I wanted to, but I won't. I'll jest say this much: if Loney Heller 'd lived two hundred year ago she'd have been in a little bonnyfire some fine morning. Mmh-huh." He nodded his head impressively and shut up one eye. "There's some strange things goes on down in that old house in the Run still,—some mighty strange things. I've saw some of 'em with my own eyes, and I'll tell you this: it would be as much as my life is worth to tell about some of 'em still. She's a queer girl, Loney is. She's the last o' the Hellers, and she owns this walley in the devil's right. You-uns knows that. Now think of this: 'fore Al Farthing could spin a thread he had to take account o' Loney. Ain't that clear 's mud? Before he could tech the Squire or Rose he had to buy her off. I tell you even the devil can't do nothin' in this walley still without askin' Loney. Now let me tell you one thing, Amos Hard'n," he lowered his voice and spoke in a shuddering whisper, "that white face you and Dan seen in the old Heller house winder that night was Loney's. 'Fore God, it was. I know it."

A shuddering "Ah-h-h-h-h!" came from the crowd.

"Yessuh, that white face was Loney Heller's. 'Fore God that's the truth, and I know what I'm saying. I could prove it if I dast to. And where did she go to? Answer that." There was no doubting the sincerity of the man. He believed what he was saying.

"Tommy rot! Oh, pshaw!" ejaculated Amos. "I'm mighty glad I'm a Yankee and hain't gut none of this infernal superstition."

"The only persons ever hung for witches in this country still was hung by Yankees," retorted Lem. "I knows some things, if my ancestors did come over in the *Cauliflower*."

"Wal, the Yankees *hung* 'em. They didn't listen to 'em with their mouths wide open like corn-poppers."

"But how about that night up in the Heller house, Amos? How about that? Dan ain't no liar; Dan's fair-minded, and what did he say? Heigh?"

"An infernal trick, done by wires and electricity. You can do anything with electricity. Al Farthing's trying to be smart. That's all there is to that."

"Oh, my! Talk about Dutch dumbness!" burst out Ulie. "By chimminy! Yar-r-r-r-r-r! e-e-e-e-e-e-e! Ho, ho, ho! Oh, my! How's that, Lem? Say, Amos, that's what I call Yankee dumb. Where's the wires? They ain't in sight, and if there was wires a man couldn't dig no trench without us knowin' it. And what about that great black ring? Hein?"

"There's an underground hole to the Farthings', or somewhere else," maintained Amos desperately.

"Oh, chimminy gracious!" Ulie was getting angry. "When did they dig it? And didn't Dan say you-uns went down cellar and jobbed every inch of the wall and stamped on the ground? Say, Amos, do have a little common sense, if you be a Yankee."

"Wal, there's some infernal trickery about it, I know that. It's jest like slight er hand: you can't tell, if you die, how it's done, but you know it's a trick all the same, and it's always easy enough when you hear it explained." Amos was in his last ditch.

"Yessuh, you're right; it *is* infernal. That's *jest* what it is. Ain't there witches in the Bible still? Heh? Ever read of the Witch of Endor? Didn't Job meet the devil walkin' up and down the earth a'ready?—But, Lord! what's the uste? By-and-by you'll be saying the Bible ain't true a'ready 'cause it's all chuckfull of fish stories."

"How do you think it's coming out, Lem?" asked one in the crowd. "What 'll Loney do with Tom? Merry him?"

"O-o-o-oh, no! No, sir! Such critters don't merry. I know Tom pretty well, and he's a decent fellow in spite of his father's dickerings with the devil. I don't know nothing about Jim, but Tom's a decent feller that's bein' jumped off of the checker-board to get Al Farthing into the king row. That's clear 's mud to me. Have yeh ever saw Loney wunst? Kinder witchy and snaky, ain't she? Ever saw anything like them eyes of hers, black and sharp 's a rat's, and that hair? 'Tain't natural. Ever notice how she don't speak to yeh, but goes off kinder ageways and soft, and sneaks out of sight? There's months at a time that you don't see nothing of her at all. Where is she then? Hein? And where does she get them clothes, let me ask yeh that? Not round here. Oh, I tell yeh there's more 'n seven devils in that critter still, and you-uns 'll know it some day. She's the last of the Heller's a'ready, and Tom's in her grip. Yessuh. She's fascinated him jest like a rattlesnake. She looks like an angel to Tom, but I tell you-uns she's a wiper,—yessuh, a wiper. I know her through and through, and I could tell a pile more if I dast to. She's like one of them awful wampires I've read about, all black and snaky, that come down in the dark and suck your life's blood before you know it. Ah-h-h!" He looked about him furtively; there was real terror in his face. He lowered his voice to a whisper. "Oh, I tell yeh, she's a hell-cat without a soul—a hell-cat—and Tom 'll wake up by-and-by like a man with the nightmare and find her grippin' his throat,—harder and harder, and he can't shake her off till he's dead,—dead with his eyes bulgin' wide open." The man was actually shaking with fear. A shudder that was audible ran round the circle.

"Say, Lem, if I knew half as much as you do about the lower regions I'd write a dictionary," snapped Amos. "I don't know of any first-class dictionary of pow-wowin' and spells and hell-catery, and here's a chance to make a fortune. But see there,—there's the preacher riding like Peter. Jest see him."

The approach of the minister called for a change of topic. Amos was an adept at this.

"Say," he continued, "I heard a good one on the preacher last week. You know somebody got into his barn a while ago, and stole every blessed chicking he had to his name. Wal, Hal Siebert that lives over to the Furnace sez to him the next day, sez he, 'Say, Reverend, it serves you jest right,' sez he. 'A Methodist minister hain't got no call to keep chickings. Don't you get chicking to eat every time you eat away from home, and that's about twict a day? Wal, give somebuddy else a chanct,' sez he. 'You've ate so much chicking now that the pin-feathers is growing behind your ears,' sez he, 'and you ought to be ashamed to look a hen in the face.' Wal, wal, Elder, you here?" He turned with a surprised look as if he had just caught sight of the man. "Which way did you come, I'd like to know? I was jest this very minute tellin' 'em that I thought you'd preach this mornin' on the good old text, 'The voice of the turkle is heard in the land,'—spring sermon kinder, don't you know? Wal, I 'spose we'll find the text out 'fore soon if we c'n keep awake."

Five minutes later not a soul was in sight, and the drowsy notes of "Duke Street" were floating out of the open windows and over the Sabbath fields.

# CHAPTER XIII

# THE POW-WOWING AT ROARING RUN

THE HABITATION OF Poppy Miller at the mouth of the Run had been seen by few of the valley people,—at least by day. The children of the region for half a century and more had been taught to avoid the uncanny place and by no means to approach it save under dire necessity, and then only in the prescribed way: at dead of night, in dark of the moon, in storm, if possible, and never by the road. No one in the region confessed to having made the fearful trip, but a strange tale it might be were all known.

The seat of power in the old cabin was Gran'maw Miller, a mysterious, dreaded personage whom few had ever seen save those who had visited her on midnight missions. Of her origin and antecedents there were only traditions. She was not a native of the valley. She and Poppy Miller had suddenly appeared one summer, so long ago that the date had been forgotten. He was manifestly "Dutch," but she was of a type utterly foreign to the region, and in half a century or more she had not once been seen outside of the limits of the Run farm. Of the surmises and conjectures of the years, that had now grown into a solid body of tradition by many accepted as veritable history, it is needless to speak.

One thing, however, was certain: Gran'maw Miller had power,—not the power that removes disease, for all must know that what brings disease and disaster will not remove it,—but the power that touches the infernal agencies. For ordinary diseases, for rheumatism, and warts, and "liver-grow'd" children, and such like, there were many pow-wowers, but when it came to dealings with the unknown only Gran'maw Miller could avail. It was firmly believed that she had in her possession one of the few copies now extant of that fearful volume, "The Seventh Book of Moses," the book which in the motherland in the old days had cost so many their lives, and which a few, it is well-known, took with them at the risk of body and soul in their flight to the New World.

Thus the little valley and a wide circle beyond it had ever their court of last appeal. Would a nix-nux have the spell removed, or a maiden win back her faithless lover, or a father rescue his wayward son,—who could avail but Gran'maw Miller? And there were dark whispers of vengeance wreaked on enemies, of lightning called from the skies, of men and women suddenly cut down by infernal agencies,—deeds too horrible even to think about. All these things men averred had been done on black nights in the Miller kitchen, and there are those even to-day who, could it be known, carry on their breasts ghastly scars of crosses and cabalistic symbolry done at midnight when the lightning was gleaming on the rocks of Roaring Run.

As to the origin of this belief, so potent in the Seven Mountains and beyond, one might say much. One might trace the incantations and witch lore to the German Palatinate, whence this race sprung; then he might study with certainty the wild fetich elements added by the African, and the still more awful lore borrowed from the Indian. But this is not a treatise.

The night of the twenty-seventh of May was dark and stormy. There was no moon; the rain came in spurts and swirls; the fog had smeared out every trace of light as with an inky thumb. From the top of Heller's Ridge and from the neighbouring gaps came down ever and anon the whimpering of the wind among the snags, rising at times to long whines. The trees along the pike shuddered and twisted, though they were as invisible as if in a cavern.

It was almost midnight. The last light in the valley farm-houses had gone out hours before; the storm and the night dominated completely the landscape. In all the region there was not a soul astir save at one single point: at the mouth of Roaring Run a woman, muffled beyond recognition, was stealing through the wet shrubbery.

She did not pause or hesitate. As she rounded a projection, guided utterly by the sense of touch, and by the snarl of the Run close on her left, a ray of light flashed into her eyes,—a single thin ray as from a dark lantern. She quickened her pace and walked more confidently. A moment and the outlines of a window became visible. The light was filtering through a hole in a blind, but it gave no hint of the surroundings. After a false step which landed her cruelly in a snarl of thorns, she found the door and knocked. The blows echoed with hollow boom.

Instantly, as if her knock had caused it, the ray of light winked out. There was no sound. She stood a moment listening, and then she knocked again. Utter silence. Suddenly there came a sharp whisper out of the dark, in her very ear.

"Who's there?" She jumped convulsively.

"Who is it?" the voice insisted sharply.

"It's me," she faltered.

"What name?"

"Rose Hartswick."

"Alone?"

"Yes. I want to see Gran'maw." The door swung open as of its own accord.

"Come in." It was utterly dark. "This way."

She followed blindly the sound of shuffling feet through what was evidently a narrow passage. A sharp turn and they came into a larger apartment lighted by a bed of coals in a fireplace. The half-light disclosed her guide, a bowed, hoary old man who walked feebly. He shambled to a corner, and, after a shaky struggle, drew out a handful of something which he threw on the coals. It smouldered a moment, then burst into flame, revealing the weasel face and snowy beard of Poppy Miller. The apartment was a kitchen, long and low, with a fireplace, an enormous affair of stone, taking up nearly all of one side.

Rose gave a single curious glance around, then centred her attention upon a figure crouched by the hearth. It was a woman, thin and bowed, incredibly old as the firelight revealed it, and smoking a corn-cob pipe. It did not move or speak.

"This here's Rose Hartswick come to see yeh wunst." The old man shuffled over to her, and spoke in an unexpectedly high-pitched voice.

"Humph!"

"I want you to help me, Gran'maw." Rose went close to her and bent over eagerly. "I'm in such trouble and I don't know what to do." She stopped; there was no response or movement.

"Can't you help me, Gran'maw?" she went on again, a growing nervousness in her tone.

"Humph!" Again silence, so complete that Rose could hear the whine of the Run outside. She fixed her eyes on the still figure and waited breathlessly. After a time she caught a low rumble:

"She lets him come; she laughs and plays; she looks into his eyes; and when he would give his soul for her, she would have him go,—and he can't!—Too late! Too late! Too late!—and she comes to me! Ha—ha—ha! She comes to me!" She broke into a mirthless chuckle, then subsided again into silence.

"But, Gran'maw," Rose cried eagerly, "I couldn't help it; I didn't want him to come." Again silence, and again the mumble of the voice.

"Ha, ha, ha! She comes here to me. She didn't want him to come. But she knew—she could see. And she danced and played, and looked into his eyes—and he's thinking of her now—to-night—he'd give her his soul, and she's to blame! and it's too late."

"But, Gran'maw, you can't help me—"

"Too late. And she would come to me and have me wave it all away. Ha, ha, ha! I make a man stop loving a woman! Ha, ha, ha! There's nothing in earth or hell to make a man stop loving a woman,—nothing—nothing at all. Oh, she can make him love her;—it's easy 's death, but when it's begun—she would stop it! Ha, ha, ha!" There was that in her mirthless cackle that was inexpressibly horrible. She continued to mutter incoherently, then subsided into silence.

"And there's no help? You mean there's no help?" Rose, in her earnestness, put her hand on the woman's shoulder, but she withdrew it instantly.

"She would send him away! There's another! I see him,—ah, there he is. The eyes,—I've seen those eyes; they have revenge in them,—eyes with revenge in them; and they have looked into hers, and she cannot sleep."

"Oh, Gran'maw! Oh, I'm afraid!"

"Oh, yes, yes, yes. Ha, ha, ha! I'll send him away,—he'd die for her, but I'll send him away—I'll send him away—Ah, those eyes! There they are! See, see those eyes!" She held out her hand shakily.

"Where? where?"

"There's but one way! It's his life,—I'll touch his life. See there! Oh, God! what's that? Ah, he lies on the floor,—and his eyes are wide open,—too bad—oh, too bad—too bad." She repeated the words over and over in a sort of wail.

"Oh, oh, Gran'maw," she gasped, scrambling to her feet and taking a swift step back, "I want to go!"

"But he shall—he shall go.—It's easy—he shall go away. It's easy—as death."

"But, Gran'maw," she broke out excitedly, "you don't understand. It's not Karl; I don't want you to touch Karl. It's father I come about,—I want you to make father—feel different. I just want you to change him." The old figure was rocking back and forth, now slowly. It was as if she were alone and had not heard Rose.

"Ah, yes, yes, yes, yes. That's good; it's good. There'll be revenge,—for she loves him; she looked into his eyes, and she cannot sleep. Ha, ha, ha! Ah, what's this? An old man?—with white hair?—oh, there's but one way,—revenge, ha, ha! revenge! revenge!"

"Oh, don't! Please don't, Gran'maw! Don't do anything. I want to go.—But, oh, it's father I come about. You won't touch him, will you? He's kind and good and jolly if you don't cross him. He'd do anything for me, but he can't be crossed. It isn't his fault; he was made so. But you haven't any idea how set he is. He's a man of iron, and he's set against—*him*, and he's going to ruin him, and he can do it—and I want you to make him stop—hating him. Oh, you can, can't you, Gran'maw?"

"And she'll look in her cap,—the cap she wore in the rain, and she'll find a hair,—a grey hair—an old man's hair." Automatically Rose looked into the cap which she held in her hand. It was her father's cap which she had taken on account of the storm. In the crown was a thick grey hair. She had it in her fingers before she was aware of what she was doing.

"Here, give it to me!" The command was like a hiss.

For the first time she saw the woman's eyes. Piercing and snaky they were fixed full upon hers, and not a foot away. The eagerness and glitter in them were wholly animal. Rose extended her hand, powerless to do otherwise. The creature took the hair and with it the handkerchief which Rose had bound about the scratch received in the thorns. There was blood in the centre.

"Oh, Gran'maw—" But the eyes of the woman, fastened full upon her, took away her powers of speech. She could only gasp and hold herself rigid.

"Wait for me." The command had in it almost hypnotic power. Then with a feeble movement the bowed figure gathered itself together with the aid of a long staff and arose to its feet. Then, taking the candle in its shaky hand, it hobbled to a door at the end of the room.

"Oh, Gran'maw, you won't harm anybody,—you won't harm father? Promise me, Gran'maw. You won't do anything bad, will you, Gran'maw?" The door closed upon her appeal.

She turned about in a tremor. The room was now in darkness, save for the coals in the fireplace. Everything was silent. She had an impulse to flee from the uncanny house headlong, nor stop until she was in her own room, but she was powerless to move. The affair had touched her deeper than she knew.

To her the affair was unspeakably awful, for, despite her good sense, she had, deep below all, more than a trace of the valley superstition. Gran'maw Miller had ever in her imagination been a fearful personage. The nurses of her childhood were responsible, and her neighbours who had whispered wild tales of "the power," and even her father, who in most ways was a true son of the valley.

Beyond the fireplace Poppy Miller, asleep now, was nodding almost out of his chair, but recovering himself each time at the critical instant. She watched him for a moment with a strange fascination. Suddenly something caused her to glance up and she looked full into the black eyes of Lona Heller. She started as she had never before started in her life, and gave a nervous scream.

"Why, why, Lona! You here? I didn't hear you."

"Here's a chair. Don't stand." She pushed a kitchen rocker in her direction.

"Oh, Lona, do you know about it? She isn't going to harm papa, is she,—or anybody? You won't let her, will you?"

"She'll do what she'll do." The girl took a low seat before the glower of the coals and began to stroke a cat that had come noiselessly from the darkness.

"But what do you think, Lona?"

"Gran'maw 'll help you," she answered evasively. "It's coming right."

"But how can it? I've thought it all over and over. Father *won't* give in,—and if he don't, it 'll kill me—"

"Better one than two." The low purring of the cat resounded through the room in the silence.

"What do you mean?" she asked, turning quickly.

"Nothing. You'll be happy; you haven't any trouble. I wish to God you *did* know what trouble was for just one day." There was a strange spurt of bitterness in the tone.

"Why, Lona!" She cast a swift look at the girl. "What—what do you mean, Lona?"

"Nothing."

"There's something wrong. Tell me, Lona." Impulsively she crossed over to her and laid her hand on her arm. There was no reply.

"Tell me, Lona," she whispered. For a single instant the girl looked eagerly up at Rose, but she dropped her glance as quickly.

"It's nothing," she said carelessly, arising with a quick movement and throwing more wood on the coals.

"But, Lona—"

"Hark! Sh-h-h-h-h!" The door opened and Gran'maw Miller hobbled out. With almost painful effort she regained her seat by the fireplace.

"Loney," she wheezed.

Instantly the girl sprang forward, scooped up in the pipe bowl a hot coal, and placed the pipe in her hand. Then, for what seemed to Rose like an hour, there was silence save for the spasmodic puffs. Rose studied the weird figure eagerly. It was much bowed, she noted, and the face had the leathery appearance which characterizes very dark people in extreme old age. The cheekbones were prominent, the eyes deeply sunken in the sockets, and the hair, despite her seeming great age, scarcely touched with grey. The silence at length became unendurable.

"Gran'maw," the girl began shakily. "What have you done? What is it? Tell me about it. What are you going to do? It's nothing bad, is it? Tell me, Gran'maw." Again there was silence, broken suddenly by the woman's voice, this time with a touch of excitement in it.

"Ah, look! It's death—death—death! Ha, ha, ha! See him. Look! see there! His eyes are wide open. See the purple in his face. Ah, revenge!—revenge!—revenge!—Ha, ha, ha!"

"Oh, Gran'maw, what is it? Tell me. Quick. What have you done?" Again Rose kneeled impulsively, but there was no answer now. The shrivelled figure seemed to bow lower and lower in its chair; the pipe dropped with a rattle on the hearth; and the head fell forward.

"Gran'maw has said all she will to-night." Lona laid her hand lightly on Rose's arm. "I'd go now."

"But, Lona, tell me what it means."

"How can I know?"

"But she won't harm him, Lona?"

"She does what she does.—It's dark,—here, let me show you the way to the pike."

"No, no, Lona. You'll get wet for nothing. I know the way as well as you do, and Pomp 'll whinny when I call." The girl made no answer, but started bareheaded out into the darkness.

"I love a night like this; it's my night." They went on in silence.

"Lona." Rose took her arm tightly and whispered the words. "What is it? Can't you tell *me*, Lona? I want to help you."

"No, no; you can't. Not even God could help me.—There's your horse.—Good-bye." There was a despairing bitterness in the tone such as Rose had never heard from human lips. She turned sharply, but the girl had disappeared.

"Lona," she called, "oh, Lona, come back." There was no answer save the rushing of the water in the gut below, and the roaring of the wind in the near gap.

# CHAPTER XIV

# IN THE WILD AZALEA

IN THE LATE spring and early summer the Seven Mountains burst suddenly from their sombre melancholy and bury themselves for a month in a wealth of efflorescence such as one may look for in vain elsewhere north of the tropics. The wild gaps and runs become choked with mighty masses of pink and white that fill even those long accustomed to it with wonder. First comes the miracle of the dog-wood, the spangling of the forest with spotless white; then the miracle of the azalea when the swart hillsides break suddenly into billows of fire; then the miracle of the laurel with its great masses of bloom like baskets of flowers set here and there amid the rocks; and then the miracle of miracles of the rhododendron which fills gap and tangle and scaur with great banks of unbroken snow. One might be contented to live eleven months in the dun solitudes for the sake of this one marvellous month of flowers.

One visiting in mid June the mouth of Roaring Run will find it transformed almost beyond belief. The fantastic weatherings are embowered in laurel; the tangle along the Run is a bank of solid bloom; and among the cedar scrubs still smoulders the last of the azalea. It is a transformation, indeed, one that no familiarity can ever strip of its semblance of miracle.

The morning after the pow-wowing at Roaring Run broke free-skied and smokeless. By midday there was no trace of the storm. The mountains lay soft and warm in the spring sun. Under its radiance the azalea shot up its fires until it dominated ridge and bottom and gap. Along the trough of Plum Run where it flowers in greatest profusion, it rolled in billows of flame, and ever among it and around it, like a deliberate contrast, glistened the stars of the dog-wood. As Tom Farthing stood on the crest of Raccoon Ridge it seemed to him as if the mountains were in gala dress; green and brown with fringings of scarlet and spanglings of white.

He was hot and restless. He had struck up into the ridges after the Sunday dinner in sheer unrest. On and on he had tramped without aim or thought. A mass of colour in the sharp of the V caught his eye and automatically he turned toward it. At one place in an angle of the rocks the efflorescence seemed to culminate. It was like a huge centre-piece or a single giant blossom. It cooled and rested him. He stood wondering a moment, drinking in the sweet reek of it, then sat down in the midst of the plot, his back against the sandstone. All was still save for the drone of the stream near by and the voice of a warbler in the heart of the tangle.

Unconsciously, for the thousandth time, he began to go over the problem which was dominating him. What had become of her? Why had she left him so? What was the mystery of it all? The brook purled on; the bird sang over and over its simple note, and his thoughts became ever more vague and more vague.

He awoke with a start. He was conscious of some sharp, sudden noise close by him, but all was silent when he opened his eyes. He was strangely confused. Everything seemed changed: the sun was lower; the shadows had shifted greatly; there was a different light in the atmosphere. A vague impression of some presence close at hand caused him to turn his head.

"Why, Lona," he cried in startled voice, "is it you? Is it really you?"

She did not answer. For a moment she stood as on that first evening by the brook-side, when he had come suddenly upon her. If he moved she would vanish.

"But how came you way up here?" He did not wait for her answer; he made a swift bound through the azalea and stood beside her. "Did you know I was here? Did you?"

"No."

"Then it's an accident? You just happened to come?"

"Yes."

"You were walking and saw this bunch of honeysuckle? Is that why?"

"Yes. I must go now." She turned abruptly in the direction of Heller's Ridge, and began almost to run through the tangle.

"Lona, don't," he pleaded. "Why do you go, Lona?" She made no answer, but bounded up the rocks.

"Wait, Lona, please," but she did not stop. It was as if she were afraid of him. She cast a swift glance back and quickened her pace. He was gaining on her. At the summit she stopped abruptly and faced him.

"We'll rest a minute here," she announced decisively, perching herself on a rock.

"Tell me, Lona, what the matter is. Why do you always run from me? Tell me, Lona." He came close to her and looked up into her face.

"There's a comfortable seat there." She pointed to a rock opposite hers. As he turned he noted that she was pale, and that there were flushed spots in her cheeks.

"You are not well, Lona. Tell me, what is it?" He did not take the seat, but came near to her again.

"It's nothing," she said absently. She was looking far out over the valley which lay bathed in the evening light. The sun was just on the horizon. The stillness of the Sabbath evening lay like a spell. From the far-away farm-houses and roads there arose no sound save the faint "Pe-pe-pe-pe" of a woman calling her chickens, and the low monotone of the Run purring with soft throat, like a kitten half-asleep by its mother. A breath of the hot clover fields, so faint as to be only half perceived, floated up over the scrub-oaks and the rocks.

"Lona, I want to tell you—"

"See," she broke in sharply. "Isn't it beautiful? It's like a great hap. Isn't it?" He followed her gaze out over the valley.

"Yes; but, Lona—"

"A hap in four colours: clover, corn, wheat, trees. The trees make it crazy work. The fences are stitches."

"Sure enough—zigzag, crazy stitches."

"Yes." For a moment they looked out silently over the valley.

The twilight was beginning to fade the picture. The great shadow of Roaring Ridge was creeping rapidly out toward Nance Mountain.

They were at the west end of the valley. The sharp notch of the Run was close to the right; just below them amid the scrub-oak tangle was the Heller cabin; and to the left of it nestled the buildings of Allen Farthing. A straight line from them to Poppy Miller's would pass close by the cabin.

"Do you know all the ridges and gaps?" she went on animatedly. "See, over there; that second ridge is the Alleghanies."

"Yes."

"The main range. Over there,"—she pointed suddenly—"is Turkey Run. That break beyond it is Blair's, with old Grayble to the left. That's the Bald Eagle, and right beyond it is the Juniata."

"Can you see the Juniata from here?"

"No, but you can see the valley. See that green spot,—that long, narrow strip of light green? See?" He was very close to her now. Suddenly he turned and caught her hand in his.

"Lona," he said passionately, "I love you."

"No, no, no, no," she gasped, "you mustn't,—you mustn't say that!" She arose as if frightened, and tried to free her hand.

"And why mustn't I,—why mustn't I, Lona?" he pleaded hotly.

"Listen to me." She turned and looked him full in the eyes and instantly he dropped her hand. "I mean just what I say. You must promise not to come again. You must promise never to come to the Run again. I forbid it."

"Forbid it?" he echoed blankly.

"I forbid it," she repeated with cold emphasis. "You'll not come again. It's best,—for *you*. Good-bye." With her eyes full upon him in a gaze that was hypnotic in its intensity, she sidled slowly over the edge of the ridge.

"Remember,—you'll obey me," she repeated, holding up her hand warningly. "Remember." He felt himself powerless to move or even to speak; he could only gaze at her absorbedly while she backed down the rocks toward the gap. Then near a jutting spur of sandstone she wheeled suddenly about and ran. On the instant he felt as if he had been released from a spell.

"Oh, Lona," he cried, "I can't. Stop, Lona." He leaped down over the rocks in reckless haste.

Just at the edge of the scrub-oaks the girl stopped abruptly and faced him. They had reached the azalea again; it flamed all about her, framing her like a picture.

"Why do you follow me?" she burst out almost petulantly.

"I couldn't help it. Oh, I don't understand it at all. Lona, what is it? Tell me,—why can't I come?"

"If I say it's *death* if you persist," she whispered intensely, "is that enough?"

"Death to you?"

"No."

"Then it's not enough," he burst out with passion. "It's not enough." By a sudden impulse he caught her in his arms.

"Oh, Lona," he cried, a torrent of passion rushing over him, "I love you,—I love you!" She made a movement to free herself, but he held her fast.

"No, no, no," she cried, as if in alarm. "I mustn't—I mustn't."

"Why mustn't you, Lona? Why can't you love me? Oh, can't you, Lona?" He crushed her to him almost fiercely and tried to look down into her eyes. She did not struggle now; she looked up into his face suddenly.

"Yes," she whispered.

"What?—What?—You love me?"

"I'd die for you, Tom."

"Why,—why, Lona!—Do you mean it? You love me?" He held her at arm's length and looked into her eyes.

"Yes, Tom." Then suddenly he felt her shudder as if with the cold; she threw up her hands to her face. "Oh, what have I done?" she sobbed bewilderedly, "oh, what have I done?" She broke away almost violently.

"No, no, no," she cried. "My God, you mustn't. I didn't mean it;—I didn't say it."

"Lona!"

"It's too late, Tom." Instantly she was calm again. "It's impossible. You must go. I can't tell you why, but you must. If you love me at all, you'll do it. Promise me that you'll not try to see me again."

"Lona, you don't know what you're saying. I can't—I won't."

"Promise me," she repeated. Her eyes, black and compelling, were on him again. Somehow he felt himself strangely helpless as she looked at him.

"But why, Lona? Tell me why," he gasped.

"Promise me."

"But—oh, Lona—"

"Promise me."

"I promise," he said faintly. "But, Lona—"

"You have promised. Remember. I shall hold you to your promise."

"Lona, you're cruel,—you're hurting me."

"I'm kind, Tom. You'll know sometime. Good-bye, Tom." He fancied there was a choke in the voice.

"Lona," he burst out passionately. "Tell me about it,—now. Lona!"

"Good-bye, Tom. Remember you've promised." She glided suddenly from him and disappeared into the rhododendron. It was dusk where he stood; the night was creeping on rapidly; the shadow of the mountain lay heavily over the little glen.

"But, Lona," he cried, forgetting everything and springing after her, "not yet; not just yet." He caught a glimpse of white ahead and ran toward it.

"Lona," he cried in real alarm, "where are you, Lona? Let me go with you. It's dark." There was no sound save the echo of his voice in the hollow gap. He rushed hither and thither in the dusk amid the rocks and the scrub-oaks, calling her name.

Then he leaped upon a jut of weathered limestone and listened. No sound save the snarl of the Run, and the jerky strain of a whip-poor-will in the near gap. There was not a breath of air. The fragrance of clover fields stole up to him mingled with the mist of the evening brook. Then right below him in the gloom he saw the old cabin of the Hellers, black and silent. An involuntary shudder, a fear of he knew not what, made a clutch at his heart. But it was only for a moment. Was that a flicker of white down there near the house? He leaped from the rock, crying, "Lona."

A moment and she was right by his elbow as if she had sprung from the earth.

"Please, don't," she pleaded in awful earnestness. "Hush-h-h-h! You promised. You must go—quick. It's death to stay here another minute."

"I don't care if it is. I'm going to stay—with you," he cried recklessly. "I'd die for you, Lona."

"Oh, no, no, no, no," she gasped, "don't say that. Hush-h-h-h. Now go, Tom, please. For my sake, Tom, go."

There was no mistaking her tone. He saw her waver a moment, then cast a shuddering glance behind her, and again she had vanished. A mad recklessness was on him; he had but a single thought. He ran hither and thither, eagerly, insanely. He looked behind every bush and rock and projection. In vain. She had disappeared like a moth.

He ran to the old cabin; the door was locked. She could not have been there; he would have seen her cross the open. He stopped and listened intently. He was within the black ring, though he did not know it.

There was a sound like a stealthy rustle near him, and as he turned he caught a glimpse of a white face,—a face as of the dead, framed in intense black, right within two feet of him. It was pressed against the window-pane from the inside, and the eyes were sharp and glittering. A sickening fear gripped him, but he sprang forward.

"Lona!" he cried.

The face disappeared like a flash.

Was that Lona Heller's face? He tried the door impulsively, then he threw his weight upon it. In vain. In a sort of frenzy he looked about him for a stone; he ran back a little. Then he heard a penetrating whisper from no particular direction, but seemingly right in his ear.

"Don't, Tom. For my sake, go."

He looked about him dizzily. It might have come from the shrubbery or the cabin. It was impossible to tell which. It was Lona's voice, but there was a tone in it that was new to him. The dead silence of the night, the atmosphere of mystery, the face at the window, the voice,—what did it mean? Then a feeling of terror over which he had no control began to creep upon him. He was no longer capable of thinking clearly. A moment and he was on his way home, walking faster and every faster, looking fearfully straight before him,

> "Like one, that on a lonesome road
> Doth walk with fear and dread,
> And having once turned round walks on,
> And turns no more his head;
> Because he knows a frightful fiend
> Doth close behind him tread."

It was a sleepless night that he spent, and his bedfellow, Jim, was sleepless too. And neither spoke a word during all the night. There are some things that part even brothers.

# CHAPTER XV

# THE MURDER IN SUGAR VALLEY

KARL KEICHLINE WAS dead; the news flew over the valleys like wild-fire. He was found on the morning of June first lying in a huddle in his back-store amid a tumble of scattered goods and packing cases. The front door was wide open, and there was a window up in the rear of the post-office room. Marks of a fierce struggle were everywhere: the safe was on its back, a great heap of horse-blankets over it, and everything was in confusion. The tin clock, which had been knocked to the floor, had stopped at the hour of one.

The post-office inspector and the coroner had arrived at noon, and had taken up the matter with vigorous hand. Nothing had been touched. The burgess, who was on the spot a few moments after the first discovery, had stretched a rope around the entire premises and had forbid any one passing it. In an hour the entire circuit of the barrier had been crowded with excited men and women, as if the place were a prize-ring. But a strange hush had been over them. One could almost hear his neighbour's heart beat.

The first step of the officials was to make a photograph of the body as it lay amid the boxes, after which they made a minute examination. There was but one mark of violence:

About the neck, reaching from ear to ear on the back, was a livid black ring.

The next sensation was the discovery near the overturned safe of a brace and steel bits, a cold chisel, a cake of putty-like soap, and a blacksmith's hammer.

Branded in the hammer handle were the initials "A. F."

There was little additional evidence. An old Agricultural Report of Pennsylvania, in which it was known that Keichline kept postage-stamps, was missing, and, according to the inspector, it should have contained some seventeen dollars in ones and twos. The money-drawer also had been rifled. Nothing else seemed to have been disturbed.

The coroner's inquest was held immediately. In scarce an hour the jury brought the report that Keichline had come to his death "from a blow delivered across the base of the brain by unknown parties who had entered the post-office intent on larceny." It was their opinion that Keichline had surprised the robbers as they were about to blow open the safe, had grappled with one of them, and had succeeded in throwing him on his back, when the other had delivered the fatal blow.

The inspector immediately offered a reward of one thousand dollars to be paid by the general government for the apprehension of the guilty parties, and the burgess after a short conference with his council offered a like amount. Then a lull seemed to come in the whirlwind of events. But it was of short duration. On the very heels of the verdict the sheriff received a telephone message from Squire Hartswick of Hell Bottom, and the excitement instantly increased tenfold.

The news had come to the Bottom like a thunder-clap. In all the history of the region there had never been such a sensation: June first was the day when Karl was to have received his final answer from Rose; Jim Farthing, it was known, was infatuated with her; the hammer with its brand could mean only one thing.

The Squire's suspicions were right. It was clear now who had been committing the robberies, and who had been responsible for the doings in the Heller cabin.

The thought came to the valley like a cold chill. As if by agreement, the men everywhere dropped their work and congregated at the store. There was no loud talk and no noisy excitement; the feeling was too intense for that. A sullen undertone, deep and menacing, came from the little groups. The uncanny element in the affair appealed to many and caused them to talk in fearful whispers. The Squire said nothing at all, but the Hartswick wrath was in his face as no one had ever seen it there before. Men glanced at him fearfully and avoided him. All through the forenoon he was a smouldering volcano: the eruption was yet to come.

It came with the report of the coroner. Suddenly he burst into furious action; three minutes after he had heard the final details he telephoned the sheriff to ride with all speed to the Bottom, and to come with a force prepared for rough work. Then, unable to wait a single instant, he rode up to the Farthing place to reconnoitre. By mere luck he came upon Mrs. Farthing in the road and learned from her that her husband and Tom had gone the day before on business to Sinking Springs, but that they were expected home before night. Jim was up in the wood-lot cutting fire-wood. The old man drove back in fierce haste.

"They hain't got back yet from their butchering," he burst in stormily even before he had reached the store. "They hain't, unless the old woman's lying. Here, two of yeh go up there where you can see the house and keep watch. Don't let 'em see yeh. But they won't come back; it's their trick to hide in the mountains till this blows over, but it won't work. Dang 'em, they can't get away now."

He bustled from the buggy and strode to the telephone, where he began giving orders like a general at the front. He called up one by one every station on the line and ordered a strict watch to be set on all roads. From Sugar Valley he got word that the sheriff would start in half an hour with a full force of deputies prepared to scour the mountains till the murderers were found. Then he turned to the crowd in the store.

"It's a clear case." He swung his fist in windy wrath. "We know who this gang is now, and damn 'em, we've got 'em. We've got every link; the motive's as clear as the light of day and so's the proof. The sheriff 'll be here against four and you must stand by us, every one of ye. We shall need ye all." He strode out of the door like an avenging fury.

For a moment there was silence; the crowd got its bearings slowly.

"Now, I ain't quite so sure," began Lem Fisher after a time. "I'd jest as quick think the Farthings wan't there as to think they was. Did ye hear about that black ring around Karl's neck still? Hein? Recollect what I told ye down to Dan's flitt'n? Didn't I say as how you'd find Karl some fine morning with a black ring round his neck and his eyes bulgin' out like he'd saw the devil wunst? Hein? Wal, suh, know what I think still? Somebody's been pow-wowin' a'ready," nodding his head mysteriously. "Umph-huh! and you don't have to be where the man is to pow-wow him. Umph-huh! See?"

"Oh, pshaw!" sneered Amos. "Let up, won't yeh, on this pesky pow-wow business. We've gut facts enough, the Lord knows, without going into that infernal rot. This thing was done by the gang that's been operatin' in this region all the spring. That's plain enough to me. They'd jest gut the safe down ready to blow when Karl, who's been sleepin' with one eye open these three months, heard the noise and pounced down on 'em. They're old hands, I tell you. They know that country postmasters have stamps ready for customers generally in some old book, and that they don't always remember to put it in the safe at night. They looked for that first thing, and they found it. They can't have been extra stout fellers, for Karl seems to have gut the best of the two of 'em for a while, jest as if they'd been *wimmen*. It looks as if he threw one of 'em and the other smashed him over the head. That don't exactly p'int to the Farthings, for they could handle Karl, arry one of 'em, jest like a fly. The main thing I can see ag'in 'em is the hammer. Then, again, nobody knows where they come from, and these breaks begun jest about the time they moved here."

"Humph!" grunted Ulie. "There ain't a jury in this State that wouldn't hang all three of 'em higher 'n Haman on half the evidence there is ag'in 'em. Not one. Rose didn't set any store by that Farthing feller. When the news was broke to her they say she turned whiter 'n milk and she pretty near keeled right over. You wouldn't think that of a girl like Rose, now, would you? but it ain't strange to me. They was goin' to be merried, she and Karl, pretty soon now, and there wan't only one way to head it off, and Jim he took it. It's all plain enough to me."

"Plain? By mighty! Why, it's *prima facie*." The Squire had puffed in again. "I've gut another piece of evidence. Dan Hubler and Ira Kemmerer sayes they met Jim in the road here with his colt driving down Gum Run way at ten o'clock last night. How's that for evidence?" He stepped across the room and rang the telephone with a snap that threatened to break the crank. "They've started," he announced, hanging up the receiver. "They've jest gone, the sheriff and a dozen young fellers. Now get ready all of you, for we're goin' to hustle that gang night and day till we get every one of 'em safe in jail. Rose, she's jest about distracted, poor girl. I never saw anybody so broke up over anything, never. And no wonder! She and Karl was to be merried on the fifteenth. I've heard of them that's dummed fools enough to think she cared for that low skunk, Farthing. I wish they could see her now. She's jest grievin' her heart out over Karl, poor girl. By mighty, I want you to stand by me, men. I'll hang the whole tribe of 'em, if it takes every cent of my property to do it." He brought his fist down on the counter like a pound of pork. The crowd had gathered densely about the old man, and no one noticed a new arrival until he was close upon them.

"How'd do?" they heard a cheery voice. All turned as by a common impulse.

It was Allen Farthing.

Instantly the same awful hush came over the room that might have come had it been the dead man himself, or his ghost. For a moment one could hear even the breathing of the old Squire.

"I've just got home from Sinking Springs. Over to Rock Creek they told me the report was that Karl Keichline had been murdered." He fumbled deliberately in his pocket, drew out a clay pipe, then leaned over and begged a match of Ulie, who produced one with amazing alacrity.

"Any evidence about who done it?" he asked, seeking out an egg-crate and puffing as unconcernedly as if his head were not thrust completely into the lion's mouth.

There was no answer, but silence ominous and deep, like that in the best room when the mourners sit about the wall and the clock strikes *one*.

The full significance of the visit was growing on the crowd. Allen Farthing had not once visited the store in six months. Why at this critical moment? Either it was an attempt to pull wool over the eyes of the town with a stupendous bluff, or it was a case of sheer ignorance: secure in the belief that no one could connect him with the crime, he had come down to learn the drift of suspicion. Squire Hartswick stood by the counter, curled up like a rattler.

"Now look here, folks." Farthing straightened up suddenly and put away his pipe. A nervous stir went over the group as if the desperado was about to begin revolver practice on the lamp chimneys and oil barrels. "There's something wrong here, and we're going to have it out—right—now. I'm going to talk fair and square, and I want you to. What's this I heard down to Rock Creek about our being mixed up in this murder? What did you go up to my house for, Squire? What's this charge you've been making? Why did you say when I come in that you'd hang our whole tribe if it took every cent of your property? Now don't mince matters; let's have it straight." There was an imperious tone in the man's voice that demanded a hearing. The old man squirmed a little under his sharp gaze.

"We've gut proof that you and your boys done this job; proof that's good and sufficient."

"For instance now?"

"You'll have jest all the chance to hear it that you want," snapped the Squire venomously. "And it won't be long either. I ain't called on to go over it now."

"You may do as you please, Squire Hartswick." There was a steel ring in the words; the man was as cool and self-contained as a surgeon. His cold eye bored the man through. "You can do just—as—you—please, but I want to tell you one thing: you are laying yourself open to mighty serious charges." He rolled the words menacingly. "I know that you've sent all over this region charging me and my boys with the murder of Karl Keichline, and I know the sheriff is on his way here this minute and all on your charge. I heard you say, sir, myself, that you'd hang our whole tribe if it took every cent of your property. Now give me your evidence."

The Squire did not flinch or squirm. He eyed the man like a wrestler waiting for an opening. He made no answer. The wrath in his face was apoplectic.

"You are doubtless aware, Squire Hartswick," the man went on after a pause, every word clear and round, "you doubtless know that unless you can substantiate these charges, you endanger yourself to a considerable degree. A man of influence can't ruin a poor neighbour in these days by false charges. That time is in the past. There is some very stringent and precise law on that point, as you doubtless know. Now you'll please accommodate me by stating the full charges against me and my boys." He stopped with cold precision, and waited for the Squire's answer.

"I shan't do anything of the sort. You'll be under arrest in jest thirty minutes and you won't leave this store before then. There'll be plenty of time for charges in the proper place." The old man was holding himself with difficulty.

"That may be; I shall make no resistance, but let me add one little thing. For some reason, God knows why, you've connected me with this wretched murder. I've got no call to defend myself now before I know the charges against me, but I don't want needless trouble either for myself or for anybody else, and to save trouble and scandal I'll simply say that, if it ever becomes necessary, I can prove beyond the shadow of a doubt that Tom and I were thirty miles from Sugar Valley last night on business that I can make perfectly clear."

"It's a lie,—it's all bluff! You can't prove it." The Squire's voice was pitched unnaturally high.

"You are acquainted with Lawyer Troutman of Sinking Springs,—a competent witness, you'll admit," the man went on calmly. "He and his wife and two boys will swear that Tom and I were in their house until ten o'clock, when we went up to bed, and that we came down and ate breakfast at six o'clock. This 'd make, as you'll admit, some lively work if we went to Sugar Valley and back—forty odd miles each way, over the devil's own make of roads, in the dark, in eight hours. Now, you've got a telephone here. I'll wait for you to 'phone the Squire right off now before I leave the store."

The old man made no move; he sat glum and black.

"Very well. The Squire's in his office by this time and you can get him if you wish. You can call my bluff in just one minute if you care to. Furthermore, I can bring one hundred of the best men in Paoli, where I've lived for twenty years and where the boys have lived all their lives till they came here, who'll give us a character that 'll be all any man could ask for. I'll give you the names of some of them who've got telephones and you can get 'em right off now on the long-distance if you want to. There's another way you can call my bluff. All right; you can do as you please. Now a man don't usually defend himself until he's given the evidence against him, but things have been going mighty strange down here and they're going to stop now, right—off—short." The words snapped like trap-teeth. "You can bring any charge you think best against me and my boys, Squire Hartswick, but I give you fair warning that it'll go hard with you if you fail to prove your case. My boys mean a good deal to me, and they are going to have fair play."

"It's a damned bluff," sneered the old man, "a devilish bluff." His face was fairly blue with rage. The veins stood out plump and black on his forehead.

"I've given you a way to call my bluff if you care to. If you don't, you place yourself in a serious position, as you'll admit. If you fail to make your case, I'll promise you here and now that it's going hard with you. I shall push it to the very limits of the law, and I'm somewhat of a lawyer myself. I know perfectly well what I'm about. Do any of you wish anything of me before I go?"

He arose and swept a keen glance over the crowd. There was that in his manner and look that awed and dominated them.

"Here, hold right on there." The Squire was regaining his self-possession. "How about Jim? The evidence all points to him. What have you got to say about Jim?"

"He was at home last night with his mother."

"How do you know he was? You wan't there."

"His mother 'll testify to it. Of course he was there."

"Wal, he wan't, that's all. Wait a minute, men. See he don't get away." He bustled over to the telephone and called for Lawyer Troutman.

"Hello! Is that you, Squire? Say, did Al Farthing and Tom spend the night with you last night? . . . Heigh? . . . . Jest what time was it? . . . . Sure, are yeh? . . ." Then the old man hung up the receiver with an angry jerk and wheeled about.

"Wal, that don't make any difference with Jim," he snapped. "That won't clear him, and all the evidence anyway is against him."

"Will you kindly explain?"

"Yes, sir, I will, and you won't want to hear it either. In the first place, as I said, Jim wan't at home last night. We can prove by two good men that at ten o'clock he was driving with his colt down towards Sugar Valley. Then he had a motive for the crime that alone is enough to convict him. He's hated Karl like hell all the spring and he's threatened him. He could have done that job himself alone; he's stout enough to. Then, as a clincher, a hammer with your letters on it was found close to the body. What have you got to say to that?" The confidence of the man had weakened a little at the recital. He turned slightly pale.

"I don't know anything about this," he said perplexedly, "but my boy didn't do it; I know that. There's a mistake somewhere."

"It's as clear as daylight. Jim's the man, and we'll have him before sundown."

"You'll have him before then." He stepped toward the door, but turned short about. "I'll bring Jim right down. There's a mistake, that's all, and I'll clear it up, Ira Hartswick, to your full satisfaction. There won't be any sneaking or dodging about this. It's going to be fought in the open, and you're going to fight fair." He went straight out through the door and no one opposed him.

There was silence for the space of ten pipe-puffs. Then Amos raised his voice.

"Wal—I'll—be—dumbuzzled!"

"He's a cold-blooded, desperate man," exploded the Squire. "He's the coolest, brazenest devil I ever met in all my life. If you can look at him one minute and not size him up as an experienced criminal you're a pack of dum fools. But he can't fool me. I called his bluff for him. See how he backed down, did yeh? He knew Jim was in a trap and he came in here to brazen us, but it didn't go. He's gut the wrong man. By mighty, I'll run this gang down if it costs my whole property." Again he smote the counter with resounding fist.

"Now, I ain't quite so sure, Squire," drawled Amos reflectively. "We'd better go a little slow, don't yeh think? The man kinder looked to me as if he was honest in what he said, and I ain't very often deceived in a man." He was rubbing his chin absorbedly, a puzzled scowl on his face. He seemed to be thinking aloud. "Now what could he want to bluff us for? That's what I don't understand. He cleared himself and Tom all right, but how could he think he was going to get Jim out of it? How was it goin' to help the business by comin' down here? By hunkey, it looks to me as if he believed Jim was innocent. I don't get fooled very often, and it looks to me as if them proofs ag'in Jim was all new to him. They kinder phased him. I'll bet a quart of beans he'll have Jim here on schedule time."

"Humph!" snorted the Squire. "Don't be a fool."

"But what's the uste arguin' about it?" broke in Lem Fisher. "Hain't I told you-uns over and over ag'in that Al Farthing didn't have to go down to Sugar Valley in order to knock over poor Karl? Hain't I told yeh a'ready? It's all clearer 'n mud to me. Don't you see how strange it was that he and Tom should be over there forty miles away on the one night of all the year when they might have to give an account of themselves? See it now, do yeh? I tells you still there's something awful about this,—something awful. There's pow-wowin' in it,"—lowerin' his voice,—"somebody's been pow-wowin.'"

"Wal, by mighty! I hope if there's goin' to be any more pow-wowin' in this valley they'll take you and pow-wow half a spoonful of brains into your old Dutch skull," exploded Amos. "Pow-wowin'! Lord A'mighty, if I ain't good and sick of pow-wowin'! Can't an old yarler hen lay a big aig in this valley but what she's been pow-wowed? Now, why don't you stop this nonsense and go to lookin' for the gang that's really been doin' this devilishness? Jim Farthing couldn't have done that job alone. There was two of 'em at least, and who was the other I want to know? You take my advice, Squire, and go mighty slow. The Farthings are out of this, and he's a dangerous man to make mistakes with."

"What about that hammer? Heigh?"

"That hammer won't hang no Farthings. They could get that hammer in a dozen ways. Almost every break I ever heard of begun by their gettin' tools out of some blacksmith shop or toolhouse. Perhaps the one that took that hammer done it to lay the suspicion onto the Farthings. I tell you, Squire, you take my advice and go slow."

"I shall go slow or fast jest as I dum please, you-uns take notice of that. It's been a mighty long time sence I've been crawling around this valley asking people what I better do. You let me tell you this, suh: Al Farthing ain't out of this yet. Nosuh." He turned with a jerk and stormed out of the room, slamming the door behind him. A small avalanche of talk, seemingly loosened by the bang, rattled about the room, but it was quickly cut short by a commotion without.

They rushed to the door in time to see the sheriff and his posse gallop up with a flourish, their horses white with foam, and make half a circle about the store front.

"Where's the Squire?" shouted the leader breezily.

"Here, right here." The old man bustled through the crowd. There was a curious, wild-western air to the scene, with its blowing horses and flannel-shirted riders. The leader sat on a raw-boned mustang that, despite its hard run, held his head high. The Squire went straight to the man.

"It's Jim Farthing we want," he announced brusquely. "No matter about the others."

"But I thought there was evidence against all of 'em. I thought they was a gang." There was a shade of disappointment in his voice.

"No. Jim's the only one in this scrape. I've gut more evidence since I telephoned. You'll know him: stout, broad-shouldered feller; about twenty-one; five feet eleven; weighs about a hundred and eighty; brown hair, grey eyes, smooth face, square jaws, good teeth; wears a brown shirt and a black felt hat."

"Where 'd we better start in?"

"You'd better go to the house first, and from there strike up into the Gap to their wood lot. He's hid somewhere in the mountains, but he can't get out. I've sent word in every direction and they're keeping watch for him."

"All right," answered the sheriff with breezy importance. "I shall want to swear in most of this crowd as deputies. We want to spread out in small groups, and—"

"God A'mighty! there he is now!" The ejaculation turned the crowd like a pistol-shot. Allen Farthing and Jim were right by the sheriff's horse.

"Here's the boy; it's all a mistake; and I want it cleared up right now. This boy is jest as innocent of this business as a child."

"Sheriff," called the Squire sharply, "that's the man. I order his arrest on the spot." The sheriff sprang from his horse and strode over to the new arrivals.

"Look here, young man, I want to put some questions to yeh and you mind how you answer 'em." The Squire, grim and black, planted himself in front of Jim and swung his fist in his face. "Where was yeh last night? Was you to home all the time?"

"No."

"Was you out with your colt?"

"Yes."

"At ten o'clock?"

"Yes."

"Driving down Gum Run way?"

"Yes."

"You'll tell the sheriff now why you took that drive at that time of night in that direction."

"Why—I went on business." There was a troubled look in his face.

"Oh, yes, that's very probable." The Squire cast a triumphant look at the sheriff. "Do you have much business at midnight these nights? Alone was yeh all the way?"

"No-o, I wasn't."

"Who did yeh have with yeh?" An intense silence had fallen over the crowd. Jim made no reply.

"Who was it?" insisted the man brutally.

"I can't tell you, Squire Hartswick."

"Can't tell me? Do you realise what it means if you don't? If you went on honest business, you'll tell who it was. Now, once again, who was it?"

"I refuse to answer."

"Oh, indeed. This is quite interesting, Mr. Sheriff. Very well, let me ask you another question. You've always liked Karl Keichline, have yeh?"

"Why, I don't know—"

"Yes or no; have you always liked him?"

"No."

"Ever had any falling out with him?"

"Why, not much. Up in the mountains one night, we—"

"Never mind the whole story," broke in the Squire harshly. "What was the last word he said to you then?"

"Why—I—"

"Tell the sheriff just what he said."

"He said he'd get even with me if it took fifty years, but I didn't—"

"Right. It takes two to make a quarrel, and what you said to him will come out in due time—"

"But, Squire Hartswick, I—"

"Oh, you'll have time enough to talk about that. We want to clear up one more point. Here, sheriff, you brought up the hammer, didn't you?" The sheriff produced it at once. "Now, have you ever seen that hammer?"

"Yes; that's our hammer." He took it into his hands and examined it curiously.

"Where did you see it last?"

"It was in our toolhouse up home."

"When was that?"

"Sometime last week; I don't remember just when."

"Have you any explanation as to why that hammer was lying near the body of Karl Keichline this morning?"

"Why, was it?" he looked up in real surprise.

"Oh, your bluff don't go. That hammer was taken into the store by the one that murdered Karl, and it's your hammer. You see, Mr. Sheriff, you've got your man."

"But, Squire Hartswick," broke in Jim confusedly.

"That's all we want to hear, young man. You can do your talking later." There was a venomous ring in the old man's voice. "This isn't all the evidence by a long shot. This feller's been infatuated with my daughter all the spring. I caught him two or three times hanging around and hiding in bushes to see her. She tried every way to get shet of him, for she was going to marry Karl on the fifteenth of this month. She was going to give him the final answer to-day. Don't you see how timely this making away of Karl was for this feller's schemes? There's not a single link missing, not one. Now, sheriff, you'd better take him right down to the jail as quick 's you possibly can. There may be trouble if you don't. The crowd here is almost a mob now, and I can't control 'em much longer."

"But, gentlemen," interposed Allen Farthing, "one word."

"No, sir; not a single word," bellowed the Squire. "You'll have time enough to testify all you know at the proper time. Here, take him away, sheriff." The handcuffs clicked on Jim's wrists.

"Here, Hal," the sheriff shouted importantly, "let the prisoner have your horse. I'll see that you get another all right. Here, sir, this way. Fall in, men." Two deputies helped Jim into the saddle. His face was pale, but he sat erect and cool. He tried several times to speak, but they cut him off brutally.

Then something in the crowd caught his eye; he started violently; but no one else noticed it. His father stood keen and defiant close to the horse, his face like an Indian's. Impulsively he laid his hand on his son's arm.

"It's all right, Jimmy. Don't lose your nerve. Remember, whatever happens, Tom and Mother and I are right with you, and we'll fight 'em till we drop, every one of us. There's a mistake somewhere, but it's coming out right. Good-bye, Jimmy." There was a tear in the cold eye, but the man stood erect and alert.

"Fall in," ordered the sheriff again in military voice.

Then the unlooked-for happened.

No one but Jim had noticed a feminine figure on the borders of the crowd. When they first saw her she was standing close by the Squire with her hand on his arm.

"Father, wait," she was saying eagerly. Every one turned at the voice, and a hush fell instantly.

"Jim didn't do it. He was out last night with *me*. I rode with him down Gum Run."

"Why—why, Rose, you—"

"Yes, I did. It was all arranged. I went up to my room and stole down the back stairs. Jim wouldn't tell because he wouldn't bring my name in. If you arrest him, then you arrest me."

"You went with him?" gasped the old man, too surprised to act or talk or think.

"Yes, sir; I did." A low murmur swept over the crowd. She straightened up at the sound of it and faced them almost with defiance in her eyes. "I tell you he never did it; he was with me."

"But—but, Rose, why did you drive—with him? And down Gum Run—at ten o'clock? I can't believe it, Rose." It was as if the old man was thinking aloud.

"Because it was impossible for him to ride with me at any other time, you've been so harsh with him." Her face was pale with bright spots in the cheeks; nervous tension was evident in every feature and movement. It was magnificent,—the lone woman amid the rough crowd of men, defending her lover and confessing publicly her love. Jim's heart beat smotheringly; his impulse was to leap from his horse and stand beside her, protecting and sheltering her. He wrenched mightily at the handcuffs, but they held.

The sheriff had edged along until he stood at the girl's elbow.

"Say, look here," he spoke sharply, "what are you riding at night for with a feller like this Farthing, when you were engaged to marry Karl Keichline?"

"I was not engaged to marry Karl Keichline." She turned to him with a look of scorn. "What's more, I never should have been. I hated him."

"Ah! then let me ask you one question: you and Jim both hated this man, and had a reason to have him out of the way before June first. Do you know anything about his death?" He peered up into her face, and her manner changed instantly.

"Why—why, no. We were back before one, and the murder, you say, was committed at one."

"Answer my question," he insisted harshly. "Did you suspect anything was going to happen when you started out with Jim? Did you have anything to do with his death? Answer me. Did you do anything either directly or indirectly towards bringing it about?"

"Oh, don't, please,—don't," she cried nervously. Then she straightened suddenly. "Jim's perfectly innocent and I know it. He didn't have the slightest thing to do about it."

"Sheriff," ordered the Squire sharply, "let the prisoner go. I withdraw all charges. My daughter's testimony is sufficient."

"But, Squire Hartswick, it's not lawful; I can't—"

"I say let him go," roared the man, "I'm satisfied. Let him go; do you hear? And, Rose, you go into the house this instant." The sheriff wavered a moment and then unlocked the handcuffs. It was not safe for an officer in that region to oppose the old Squire if he had ambitions for re-election.

"That's all there is to do here, sheriff. If I want you, I'll send for you. Good-day, sir." Then he turned to the Farthings, his face the colour of raw liver.

"This ain't the end, sir, by any manner of means, remember that," he hissed. "You just remember that."

"You are right; it's not the end, Squire Hartswick." Allen Farthing was still cool and alert. "I shall try to find the real criminal in every way in my power, and when's he's found I shall have a word to say with you. You can't fool with my boys with impunity, I can tell you that." He turned sharply about and strode away; the Squire hastened toward the house.

The first comment was from Lem Fisher:

"What did I tell yeh? Heigh? Didn't I tell yeh there was pow-wowin' in this? Don't you see it now a'ready? Rose is spell-bound and haexed. You can see it in her face with your eyes shut. Did you see her eyes when she stood there? Those eyes were jest like Katie Barndollar's. And what did I tell yeh wunst?"

The next comment was from Amos:

"Wal—I'll—be—dumbuzzled!"

# CHAPTER XVI

# THE MOB AT HELLER'S GAP

SQUIRE HARTSWICK WAS first of all a man of action. He struck when the iron was hot and he struck hard. He formed his theory instantly and acted instantly. Rose was ill: the shock at the fire had unbalanced her; she was not responsible for her behaviour. Dr. Kuack, the family physician, who was consulted within an hour after the scene at the store, confirmed the theory. By no means must she stay for the funeral; it might upset her completely. She must have change of scene, and above all expert treatment and care. Therefore on the very next morning her father took her to Pittsburg, where her mother's sister resided, and secured for her a trained nurse, and the best medical counsel in the city. It was useless for her to protest or resist; it was her father's will.

Thus moved the tragedy, and in the interludes the chorus on egg-crate and biscuit-box commented and conjectured and philosophised. The Squire, strangely enough, sided now with Lem Fisher. Rose clearly had been spell-bound; she had been haexed by the Farthings; and it was driving her to physical ruin and madness. It was like hypnotism, he averred; she was at the mercy of the Farthings, and was not in the least responsible for her words.

The Squire, however, talked very little; yet all took note that the black look on his face deepened with every day. He studied absorbedly the details of the Keichline murder and of every one of the robberies. He was absent for days at a time. To those who knew him there could be only one result: if the Farthings were even remotely guilty, they would suffer and to the full extent of the law. The culmination was bound to come, and soon. There was tragedy in the air; it haunted the valley all through the June days like a premonition of war.

But before the Squire had his case complete, something took place utterly unlooked-for and unprecedented. On the night of the second of July, the Squire's own store was entered. The audacity of it was beyond belief: while the hunter was scouring the woods, the hunted was in his cabin making free with his possessions.

It was a cool, carefully engineered job, done by some one familiar with local conditions. It had come on the one night in three months when the store had not been guarded. In a benevolent moment the Squire had consented to let his clerk, who usually slept in the office, go home to see his sick mother. That this time of all others had been chosen showed clearly that the gang had been long in the near vicinity, watching night after night for their chance.

Furthermore, one, at least, of the breakers had previously been inside the store and knew the geography of the place,—that was evident from the way in which they had proceeded. They had known too what few in all the valley suspected, that the Squire kept in his back-store a large mastiff, which at night was allowed to roam about the office room. Tom Farthing had seen this dog, so the Squire alleged, one rainy day when at the store for coal-oil. Failing to find any one, he had sought the clerk in the back-room and had remarked on the dog.

That was clue number one.

The thieves, it seemed, had thrown to this dog a piece of meat, undoubtedly drugged. The remains of the piece were still on the back-room floor, and the evidence of the drugging was the behaviour of the dog. The Squire declared that he had never known him to act so numb and listless. The thieves had entered by a small window which the clerk admitted had been left unhasped. Clue number two was a pocket handkerchief found near the safe.

In one corner were the initials "J. F."

There were other startling details. The gang had evidently started to blow open the safe. They had rolled it into position, had covered the top with horse-blankets, and had left behind a chilled steel bit and a brace of peculiar mechanism. Evidently something had scared them at the critical moment. They had taken an old book in which the Squire had kept his stamps; they had rifled the money drawer; and had carried away, as far as could be ascertained, a suit of ready-made clothes, a woollen blanket, twelve cans of salmon, two boxes of cigars, and a pair of shoes,—a curious assortment, but one in keeping with the plunderings in other places.

As the news spread through the valley, the farmers once again dropped their work and flocked in to the centre store. An excited crowd had gathered on the front porch, discussing the news in low voices as if the thieves were still near at hand. Squire Hartswick was dangerously cool. The post-office inspector could not come until late in the week, and the old man was conducting the case himself. He examined with utmost care every trace left by the robbers, and he made arrangements with cold precision.

"Be careful, men," he counselled calmly. "No mistake this time. We've got him now dead sure, and there'll be no bluffing. The sheriff's out of town and can't get here until five this afternoon, and we must be mighty careful not to let Farthing know what's coming. We must catch him red-handed with the plunder right on him."

"I doubt if you can do it, Squire," protested Ulie. "It's hid up in that old cabin still, I'll bet yeh anything, and we don't dast to go there."

"You wait and see. If it's hid within ten miles we'll find it. We'll begin with his house and barn and the cabin and keep up the search till we've run over his whole property. I tell you we've got 'em this time." The Squire's unnatural calm was more exciting to the men who knew him than any amount of bluster would have been. It was the hush before the typhoon.

Amos alone seemed to be unimpressed. He sat and smoked slowly, but there was a little knot between his eyes that no one had ever seen there before.

"As I said before, Squire," he said at length, "hadn't you better kinder go slow? You say this job is jest like the Sugar Valley job and done by the same gang, but the Farthings cleared themselves of that."

"Who says they did? What's your proof that Jim Farthing wan't in it?"

"Wal, Rose—"

"Pshaw! That don't prove nothing. She wan't responsible; the doctor says so. The Farthings had her right in their power. Didn't you see how Al Farthing's little black eye was on her every minute, and how wild and flustrated she looked? Her story is absolutely unreasonable on the face of it. Then how about the handkerchief?"

"Then letters can stand for a good many things besides 'Jim Farthing.' How do you know but the one that done this job left it there jest on purpose to turn suspicion onto Jim? It's easy enough to mark a handkerchief."

"What do yeh mean?" roared the Squire, wheeling upon him instantly. "That's rot. Things may happen once, but they don't twice. Talk common sense, if you're going to talk here. We ain't boys."

"All the same, Squire, you let me advise you to go slow,—mighty slow. You've got a cool, clean-cut, clever man to deal with, and he'll euchre yeh unless you've got both bowers and the joker right in your hand. The day he cleared himself here in the store, sez I to myself: 'The man that deals with Al Farthing's got to play square and keep his head.'"

"Humph!" snorted the old man. "You'll see some things before you're much older. He's tackled the wrong man for once in his life. You wait and see."

"All right; I've said my say." Amos leaned back resignedly and went on with his smoking.

"Say, I agree with Amos in one thing, Squire." Lem Fisher was nervous and excited. He gesticulated almost convulsively. "You keep out of this, Squire; don't you tech him wunst. Don't you dast to. You can't ketch this here Farthing, sheriff or no sheriff. I don't care if you seen him with your own eyes still right here in the store wunst, stealing things, he'll clear himself a'ready. He's a haexer and you've gut to fight fire with fire still. He'll tech your life next."

"That's right, Squire," chimed in Ulie. "He'll haex you sure 's death."

"Humph!" grunted the old man.

"I tell you it ain't no small matter; no, it ain't. Nosuh." Lem was tremendously in earnest. "Jest you see what he's did to Rose a'ready. She's hed the run-down all the spring still, jest as I told you-uns she'd have. When I seen her that morning you took her away I didn't know her. She was that pale,—paler 'n a winter ghost,—jest like Katie Barndollar when she was haexed with the oppnehmer. She won't last the summer out still; you can send her to Pittsburg or Rooshey, I don't care. Again you leave the Farthings be, it 'll be too late a'ready yet. I tell you, Squire, you are the next one; you're liable to go any minute like poor Karl, with a black ring round your neck. I'm your friend, Squire, and for God's sake you take my advice. You go,"—lowering his voice to a shuddering whisper,"—you go to Gran'maw Miller's this werry night,—this werry night, Squire. 'Fore God's, it's your only chanct."

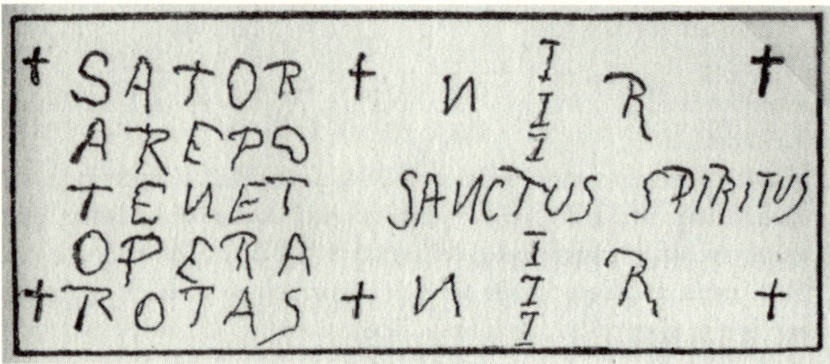


"Oh, I'm all right, Lem." He spoke with an indulgent tone. "I carry words against him. See here." He fished a slip of dark paper from his inner pocket and handed it over to the circle.

"I don't know about this, Squire." Lem examined it with the air of an expert, and the others crowded around to look over his shoulder. "That's for still-bindin' a thief wunst. This won't stand ag'in Al Farthing. Nosuh. You take my adwice, Squire, and go this werry night. It's your only chanct."

"Oh, don't you worry, Lem. You don't know where I got them words."

"I don't care where you gut 'em; they won't stand." He mumbled a moment, then relapsed into silence.

The hours passed slowly. Some of the men went home to dinner; others lunched at the Squire's expense. They discussed in detail all the robberies and inferred and deduced and conjectured. The Squire dwelt much on Karl Keichline: his character, his abilities, his tact and honesty, and his lovable qualities generally. He worked himself into a passion of indignation and pity. The "poor boy" had been like a son to him; he was beginning to lean on him and love him. "I'm getting to be an old man," he went on pathetically. "The cares of my business are weighing upon me, and now I'm all alone." There were actually tears on the old man's cheeks as he went on, and a thrill of real pity came over the crowd. Karl had been a general favourite everywhere.

It was four: forty-five when the sheriff and posse with pomp and dash swung up before the store. The details of the raid had all been carefully planned over the telephone, and they delayed only a moment. Leaving their horses they struck out with the crowd for Heller's Gap.

Twenty rods from the Farthing place a great silence came over them. The excited mumble of voices fell to a whisper and then, a few steps further on, died out entirely. There was no movement about the house and not a sound, though they listened intently. Squire Hartswick and the sheriff held a whispered council of war, and then the sheriff, with the air of one leading a forlorn hope, advanced to the front gate.

"Hello!" he cried. "Hello, in there!"

No response.

"Say, watch them upper winders still," whispered Ulie sharply, keeping well in the rear. "You'll see a gun berrel in less 'n one minute. Get out of line of the sheriff. Quick!" he ordered excitedly.

"Try 'em again," called the Squire, well in front and remarkably cool. "Here, let me try 'em." He went through the gate and bellowed lustily:

"Hello in there! Hello, Farthing!" A murmur of admiration arose behind him. Only a brave man could do that. Suddenly he advanced and knocked loudly at the front door. There was a sharp sound from within, causing Ulie and several others to duck out of sight.

"Watch for a gun," he shouted. "Watch the winders there. Get back there, Squire; quick!"

Then a small, pleasant-faced woman, with sleeves rolled up, with flour on her hands, and with a towel knotted about her head, appeared at the door. She took a startled step backward when she saw the crowd.

"Why, what's the matter?" she gasped. "What's happened?" She put her hand up to shade her eyes, and examined the scene with bewilderment.

"Is Mr. Farthing at home?" The sheriff stepped forward with business swing.

"They're up in the Gap peeling bark," she answered. "But what are you all here for? What is it? What's happened?"

"We suspect that your folks had something to do with that break last night, and it is our duty to search your premises."

"Break? Why, what do you mean?" She took a step nearer the sheriff and looked up at him appealingly.

"My store was broken into last night and robbed, and we've got proof that your people were the ones that done it," broke in the Squire brutally.

"Why—why, our people break into a store?"

"That's what I said. Now to business. We've got a warrant to search your premises, and we're going to do it. Come on, sheriff."

"Why, certainly," she said briskly. "You are welcome to go anywhere you wish and search."

"Here, Johnson and Carpenter, come in here with us," ordered the sheriff authoritatively. "Squire, I shall want you. The rest of you stay where you are." That four followed Mrs. Farthing into the house. In half an hour they appeared at the door.

"Nothing in the house," announced the Squire briskly. "We are going to try the barn now." For ten minutes more there was no movement. Then Johnson and Carpenter came out at a side door.

It was evident from their looks that something had happened.

"What is it?" called several in chorus.

"Nothing; only we've found the kit. We've gut the whole layout." They did not wait for further explanations, but pressed toward the barn with a rush. Several entered, and the others crowded the door.

"Keep out of here!" yelled the sheriff.

They fell back, but immediately crowded forward again. After a moment they were in the middle of the barn floor. The Squire and the sheriff were in one corner. From under a heap of hay they were pulling out one by one various articles. A pair of rubber boots, a suit of clothes, a blanket, and a number of cans of salmon lay in a heap beside them.

"Only eleven here," announced the Squire as coolly as if he were taking account of stock. "They had salmon for breakfast. Ah, see here!" He was blowing the chaff from a large, thin book. "That's my stamp book; stamps still in it. Here, sheriff, count 'em; there ought to be seven dollars' worth in ones and twos."

The sheriff took the book and ran over the number of stamps between the pages. There were seven dollars and twenty cents' worth. The Squire was still fumbling in the hay. A sharp exclamation turned all eyes in his direction.

"Good God! see here!" His voice fairly broke in its excitement. "That's Karl Keichline's stamp book, took the night he was murdered. Here, sheriff, look at it for God's sake."

"By mighty, you're right," cried the sheriff excitedly. "That's it. Look here: 'Report of the Secretary of Agriculture, 1886.' See, the cover's loose and there's the blot on the front. Stamps all gone. Yessuh, that's the very book." He continued to handle it in a dazed sort of way. There was an absolute hush about him in the barn. They stood gaping at the book, and no one breathed.

"Any of you remember what I said?" spoke up the Squire at length, with the tone of the man who says "I told yeh so" after the event. He had arisen, and he gesticulated heavily as he talked. "Them Farthings can't bulldoze and bluff me. I knew all the time Jim Farthing killed Karl; I knew it as well as I knew I was alive and breathing. And you thought the old man was mistaken, did yeh? Where's Amos? Heigh?" There was a rasping sneer in his voice. Amos had not deigned to accompany the searching party; he was at home and at work.

"I don't seem to see him, do you? Wal, suh, all I can say is that you folks are in luck, the biggest kind of luck, and all because I didn't lose my head and be bluffed out of what I knew. I tell yeh a den of murderers in your backyard ain't safe. We've found goods in this haymow from three different breaks, and there's more under there. You can all thank your lucky stars you're alive, that's all. Poor Karl,—he knocked him over jest like a chicken." He made a dash at his eyes with his coat-sleeve.

A wave of indignation was gathering in the crowd sinister and deep. They had been angry when they started from the store, and the sight of the stamp book infuriated them. The low murmurs grew in a moment to angry denunciation, then quickly into cries of hate and vengeance. They had not the slightest doubt that they stood in the retreat of the veritable murderers. Fear, self-protection, apprehension of they knew not what mingled with their feelings for Karl to lash them to madness. Little knots gathered here and there, arguing excitedly. Then all at once a single voice raised the wolf-cry and they were beyond reason.

"Lynch 'em!"

"Quick, men. Catch 'em before they can run." Angry yells from the pack greeted the cry. A dozen voices took it up.

"Don't give the ole woman time to warn 'em."

"Jim Farthing's the man. Dang him!"

"He's the murderer."

"Hang the hell-hound,—hang him before he has time to kill somebody else."

"Lynch him!"

"The whole damn bunch of 'em."

A few mad spirits can make a mob of any multitude, and a mob is a piece of hell.

"Shoot 'em!"

"Hang 'em!"

"Lynch 'em!"

"Here, get the ropes; somebody get some halters."

"Cut the rope off'n that rig."

"Come on; we'll learn the hell-birds."

The mob-frenzy had seized the crowd in full grip. In a yelling, cursing, boiling mass they swung out of the barn and up the trail toward the Gap, cruel as wolves on a scent and as hot to destroy. The sheriff pleaded, and argued, and threatened, but he might as well have argued with the freed waters of a dam.

"What is it? What's the matter? Where're you going?" demanded Mrs. Farthing helplessly, standing by the gate and wringing her hands in growing terror. A hideous yell, mingled with insults and curses, was the reply.

"Oh, don't be hasty! Oh, please don't, gentlemen! There's some mistake. Oh, my God, don't do it! Oh, sheriff, stop 'em. Don't let 'em do it. My God, stop, men; don't do it." But they swept by her like wolves. Wholly beside herself now with terror, she bounded after them, begging and demanding, laying her hands on the shoulder of this man and that in wild entreaty. But they pressed on, heedless of her anguish.

Tom Farthing, standing on a freshly felled tree, heard the roar coming up the Gap and paused to listen.

"What's that, Jim?"

"Sounds like a crowd." They both listened intently. Their father had left them an hour before for the Wild Meadows to examine some trees to be cut later.

"What's a crowd coming up here for?"

"Say, 'tain't Fourth of July, is it?"

"Why, no; to-day's only the second."

Suddenly a woman darted out of the bushes and made straight at Tom.

"Why, Lona—"

"Quick, Tom. Run!" she panted.

"Run?"

"They're after you—you and Jim. They've got ropes. They'll hang you both. Come,—quick!"

"But we haven't done anything. Why should we run?"

"That don't make any difference. Quick! They won't listen to anything. Hear that? Oh, come!"

"If we run, it will be confessing we done something."

"If you don't, you'll be hung in two minutes. Oh, Tom—"

A hideous yell arose below them. They had caught sight of the boys through the rhododendron and had broken into a mad rush like a pack of hounds at the sight of their victim.

"Quick, Tom," she gasped. "For my sake, Tom." Her panic was contagious. He looked into her eyes an instant and turned with her. Jim still wavered, but a fresh yell from behind sent him after Tom and Lona. Then the wild panic of the animal that turns its back came over them,—that mad, undefinable fear that grips the heart as with iron and sends the fugitive on and on till he drops in his tracks. They ran for their lives, spurred on by the yells that came up from behind.

The mob had again caught sight of them and it was straining every nerve in mad pursuit, the younger and more active in the lead. They crashed through the rhododendron snarl like a stampede of cattle, tripping and pitching headlong, bruising themselves on the rocks, and tearing clothes and hands and faces in their pursuit. The fugitives had cleared the bush line and were in plain sight now among the rocks halfway up the ridge. The sheriff, forgetting his duty to restrain the mob, in the excitement of the chase drew his revolver and fired.

"Halt!" he cried. "Stop in the name of the law," but they fleeted on.

"Take 'em dead or alive!" he roared, emptying his revolver in mad fusillade.

There were three figures, as there should have been, but one, as he stood for an instant sharply cut against the sky-line, seemed to look queer. It was as if he were a woman, but they were too excited to speculate. It was Allen Farthing and his boys. No one dreamed of anything else. At the top they caught sight again of the trio almost down to the tree-line.

Suddenly, just as the three came to the turning point, where, to reach the Gap, they must turn sharply to the right, the pursuers saw them come to a full halt. It was as if they were weighing the chances between the Gap and the road to the pike. For a single instant they hovered in indecision, then they turned sharply to the right.

Could the mob have known it, that pause and that sudden decision marked the crisis in the life of Lona Heller, and the turning-point in the valley's history.

"We've got 'em," yelled the sheriff. "Here, six or eight of you cut across to the pike and head 'em off. They can't get through the Run before we can catch 'em." They were indeed gaining on their prey. When the foremost runners reached the scrub-oaks at the border of Poppy Miller's farm they caught what seemed like glimpses of a single fleeting figure almost in the entrance of the Run. They redoubled their yells and flew down the rocks.

The fugitives had disappeared.

They ran quickly to the mouth of the Run; no one had gone through. They spread out in a large circle and surrounded the whole area of Poppy Miller's farm. It was evident that the three had hidden somewhere among the brush and rocks. They slowly closed in, searching every inch of the place. In ten minutes they met in the centre.

They had found no trace of the Farthings.

They looked into each other's faces in wordless amazement. The detachment that had been sent down the pike came up. No one had escaped that way. They were still in the valley; escape was impossible.

"Poppy Miller's house," shouted a voice.

"Ah, Poppy Miller's." The thing was plain now.

"Come on," ordered the leader. In a twinkling they had surrounded the little cabin. The sheriff strode to the door and shook it vigorously. It was barred on the inside.

"Here!" he roared. "Open in the name of the law. Open up or we'll smash the door." There was no movement within.

"Come on, boys, Get a log and stave her down." Some half a dozen of the Sugar Valley men seized an old tree-trunk from the woodpile and ran with it full tilt against the barricaded entrance. It crashed down like a rotten shingle.

"Come on, you six fellers; the rest of you stay out and surround the house. Watch sharp now."

They sprang forward, but at that moment an unexpected figure appeared at the doorway,—an old woman, unspeakably old, bowed over a staff, her face shrivelled and brown as a baked apple, her hair in strange contrast almost coal-black, and her eyes small and piercing as a rat's.

"What you want here?" she called in a shrill falsetto. "I warn you; don't you come in here."

"You're hiding the Farthings, Gran'maw," spoke up the sheriff, a trace of awe in his voice. "I'm the sheriff; you're resisting the law. We must search the house."

"Have you got a search-warrant?" she asked shrilly.

"Why, no-o." The demand paused him.

"Then, if you come in here, you break the law." The sheriff hesitated a moment and then turned back.

"Danged if I know whether it's necessary or not," he muttered. "Where's Squire Hartswick? He's a justice; he can make one right here. Where are yeh, Squire?" The old man, who had been left hopelessly behind in the race, came puffing up, his face like a plum pudding. A sheet of paper was improvised from an old envelope, and the Squire proceeded to execute the warrant in due form.

"Here—look ahere wunst, you-uns take my advice," chattered Lem Fisher. "You get out of here jest as quick 's you can. The devil's in this business. See her? See there! My God, men, she's weavin' a brauch over us a'ready. God A'mighty, look at that wunst. I'm goin' home. Come on, Ulie. I ain't called on to fight the devil." He turned square about and crept away down the pike. Ulie and several others followed him. The old woman, still standing in the door, was swinging slowly from side to side, her eyes fixed on the far distance, and muttering incoherently under her breath.

"All ready, come on, fellers." The sheriff and the young men from Sugar Valley advanced hesitatingly toward the house. It was plain that they did not relish their job, but *noblesse oblige*. Were they not the sheriff and his sworn deputies? The eyes of the county were upon them.

"We've got the warrant, Gran'maw," he said in velvet tones. She turned squarely about and hobbled out of sight.

"Come on, Squire, I want you to go in with us."

"No,—no. I'm too hot and tired. You'll make it all right alone."

He took a seat on a stone at the rear of the group. The seven turned and went into the house without another word. A sort of sigh, like the drawing in of the breath by the crowd before the fall of the fatal drop, went up. Every atom of the mob spirit had oozed out. Not a man but felt like sneaking home.

"Last we'll ever see of them," shuddered a voice.

"Gee! I wouldn't go in there for ten farms."

"It's devil's business; I'm goin' home," said another.

Then for what seemed like hours and days there was silence,—awful and complete save for the gibbering of the water in the gut almost at their feet. The gloom of the uncanny hole was falling heavier and heavier on their spirits. Most of them were looking about furtively at the black shadows that were beginning to creep under the cedars, at the hideous caricature faces leering from the limestone jags, and at the black barrier of the ridge behind which the sun had already disappeared. Few there had ever before seen the place by day. They breathed a real sigh of relief when the form of the sheriff appeared at the door.

"They can't be found," he said in a queer tone.

A murmur of superstitious horror broke from the crowd. Many, looking neither to the right nor the left, sneaked out to the pike and crept home in twos and threes, scarcely speaking all the way, but each thinking hard the same thought. The sheriff and the Sugar Valley men went again into the Run, and searched for an hour amid the gathering darkness. Then they too went down the pike without a word. There was nothing to say.

The Farthings had disappeared as if the earth had swallowed them up, and of all places in the world, in the black mouth of Roaring Run.

## CHAPTER XVII

## THE HOUR OF THE POWERS OF DARKNESS

THE NIGHT FOLLOWING the day on which the Farthings disappeared stands as the blackest in the valley annals. Few who have not passed their childhood amid the dark whisperings of witchcraft and the evil eye and of unseen presences which lurk to do evil, can imagine the terror that fell upon many throughout the region after the event at Roaring Run. The group that met at twilight at Squire Hartswick's store was small but select. The sheriff and the Sugar Valley deputies, who were to spend the night at Hartswick Hall, were sitting glum and surly on boxes about the door. The Squire was in a chair in the doorway, silent and moody, smoking his corn-cob; Lem Fisher, to whom the world presented as many devils as ever it did to old Cotton Mather, was centre and spokesman, warmly seconded by Ulie Dribelbis and old Jake Kisterbock.

The powers of darkness were having their hour.

"Do you-uns s'pose one minute that three grown men could hide themselves in the rocks of that little hole so that a hundred couldn't find 'em? Heigh? Is that reasonable wunst? They couldn't get out of there; you know that. Abner Moritz was right clost to 'em still and he knows they didn't go down the Run. I tell you a haexer like Farthing don't get ketched less he wants to. Nosuh."

"What did he run for?" asked Amos quietly. "Why didn't he stand jest where he was peeling bark and haex the whole gang? What was the use of running himself half to death? Why didn't he jest drop out of sight in his tracks and save all the hard work of runnin' over the ridge?"

"Huh! That's all a Yankee knows. W'y that's clearer 'n mud still. He run 'cause he didn't have nothing to haex with. A haexer has to have tools jest as much as a blacksmith. They must have locks of hair, and pieces of Bibles, and keys, and blood, and what not. Now can't you see it? If it had been you or we, wouldn't we have struck for the Wild Medders instead of goin' it for a man-trap like the Run? I tell yeh he was strikin' for Gran'maw Miller. While you-uns was a-foolin' round she had time enough to hide a nation."

"Yas, and why did she stop you off at the door and make yeh get a warrant?" broke in Ulie. "Wal, I'll tell yeh why." He closed one eye and nodded his head knowingly. "She had to have time to work her spell. Did you see her weavin' that brauch? I tell you-uns if we knew the bottom of this business we'd be scairt. Something awful's comin'. We don't know who's turn it is next, but it's one of us."

"Yessuh, he's right." Lem Fisher took up the argument with unction. "That brauch meant death. I've saw it twicet in my life a'ready and what's twicet is thricet. There's goin' to be an awful death in this walley until twenty-four hours still. You-uns take notice of what I say."

An awed silence fell over the group. At length old Jake Kisterbock spoke with faltering voice.

"Let me tell you-uns somesing wunst. When I got hum this afternoon, my woman comes to the door with a face like a dish-clout still, and she sayes, sayes she, almost yammerin', 'Come in here wunst.' Then she takes me into the bedroom and sayes she, 'Keep still wunst.' It was still as the grave. And then—oh my Lord!" He leaned far over the group, his eyes glittering like a child's. "The death watch was tickin' there in the wall. 'Tick-tick-tick-tick-tick,' right by the headboard. 'It's death,' sayes the woman, fallin' over on the bed and cryin' like as if the life was goin' out of her still, 'It's death, death, death.' Yessuh, I've heard it before, and it always brings death in this walley until twenty-four hours."

"I don't want to scare yeh, Squire." Lem Fisher spoke deferentially. "But the signs do pint at you."

"Humph," he grunted.

"Recollect that apple-tree that blowed late last fall in your yard? Recollect how the pee-wee flew into the store here? Recollect how, down to Karl's funeral, the wagon clipped right in ahead of yeh in the procession? Then what have I told yeh about these Farthings? You go this werry night, Squire, and do what I told yeh. It may be too late now."

He made no answer.

"Say, Lem," spoke up Amos, "if Al Farthing can do all you claim he can, then why's he workin' every day on that old farm?"

"Oh, his farmin' is jest a blind. I'll bet he's gut money like water in the creek. Now if there ain't no haexin' about this, where *did* the Farthings go? You tell me that."

"I ain't explainin' jest yet, but there's an explanation all the same, and it's comin' out. Al and his boys are pretty wide-awake chaps; they've hunted all over these ridges and they know every square rod. They knew how to get through the Run, that's all. You fellers was so excited you didn't know what you *was* doin'. You can't come any of your miserable witchcraft on me."

"If the Farthings was innocent, why did they run?"

"They showed horse sense by runnin'. When a crazy, hot-headed crowd of lunatics gets after yeh, run I say, for dear life, and do your explainin' next week."

"An innocent man don't run, I'll tell you that," said the Squire sullenly. "How are you going to account for that stuff in his barn?"

"I ain't going to give my verdict till the evidence is all in. But there's a good deal to be cleared up yet 'fore I'm satisfied, I'll tell you that. Say, Mr. Sheriff." He turned about suddenly and faced the man. "What are you goin' to do to-morrow? How are you plannin' to ketch 'em? Gut a watch set round their house, I spose."

"Why, no; I hain't."

"Wal, now, that's kinder strange. Say, wouldn't it be sort o' natural for some on 'em to sneak back there to-night for somethin' to eat? What *are* yeh doin' to ketch 'em? All I can see is you are settin' right here listenin' to old women's stories about pow-wowin', while they're hustling out of the region lively,—that is if they want to."

"What can you do when men disappear into the air?" argued the sheriff.

"Say, that's a smart question for a sheriff of a county to ask, now ain't it,—a regular old woman's question. If they've disappeared, then it's your business to find 'em and not squat down here listenin' to witch stories. If you're that cut, you won't be elected next fall; I'll tell yeh that. We want a man for a sheriff, not an old woman."

"Perhaps you'll condescend to enlighten us just a little," answered the sheriff with withering sarcasm. "Perhaps you'll be gracious enough to do the county the favour of dropping a few offhand little hints as to what the officers ought to do in this case."

"Sure. No trouble at all," he answered serenely. "You left a guard round Roarin' Run, I 'spose? You are ready to swear, you say, that they didn't get out of there, so it stands to nature they must come out sometime. Got a right smart guard all around it, I 'spose."

"Why, no—."

"Went through the Run gap, I 'spose, and looked for tracks up and down the banks for half a mile?"

"What's the use?" he answered hotly. "They didn't go through that gap, and you know it. There hasn't been any tracks through that gap since the rain."

"Mmmm! So I hear. And you hain't got nobody up round the Farthing house? Pretty efficient sheriff we've got in this county. What have yeh been doin'? Consulting the authorities on pow-wowin'. I swann, I believe I'll run for sheriff myself next fall."

There was the sound of brisk footsteps; a large man was approaching rapidly.

It was Allen Farthing.

Lem Fisher started from his seat and stole into the back store as if the devil had come. The sheriff arose, but said nothing. All looked with hanging jaws as if the man held a cocked revolver in either hand.

"I understand, gentlemen," he began at once, "that you have been in search of me. I was over in the Wild Meadows until six o'clock. When I got home I learned about your visit and came down as soon as I could get away. Now, gentlemen, what can I do for you?"

"It's a lie!" The words came from the Squire in a smothered heap. "We've got a dozen men right here who saw you in the gap this afternoon, and saw you run over the ridge. That talk don't go here."

"I arrest you, sir, in the name of the law," said the sheriff theatrically. "Hold out your hands."

"There's no need of irons, Mr. Sheriff; I shall not resist or try to escape."

"Hold 'em out," he ordered sharply. The man obeyed without a word, and the sharp "click-click" was distinctly heard by all.

"Did I understand you to say that you was not with the boys this afternoon when they run over the ridge?" asked Amos, elbowing his way to the prisoner.

"No, suh, I was not. You scared my wife almost to death, but she had sand enough to follow the mob, and she said the boys and somebody else that looked to her to be a woman, ran down into Roaring Run and got through the gap. I don't know a thing more 'n that." The sheriff squirmed uneasily at the mention of the escape through the gap.

"What did the boys run for?" cross-examined Amos.

"I don't know more 'n you do. They probably got into a panic, and from what my wife says there was reason for it. They'll come back; they'll be here in time for the hearing. And here, Squire Hartswick, I demand a hearing to-morrow morning. And I wish somebody'd be kind enough to run up and stay with my wife. She's all alone and frightfully nerved up. Won't somebody do it?"

"I'll go," volunteered Amos quickly. "Glad to go. Don't you worry one mite, Mr. Farthing."

"I won't forget this, Amos," said the man feelingly. Amos arose and left the store.

"Got a place for him, Squire? I've got a guard." There was a business ring in the sheriff's voice.

"Yes; oh, yes. This way." The Squire bustled out into the darkness, followed by the sheriff and his prisoner. The men from Sugar Valley arose and fell in behind.

For a time there was silence among the little group huddled about the store door. Then the voice of Lem Fisher was heard from behind.

"I see it. It's clearer 'n mud now. Al Farthing wants to get into that house still. He's goin' to spend the night there. Jest you mind what comes of it. S'pose you can tie a haexer with handcuffs? Nosuh. The devil's in it. There'll be a dead body in that house against to-morrow still. You notice what I say."

It was fully ten o'clock when Amos finally started up the turnpike for the Farthing place. The summer night lay dark and sultry upon the valley. There was the threat of a thunderstorm; the heat lightning played in ghostly flickers across the south; and the clouds lay in snaky swaths, with here and there livid patches where the stars struggled feebly through. Save for the nervous notes of a whip-poor-will in the near meadow, and the steady drone of the waters in the Run, the night was silent.

Then Amos caught another sound, and straightened up to listen,—the sound of a horse and buggy approaching at furious rate. The horse was evidently speeding as on a race-track, and he was coming nearer every instant. Automatically Amos stepped into the ditch and held up his lantern. A moment and the wild whirl-wind was right upon him, then it was gone, and the hoof-beats and roaring wheels came fainter and fainter from the distance. It was dare-devil riding in a night like that. The lantern had showed him a single figure in the buggy, but whether a man or woman he could not tell. Who could it be plunging into the night in that mad fashion? Life indeed was becoming strenuous in the little valley.

He poked ahead again. As he came near to the Farthing place he caught the glint of a light in the yard, and made out a figure beside it,—a woman.

"Hello, there," he shouted reassuringly. "It's me, Amos Hard'n. Don't you go to work and get scairt."

"Oh, it's you, Amos?" Mrs. Farthing's voice. "I'm awful glad you've come. I'm worried 'most to death. Where's Allen? Is he all right?" She came close and looked into his face.

"Snug's a bug," he explained jovially. "They up and arrested him, but he's jest as safe as I em,—jest exactly. Don't you worry about him." His cheery manner was reassuring.

"I can't understand it," she went on rapidly. "Jim came in jest a minute ago on the run after the colt. He said he was going to Gum Stump after Doctor Kuack. He said Tom was all right, but I must go quick as I could down to Miller's, for Loney was jest alive. Then he hitched up the colt and drove off the next minute."

"Sho! What 'spose he meant? Say, I'd better harness right up, hadn't I?"

"Yes, I think you had. I'll run in and get my medicine box; I'll be ready when you are."

He bustled into the barn and in five minutes they were driving down the pike.

"I vau, M's. Farthing," he began. "This whole thing beats the Dutch, now, don't it?"

"What's it all about, Amos?" Her voice had a quiver in it. "It come so sudden. I can't think or straighten it out. Seems like some kind of a nightmare."

"Wal, I'll tell yeh, M's. Farthing; it's jest like this." Thereupon he detailed with fulness all that he knew of the matter from the first. Before he had finished, they were driving up the crazy road to Poppy Miller's house.

The door was open and a light was shining out. Then a voice, eager and anxious, came from the darkness:

"Is that you, mother?"

"Yes,—are you all right, Tom?"

"Oh, I'm glad you've come. Right in this way. Don't stop for anything." He almost lifted her bodily from the seat, and they rushed together into the house, closing the door behind them.

At once all was dark and silent. Amos sat for a moment gazing blankly at the place where they had vanished, then he swore softly.

"Wal—I'll—be—dumbuzzled!"

But nothing could long disconcert Amos. It was evident that Mrs. Farthing's stay was to be no short one; it was equally evident that nothing was required of him,—at least for the present. Accordingly he found a place for his horse, sought out a comfortable seat, and lighted his pipe. Thus fortified, he prepared for a long siege. Mosquitoes sang their shrill songs about him, a whip-poor-will came at length within a few feet of where he sat, so near that he could distinctly hear the "chuck" at the end of each bar of his score. The near Run filled the night with its drowsy monotone. Amos leaned against the side of the house, and then dozed off with his pipe still in his mouth.

He was awakened by a stealthy step very near him, but, though bewildered, he did not move or make a sound. A man crept silently through the yard, opened the back door of the kitchen, and passed in. That was not Tom's step nor Poppy Miller's. He listened intently and after a time heard the mumble of a voice within, but he could catch no syllable. There was something strange about the affair.

Perhaps he could peer in at a window, but the windows were not easy to locate in the old structure. Two he found after cautious reconnoitring, but they were closed and tightly blinded. Then he stole to the other side and found a window partly open. He lifted himself cautiously.

It was the window to what appeared to be the pantry. The apartment beyond seemed to be feebly lighted, as with a candle.

All was silent. Then, by listening hard, he heard a low sound as of some one muttering disjointedly, but he could make out no words. Suddenly sharp and clear rang out Squire Hartswick's voice. There was no mistaking it.

"But who put it on, I want to know?" There was both fear and anger in the tone. "Who was it? Did Al Farthing put it on?"

Again Amos heard nothing save the low monotone.

"Here, damn it! quit that! Look me in the eye, and stop that jabbering! You can't scare me, you blasted old witch, with any such rigmarole 's that. Speak up, or I'll put you where you belong. You mean Rose came here?"

The reply was audible now. It arose in a wailing tremolo, and it gathered force as it went on until it became almost a shriek.

"Ha, ha, ha! she comes here. She comes to see me. And shan't I help her when she loves the very air he breathes, when his eyes have looked at her and she can't sleep, when he'll have his revenge? Ha, ha, ha! Let him look to his daughter,—is she well? is she happy? is she fair now?"

"Here, quit it; do you mean Jim Farthing?"

"Ah, look,—look—see! The old man, her father,—let me count his hours. One, two, three, four—"

"Stop, you damned hag! stop!"

"Five,—six,—seven—oh, it's not long enough to be worth the counting—"

"What—"

"Then she'll marry *him*,—ha, ha, ha! she'll marry him, and they'll divide it up,—oh, it 'll be merry! All these years he's slaved for 'em and sold out his very soul for 'em. And she'll marry him.—See, those eyes, there's revenge in 'em. Ah, my God! Matthew Heller, you've got revenge."

"Stop!" thundered the old man, but at that moment there was a commotion in front. Amos turned automatically.

"Run right in, doctor; don't stop to rap." It was Jim's voice.

The kitchen door opened softly, and Squire Hartswick stole around the house and down the road, passing not six feet from the man under the window.

"Off after the sheriff, I'll bet yeh," mumbled Amos under his breath. Then he went out to interview Jim.

# CHAPTER XVIII

## IN THE HEART OF THE LIMESTONE

IT WAS TEN o'clock when Jim left the Farthing place with the colt; it was five minutes to one when he swung into Poppy Miller's yard, a record that has never been equalled even by daylight. The colt was streaming wet and dripping foam, and she was blowing heavily. Jim began upon her instantly, freeing her from the buggy and harness and rubbing her with vigour. It was at this moment that Amos appeared.

"Why, you here, Amos, at this time of night?"

"Yes; brought your mother down. But what ails Loney? I hain't seen a soul."

"She's shot. Here, grab right hold and help rub her down; she's about blown."

"Who shot her?"

"Don't know him." He was rubbing away for dear life.

"What do you mean, Jim? Say, what's this all about? Tell a feller, won't yeh?"

"There's a cave down there," jerking his head toward the Run. "Lona took us in there when the mob chased us."

"Naw. You're jokin'. There ain't no cave."

"Well, there is, and it's fixed so you couldn't find it in a year. Where's father?"

"Down to the Squire's; they've arrested him. But who shot her?"

"After we'd been in the cave an hour or two we heard somebody coming from the other end. Lona made us run, but we broke the lantern and they saw us."

"Who did?"

"Two fellers with a lantern, a big one and a little one. The big one swore when he saw us, and started to shoot Tom. Lona jumped for him and the pistol went off and hit her. Say, I'm going in to see what the doctor thinks." He bounded off into the darkness and Amos heard him open the door. After a moment he returned. "Doctor hain't said anything yet. Mother don't think there's much chance."

"What did you do when he shot?" Amos was getting his bearings slowly.

"I made a rush for him, and got the better of him after a while. Tom seemed kind of phased like. We tied the feller, though."

"Sho! And where is he now?"

"Tied in the horse-stall there." He jerked his hand toward the old barn.

"Jimminy! you mean to say he's there now? By gum, le's go and see the critter."

"I can't leave the horse, but you can take the lantern."

"Wal now, I kinder guess I will. Sure he's tight?"

"He's got all the ropes on him there is about the place, and half the straps in the harness."

Amos took the lantern and poked into the barn cautiously. In an old stall, tied cruelly to the manger and the side rails so he could neither sit nor lie, stood a powerfully built man swathed like a mummy in ropes and straps. Amos raised his lantern and looked him over much as he would the man-eater in a circus.

"Say, for God's sake, Rube, can't you let up a little on some of these straps? My arms are all dead."

"Wal naow, I 'spose I could." He continued his examination, cocking the lantern this way and that critically.

"Here, loosen this rope on the right, won't yeh? It's pulled tighter 'n hell. Say, won't yeh?"

"Wal naow, that depends." Amos continued his investigation like a judge at a county fair scoring the fat pig. The man had once been very good looking. He had a square, full face and a large moustache, but there were marks of dissipation in the eyes, and there were brutality and weakness about the mouth and jaw. His reddish hair was rumpled, giving him a desperate look.

"Look here, Rube." He lowered his voice confidentially, and spoke in an oily tone. "Want to earn five hundred?"

"Five hundred what?"

"Plunkers—greenbacks—dollars. Five hundred dollars."

"You bet I do. I'd stand on my head in a tar berrel for half the money."

"Then here's your chance. You ease up on the ropes here so I can get 'em off, and I'll pay you five hundred dollars."

"Give me your note, or send a registered letter?"

"No, the money's in your hands, every dollar of it, before you untie a single rope."

"Sho! Then you must have it in your pocket. Guess, seein' you are pretty well tied, I'll sorter help myself. It's hard work to untie knots." He climbed over the rail into the stall and put down his lantern.

"Oh, I hain't got it with me."

"I kinder 'sposed you hadn't."

"But I can tell yeh where it's hid, not far from here."

"Pretty slick naow, ain't yeh?"

"Honest now, that's straight. There's five hundred, and it's yours the minute you untie these ropes."

"Say, mister, I'm green,—greener 'n ten car-loads of calves, but I ain't green clean through."

"Here, wait. I'll tell yeh what I'll do. You unhitch me so I can walk,—you needn't untie my hands, and I'll show you where it is. Then, when you've got it, you can untie me and I'll skip. See?"

"What sort of place is it hid in?"

"It's a cave, and not a great ways off."

"Is it cash? Legal tender? Greenbacks? Gold bricks?"

"It's part cash and part postage stamps, that's just as good. Come, quick now; untie these side ropes. Such chances don't come only once in a lifetime."

"Wal, naow, you kinder interest me, darned if you don't. Now you mention it I do need five hundred pretty bad, but I guess you'd better stay right here. I've heard tell about that cave, and I reckon I'll try it. I'm kinder 'fraid you'd ketch cold goin' in there with your hands tied." Amos climbed deliberately back over the rail.

"Say, I'll double it. Come on, Rube. You won't find it if you do go in there. Can't nobody but me find it."

"Oh, now don't worry. I'll find it all right. I'm awful good on findin' things; you hain't got no idea. Say, if one leg gets to achin' too bad, why you jest stand a while on the other." A spurt of curses came from the man, but Amos did not pause.

There was no one in sight.

He took up the brush and began to rub again at the colt, but Jim appeared after a moment.

"How does she seem to be?"

"She ain't conscious yet. Not much hope."

"Say, le's you and me go into that cave. That feller in the barn says it's chuckfull of money and postage stamps."

"All right; we may catch that other man. Wait till I get that revolver."

At that instant a harsh voice rang suddenly out of the darkness behind them, causing both men to jump convulsively.

"Halt there! Throw up your hands. Up with 'em, or I'll shoot." Automatically they obeyed.

"Jim Farthing, I arrest you in the name of the law." The sheriff stepped quickly forward and slipped on the handcuffs. Then Squire Hartswick puffed into the circle of light.

"You here, Amos? With him? Why, what does this mean?"

"I come down with M's. Farthing, and I've found out some things sence I've been here, too. Here, sheriff, I demand an investigation right off." Amos pressed eagerly forward. "That was Loney Heller that run over the ridge with the boys. She hid 'em in a cave down here in the Run. There was some men in it, and they shot her."

"Cave? You're raving crazy, Amos." The Squire came near and looked curiously up into his face.

"It's God's truth. The doctor's in there now, and the one that shot Loney is here in the barn tied. If you don't believe it, you come and look at him." They followed him into the barn. The man stood sullen and defiant and made no reply to the sheriff's questions.

"That man tried to hire me. He offered me five hundred dollars in postage stamps if I'd let him go. He said it was hid in that cave."

"Cave?" snapped the Squire. "That don't go. I've lived here all my life, and I should have known if there was a cave."

"But we can prove it in two minutes, Squire Hartswick," broke in Jim eagerly. "It's only a few steps."

"Now that's fair," assented Amos. "Come on. I'm jest dyin' to see it."

"Nosuh, it's a trap."

"It ain't no such thing, Squire. Now you look ahere. That feller there is the one that's been doin' these robberies. You can see that by the looks of him. They have got a cave down there that we don't know anything about. I say it's nothing more 'n right that we take a look at it,—at the outside of it, if nothing more. Come on, sheriff."

"That's fair," assented the man. "There's no risk in doin' that. Come on, Squire. Now, Farthing, no monkey business. I've got a revolver here, and I'll plug you the minute there's foul play." The Squire hesitated a moment, then followed the trio into the Run.

Over Central Pennsylvania lies a blanket of limestone, five hundred and more feet thick. Imagine from the top of this a mighty layer lifted like a slice from a loaf, and behold a chaotic landscape of winding caverns sparkling with stalagmites, huge chambers frescoed in myriad colours,—a section of a sponge, a cut across an ant-hill.

Those born on the granites and the schists never overcome their wonder at the limestone. Its vagaries are ever new and astounding. Great streams burst out of the mountain gaps, wind awhile through the alluvial, then are sucked down suddenly by the maw of a sink-hole; again miles away they burst into the daylight, boiling springs with mighty rush of water sufficient to turn great mills. Farmers ploughing in the field sink out of sight in a twinkling, horses and all; a field as smooth as a floor, suddenly in an autumn flood springs a leak; there is a sink-hole in the centre, and by night there is a yawning gulf down which has disappeared the fertility of many square rods of tillage; great towns have no sewerage outlet, the whole torrent from countless sewers being discharged into some sink-hole. Sometimes a whole field, acres in extent, begins to settle. Down and down it goes until it has become a gulf with precipitous sides. In the famous Sinking Valley there is a plot twelve acres in extent, which began to sink in 1864, and to-day it is a chasm a quarter of a mile in depth. And still it is pulling gradually down acre after acre of the fertile land.

It is the country of the weathered and grotesque out-croppings, of thin soil,—a mere crust over the rock mass,—of sink-holes, and ice caves, and blind caverns,—millions of them unmeasured, unsuspected by man.

"Here we are," said Jim at length. "The mouth of the cave is in that rock heap." They threw the light of their lanterns into a jagged fissure lying low amid the tangle of juniper. "See that big stone? Give it a push on the left side."

Amos bent over and pushed the stone. It rolled back noiselessly, disclosing a black void.

"I swanny now! That's mighty neat, ain't it?" He looked up at the ring of faces. "A feller might hunt a week and not find that. Le's go in."

"Nosuh! It's a trap. Don't you go in there." The old man spoke decisively.

"It's a cave all right." Amos flashed the rays of the lantern far into the hole. "And it's where them robbers have made their head-quarters jest as sure as you stand there. Come on, sheriff; if you do your duty you'll go in."

"Now I don't know," he said hesitatingly.

"Wal, I'm goin' in whether or no, and I'm goin' to run for sheriff next fall. Here, give me your revolver."

"All right, we'll go in. Amos, you go ahead; Jim, you go next, and remember I've got my revolver right in my fist. At the very first sign of monkey business I'll shoot yeh as quick as I would a rattler. Squire, you come on behind with your lantern."

"Nosuh. You don't catch me in there," he snapped, but Amos was already out of sight. Jim, impeded greatly by the manacles, was following closely. Then the sheriff crept into the narrow opening and the Squire stood alone. All was silent save for the waters of the Run, which gibbered and hissed at his feet. He stood a moment undecided; then he too crawled in.

The place was damp and narrow at first and so low in places that they had to bend almost double, but all at once they emerged into a chamber as broad and high, judging from what they could see in the dim light, as a barn. The roof seemed to be made up of innumerable points like icicles, wet and gleaming, some a brilliant yellow, others dull and lustreless. The floor was jagged and irregular, made up of blunted stalagmites and broken fragments from the roof. The walls near them glistened under the light of the lanterns as if freshly smeared with paint. Amos was the first to break the silence:

"Wal—I'll—be—dumbuzzled!"

"Lona took us to this room," explained Jim, gesticulating with his head. "See, there's the remains of our lantern; she found it at the entrance and took it in. We sat on those rocks right there, and she seemed nervous and excited. She made us keep as still as death, and every little while she would say, 'Hark!' and listen as if she expected to hear something awful. She went out to the entrance two or three times, and she came back saying we couldn't go out just yet, but that we must go the very first minute we could. After a long while we heard a noise way off in that direction. She jumped up as if the roof was coming down, and told us to run out for our lives. We started, and Tom smashed the lantern against that rock there. We tried to get out, but lost the direction, and while we were trying to find it, two men with a lantern came right round that rock there."

"Was there two of them?" asked the sheriff.

"Yes; the one up there in the barn and a little black-haired one. Tom stood right there, and Lona stood there. The minute the big one saw them he stopped short a minute and started as if he was going to run, then he began to swear. He pulled out his revolver and said he would shoot Tom like a snake and me too. Then Lona made a dart for him and tried to get the revolver and it went off. I made a leap for him and landed him right there on that flat place. The little feller stooped over Lona a minute and then run."

"He's in here now, then?" exclaimed the sheriff, getting excited. "Let's see what's in beyond there."

He cocked his revolver, and they pushed on cautiously, pausing now and then to listen. There was no sound save the slow dripping of water somewhere off in the darkness, echoing in the hollow void like blows on a tun. The passage grew larger. At length they came out into another chamber somewhat broader than the other. At one side of it there seemed to be a door in the solid rock.

They investigated closely. A branch of the cave had been walled up at some time with stones and mortar, and a narrow door made of two solid oak logs hewn smooth was fitted into the wall as if a part of it. It was evidently locked: for there was a large key-hole. They kicked on it and pounded on it with stones, but it was like pounding on the side of the rock.

"We'll let this go for a while," said the sheriff decisively. "Let's see what else there is." Again they pressed on and on through the narrow passages. Then they came apparently to the end. Another doorway it was, but this one yielded easily, and they found themselves in a spacious room with boarded walls and floor, and a confusion of roughly made furniture. A ladder at one end disappeared into the darkness of the roof. There were cupboards and closets, a bed and tables and chairs.

The nature of the place was evident at a glance. They were in the home of the robbers: there could be no doubt of it. Blankets, clothes, shoes, canned goods,—everything that had been taken during the winter lay scattered about the room. Amos bustled here and there, feverishly opening cupboard and box, and dragging out their contents, while the sheriff identified them.

"Yessuh; there's the very blanket they took down to Snyder's, and there's the fur overcoat they got at Heisler's." It was impossible to identify the canned goods, but canned goods had been taken at nearly every place entered. Amos at length pulled out a drawer in an old, homemade dresser.

"Look here," he cried, holding up a dingy book.

"Here, let me see it." The sheriff sprang toward him excitedly. "My God, that's the Keichline stamp book. How's this? There wan't two."

"Let me see it," asked the old man grimly.

"It's the same book. See there, and there."

"Humph!"

"There's something strange about this. I'll take that right along with me. The stamps are still in it."

"Here, look here, sheriff." Amos's voice came from high above them.

"Where are yeh, Amos?"

"Up the ladder. Come up, quick, for God's sake."

"Here, Squire, you keep your eye on Jim. I'm going up." He disappeared up the ladder as if on an errand of mercy.

"Where are you, Amos?"

"Here." He looked up and saw the excited face of the man peering down at him through a round hole the size of a barrel-head. "Come up through, sheriff." In a moment they stood together in what seemed to be a cellar. A round lid was standing up, hinged at one part like the cover of a coffee-pot.

"Say, the whole thing's clearer 'n daylight. Look here." He closed the lid, which fitted with utmost nicety. The top of it was of the same composition as the earth floor. Without the most careful inspection one might not tell there was any opening.

"I've been here before. This is the cellar of the old Heller house. The whole thing's clear 's mud, as Lem sez. The gang's been here all winter, and of course there needn't be any track in the snow. Here's where they went the night Dan and I chased 'em. I 'spose they had to do their cookin' up there on account of the smoke. Pshaw, it's easy, ain't it? The reason why snow don't lay around the house is on account of the warm air that comes up from the cave. My senses, won't I knock out Lem's pow-wowin'? Come, le's down 'n tell the Squire."

They found him wrathful and excited.

"He tried to kill me," he cried. "If he hadn't had his hands tied he'd have murdered me, sure."

"You see that stamp book?" Jim was standing by the table, the book before him. "The minute you got out of sight the Squire took out his knife and begun to scrape off some of the marks. I stopped him, that's all. Lona said you found that stamp book in our barn, and I don't want this one altered."

"It's a lie," shouted the old man. "He tried to kill me."

"Wal, Amos, you take charge of it now, and you be careful of it. It's a valuable find." There was a business ring in the sheriff's voice. "Come on. We'll go back now." They started out together through the winding passages, the sheriff explaining to the Squire what they had found at the end of the ladder.

"That clears the whole thing up then." He stopped suddenly and faced them with animation. "Al Farthing knew all about this, of course. He had these two old partners of his in there, and could sneak in and out just as he wanted to. You remember, Amos, how he slipped in onto you and Dan that night in April. Clear enough now you see it, ain't it?"

The others made no reply. They wound silently out through the marvels of the cavern, out into the dark warm of the summer night. There was no hint as yet of light in the east. All was silent save the boom of the Run, and the sighing of a little breeze in the rhododendrons and cedars.

## CHAPTER XIX

## THE LAST OF THE HARTSWICKS

IT SEEMS TO be a rule of nature that like shall seek like, and that they shall move together in swarms. Hence a variety of proverbs: "Birds of a feather," and "It never rains but it pours," and "Misfortunes never come singly." Life drones on for a man's-age without jar or change, when, all unheralded, the break comes, and shocks and horrors crowd one upon the heels of the other.

Thus the little valley stagnating among the hills, with no change in a year save the weather and the season and the moon, all of a sudden crowded into twenty-four hours a lifetime of sensations. The robbery, the discoveries at the barn, the mob, the vanishing of the fugitives, the tragedy of Lona, the cave, the solution of the century-old Heller mystery, the strange captive,—all jammed into a matter of hours, and the end not yet.

Squire Hartswick, however, was not philosophising. His capacity was one idea at a time, and he drove the tragedy on with relentless precision. By daybreak he had Jim and the stranger safely imprisoned in the Hartswick mansion, and was driving arrangements by telephone for the preliminary hearing. It would of course be a mere matter of form, and soon over, and the sooner the better: for the prisoners must be safe in the county jail before night. But the justice before whom the hearing was to be held could not arrive before ten, and the Squire fretted and fumed.

By eight o'clock the space about the store was crowded as if for a farmers' picnic. Every available place for hitching, for rods up and down the road, was taken. The people were even scattering into the Hartswick grounds.

The morning, however, was eventless until shortly after nine, when a strange hush came over the multitude—a hush so instant and complete that those within the house noted it and looked out. Squire Hartswick even ran to the porch. An unfamiliar buggy was on the driveway, and the woman by the driver,—there could be no mistake,—was Rose Hartswick. The Squire rubbed his eyes, and fumbled for his spectacles. Then he bustled out to meet her.

"Why, Rose——"

"What does this crowd mean, father? Quick; what's happened?" She leaned far over in her eagerness.

"How did you get here? What are you here for?" he blurted out almost brutally.

"I came because I was needed. Now tell me what you're doing. Tell me." There was a dangerous light in her eyes.

"Go to your room, Rose. I'll see you there." He turned abruptly and started toward the barn.

"Father!" she called commandingly, but he did not stop or turn. Then she saw her mother's face at a window, and ran quickly up the path.

"Rosie,—why, Rosie!"

"Tell me, mother, what is it? What's happened?"

"The sheriff's here, and they are going to have a trial."

"What for?"

"Somebody broke into the store, and they've arrested Jim Farthing and his father."

"What proof have they got?" She was fairly shaking in her excitement.

"They found the goods in Mr. Farthing's barn."

"The goods stolen from father's store?"

"Yes; and they found Karl's stamp book there, too."

"Where's the sheriff? I must see him this instant."

"He's in the dining-room,—but, Rose." But she had disappeared into the dining-room where the sheriff was making preparations for the coming trial.

"Are you the sheriff, sir?"

"I have that honour, madam," he replied importantly.

"Then you'll allow me to attend the trial. I have important evidence."

"You'll have to speak to the judge, madam."

"All I ask is to be allowed to remain in the room; will you allow that?"

"All right; sit right here. We'll be ready in a minute." He placed a chair for her near the window.

There was a commotion in the front hall; the justice had arrived,—a florid, stout old gentleman, with a stern eye. Squire Hartswick, who was with him, stopped short when he saw Rose, then strode over to her angrily.

"This ain't no place for you," he whispered sharply. "There won't be only men here. Go to your room at once."

"I shall stay right where I am, father," she replied calmly.

"What?—what's that? Indeed, you won't stay here: I forbid it."

"You have no authority." She looked at him coolly, and settled back in her seat.

"We'll see about that. Here, sheriff, conduct this lady out where she belongs."

"I told her that she might stay here, and she may unless the judge orders differently."

"Squire Myers, are you going to allow women spectators in this court? I don't care to have my daughter here during the trial."

"I have important testimony, very important testimony," she said earnestly.

"Let her stay." The old man dropped into his seat with a look on his face of mingled wrath and apprehension.

The justice took his place at the head of the dining-room table, and arranged half a dozen sheep-bound volumes before him.

"Let the prisoners be brought in," he said.

There was a moment of silence, then the entrance of the sheriff, the three prisoners, and the six deputies. Jim, erect and alert, cast a curious glance about the room, and stopped short as his eye fell on Rose. A tide of colour leaped to his face, and ebbed as quickly, leaving it deathly pale. Rose gave no sign: she sat motionless and impassive. Then the group seated itself at the end of the table opposite the justice.

The trial, like all rural hearings, was to be an informal affair. The charge was to be brought against the prisoners, each was to have a chance to speak for himself, and then the justice was to bind them over to appear at the next term of court. He announced in due form the nature of the three cases. The first would be that of James Farthing, charged with breaking and entering the store of Squire Hartswick, and also of entering the post-office in Sugar Valley, and causing the death of Karl Keichline, the postmaster.

Squire Hartswick, as complainant, opened the case at some length. He began by establishing the motive. He told minutely the relations between the two men, dwelling particularly on the quarrel at Moon Run. His daughter, he averred, had planned to give Karl the final answer on the day which had followed the murder. This had been the immediate cause. Jim had been seen driving toward Sugar Valley on the night of the tragedy. A hammer with "A. F." burned into the handle had been found near the body. As to the testimony of his daughter at the time of the first arrest, it was unreasonable and fantastic. She was temporarily deranged mentally as a result of her narrow escape at the forest fire. He had with him the opinion in writing of an expert. Then he went over the details of the robbery of his own store. He passed to the justice the handkerchief with Jim's initials, and he described the findings in the Farthing barn. He produced Karl Keichline's stamp book, and identified it by the printed description. He touched upon the cave episode. The fact of a robbers' retreat under the very noses of the Farthings threw upon them suspicions of the darkest kind. When Amos and Dan Tressler had once late at night investigated the cabin, they had found Farthing there. The finding of the second stamp book was a mere coincidence. In 1886, when Eli Smith of Sugar Valley was the representative at Harrisburg, he had sent a copy of the Agricultural Report to every farmer in his district. It was doubtless the most widely distributed book in the locality. Nearly every household had one. Beyond a doubt many other postmasters had used it for stamp purposes. At one time he did himself. It was a mere coincidence, and could not in the least take away from the grave suspicions which the finding of two hiding-places for plunder on the Farthing property had created.

The Squire took his seat with the air of one who has proved his case. James Farthing was called and sworn.

He arose cool and alert, and he told his story in a convincing manner. He knew nothing of any of the robberies. He did not even know that the Squire's store had been robbed, until after his flight over the ridge. As to the goods in the barn, he could not even guess how they came there. That was not his handkerchief; he had never had one like it. All of his linen was marked with an indelible stencil, and he showed the mark on the handkerchief which he had in his pocket. He told graphically the events of the preceding afternoon, the flight into the cave, the shooting of Lona, and the exploration of the cave later in the night. As to the murder of Karl Keichline, he was miles away at the time it occurred.

"Where was yeh?" cross-examined the Squire.

"I rode down Gum Run."

"How far did you go?"

"To Gum Stump."

"What time were you there?"

"At eleven o'clock."

"Can you prove it? Did any one see you?"

"Yes, sir."

"Who?"

"I'd rather not say."

"You have witnesses, and yet when it might save you from the gallows, you refuse to tell who they are?"

"Yes."

"Do you mean Rose?"

"She was with me."

"And you have other witnesses, and refuse to give their names?"

"Yes."

"You will note this fact, your honour. We have nothing but his bare statement. If he had witnesses, wouldn't he produce them? I have no further questions."

"Your honour, may I be called at this point?" asked Rose with a quiver of nervousness in her voice.

"Have you important testimony on the point at issue?"

"I have."

"Let her be called. You may testify, madam."

"Your honour, I object." The Squire was on his feet instantly. "I have with me expert opinion—here, look at this—that says she is not in a mental condition to testify. She must have run away. I gave express orders for her to be carefully guarded."

"But, your honour, I have with me certain documentary evidence of great importance."

"You may present it."

She arose and advanced to the table with firm step. She was pale, but there was that in her eyes which warned all who knew her that something unusual was coming. She was looking straight at her father, as if he alone were the court. She held a paper in her hand.

"Mr. Farthing has told the truth. I was with him at Gum Stump at eleven o'clock, and we had witnesses. This certificate will show you that we were married by Preacher Gregg there at the parsonage on May 30th. If you send for him, he will testify as to the hour. This was the reason why Mr. Farthing refused to name his witnesses." She passed the slip not to the justice, but to her father. A silence as of death was in the room.

"You married him?" he gasped.

"Yes, I did. I hated Karl Keichline; I tolerated him at first just because your heart was set on it. But I couldn't marry him, I found that out; I couldn't drive myself to do it. And I had got to give him his answer on the first of June. If I said *no,* I knew what would happen. You wouldn't rest night or day until you had ruined Jim completely, and you had the power to do it. Then you would have forced me to marry Karl. There was only one hope, and we took it. I thought that after he was actually my husband you would forgive us. I should have told that day at the store, but you withdrew all your charges. Then you hurried me away to Pittsburg, but Amos telegraphed me."

"Amos telegraphed?" he repeated, as if his mind had refused to act.

"Yes, I got a telegram from Amos yesterday at five o'clock, saying, 'Come instantly.' I don't know how I got away, but I did, and I caught the last train and rode all night."

"What about that admission you made at the store that day, Miss Hartswick," spoke up the sheriff. "You virtually admitted that you knew something about the murder."

"Why—why—I'll tell you." It was evident instantly that he had found a weak point. For the first time she seemed to lose her self-possession. She composed herself, however, after a moment. "It was like this. I went down to Gran'maw Miller's, and she frightened me. She said somebody 'd die,—and it was because I went there. It came out just as she said. But, oh, I told her not to."

"Oh, pshaw!" ejaculated Amos from the doorway.

"Your honour," spoke up the Squire suddenly, "I withdraw all my charges. Let the prisoner go."

"I'm judge here," answered the officer sternly. "I'll make my ruling at the end of the trial. Let the next prisoner be called." The sheriff tapped the man on his shoulder, and he arose sullenly.

"What's your name?"

"John Clinca."

"John Clinca, hold up your hand and be sworn." The fellow obeyed slowly.

"Do you plead guilty or not guilty?"

"I don't plead."

"Mr. Clinca, you're in a bad position. There is evidence to incriminate you not only in robbery, but also in murder. The question with you is only concerning the degree. Who was associated with you? If you make a clean breast of it, it will not in any way harm your case."

"If I turn State's evidence, will it clear me?" he asked, looking up for the first time.

"It will not harm your case, to say the least. I advise you to do it."

"The man that helped do these breaks was Leon Heller."

"Leon Heller?"

"Loney's brother."

"Did you make the break at Keichline's? Of course you did, or that stamp book would not have been found among your effects."

"Your honour, I object." The Squire partially arose, but the justice did not notice him.

"I say you have no hope of trying to escape this charge; you made that break, isn't that true?"

"Yes," he admitted sullenly.

"Did you kill Karl Keichline?"

"It was in self-defence." He spoke eagerly. "He had Leon down, and was chokin' the life out of him. I tried to yank him off, but I couldn't break his hold. Leon was chokin', and I grabbed that pipe and swatted him. I didn't try to kill him, so help me, I didn't, and I didn't know I had till next day. He so near finished Leon that I had to carry him all the way home."

"Did you break into Squire Hartswick's?"

"No."

"Have either of these prisoners here associated with you?"

"No."

"Do you recognise this book?"

"Yes; it's the one we got at Keichline's."

"Sure?" The prisoner examined it attentively.

"Yes."

"Your honour," spoke up Amos, "here's the book we found in the cave. The sheriff gave it to me last night to take care of." He handed it to the judge, who passed it to the prisoner.

"Are you sure *this* ain't the book?" the judge asked.

"I can't tell 'em apart. They look jest alike."

"Your honour," interposed Amos again, "Karl Keichline's clerk is outside. I ask that he be called to identify the book."

"Bring him in," commanded the judge. The sheriff went out, and came in immediately with a nervous young man who was duly sworn.

"Here are two books. Will you tell the court which of them is Karl Keichline's stamp book?" The young man picked up one of them instantly.

"That's the one," he said with decision.

"How do you know?"

"I used it every day for years; I know by the looks of it."

"It's the book found in the barn," announced the Squire.

"Nosuh, it's not," retorted Amos; "it's the other."

"You've got 'em mixed up; you can't tell now which is which," he sneered.

"Your honour," spoke up Jim deferentially, "I haven't examined the book found in the barn, but the one found in the cave has a knife-cut on the back, where the Squire tried to mutilate it last night when I stopped him."

"Here—here; I object," thundered the Squire.

"Yas," interposed Amos with a drawl, "and if you turn to page 186, you'll find a little piece of paper with some of my writin' on it. I kinder thought they might get mixed up."

"Then the book found in the cave is the genuine one," announced the judge decisively.

"Say, your honour, may I speak?" pleaded Amos.

"If you have any evidence bearing on this case."

"Wal, now, I ain't very much on stickin' my nose into other people's swill berrels. I've allus cal'lated it was a man's first duty to mind his own business, but it sometimes takes judgment to tell when you're mindin' it. I'm willin' the Squire here should fight the Farthings here till there ain't anything left of arry one of 'em but yeller fuzz. I sorter like to see a good fight goin' on, but if folks, cats, or roosters fight before me, they've got to fight fair. I won't stand round with my hands in my pockets, and see a man licked with a foul hold. Now it looks amazingly to me as if the Squire broke into his own store, and hid the goods there in the barn himself, and doctored up that book so as to get Jim here convicted of murder."

"Here,—here, Judge, I protest," broke in the old man excitedly. "That ain't evidence. That's personal spite. I protest." He sat down, his face fairly purple; his hands working convulsively.

"You're out of order; you'll be seated, Amos," ordered the judge sternly. "Allen Farthing will arise and be sworn."

The man arose calmly and took the oath, the Squire eyeing him all the time like a cornered lynx. The old man was labouring under high excitement; the veins in his face stood out like purple cords.

"I know nothing about this business," the man began in clear tones. "I've had no connection with it whatsoever. I've already proven to the Squire's satisfaction an alibi for myself and Tom, and now an alibi has been proven for Jim. We, therefore, are concerned in no way with the Keichline murder. Moreover, this man here confesses that he did it himself. An alleged robbery is committed in the Squire's store. He bases his suspicions on the finding of a handkerchief that we can easily prove never belonged to any of us. He leads the sheriff to the hay-mow in my barn, and uncovers the goods and the Keichline stamp book. If that's the genuine stamp book, then the same parties that stole the book stole the goods, but, remember, we are free from all connection with the Keichline business. The true stamp book is found in the cave, and there can be but one conclusion: the book found in my barn is a counterfeit, made deliberately to throw suspicion onto me and my boys. I do not lock my barn at night, and it could easily have been put into my hay-mow by any one who had wished to do so.

"Now, what's the motive? You all know that the Squire has hated me all winter, because I opposed him honestly in trade. I can call witnesses by the score who could tell how he has tried to throw suspicion on me and rob me of my good name. I heard him say myself that he would ruin me if it took every cent of his property to do it. I came into this valley a year ago with only one thought, and that was to settle down and pass a peaceful and helpful old age. And I'm going to tell you just why I came. I was born in this valley. You have heard of me, some of you. I left the valley because of Ira Hartswick here. He was jealous of me because I took the lead of the boys. He insulted me, and I thrashed him, as he deserved. Instead of taking his licking like a man, he went home blubbering, and lied to his father. The old man swore he would prosecute me for assault and battery with intent to kill. He sent for the sheriff, and I knew what was coming. You all know, and I say it fearlessly in the man's very house, that no jury in this region would have dared to bring in a verdict against the will of old Hiram

Hartswick. I was young and inexperienced, and I ran away. I enlisted in the army, was wounded at Gettysburg, and the papers got it that I was dead. I did not correct the report. After three months in the hospital, I was honourably discharged. Then I drifted to Paoli, and, wishing to cut myself off wholly from my past, I called myself Allen Farthing. That's the English for the German Heller. I didn't change my name, I simply translated it into English, just as the Zimmermans over in Sugar Valley have changed their name to Carpenter. I lived in Paoli till I saw the old farm advertised for sale in a Philadelphia paper. Then a longing to get back to the old valley to spend my last days came over me. I have always dreamed about the old place, and pined for it, and the temptation was overpowering. I bought it, as you all know, and I said nothing of my past simply to avoid unpleasantness. I'm a man of peace, and I knew that, if once Ira Hartswick recognised me, peace would be impossible. But it seems that even then I was not to escape trouble. The Squire has persecuted me every minute since I have been here, and now he has tried to hang me and my boys. He might have done a good deal to me without my retorting, but when anybody touches my boys, I fight. He's gone one step too far. Now I'll see him to the end of this business, if there's any law in this State to cover this crime. There's been enough evidence brought in here this morning to prison the man. He knows that. He's in a corner of his own making, and I'll see to it that he don't get out easily."

"It's all a lie," roared the Squire, fairly shaking in his wrath. "It's a miserable trick, the whole of it. You know that ain't Al Heller. He's dead, and I can prove it. It's a trick, and a thin one. It won't work."

"Al Heller is not dead," said Farthing, looking him straight in the eye. "Recognise that watch? Recollect that picture in the back? Remember any little story connected with that picture? Remember what I said to you when you tried to get that picture and didn't? Remember what you called my father and my grandfather, and what I did to you for it? Oh, no, Al Heller isn't dead. If he is, then this is his ghost." There was an awkward pause, during which all eyes were fixed on the old man.

"Squire Hartswick," said the judge solemnly, "what have you to say in view of the evidence against you that has been brought out here?"

"Father, you are not well." Rose sprang to her feet anxiously and went over to his side. "Don't, father, Let me get you some water."

"It's a lie from end to end," he gasped, rising to his feet. "It's all a miserable lie, got up by that Farthing to ruin me. But he can't do it. It won't work. I'll prove it yet that he killed him! I'll make him suffer——" His face was twitching violently. He took a step toward Farthing, then fell in a heap on the floor. Rose was by his side instantly.

"Water! Bring water!" she ordered. "Amos, quick! Get the pitcher from the sideboard there. Quick!" Amos seized the pitcher, and they sopped the water into his hair and face.

"Stand back. Give him air. Here, Jim. Amos, carry him in onto the bed. Be careful with him. When you get him in there, Amos, you telephone for Dr. Kuack just as quick as you can." Mrs. Hartswick came bustling in, the image of helplessness, but Rose set her to work instantly. In a moment she had the entire household at her command.

After the little procession had left the dining-room, there was a moment's hush. Then the judge spoke up sharply:

"Sheriff," he ordered, "let the Farthings free. I bind John Clinca over without bail to await the next term of court. The court is adjourned."

When the news flew out among the crowd, there was almost a panic. The horrors of the past few days had culminated. It was as if a bombshell had fallen into the little community, and had changed completely all of the old landmarks.

Squire Hartswick lingered on for three days, then passed away, never once regaining consciousness. The old king was dead, and a new king reigned in Hell Bottom.

# CHAPTER XX

## THE REVENGE OF MATTHEW HELLER

THE AUTUMN LANDSCAPE in the Seven Mountains is sombre rather than gay. There are few rock maples to furnish the vivid yellows and scarlets. Here and there a sassafras adds its splash of ochre, and a chestnut or a shell-bark varies the scene with its pale lemon, but the ruling tints are dull. The scrub-oak, which dominates every scene, turns late in the season to a russet brown, and then at length to a livid red and purple, as if the year had to force the tree to obey the season, and strangle it into submission. Late into the winter and even into the spring, the snags that twist themselves among the rocks cling with desperate grip to their old leaves, loath to disclose their deformity; and these yellowed and tattered rags give to the winter ridges an indescribably desolate and lifeless aspect.

But the Indian summer transfigures the mountains, and drives away for a time every trace of sombreness. The haze settles down like a veil over the ridges, concealing the sharp angles and ragged gaps and scrawny trees, until the ranges lie vague and dim, like summer clouds.

It was Sunday, the last day of October, and the flood-tide of the year. There was not a movement in the landscape; all was still as if the world were dead; even the voice of the Run, which so dominates the little valley, was lost in the haze.

"Beautiful! beautiful!" whispered Tom Farthing, looking down at the frail figure beside him. "Isn't it beautiful?"

"Yes, too beautiful to last." There was weakness in the voice. She was half reclining amid pillows, wan and wistful-eyed, but fairer than he had ever seen her before. He looked into her face and drove more softly.

"No, no, Lona," he pleaded, "don't say that. Please don't." Then they were silent again, while the great sun shone on them and the soft haze folded them into a little world where they two were alone,—utterly and forever, it seemed, in that golden light,—they two, and alone.

"Why, Tom, where are you taking me?" she asked suddenly, arousing herself and looking about her.

"Oh, I'm just letting the horse go."

"But, see,—the old cabin! He's taking us to the old cabin!" She looked up into his face as if in sudden alarm.

"And why not?"

"Tom,—please! Oh, you don't know—"

"But let's not go home now, Lona," he broke in pleadingly. "It's too beautiful. Let's go in; you can rest a long time before we start back. We can be all alone,—and it's so beautiful."

"But, Tom—"

"All ready." He had alighted and was standing by the wheel. "Come." He lifted her unresisting from the buggy, and carried her as if she were a child in to the old sofa.

"One moment; I'll get the pillows—There, you can rest now just as if you were in your own room. Can't you?"

"Yes; but, Tom—you don't know—"

"And I don't care," he burst out with passion in his voice. "Oh, Lona, I don't know anything, only that I love *you*." He knelt impulsively, so that he could look up into her eyes, and took both of her hands in his. "I wouldn't say it while you were sick; I couldn't; but you're better now, aren't you? and I may say it now, mayn't I?"

"Tom, I must tell you something—"

"No, no, don't," he pleaded.

"But I must,—I must,—and you'll hate me—"

"Lona!"

"It's my brother,—Leon—"

"Oh, is that all? That's nothing. I know all about that. It's just nothing at all."

"Wait!" She sat up suddenly among the pillows and looked into his eyes almost fiercely. "It *is* something, and you will hate me. Listen to this: I knew all winter they were in the cave; I knew all about the robberies, and the death of Karl Keichline."

"Ah!"

"I always knew Leon wasn't drowned. I've been away with him on the road—to the city. We're of gipsy blood; it came from Gran'maw." She poured out the words impetuously, as if eager to tell the worst. "Leon fell in with Clinca, and—and they got into trouble. They had to run for their lives. I knew they were in the cave,—I knew it all the time,—and, oh, you'll hate me!"

"Lona,—you're ill,—don't tell any more, please."

"He was my brother,—my twin, and he wasn't wicked,—only wild. It was Clinca,—he had him in his power. Oh, my God, how I hate him!" She was sitting bolt upright now. There was a dark flush of red in either cheek, almost ghastly as it burned in the pale olive. Her eyes glittered in their beady blackness.

"Lona,—please!"

"He said he loved me." The words came almost in gasps. "I couldn't avoid him. He said we must be married. He had me in his power. He said he would give up Leon or kill him if I wouldn't marry him. He told me so, and he could have done it."

"Why didn't you tell me, Lona? I told you I'd help you."

"I couldn't. He saw you that night. He swore if he saw us together again he would kill you in a minute and hide you in the cave. And he would have done it; he was capable of it; and not a soul would have known. I couldn't tell you. My father made me swear when he was dying that I would never tell the secret to any human soul. He told me the moment I betrayed it, Matthew Heller's fingers would clutch my throat. Oh!"

"And you told Clinca?"

"Never. It was Leon. Father told him when he did me. Hark! Oh, my God! What's that?—Matthew Heller!" A half-heard thud came up from below them. The girl was rigid, her eyes full of unspeakable fear.

"There's some one in the cellar," he announced after a tense moment.

"Oh, Tom—come—quick!" She made a movement as if to fly from the haunted house, but he held her in his arms. It was as if there was a shuddering presence in the room brooding over them almost threateningly.

"There's more than one," he murmured intensely, listening as if for some ghostly visitant. "There's a *woman* there. Ah!" Clear and distinct there came up through the floor a familiar intonation. There could be no mistaking it.

"Careful that old pot-lid don't swat yeh."

"Amos."

"Oh!" She fell back half in a faint from the sudden revulsion.

"You say this leads up to the kitchen?" It was Rose's voice. A moment later she opened the door.

"Why,—why, Loney! Is that you? You here? Why, Loney, you're pale 's a ghost.—Here, Jim, Amos,—Loney and Tom are here." The two appeared at the door simultaneously.

"By gummy, ain't this bright though after that darned hole!" Amos set down his lantern and looked about him blinkingly. "And so you're up here, are ye, Tommy? And Loney, too, by George! Good,—good enough! Say, old man, when's the happy day? You want to give me time to wash my neck and get a new pair of calf-skin boots."

"Uncle Amos!"

"I hain't said nothin'. All I said is that this is a happy day,—fine weather,—couldn't have better. Makes me feel jest like a boy. I vanny, if it wan't Sunday I'd dance ye a clog right on this old shanty floor. Tain't wicked to sing hymns though on Sunday is it? Wal, then, here she goes:

"Hooray fer Penn-sil-way-ne-ar wunst
Where folks is fat and cam;
Hooray fer scrapple, schnits, and krout,
Unt peegs what takes t'e pam.

Hooray! How's that fer Ike Watts? I tell you that beats the pomes of Lole and Scott's *Marmelade* all to ponhoss a'ready. Hein? But I've gut to hev more air; it's close in here. Hooray fer Pennslywania!—" He swung hilariously out at the door, and they heard his song far down among the scrub-oaks.

"It seems good to see you out again, Loney. This is your first ride, isn't it? Glad of it." Jim crossed over behind the sofa and took her hand cordially. Tom looked over at them with beaming face.

"Loney's doing fine," he cried. "Doctor isn't coming any more, unless he's sent for. He says she'll be well 's ever by Christmas."

"Oh, I'm not sick now." She looked up at the group about her with a wan, faint smile, but her eyes were near to tears. "You've all been good to me."

"You must come now to see Jim and me and you must stay a week. We insist upon it." Rose seated herself by the girl impulsively and took her hand.

"That's it," echoed Jim. "Mother Hartswick spoke of it only this morning."

"I'll be glad to come," she began feelingly, but at that moment the voice of Amos Harding rang suddenly in from the scrub-oaks.

"Heigh, folks, look o'here! Here's where you get your gen-u-wine happiness! Heigh, all come out and see the happy couple. Caught 'em right out on their honeymoon." He was leading in high glee Ulie and the late widow Kuhn.

"Come right in and see the folks. Don't be bashful. Here, people, salute the happy couple; salute the blushing bride."

"I hain't goin' in there still." At the edge of the black ring Ulie had halted suddenly. "We've gone fer enough, Amos."

"Oh, come on with yeh. There ain't no speerits in there now; I've pow-wowed and haexed 'em myself. Come on." He pulled them with a great show of force into the cabin. "Say, good-lookin' couple, ain't it? Honest now, did you ever see a handsomer one?" He stood off critically, his head on one side. "And it's all account of *me*. I tell you, folks, this is my masterpiece. M's. Dribelbis, you've got a good deal to thank me for."

"Oh, pshaw!" The bride snapped out the words with killing sarcasm.

"Wal now, you look o' here," continued Amos solemnly, "do you remember how wild Ulie was for one spell? Wal, suh, when he was right at the height of his craziness I took him and give him a little talk. 'Ulie,' sez I, fatherly like, 'you're blinder 'n a beat. Here you be a-runnin' hither and yon, like a hen with her head off, after this silly young thing and that silly young thing, and you've looked plum over the best lookin' and pertest young woman in these here valleys,' sez I."

"Oh, you git out," flirted the bride girlishly.

"Honest now. You jest ask Ulie here. Say, didn't I, Ulie? 'You take my advice, Ulie,' sez I. 'You play your trump cards on the widder Kuhn,' sez I. 'You don't stand much show; she's smarter 'n white lightnin' and she can hev the pick of the valley the minute she turns her hand over, but you try her,' sez I. 'It 'll take careful courtin',' sez I, 'and you may hev to ask her a dozen times, but you hang right to it. You've gut the bare ghost of a show,' sez I, 'but I'll tell you one thing on the square. If my beloved companion should suddenly be called up yonder, you wouldn't hev no more show than a snow-bird in tophet,' sez I."

"You're a soft old squash-head. Thar!" she snapped, simpering the while in spite of herself.

"Wal now, that ain't no joke neither; but then squashes ain't the worst things in this world. And there's others jest as bad. Say, Ulie, how's your pow-wowin'? Faith good? I'll tell yeh one thing, M's. Dribelbis, you're goin' to have the benefit of dretful good pow-wowin' down there. Dretful good. Ain't that right, Ulie?" The man squirmed uneasily.

"Well, everything ain't settled yet, not by a jugful a'ready," he snapped. He was nervous in his strange environment. He had been looking about him with curious eyes, and at times he stole cautious glances at Lona.

"Wal, what hain't for instance?"

"If he's Al Heller, then wan't he bo'nd and raised in this here old house wunst?"

"Sure!"

"Then didn't he know about the cave a'ready?"

"How about that, Loney?"

The girl on the sofa sat suddenly erect, her pallid face amid the intense hair making her look like some unreal creature in the grim old room. Ulie made a movement as if to escape.

"Here, hold right on!" Amos caught him by the coat and pulled him back. "I want you to hear Loney pow-wow jest a little mite. All right; let her go, Loney."

"There's nothing strange about this house." She faced them as if explaining the matter not alone to Ulie, but to all. "Matthew Heller was the first white man who ever came into this valley. It belonged to him. He came in the winter through the Gap. There was a strange bare spot in the snow, and he camped on it, and later made his log-house on it. When he dug his cellar, he found the cave, and when he had trouble with Mr. Hartswick he fixed up the two ends. He walled up one branch, and most of the family are buried there. That's our family secret."

"Hear that, Ulie?"

"Every one of us has had to swear not to betray it. The children were never told until they were sixteen, unless their parents died. That's why Uncle Allen never knew it. He left the valley before he was sixteen."

"Don't that answer ye, Ulie? By mighty, where does your pow-wowin' and haexin' come in now?"

"Wal, that don't explain everything, I'll tell ye that," snapped the man doggedly.

"Course it don't. Say, we couldn't get the pow-wowin' out of your Dutch skull if we opened it up and slathered it out with soft soap and water."

"Come, wife, we must be goin' a'ready." Ulie was clearly uneasy. He was watching Lona as if she might at any moment bring an infernal spell upon him. "Good-bye, folks." He was backing cautiously out into the sunlight.

"What's your rush? Wal, I don't know 's I blame yeh. Go it while you're young. It's a long time 'tween honeymoons."

The two disappeared, simpering and giggling, into the scrub-oaks.

"That's a strange story, Lona, fearfully strange." Rose drew nearer to the girl.

"And can you blame us? Every one who has borne the name of Heller has had to repeat that curse of the old settler, and the curse was never to be lifted until Matthew Heller had his revenge, until his lawful heir was king of the valley lands."

A hush fell over the little group. The intensity of the girl, and the strangeness of the place, awed and silenced them. A cloud covered the sun, bringing into the room a shadow that was almost like a personal presence. Even Amos felt it and was silent. Rose was the first to speak. She was crying softly.

"And he's had his revenge," she said brokenly. "He's had his revenge."

Again there was silence. It was as if the spirit of the grim old settler was enveloping them as with a smothering garment. The darkness increased visibly.

"But the curse is removed now, Lona." She looked up suddenly with bright eyes. "It was said that no Hartswick could ever enter this house and live, but I shall live. The curse is gone. Old Matthew Heller at last has his will.—Jim,—Oh, Jim!" She groped dizzily in his direction.

"What,—Rose! Are you ill?" He caught her in his arms.

"No, no. It's you, Jim; you are the king now,—king of the valley lands,—my king." She spoke the words almost in a whisper.

There was silence for ten heart-beats,—silence so intense that no one breathed. Then Jim spoke like a judge in the deathlike stillness pronouncing doom.

"And I shall share it with those of Matthew Heller's blood. We're together, Rose, at last; the two houses are together now. We'll keep the valley lands, you and I, but we'll give the store to Tom, won't we, Rose? It's yours, Tom,—and Lona's, if she will."

"Tom!"

"And you'll share it with me?"

"If I may," she whispered.

"If you may! My God! If you may!"

"Look,—look!" Lona was sitting bolt upright, an expression of wonder in her eyes.

"What is it, Lona?" they all asked together.

"See! The old deed." She pointed to a yellowed parchment nailed above the fireplace. The sun, suddenly free from the cloud, had darted a ray full upon it. The dark presence was gone; the room was radiant with light.

It was the old deed that gave to Matthew Heller and his heirs forever the whole of this valley bounded by the ridges and the gaps.

"And it's good again, Lona," Tom whispered softly. "The old curse is gone forever; the heirs of Matthew Heller at last have obtained their rights; and all because one little girl, standing all alone, did what her heart said was right."

And the ray of the Indian summer, increasing as the sun sank lower in the west, lighted up the old deed until it seemed printed in letters of gold.

THE END

# NOTES

For references in the original text that are unfamiliar or unknown to the contemporary reader, additional information in the form of explanatory endnotes is provided. Each of the notes is headed by a page-line number reference and the word or phrase from the text in italics.

## CHAPTER I

7:3 *Seven Mountains.* A range of mountains within the Pennsylvania stretches of Appalachia. The range divides Mifflin County on the south and Centre County on the north. Pennsylvania folklorist Henry Shoemaker (*Allegheny Episodes*, 290) counts Path Valley, Short, Bald, Thick Head, Sand, Shade, and Tussey Mountains as composing the Seven Mountains range. However, local author Jeffrey Frazier (*Pennsylvania Fireside Tales*, 3) disagrees and includes Sand Hole Ridge, Front Mountain, Spruce Mountain, Long Mountain, Broad Mountain, Sand Mountain, and Bald Mountain. A mountain range generally described as Seven Mountains is viewable from Route 322 between State College and Lewistown, near the Laurel Creek Reservoir.

7:7 *pantograph.* "An instrument for the mechanical copying of a plan, diagram, pattern, etc." (*OED*).

8:18 *better known on the local maps as Hell Bottom.* Exact locations in the text are fictitious. An undated newspaper editorial titled "Bellefonte and Centre County Becoming Famous in Literature" contained in the Fred Lewis Pattee Papers claims that Hell Bottom is actually Bear Meadows within the Rothrock State Forest (Fred Lewis Pattee Papers, 1821–1954). However, in his preface to the Penn State (second) edition, Pattee (*House*) writes: "There is no Hell Bottom among the Seven Mountains, and no Roaring Run,—at least no regions that go by those names."

8:20 *butchering day.* Butchering day was a major work-centered festivity on the Pennsylvania Dutch farm. Fires were started before daylight in preparation and the entire day was spent socializing and working.

8:22 *in the up.* The early Quaker author on the Pennsylvania Dutch, Phebe Earle Gibbons, details the "up-going" and "down-going" superstitions in her essays (Gibbons, *Pennsylvania Dutch*). The Pennsylvania Dutch placed an emphasis on the moon with regard to many activities on the farm. The moon was important for its position in the zodiac, its phases, and even its distinctive image in folk motifs (Winkler, "Pennsylvania German Astronomy"). A number of folkloristic beliefs are associated with the stages of the moon cycle. Generally, when the moon was increasing toward full, things grew better. When it was decreasing toward the new moon, things withered or were stunted in growth. As a result, crops were planted in the increase and fingernails cut in the decrease. The "up" and "down" of the moon refer to the position of the horns in the crescent moon, which was noted in the almanac. When the horns pointed down, the Pennsylvania Dutch put shingles on roofs and planted willow trees. In the up, they plowed soil to ensure that it stayed up and loose (Barrick, "Moon-Signs").

8:26 *Dutch.* The Pennsylvania Dutch are an American ethnic group; they immigrated to areas of southeastern Pennsylvania from southwestern Germany, Alsace, and Switzerland before the American Revolution. Two distinct groups among the Pennsylvania Dutch are the "church people," or "gay Dutch"—adherents to (predominantly) Lutheran and Reformed faiths—and the "sectarians," who are Amish and Mennonites. Some use the term "Pennsylvania German," which was applied later.

8:26 *Baer's almanac.* The almanac was an essential part of the Pennsylvania Dutch library. The almanac contained important information on weather, saints' days, and phases of the moon. It was a primary tool among the Pennsylvania Dutch to determine their actions in daily life—planting, butchering, cleaning, and the like (Yoder, "Almanac Album").

8:30 *schnittin'.* From the Pennsylvania Dutch *schneide,* "to cut." Similar to a butchering day, a schnittin' was a social and work frolic. The work centered on peeling and cutting apples. The cut pieces were then used for making apple butter. They may also have been dried and used in pies and *schnitz-un-gnepp* (schnitz [dried apples] and dumplings with ham). The schnitz were valuable to the Pennsylvania Dutch and occasionally used as payment (Yoder, "Schnitz").

9:4 *scalding-tubs.* One of the first steps in the butchering process is to cover the hog with resin or ashes and add boiling water to loosen the bristles and dirt (Dieffenbach, "Butchering Day"; Eaby, "Country Butcher").

9:5 *scraping-tables.* After the hog is covered with water in the scalding trough, scrapers and knives are used to remove the bristles from the skin (Dieffenbach, "Butchering Day"; Eaby, "Country Butcher").

9:22 *Bet yeh that's old Miff still.* The Pennsylvania Dutch speak a language derived from several German dialects, which leveled in colonial Pennsylvania. The language remains the first language of most Old Order Amish and Old Order Mennonites. Pennsylvania Dutch English often places adverbials like *still* in places that mainstream English does not (Huffines, "English"). Pattee flavored his dialogue throughout the text with examples of English influenced by Pennsylvania Dutch. Contemporary reviewers both lauded and despised his language efforts.

9:25 *wunst.* From the dialectal English *once.* Another example of stereotypical Pennsylvania Dutch English.

9:30 *warmus.* From the Pennsylvania Dutch *Wammes,* "work/warm jacket." In addition to Pennsylvania Dutch English, Pattee included words from the Pennsylvania Dutch language, which resulted from a dialectal leveling in colonial Pennsylvania among the European immigrants. It resembles German dialects spoken in the Palatinate.

9:36 *How gehts.* A bizarre combination developed to mean "how is it going," from both Pennsylvania Dutch and English.

10:22 *Pet day*. From Scots and Irish dialectal English, "a fine day in the midst of a spell of bad weather" (*DARE*).

11:1 *dretful*. From the English *dreadful*. An example of Pennsylvania Dutch English showing syllable final hardening. Instead of a voiced sound *d*, the Pennsylvania Dutch may devoice it as a *t*. This is a common feature of both Pennsylvania Dutch and standard German (Huffines, "English").

11:37 *wuts*. From the Pennsylvania Dutch *Wutz*, "pig."

12:11 *you-uns*. Second person plural marker in much of Central Pennsylvania (Yoder, "Discovery"). In some areas, this form is elided to *yinz*.

12:32 *tramps*. Tramps were a familiar sight in the Pennsylvania rural countryside. Tramps were homeless wanderers of many ethnic backgrounds. They were sometimes employed briefly on the farm, fed, and housed (Dieffenbach, "Tramps").

13:1 *yetst*. From the Pennsylvania Dutch *yetzt*, "now."

13:7 *Ira Hartswick*. Hartswick is a familiar name in State College, Pennsylvania, history. It is likely that Pattee took local names and incorporated them into his text. Today Hartswick Avenue is found in State College's historic College Heights neighborhood.

13:19 *inwited*. From the Pennsylvania Dutch English *invited*. Pattee exposes the stereotypical *v* and *w* confusion among the Pennsylvania Dutch (Huffines, "English").

13:23 *kreiseled*. From the Pennsylvania Dutch *gegreiselt*, "nauseated."

13:26 *I don't care a chincapin*. A chincapin is a small nut produced by the dwarf chestnut tree (*Castanea pumila*); the word can also refer to the tree itself. This phrase is not common usage, though perhaps means "I don't care much."

13:33 *awmnick*. From the Pennsylvania Dutch English *almanac*.

17:7 *swain*. "A country gallant or lover" (*OED*).

18:11 *overshot*. On a Pennsylvania Dutch barn, the typical structure had a bank at the rear leading to the threshing floor. The second floor extended beyond the first to provide protection to the animal stalls on the ground floor. This extension is called an "overshot" or, more commonly, a "forebay" (Ensminger, *Pennsylvania Barn*).

18:20 *red rag*. Something that infuriates.

20:34 *apple-butter*. Apple butter was the result of many schnittin' or schnitzing parties among the Pennsylvania Dutch. Fresh apple schnitz, along with spices, cider, and sugar, were cooked down into a thick brown mixture (Grim, "Old Fashioned Applebutter"; George, "Apple Butter"). Traditionally the cooks constantly stirred the mixture from afar with large stirrers.

20:35 *spreads*. Pennsylvania Dutch tables were known for the many types of accompaniments that were spread on pieces of bread. Local color author Helen R. Martin used a similar stereotype of *spreadin's* in her works on the Pennsylvania Dutch. Examples of spreads include apple butter, fruit preserves, and *Schmierkaes* (cottage cheese).

20:36 *Pennsylvania salve*. Pattee is doubtless referring to apple butter.

## CHAPTER II

29:18 *nixy.* From the Pennsylvania Dutch English, "the least bit."

29:21 *Buff Cochin.* A breed of chicken.

29:41 *a brauch.* From the Pennsylvania Dutch *brauche,* "to powwow." Powwowing is described below.

30:1 *haexed.* From the Pennsylvania Dutch *hexe,* "to bewitch." Pattee is conflating the terms *brauche* and *hexing.* Yoder ("Official Religion") describes both as "occult phases of folk religion," but distinguishes occult folk healing (*Braucherei*) from witchcraft (*Hexerei*). Powwowing (or Braucherei) was widely practiced to varying degrees among the Pennsylvania Dutch (Dieffenbach, "Powwowing"). Kriebel (*Powwowing,* 16) defines *powwowing* as "an unofficial traditional magico-religious practice—originating with and chiefly practiced by the Pennsylvania Dutch and emphasizing healing of humans and animals, but with other goals as well—that uses words, charms, amulets, and physical manifestations to achieve its objectives." The powwow practitioner relied on several books for ritual inspiration: the Bible, the Sixth and Seventh Books of Moses, Johann Georg Hohman's *Der lang verborgene Freund,* and *Albertus Magnus: Egyptian Secrets* (Shaner, "Recollections"; Yoder, "Folk Medicine"). Powwow's rituals include the verbal (e.g., utterance of a spell), the somatic (e.g., placing hands on the patient), and the material (e.g., the use of eggs or string) (Kriebel, *Powwowing*).

30:1 *liver-growed.* From the Pennsylvania Dutch *aagwachse,* "liver grown, hidebound." Liver grown was a common complaint among the Pennsylvania Dutch that was treated with powwowing. Symptoms included defined ribs, protruding abdomen, and abdominal pain. Treatment included measurement with a red string or passing a child through table legs (Kriebel, *Powwowing,* 226–27). Aunt Sophia Bailer treated liver grown by rubbing lard on a person's chest while reciting a spell (Bailer, "How I Learned"). Others used hog fat massaged into the back (Millspaw, "Witchcraft").

30:1 *run-down.* Most likely a reference to general malaise, fatigue, or even malnutrition.

30:2 *oppnehmer.* From the Pennsylvania Dutch *Abnehme,* "take-off." The major symptom is weight loss. A typical treatment was measurement of the patient (Kriebel, *Powwowing,* 227).

30:9 *haexer.* One early review of the book published in the *Pittsburgh Gazette* complained that Pattee's unfamiliarity with the language created some unknown forms. Instead of *haexer* the reviewer suggested *hexemeister* for "wizard." However, in Pennsylvania Dutch *Hexemeeschder* more closely refers to a sorcerer or magician. Pattee most likely meant *Hexedochder,* "witch doctor," instead.

## CHAPTER III

35:8 *sulky.* "A light two-wheeled carriage or chaise (sometimes without a body), seated for one person" (*OED*).

35:12 *cultivator.* "An agricultural implement for breaking up or loosening the ground and for uprooting weeds between the drills of crops" (*OED*).

35:13 *horse rake.* "An agricultural implement consisting of a toothed bar mounted on wheels and drawn by a horse" (*OED*).

## CHAPTER IV

41:7 *the dishes had been "dried."* It is unclear why Pattee put this standard verb in scare quotes.

41:18 *redded up.* A fusion of several dialectal English terms meaning "to clean up." Mostly found in Northern Midlands dialect area, especially Pennsylvania (*DARE*).

46:9 *Centre County.* A county in Central Pennsylvania to the north of the Seven Mountains range and home to Pattee while he was a professor at The Pennsylvania State College (now The Pennsylvania State University).

## CHAPTER V

49:20 *chicken and waffle supper.* A popular dish served in Central Pennsylvania consisting of waffles covered in shredded chicken stewed in gravy.

50:7 *Front doors are of little use in the Seven Mountains.* Front doors typically served official functions among the Pennsylvania Dutch. Side or back doors, usually leading into the kitchen, were more unofficial and familiar entrances for friends and family.

50:36 *Altoona.* A city in Central Pennsylvania's Blair County. It is located approximately 130 miles (north)west of Pennsylvania's capital at Harrisburg.

52:6 *Bright, sunny days will soon pass away.* Lyrics from the song "The Spanish Cavalier" (Hagans, "Spanish Cavalier").

52:17 *I'm off to the wars; to the wars I must go.* Lyrics from the song "The Spanish Cavalier" (Hagans, "Spanish Cavalier").

55:25 *Good-night, ladies, we're going to leave you now.* Lyrics from the folk song "Goodnight, Ladies" (Christy, "Goodnight").

57:26 *Not by a long chalk!* "Not by any means" or "not by much."

62:31 *like one in a brown study.* Like someone who is daydreaming.

## CHAPTER VI

64:14 *Amos was a Yankee, a native of Connecticut.* Amos is not only the most logically minded of the group but also, in the end, the Farthings' saving grace. It may not be a coincidence that Pattee, like Amos, was a native of New England—Pattee hailed from New Hampshire. Pattee's later autobiography was in fact titled *Pennsylvania Yankee.*

65:10 *I swann.* From the dialectal English "I swear."

## CHAPTER VII

75:1 *All Fools' Day in the Seven Mountains is the time for "flitt'ns."* A flit, or wagon, was used for containing household and farming items for a move (*DARE,* s.v. *flit* and *flitting;* Yoder, "Discovery," 191). The traditional day for moving among the Pennsylvania Dutch was April 1.

75:8 *reapers and mowing machines dragged along behind "hay-ladders."* Although Pattee was a professor of American literature, he was raised on a farm in New Hampshire.

75:12 *schnittings, infares, apple-butterings.* A listing of several important social events among the Pennsylvania Dutch. An infare is a frolic for a new house.

78:25 *scrapple.* Weaver (*Country Scrapple,* 1) defines *scrapple* thus: "For the uninitiated, scrapple is a mixture of meat and flour cooked in meat stock until it thickens. It is allowed to stiffen and set like Italian polenta, then is sliced and fried in a skillet until brown and crispy on both sides." Scrapple remains one of the most popular ethnic dishes in the historic Pennsylvania Dutch areas of southeastern Pennsylvania.

78:26 *ponhoss.* From the Pennsylvania Dutch *Pannhas,* "scrapple." Pannhas and scrapple are variations of the same food item. Some claim that Pannhas contains more meat and less flour than scrapple (Weaver, *Country Scrapple,* 113).

78:26 *schnitts-and-knepff.* From the Pennsylvania Dutch, "dried apple and dumplings." Pennsylvania Dutch dish made with dried apples, dumplings, and ham. The first known reference to the dish as *schnitz-un-gnepp* is in a newspaper from 1828 (Yoder, "Schnitz").

79:12 *Susquehanny.* The Susquehanna is a major river in Central Pennsylvania. It empties into the Chesapeake Bay.

79:13 *brown-bread and Injun puddin'.* Pattee was a central Pennsylvania transplant. As a native New Englander, he incorporated his own knowledge of northeastern culture into the text. Brown bread is a quick, sweet bread made of varying parts of Indian meal and rye meal. It is also known as *ryaninjun,* hinting at the two main ingredients. Indian pudding is an Indian meal-based pudding flavored (often) with spices, molasses, and raisins. They are both popular in traditional New England cuisine (*Yankee Magazine Cookbook,* 114, 183; Stavely and Fitzgerald, *America's Founding Food*).

79:17 *biled dish.* From the New England English *boiled dish.* Boiled dinner is popular in New England cuisine. Traditionally pork or corned beef was boiled with root vegetables in one pot. Unlike in other parts of the United States, boiling was the most common way of preparing beef in New England in the early nineteenth century (Zanger, *American History Cookbook,* 70; Stavely and Fitzgerald, *America's Founding Food*).

80:6 *won't come off more'n a Dutchman's hat at a funeral.* It was customary among the early Pennsylvania Dutch men (at least those closest to the deceased) not to remove their hats during a funeral (A. Shoemaker, "Male Mourners").

80:8 *widder Kuhn.* From the dialectal English *Widow Kuhn.*

81:20 *A Saturday flit makes a short sit.* Moving on a Saturday invoked the superstition that a couple would not remain long at their new home. Don Yoder relates a Centre County version: "Friday flit, short sit; Saturday flit, shorter yit."

83:40 *cur.* "Figuratively, as a term of contempt: a surly, ill-bred, low, or cowardly fellow" (*OED*).

## CHAPTER VIII

88:1 *Wuts, wuts, wuts, wuts.* From the Pennsylvania Dutch *Wutz,* "pig." When used in succession, it is a call to pigs.

88:29 *onion snow.* From the Pennsylvania Dutch *Zwiwwelschnee,* "the last snowfall or snowfalls of the year after the onions are already planted" (A. Shoemaker, "Folklore").

88:36 *plant 'em in the down so t'ey'll strike down wunst.* Another reference to folklore related to moon phases. See endnote to chapter II, 2:9. The Pennsylvania Dutch regularly planted "in the down" for root vegetables and bulbs (Barrick, "Moon-Signs").

89:9 *What are the signs for planting.* The Pennsylvania Dutch placed great importance on the position of the moon in the zodiac signs. Almanacs, which were prevalent in Pennsylvania Dutch homes, contained references and diagrams of moon signs; the belief in the effects of moon signs on agriculture, however, is ancient.

89:10 *Plant your taters and turnups in the sign of t'e scales.* Planting in Libra will yield a heavy crop, especially of potatoes (Barrick, "Moon-Signs").

89:11 *Plant cowcumbers in t'e sign o' t'e twins.* Planting cucumbers in Gemini is recommended for a good crop (Barrick, "Moon-Signs").

89:13 *plant 'em in t'e fishes wunst, or t'ey'll be so watery.* Another well-known planting belief is that potatoes planted in Pisces will be waterlogged (Barrick, "Moon-Signs").

89:15 *unnergehende.* From the Pennsylvania Dutch, "decreasing."

89:15 *beans and peas and such truck must be put in when t'e moon's in t'e up.* Beans and peas are to be planted in the waxing moon so that they climb up the poles or trellis (Barrick, "Moon-Signs").

89:18 *Plant cabbage in t'e Lion still.* Barrick's ("Moon-Signs") informants suggest that cabbage should be planted in Aries. In almanacs, human body parts were assigned a zodiac sign. The human head corresponded with Aries. In other words, to get a good "head" of cabbage, plant them in the sign of Aries.

92:21 *some nigger shack down South.* Pattee's language here was common in literature and some vernaculars of the time.

## CHAPTER X

111:13 *steel maul.* A hammer (*OED*).

## CHAPTER XI

122:9 *Jacqueminot.* "A red-flowered, hybrid perpetual variety of rose" (*OED*).

122:21 *daughter of Herodias.* The daughter of Herodias was Salome, whose infamous dance of the seven veils occurred in conjunction with the beheading of John the Baptist.

125:16 *spring fever.* A syndrome causing listlessness at the start of spring.

127:5 *jonquil.* "A species of the *Narcissus* flower" (*OED*).

## CHAPTER XII

133:36 *hoss-fly.* From the dialectal English *horsefly.*

134:32 *gets his Bible and key and silk threads.* Powwow doctors regularly used the Bible and threads in healing rituals. The Bible provided verses and prayers for cures. Thread healed and diagnosed illnesses. In most cases it was used as a measuring device or was knotted for cures. Measuring a person with a string or thread was a common part of the curing of *Abnemme* (take-off) (Kriebel, *Powwowing*).

135:37 *Tommy rot.* "Nonsense" (*OED*).

135:39 *The only persons ever hung for witches in this country still was hung by Yankees.* An allusion to the Salem witch trials (1692–93), which took place in Massachusetts.

135:41 *Cauliflower.* A humorous play on the *Mayflower,* which bore New England stock as opposed to those of Lem's Pennsylvanian ancestry.

136:9 *Talk about Dutch dumbness.* The common stereotype of the "dumb Dutchman" persists even today. When individuals were speaking only Pennsylvania Dutch, outsiders viewed them as isolated and unfriendly. As younger bilinguals entered common schools, teachers and fellow students punished their varying proficiency in English both verbally and physically. The Pennsylvania Dutch are viewed in literature as stubborn, backward, and unwilling to assimilate.

136:25 *Witch of Endor.* A woman who conjured up the ghost of Samuel in Samuel 1:28.

136:26 *Didn't Job meet the devil.* An allusion to the devil observing Job on his travels on the earth in the first chapter of the book of Job.

137:39 *Duke Street.* Title of the music set to the hymn "Jesus Shall Reign."

## CHAPTER XIII

138:20 *all must know that what brings disease and disaster will not remove it.* Gran'maw Miller was not a powwow doctor, who cured diseases. She was probably a feared "witch doctor"—able to counteract powers of witchcraft (Yoder, "Folk Medicine," 98).

139:7 *The Seventh Book of Moses.* The Sixth and Seventh Books of Moses are "pseudo-cabalistic" texts used for powwowing (Yoder, "Folk Medicine," 99). Many powwowers claim not to even own a copy of the books, as their spiritual weight is too powerful (Kriebel, *Powwowing*).

139:12 *nix-nux* (also *nix-nutz*). "Good for nothing." (*DARE*)

139:20 *crosses and cabalistic symbolry.* Witches were supposedly covered in scars from charms used against them by witch doctors.

139:22 *origin of this belief.* Many of the charms used in Pennsylvania Dutch powwowing have origins in medieval charms of central Europe (Yoder, "Folk Medicine").

139:24 *German Palatinate.* A number of the first Pennsylvania Dutch settlers came from the Rhineland-Palatinate region of Germany, though others came from Switzerland, Hesse, Alsace, and neighboring regions.

139:25 *fetich.* Usually "fetish": an incantation or object believed to be magical.

## CHAPTER XIV

148:26 *Pe-pe-pe-pe.* From the Pennsylvania Dutch *bie, bie, bie!,* a call to chickens.

148:31 *hap.* "A covering" (*OED*). According to Don Yoder, a hap is "a bed covering, more primitive and less artistic than a pieced quilt" (personal communication).

149:9 *Turkey Run . . . Blair's . . . Grayble . . . Bald Eagle . . . Juniata.* Blair, Bald Eagle, and Juniata are common geographic names in Central Pennsylvania. The Bald Eagle Mountain lies just north of Pattee's home in State College, Pennsylvania. The other place-names are either lost to time or fictitious.

152:25 *Like one, that on a lonesome road.* Stanza from Samuel Taylor Coleridge's 1798 epic, "The Rime of the Ancient Mariner."

## CHAPTER XV

156:14 *hang all three of 'em higher 'n Haman.* According the book of Esther, Haman was hanged from his own high gallows because he had tricked King Xerxes.

159:9 *Paoli.* A town in Chester County, Pennsylvania, near Philadelphia.

## CHAPTER XVI

171:10 *euchre.* "To outwit" (*OED*).

171:10 *you've got both bowers and the joker right in your hand.* An allusion to the card game euchre.

171:34 *Rooshey.* Most likely Hershey, Pennsylvania.

172:2 *He fished a slip of dark paper.* Charms for protection were common in powwowing. The most famous is the Sator square, which has ancient origins. The words read the same backward, upward, and downward. The Sator square (on the left of Pattee's image) is included in *The Long Lost Friend* as a means to extinguish fire without water (Hohman, *Der lange verborgene Freund,* 60). The second image (on the right) is another common charm used against evil spirits and witchcraft.

175:10 *hay-mow.* "A stack of hay or the compartment of a barn in which hay is stored" (*OED*).

179:14 *noblesse oblige.* "Privilege entails responsibility" (*OED*).

## CHAPTER XVII

181:11 *the world presented as many devils as ever it did to old Cotton Mather.* Cotton Mather (1663–1728) was a New England Puritan minister who had an influential role in the Salem witch trials.

182:7 *They must have locks of hair, and pieces of Bibles, and keys, and blood, and what not.* Pattee is drawing on the belief that one needed intimate items associated with the soon-to-be-victim of a hex.

182:39 *Recollect that apple-tree that blowed late last fall in your yard?* A series of accounts that stereotype the Pennsylvania Dutch preoccupation with superstition. All are intended to foretell some sort of bad omen.

186:31 *beats the Dutch, now, don't it?* Something that "beats the Dutch" is "extraordinary or startling" (*OED*).

## CHAPTER XVIII

193:27 *the famous Sinking Valley.* Sinking Valley is in the area of Tyrone, Pennsylvania, in Blair County—twenty-six miles south of State College and twenty-three miles north of Altoona. If this is the correct Sinking Valley, Pattee's text covers a large area of land in Central Pennsylvania, spanning the Seven Mountains in Mifflin County, Bald Eagle Mountain in Centre and Huntington Counties, and Sinking Valley in Blair County.

## CHAPTER XIX

207:6 *That's the English for the German Heller.* From the German *der Heller;* refers to a small sum of money and even an old German and Austrian coin—similar to the English farthing, which was one quarter of a penny.

## CHAPTER XX

212:20 *Hooray fer Penn-sil-way-ne-ar wunst.* A fictitious song using elements of Pennsylvania Dutch folk culture and speech.

212:24 *Ike Watts.* Humorous contrast with the preceding earthy song. This is likely a reference to Isaac Watts, the originator of English hymnody (1674–1748).

212:24 *pomes of Lole and Scott's Marmelade all to ponhoss.* A reference to the poems of James Russell Lowell, well-known Fireside Poet, and Walter Scott's epic *Marmion.* Amos articulates his pride in the elements of rural Pennsylvanian culture, clinging to religious hymnody and local cuisine (scrapple). Literature, such as Scott's *Marmion,* and even the works of a New Englander, Lowell, are foreign to him—indeed, Pattee plays on the word *Marmion* to emphasize this.

212:37 *no more show than a snow-bird in tophet.* Tophet was a place in Jerusalem where children were burned (Jeremiah 7:31). *Tophet* is also an allusion to hell in some literature.

# BIBLIOGRAPHY


Bailer, Aunt Sophia. "How I Learned 'Powwowing.'" *Pennsylvania Dutchman* 4 (June 1952): 8.

Barrick, Mac E. "Moon-Signs in Cumberland County." *Pennsylvania Folklife* 15 (Summer 1966): 41–43.

Cassidy, Frederic G., and Joan Houston Hall. *Dictionary of American Regional English (DARE)*. Cambridge: Belknap Press of Harvard University Press, 1985–.

Christy, Edwin Pearce. "Goodnight, Ladies." 1867.

Dieffenbach, Victor C. "Butchering Day on the Farm." *Pennsylvania Dutchman* 4 (January 1953): 14–15.

———. "Powwowing Among the Pennsylvania Germans." *Pennsylvania Folklife* 25 (Winter 1974–75): 29–46.

———. "Tramps of My Youth." *Pennsylvania Folklife* 10 (Spring 1959): 8–13.

Eaby, Thelia Jean. "The Country Butcher." *Pennsylvania Folklife* 32 (Summer 1983): 29–31.

Ensminger, Robert F. *The Pennsylvania Barn: Its Origin, Evolution, and Distribution in North America*. 2nd ed. Baltimore: Johns Hopkins University Press, 2003.

Fetterly, Judith, and Marjorie Pryse. *Writing out of Place: Regionalism, Women, and American Literary Culture*. Urbana: University of Illinois Press, 2005.

Foote, Stephanie. *Regional Fictions: Culture and Identity in Nineteenth-Century American Literature*. Madison: University of Wisconsin Press, 2001.

Frazier, Jeffrey R. *Pennsylvania Fireside Tales*. Vol. 1. Centre Hall, Pa.: Egg Hill, 1996.

George, Marie. "Apple Butter . . . Then and Now." *Pennsylvania Folklife* 33 (Summer 1984): 162–64.

Gibbons, Phebe Earle. *Pennsylvania Dutch and Other Essays*. With introduction by Don Yoder. Mechanicsburg, Pa.: Stackpole, 2001.

Grim, Rita. "Old Fashioned Applebutter Making." *Pennsylvania Folklife* 26 (suppl. 1977): 46–47.

Hagans, George W. "The Spanish Cavalier." 1881.

Hill, Susan Colestock. *Heart Language: Elsie Singmaster and Her Pennsylvania German Writings*. University Park: Penn State Press, 2009.

Hohman, Johann Georg. *Der lange verborgene Freund oder: Getreuer und christlicher Unterricht für jederman, enthaltend; Wunderbare und probmäßige Mittel und Künste, sowohl für die Menschen als das Vieh*. Reading, Pa.: Hohman, 1820.

Huffines, Marion Lois. "The English of the Pennsylvania Germans: A Reflection of Ethnic Affiliation." *German Quarterly* 57 (1984): 173–82.

Kriebel, David W. *Powwowing Among the Pennsylvania Dutch: A Traditional Medical Practice in the Modern World*. University Park: Penn State Press, 2007.

Lutz, Tom. *Cosmopolitan Vistas: American Regionalism and Literary Value*. Ithaca: Cornell University Press, 2004.

Martine, James J. *Fred Lewis Pattee and American Literature*. University Park: Penn State Press, 1973.

Millspaw, Yvonne J. "Witchcraft Belief in a Pennsylvania German Family." *Pennsylvania Folklife* 27 (Summer 1978): 14–24.

*Oxford English Dictionary (OED)*. 1989. 2nd ed. Oxford: Oxford University Press.

Pattee, Fred Lewis. *Compelled Men*. New York [etc.]: Association Press, 1913.

———. *The House of the Black Ring*. Penn State ed. State College, Pa.: Pattee, 1924.

———. *Penn State Yankee: The Autobiography of Fred Lewis Pattee*. State College: Pennsylvania State College, 1953.

Pattee, Fred Lewis, Papers. 1821–1954, Accession 1950–0006R. Rare Books and Manuscripts, Special Collections Library, University Libraries, Pennsylvania State University.

Quick, Graeme, and Wesley Buchele. *The Grain Harvesters*. St. Joseph, Mich.: American Society of Agricultural Engineering, 1978.

Robacker, Earl F. *Pennsylvania German Literature: Changing Trends from 1683 to 1942*. Philadelphia: University of Pennsylvania Press, 1943.

Shaner, Richard H. "Recollections of Witchcraft in the Oley Hills." *Pennsylvania Folklife* 21 (suppl. 1972): 39–43.

Shoemaker, Alfred L. "Folklore on Snow." *Pennsylvania Dutchman* 5 (February 1954): 5.

———. "Male Mourners of Old Kept Their Hats On." *Pennsylvania Dutchman* 1 (June 9, 1949): 2.

Shoemaker, Henry W. *Allegheny Episodes: Folk Lore and Legends Collected in Northern and Western Pennsylvania*. University Park: Penn State Press, 2007.

Stavely, Keith, and Kathleen Fitzgerald. *America's Founding Food: The Story of New England Cooking*. Chapel Hill: University of North Carolina Press, 2004.

Weaver, William Woys. *Country Scrapple: An American Tradition*. Mechanicsburg, Pa.: Stackpole, 2003.

Winkler, Louis. "Pennsylvania German Astronomy and Astrology II: The Moon." *Pennsylvania Folklife* 21 (Summer 1972): 23–27.

*Yankee Magazine Cookbook*. New York: Harper & Row, 1981.

Yoder, Don. "Almanac Album." *Pennsylvania Folklife* 17 (Winter 1967–68): 12–19.

———. *Discovering American Folklife*. Mechanicsburg, Pa.: Stackpole, 2001.

———. "Official Religion Versus Folk Religion." *Pennsylvania Folklife* 15 (Winter 1965–66): 36–52.

———. "Schnitz: In the Pennsylvania Folk-Culture." *Pennsylvania Folklife* 12 (Fall 1961): 44–53.

Zanger, Mark H. *The American History Cookbook*. Westport, Conn.: Greenwood Press, 2003.